I0662345

LINCOLN

BOOK 2 IN THE ANGELBOUND LINCOLN SERIES

CHRISTINA BAUER

COPYRIGHT

Monster House Books
Newton, MA 02135
ISBN 9781946677204
First Edition

Copyright © 2019 by Monster House Books LLC
All rights reserved. This book or any portion thereof may not be reproduced or used in any
manner whatsoever without the express written permission of the publisher except for the use
of brief quotations in a book review.

CONTENTS

DEDICATION

For All Those Who Kick Ass, Take Names
and Read Books

FOREWORD

Dear Reader,

In prepping for this novel, I researched similar titles. Basically, I read an ass-ton of books that were rewritten from the love interest's perspective. In the volumes I reviewed, most authors took their original work and kept it, beat for beat, but built out new internal dialogue.

Which isn't easy to do.

Trust me, I tried.

So I need to be straight-up here.

There's no way I could write that *beat for beat* book. Don't get me wrong: in some places, that approach worked fine. But in the interests of full disclosure, here are five ways that LINCOLN is different from other *rewritten from his point of view* books that you may know and love. You are hereby warned about what you're getting into, and I won't feel offended if you decide to click the *return* button at this point.

Difference Number One. If you follow my work, then you know I love a good twist. In ANGELBOUND you may have thought that Lincoln was an anti-demonic douchebag.

Spoiler Alert

Lincoln is a good guy. Seriously. That was true when I wrote the original ANGELBOUND, which is why Lincoln fell for his girl before they officially met, Walker shared that Lincoln was obsessed with Myla, the anti-Acca treaty was a theme, and so on. I'm super happy to have this chance to set the record straight. That said, if you really liked him as a anti-hero? Oops. I really tried to make him that, but Lincoln can be stubborn as fuck. As Camilla says in the book, he's a "nobleman. Noble plus a man." Boom.

Difference Number Two. A lot of the drama in ANGELBOUND was about Myla's mother, friends and school. That's not Lincoln's world and it didn't feel authentic to have him worrying about Cissy's jealousy or whatever. Our guy's got his own shit to deal with. In this book, I focus on scenes and themes where Lincoln and Myla were together. The rest is new stuff (more on that later.)

Difference Number Three. Even when a Lincoln-Myla scene was spelled out in ANGELBOUND—and I keep it in LINCOLN—I didn't recount every last beat unless I could add something really significant. In other words, many things that Myla noticed in detail (like the nuances of negotiating with the Oligarchy) just aren't big deals in Lincoln's experience. For instance, treaties are his world. He'd be more concerned about how Myla was handling things versus anything else.

Difference Number Four. There's a new story about Myla which only takes place in Lincoln's point of view. He's more than just a handsome face, damn it! Our guy gets an adventure of his own.

Difference Number Five. In this book, I really wanted to give y'all an inside look at Lincoln's daily life. In writing ANGELBOUND, I had to build out Lincoln's world, such as his friendship with Walker, the anti-Acca treaty, seeing Myla at the lake fighting doxy demons and so on. That gave ANGEL-BOUND's world texture and logic, but I couldn't include it directly on the page. Now this is Lincoln's chance to shine. Huzzah!

SIDE NOTE: This book ended up long. As you may know, I tend to write books out of sequence and I never know which ones will be huge or short. I used to beat up on myself about it, but I've gotten to a place where I'm just happy that I can create things people want to read. As Myla would say, *meh*.

With that, I'll stop with the caveats and let you get to the book itself! I hope you enjoy it.

Best,

Christina

AUTHOR NOTE

Dear Readers,

Forty-eight months and a million years ago, I outlined the story of Lincoln *before* he met Myla ... a tale that became DUTY BOUND.

Key fact: If you're hungering for Lincoln's voice *in tandem with* some serious Myla interaction, then there's book 2 in this series, LINCOLN.

But I digress.

Back to DUTY BOUND.

In the years since ANGELBOUND was released, I've been thrilled by the ongoing love for all things Lincoln and Myla. My readers even voted to have Lincoln's story told—and since I love to make readers happy—here it is!

I hope you enjoy it :)

Christina Bauer

LINCOLN

*B*efore me looms a dissolus demon. Think about a waist-high glob of mayo—only both alive and deadly—and that's the general idea.

No face.

No limbs.

Just mega-bacteria with attitude.

For hours, I hunted this creature through the forests of Purgatory. Why? I'm both part angel and a demon hunter. *One of the thrax.* Killing monsters is what my people do. Now I've cornered this slime ball (as in a ball literally made of slime) against the back wall of the royal stables.

All that remains is the kill.

This won't be easy.

Little by little, I pin the dissolus against the wall with my body. The white goo of the demon's exterior smears across the legs of my Kevlar armor. The creature's round form pulses, heartbeat style. Reaching forward, I slip my hands through the monster's outer layer, careful to keep my palms tipped at precisely forty degrees. Unless I use that exact angle combined with slow speed, the demon's interior will transform from ugly slop into deadly acid.

Then I'll be dissolved in seconds. Painfully.

Sweat beads down my spine as I search inside the monster. My goal is to find the creature's nucleus—the equivalent of its heart—which is solid, transparent and egg-shaped. I shift my arms inside the demon's gooey interior. Slurping sounds ricochet through the air. Across the stables, a horse whinnies. Adrenaline spikes through my system. There's a time limit here. If I don't grab the nucleus fast enough, then the demon's insides will turn acidic anyway.

Again, death. Not a fan.

It's an effort, but I somehow keep my motions slow and steady. All thoughts collapse into a single goal: Grasp the nucleus.

A familiar voice breaks up the quiet. "Interesting monster, eh?"

Seriously?

That's Aldred, the Earl of Acca and an extraordinary scumbag. At this point, he and I are the only people in the stables, if you don't count the demon. Aldred's a portly fellow, middle aged with thinning hair and long jowls. His clan, the House of Acca, is a perennial pain in my royal backside. While I spent hours hunting the dissolus, Aldred followed behind at a safe distance. All the while, he released a steady stream of chatter.

"I said," Aldred really drags out the word *said*. "Interesting monster, right?"

"*Interesting* isn't the word I'd use," I reply.

"What can I say?" Aldred steps beside me, scanning the scene. "I'm an earl, not a walking thesaurus."

For a moment, I see myself in Aldred's eyes. I'm Lincoln Vidar Osric Aquilus, High Prince of the Thrax. My family rules the land of Antrum, which is hidden far below Earth's surface. The rest of the After-Realms consist of the angels in Heaven, demons of Hell, quasi-demons in Purgatory, and the ghouls of the Dark Lands. At eighteen, I'm tall and broad-shouldered with brown hair and mismatched irises. I also happen to be leaning over a possessed blob of white goo the size of an engorged Hippity Hop. Being a demon hunter is rarely glamorous. Neither is being royal, for that matter.

"This is taking too long," declares Aldred. With mincing steps, the earl creeps up beside me.

"Stay back," I warn. "That's for your own safety."

"No, I shall kick it for you."

"Absolutely not," I counter. "You'll end up losing your leg, and that's if you're lucky."

Aldred holds his hands palms forward, in the universal motion for, *it's not my fault.* "No need to get testy."

Frustration sends my thoughts reeling. How did I end up here anyway? The answer flickers through my mind like images on a carousel. On orders from Verus, the Queen of the Angels, my family and I are temporarily residing in Purgatory, along with all our court. Since my people enjoy a medieval lifestyle, we've constructed cabins in Purgatory's Alighieri Woods. This morning, a dissolus broke free from our royal menagerie. Cue me chasing the monster through the forest while the earl follows behind.

Which brings me to the present moment and imminent death.

At last, my fingers brush against the creature's hard nucleus. *Yes!* Normally I give demons a chance to retreat before killing them. However, dissolus have the mental powers of paramecium. To them, attacking is nothing personal—it's just what they do.

Time to end this.

Tightening my grip on the nucleus, I yank with all my strength. The clear sphere breaks free from the gelatinous demon. For a moment, the dissolus quivers in place. Then—SPLASH—it collapses into a puddle of translucent sludge. The scent of rotten eggs fills the air. In my right hand, the nucleus transforms into a bright white orb before vanishing altogether. The gooey entrails covering the floor also disappear. Easy cleanup; that's one benefit of this demon type.

I exhale a long breath. "And *that's* how to kill a dissolus."

"Glad I was here to help," declares Aldred. "We make a great team." He moves to stand directly in the main aisle of the stables. In other words, blocking my departure. I've seen this action from Aldred before.

"Is there a particular topic you wish to discuss?" I ask.

"As a matter of fact, yes. Now that we've spent the morning together, I thought we could talk, man to man."

I tilt my head. "Go on."

Here it comes. Another discussion about my marriage contract.

For weeks, Aldred has been pestering me to sign a betrothal contract with his daughter, Lady Adair. At one time, I might have been interested. Now, not so much. The local residents of Purgatory are quasi-demons, and one of those ladies happens to be an excellent warrior named Myla Lewis. As of this moment, it's been eight days, six hours, and thirty-two minutes since I last saw Myla. At the time, she was fighting off Doxy demons in a nearby lake. Her battle technique displayed the perfect combination of beauty, intellect and lethal power.

Ah, Myla.

Long story short, I'm no longer interested in signing a marriage contract. Instead, my time's been consumed with researching a certain Miss Lewis. To that end, I've learned she's fighting in Purgatory's Arena tomorrow morning. I plan to sneak into an access corridor and watch her battle from a distance. The very idea makes my heart soar.

Aldred clears his throat, breaking up my thoughts. "Did you hear what I said?" he asks.

"No," I reply. Evidently, the earl was blabbing away while I contemplated Myla. Even so, I doubt I missed anything. There's only one topic of interest to Aldred these days.

My marriage.

"Please repeat your statement," I say.

Aldred makes a great show of scanning the stables. "I've news for you about Minister Devak." He narrows his eyes to conspiratorial slits. "Great information."

This is what humans call a *red flag*. Why the concern? I've been working on what I call an anti-Acca treaty. By uniting the armies of Kamal, Horus and Striga, I'll have enough warriors to make Aldred kowtow on any number of topics, including my marriage to Adair. Of all those houses, my negotiations with Minister Devak—and therefore the House of Kamal—are the farthest along.

"And?" I prompt.

"Devak's been asking around." Aldred lowers his voice. "About quasi warriors."

A chill rolls up my limbs. Can Devak be interested in Myla for some reason? When I next speak, it's an effort to keep my voice calm. "What is Devak's precise concern?"

"Wouldn't *you* like to know." Aldred smirks.

At this point, that smug grin of Aldred's tells me two things. First, the earl knows exactly what Devak is up to, and second, Aldred wants something in exchange for the information.

I stifle the urge to roll my eyes. "Name your price, Aldred."

The earl exhales a long-suffering sigh. "I might confide everything, but it's sensitive information … the kind you share with *family*, you know?"

Meaning: ink my betrothal contract and I'll tell all.

I chuckle. Aldred always overreaches in negotiations. However, what he lacks in finesse he more than makes up for in persistence. "I am *not* finalizing a contract merely to discover Devak's plans."

"Please; I never expected you to sign this very second," lies Aldred. No doubt, the man keeps the document in the folds of his tunic along with a quill, just in case. "But perhaps you can commit to spending more time with my sweet Adair? If so, then I might feel like sharing."

Aldred thinks he's being sneaky, but I already made this decision last night. "Mother is organizing a garden party at the Ryder mansion. My plan is to request Adair's company for the event." After all, I've said all of five sentences to the girl. We may be compatible. It's a long shot considering my blooming obsession with Myla Lewis, but there it is.

Aldred rubs his palms together. "Excellent, I'll tell Lady Adair today."

"Your turn," I state. "What about Devak's interest in quasi warriors?"

Aldred bobs his thick eyebrows. "No doubt, you're aware how the court itches to hunt local demons."

My eyes widen with shock. "No, I wasn't." A memory flashes through my mind.

I'm fifteen and late for monitoring a demon patrol in the Canadian Arctic. As I exit the transfer platform, a woman's screams echo through the cold air. I race out of the ice station and onto a sheet of white tundra under a grey sky. Freezing winds batter my body. Before me, a dozen Acca warriors tear apart a Vantys—a harmless she-demon who's equal parts human and reptile. Aldred stands behind them, pumping his fist in the air. Fresh sprays of blood darken the snow. I race over, my young voice bellowing.

"Stop!"

But the Vantys is already dead. And Aldred's men have placed her head on a pike.

"This is disgraceful," I announce. "We are thrax, not a mindless mob."

Blinking hard, I try to wipe out that recollection. However, the image of a severed head stays seared in my mind. Thrax should act as ethical warriors, yet Aldred transformed them into something else. There's no avoiding the truth. With the wrong encouragement, my people can do terrible things.

And now, their baser instincts may be focused on Myla. I shudder. I'd been actively avoiding thoughts of any future with Myla. Contemplating her in the present was just too enjoyable. But now? I must consider the risk my people pose to her, myself included.

"You know us thrax," continues Aldred. "We're always seeking a new challenge."

Protective energy runs up my spine. I round on the earl. "The Queen of the Angels herself, the oracle Verus, sent us here to interact with the quasi population, not hunt them down."

"Bah." Aldred waves his hand dismissively. "It's only a matter of time before some quasi marches into our camp, looking for trouble. After all, they're semi-demonic. It's in their blood. And once those quasis come after us, then we'll have to protect ourselves. It's only right."

Images of Myla appear in my mind. She did indeed sneak into our compound, but only because she was on the trail of a mutual enemy, the Doxy demons. A weight of worry settles into my stomach. What if someone other than me saw her? Aldred is correct; my people would kill first and ask questions later.

"You still haven't shared specifics on Devak and quasis," I point out. "What did he say, exactly?"

"Devak's asking about Purgatory's Arena."

My heart sinks. *That means he's focusing on warriors like Myla.* "What's his interest?"

"My guess? Arena warriors are the best fighters. Here's the thing. Maybe you and I can team up." Aldred grins, showing off his mouth of yellow teeth. "Together, we could claim the first official quasi kill."

At those words, anger zings through my nervous system. "Let me make one thing absolutely clear." I prowl toward Aldred, my voice deep as thunder. "Hunting the local population is off the table, whether they are Arena warriors or not. If you or anyone else speaks of this again, I'll have you shipped back to Antrum and tossed into the dungeons." For every final word I speak, I tap Aldred on the center of his chest. "Do you understand?"

"All right." The earl forces another laugh. "No need to get sensitive."

I glare at Aldred with a look that says, *I'm done here.* "The dungeons, Aldred. I mean it."

Without waiting for a reply, I storm past the earl and out of the stables. Hunting quasis? *Outrageous!*

Suddenly, I wish my parents weren't away on a demon hunting excursion. I'd like nothing better than to open a formal inquest, find out who's threatening quasis, and then fill our dungeons to overflowing. But starting an inquest is serious business. For the process to have teeth, my parents must sign off. And they won't return for at least four days.

Ah, well. Better to wait and do this correctly, much as I hate that fact.

All the way back to my cabin, my thoughts race through everything I've just learned: that Aldred is still pressing my marriage to Adair ... the fact that my own people might be targeting quasi warriors ... and how the entire situation could place Myla in danger. It all adds up to one terrible conclusion.

If I'm not careful, Myla might end up dead. That's not an option, so I take a silent oath.

With all my mind and body, I vow to protect the woman who already holds my heart.

I spend a restless night brainstorming ways to punish Aldred and therefore, I can't sleep. The fact that I'm about to see Myla again doesn't help.

Finally, early morning arrives. I tiptoe out of my cabin, mount my horse Nightshade, and slip away from camp to ride across rolling hills of yellowing grasses. The scent of mist and decay fills the air. My trip soon ends at the back of a deserted parking lot. Lines of weeds poke up through the asphalt. Lonely car hulks sit at odd places and angles. A chipped wooden sign reads, *Purgatory's Arena*. Like most things here, the main structure is a tad run down.

On second thought, make that *exceptionally run down*.

The Arena is little more than a pile of ruined bricks. Moss peeps out between the gray stones of the building's facade. In all honestly, the place looks held together with popsicle sticks and glue. Still, all that matters is how a ghoul named IK-3 will meet me at the back access door.

From there, I sneak in and see Myla. The thought must be a little distracting, considering how Night swings her head in my direction. She glares at me with her big round eyes as if to say, *are you paying attention here?*

"Yes, yes," I reply. "That way." I gesture and click my tongue. Night takes off around the back of the Arena. Sure enough, I discover a boarded-over door marked, *No Admittance*. My contact—a night guard named IK-3—awaits outside.

Ike (he loathes his ghoul name) waves as we approach. "Hey, glad you could make it." Ike is tall and lanky, with incredibly pale skin, which is appropriate considering he's one of the undead. His heart-shaped face is dotted with freckles that somehow survived the ghoul-conversion process. As a matter of fact, he looks more like a skateboarding human than an undead ghoul.

"Thank you for your help, Ike."

"Hey, just happy for the worms, you know." Ghouls love worms; I sent Ike a case. *Yes, he's been that helpful.*

Ike pushes open the blocked door. "This hallway has been under construction for years. You can watch from here and no one will know. Best-kept secret in the Arena."

"Thank you."

Ike stares at Night. "You need help with your horse?"

"Night can take care of herself, right girl?"

My horse sniffs; a plume of purple smoke curls out of her nostrils. Night casts minor spells, and this magical puff is but one example. One moment, Night is here. The next? *Gone.*

"Whoa," says Ike. "Cool."

"Horses from the House of Striga are all like that." The reason why is simple: Striga's home to our most powerful witches and warlocks. "If you'll excuse me."

"Knock yourself out."

I step into the hallway and the first thing that strikes me is the scent of stale cigarette smoke. *Seems like the best secret in the Arena is rather well known.* The floor is littered with cigarette butts, empty coffee cups, and drained containers of cough syrup. Add in a worm farm and this would be the ideal spot for a ghoul rave.

The corridor winds a bit before opening out onto the Arena proper. Pausing at the end of the passage, I lean against an arch that leads directly to the Arena floor. Beyond it, tiers of stone benches loop around an oval battleground. Like the Arena's exterior, the inside is a mishmash of mold, cobwebs, and cracked stone. Nothing fancy, but it could be Hell itself and I'd still sneak in. I smile.

Myla's fight starts any minute.

A low hum sounds in the corridor. *Someone's opening a ghoul transport portal.* Moments later, a dark rectangular shape appears just within the passage. Out of it steps a ghoul who's tall, lean, and deathly pale. As always, the strong bone structure of his face is perfectly framed by a buzz cut and sideburns. His official name is WKR-7.

I call him Walker.

As my best friend, Walker takes it upon himself to help my royalness avoid trouble. Today, that means using his ghoul powers to track me down. He's well-intentioned, if a little intrusive.

While Walker strides closer, the portal vanishes behind him. "How very odd," he says.

"And *hello* to you too," I deadpan.

Walker folds his arms over his chest. The long sleeves of his dark robes sway with the movement. "You're not in royal gear this morning."

"True." Usually I wear leather pants, tall boots, chainmail, and a dark velvet tunic. *Classic thrax gear.* "Here's the thing. Today I'm blending in with the general populace." In this case, that means sporting jeans, hefty boots, and a *Purple Rain Tour* T-shirt. I also keep a small assortment of weapons hidden on my person.

Daggers. Don't leave home without them.

"Blending in?" repeats Walker. "You've the mismatched eyes of a thrax."

"And I've no tail. Don't forget that part." Like me, Myla is around eighteen years old. Unlike me, she has a long thin tail that's covered in dragon scales. *So intriguing.*

Walker narrows his eyes. "What are you *really* doing here?"

I purse my lips, contemplating. *Do I tell Walker about Myla?* So far, I've avoided sharing anything major with him. Not that I think my friend will be judgmental or share my secret. It's more that my feelings for Myla are a bright spot in an otherwise grey life. Telling someone else might dilute the color. But as of yesterday, I can no longer stay silent. My own people may be hunting quasis, so Walker must know everything.

In a minute.

A little teasing is part of our bro code.

"You know I'm stuck in Purgatory for a few months," I reply. "Thought I'd catch an Arena match."

Lately, I've been rather busy learning the minutiae of Myla's lifestyle. Purgatory sorts souls into Heaven or Hell, either through *trial by combat* or *trial by jury*. As an Arena warrior, Myla fights evil spirits who want passage to Heaven.

"Arena fights are private events," says Walker. "How did you discover this one?"

"Would you believe me if I said it was a coincidence?"

"Not at chance." Walker sniffs. "You recently asked me about quasi girl fighters with dragonscale tails. Now I find you skulking around an access hallway to Purgatory's Arena, right before one such fighter will do battle."

"Me? Skulking?" I open my mouth in mock-surprise. "I'm more of a sneak."

Walker doesn't even crack a grin. "I repeat, how did you find out?"

"You won't drop this, will you?"

At last, Walker smiles. "I can wait for all eternity, if you like."

He's not kidding. Walker once followed me—silent and glowering—for three solid days because I wouldn't tell him where I hid the cough syrup (ghouls love that stuff, along with coffee, worms, and smokes.) Walker didn't back down then; he definitely won't now.

"Well?" asks my friend.

Time to fess up.

"This morning's match was revealed to me after—" I look up, my mouth making silent calculations "—bribing eight different government officials, beginning with the Ghoul Minister and ending with an arena night guard called IK-3. Along the way, I even discovered a name." I can't help but smile as I speak this next part. "Myla Lewis."

Walker glares daggers in my direction. "Leave Myla-la alone."

A pang of jealousy moves through me. *Walker has a nickname for her?* When I next speak, my voice comes out far lower than I'd like. "How do you know her?"

Walker's features turn unreadable. "My people rule this land. Sometimes I help out."

"There's more to it than that." I step nearer. "Isn't there?"

"You know my kind. Lots of rules. Our regulations require that Arena warriors travel via ghoul portal." Walker gestures to the walls around him. "Between all the evil souls and demons running around this place, I'm one of the few ghouls who can handle themselves."

Logical enough. Like me, Walker is a descendent of the archangel Aquila and a well-trained fighter.

"So you take Myla to her matches," I recap.

"Precisely. We barely say much beyond *hello* and *goodbye*."

Which could be true, except for the fact that Walker never uses nicknames. Point of fact: he still calls me Lincoln, and I've known him my entire life.

My friend is definitely hiding something.

I scan Walker carefully. "If that's true, then why not tell me about Myla before? I specifically asked you about quasi Arena fighters who were women."

"It's not that easy." Walker's gaze locks with mine. When he next speaks, all the seriousness in the world is etched into the lines of his face. "I'd tell you everything if I could."

Some history on Walker: He's forever getting involved in tricky situations. Binding oaths, soul saving, magical contingencies ... Walker has his undead hands in everything. Plus, I know this particular look of his; my friend is telling the truth. He can't share when it comes to Myla.

I give him a solemn nod. "I understand."

Even so, there's no way Walker *barely knows* my girl. There's more to the story and I intend to uncover every last detail. After all, hunting beings and information is what I do best.

"Most appreciated." Walker pauses for a long moment. "And since you snuck in to watch Myla's fight, I'm guessing you haven't met her formally."

"That's correct." *And I loathe that fact.*

"Myla's part demon, so I'll also assume you won't introduce yourself either."

A weight of sorrow settles into my soul. "Correct again." Considering the situation with my people wanting to kill her, having any kind of relationship seems far from reasonable.

Walker eyes me for a long moment, then he shakes his head. "Still, I don't like this. From the little I know about Myla, she could easily be taken with you. The fact that you're lurking anywhere near her? That's simply inviting disaster. What if she falls for you and gets her heart broken? I can't allow that."

If I felt a small flare of jealousy before, that emotion now blazes into full, white-hot envy. "And why would you care?"

"Again, not answering that."

My hands curl into fists. Clearly, my friend knows Myla far more than he lets on. *Does he want her for his own?* Closing my eyes, I force my mind to calm. Getting green-eyed over Walker will accomplish nothing. My vow is to protect Myla, even from me.

When I next speak to Walker, I work hard to act neutral. "You seem to know Myla well."

Walker shrugs. "I know the quasi people."

"If Myla and I were ever to meet, how would you suggest I ensure she doesn't …" I pinch the bridge of my nose, trying to find the right words.

"End up like you?" asks Walker.

I level him with a dry look. "Precisely."

Walker rocks on his heels. I've seen this move before; my friend is in deep contemplation. At length, Walker speaks once more. "You're excellent at containing or faking emotion when necessary. If you ever encounter Miss Lewis, you should play the haughty thrax. Look down on her demonic side. She'll hate it—*and you*—forever."

The words slam into my heart. *Myla will hate me forever.* How could I act in such a foul manner, even if it is for Myla's benefit? My shoulders tighten with worry. When I first saw Myla, I was surprised to discover her heritage as a quasi demon. I'd never met one before. But after learning more, things have changed. Now I don't see Myla as anything but her beautiful self.

All of a sudden, that memory appears again.

The Vantys.

A bloody head stuck on a pike.

Bands of worry tighten around my throat. It doesn't matter that Myla is an excellent warrior; no one can fight off an entire mob of thrax. Taking in a deep breath, I force my spine to straighten. *This isn't about me. It's about what keeps Myla away from harm.* And considering the recent news from Aldred, safe is where I'll ensure she stays, no matter what.

Walker tilts his head. "Is that possible, Lincoln? If it comes to it, can you play the villain to keep her away?"

"I can and will." Turning from Walker, I stare off into the empty Arena. Pain radiates through my chest, sharp as a blade driving though my rib cage, and I'd know the sensation. I've been stabbed no less than thirty-seven times. Even so, none of those cuts reached this level of agony.

Why does caring for someone have to hurt so much?

Stepping to my side, Walker sets his hand on my shoulder. For a long minute, my friend's all-black eyes carefully scan my face. "Oh, Lincoln," my friend says at last. "I've never seen you this miserable. You've become deeply attached, haven't you?"

For a long moment, I can't find the words to explain. Then, the truth falls from my lips on its own. "There's no one else in the world like her. Seeing

Myla?" I throw my hands apart and make an explosion noise. "She blew apart everything I thought I knew. A woman fighter who laughs while taking down demons? I'd no idea someone like that even existed. Thoughts of her simply consume me."

Walker gives my shoulder a squeeze. "Perhaps you should skip this morning's match."

"And miss torturing myself?" I smile, but there's no joy in it. "Not a chance."

My friend gives me the side eye. "You won't drop this, will you?"

"As a wise ghoul once told me, *I can wait for all eternity.* Or long enough to make you late in transporting Myla." Like the rest of his people, Walker loathes missing schedules.

At last, Walker lowers his hand. "In that case, I'm off for transport duty."

"Be safe. You carry precious cargo." My voice warbles a bit when I say that last part, and I don't care.

"I will."

Another hum sounds as Walker opens a fresh ghoul portal. Within seconds, my friend is gone. Long minutes tick by. Eventually, the Arena's emcee takes to the floor, along with a handful of workers. I count quasis, demons, and ghouls in the mix. Still, there's no sign of Myla.

A realization hits me. I became so jealous, I forgot to tell Walker about the threat to Myla from my people. I pause, wondering if I should chase after Walker. *Probably not, at least for now.* The conversation should wait until I'm perfectly calm and rational. And that's not now.

Finally, a rectangular hole appears at the arena's center. My heart thuds at double speed.

This is it.

A moment later, Walker steps through the dark portal. After that, *she* walks out behind him.

Myla.

I devour every aspect of her. Long auburn hair. Soulful brown eyes. Amber skin. Lovely, feminine curves. Predatory tail. Perfection.

Once Myla steps away from the portal, her face pales. It makes sense— ghoul transport can make anyone nauseous. Every instinct I have screams for me to approach her, making sure she's all right. Gripping the uneven stone wall, I force my body to stay put. It isn't easy.

Across the Arena, Walker checks on Myla. I can't hear the words he speaks, but the effect is clear. Within a few seconds, Myla stands upright again. Color returns to her luscious skin. As she recovers herself, an aura of energy seems to pulse around her.

Light.

Power.

Confidence.

She's magnetic.

The emcee must sense it too, since the ghoul decides to approach her. This master of ceremonies is an especially awful character with pointed teeth and a bad attitude. Once again, my protective instincts soar. My heart demands that I place myself between the two of them. Yet my intervention isn't needed. Myla's full mouth quirks with a smile as she faces off against the emcee.

I shake my head and grin. *This woman.* She's fearless. Intelligent. Passionate. Just watching her awakens something inside me—a corner of my soul which craves that same ferocity for life. All the while, her presence also soothes me in ways I hadn't even known I'd been hurting. All of it adds up to one conclusion: my waiting and scheming has been worth it.

Here she is. My Myla.

The wisp of a breeze strikes up behind me, interrupting my reverie. *That's odd.* This tunnel is a sealed off behind a heavy wooden door. What could start any wind? Turning away from Myla, I scan the darkened corridor. The reason for the change of air becomes clear.

The ghost of an elder thrax now hovers in the shadows. An ethereal breeze twists around him, making his formal tunic flutter against skeletal form. A long white beard cascades to his waist. The specter is instantly familiar.

"Minster Devak?" I ask.

Yesterday, I'd discussed this very thrax with Aldred.

And now he's dead and visiting me in spirit form.

Now this is unexpected.

*M*inister Devak's ghost hovers before me in all its semi-transparent glory.

It's almost beyond belief.

Yet not quite.

Was it just yesterday that Aldred and I discussed Devak's interest in hunting quasis?

Why yes, it was.

Since then, I've received no formal notification of the minister's death, which makes this ghostly encounter rather unusual. Not that I haven't met spirits before. Occasionally a ghost visits me before moving on to Purgatory. However, I'm always last on the list after the spirit presents itself to loved ones.

And the key concept here is *loved ones.*

The minister and I were never close outside of his official duties. It's odd for his ghost to find me so soon.

"Yes, it's me," replies Ghost Devak. "I just died a few minutes ago. Oldest thrax to pass away on record."

I nod. "Are congratulations in order?" Chatting with new ghosts is always tricky. You never know their mood.

"I lived a full life and now head off to my eternity. I am pleased."

"That's good to hear." *And I mean it.* "What brings you to me?"

Ghost Devak sighs. "My earl has signed the latest version of our anti-Acca treaty."

"Excellent." *One house down, two more to go.* "Though I doubt you're visiting me to share that piece of information."

"It's like this …" Ghost Devak pauses. "I've been chosen by the Tithe."

My brows lift. *That's not what I expected to hear.*

The Tithe is an immortal thrax warlock who fulfills your greatest wish, assuming you're both worthy and part-angel. Want a pile of gold? The Tithe will make it happen. Hope your enemies will disappear? No problem; the Tithe will handle it. In return, you agree to serve him through all eternity. The Tithe began life as a sculptor, so he places your ghost inside an effigy, which is a lifelike statue of your best self. You then spend forever as a happy resident in his so-called Tower of Wonders. In my mind, it's too good to believe, but my people like the idea of a *fairy godfather type* who solves all their problems. Plus, in this moment, the Tithe really doesn't interest me.

Myla's safety does.

A thread of unease winds through me. There's something unsettling about this ghost appearing ... the Tithe becoming involved in the minster's afterlife ... and Aldred's news regarding Devak and quasi hunting.

I haven't been a warrior my whole life not to recognize danger when it stands before me. And this situation with Devak positively overflows with menace.

"Selected by the Tithe," I repeat. "How nice." Yet as I say these words, my tone is more *ice* than *nice*. "I understand you've been asking about quasi fighters."

Ghost Devak's weathered face creases into a grin. "Yes, I was asking on behalf of my master. There's a particular quasi he wishes to hunt. It won't be easy, so no one can intervene." Ghost Devak stares at me pointedly, as if there's zero question who he expects to intervene. *Me.*

I keep my features still. Yet inside, my heart thuds with worry. *Please, don't let his target be Myla.* It's already bad enough that Aldred has taken an interest in my girl. I don't need a sketchy warlock after her as well.

"And who is his chosen target?" I ask.

Ghost Devak's grin widens. "The Tithe plans to hunt down the demon Myla Lewis. You must allow him to claim this quarry."

The way Ghost Devak speaks, it's as if hunting a woman were nothing more than swatting a fly. His casual tone transforms my sense of concern into something else. Pure rage now heats my blood. When I speak again, my voice drips with menace. "Why Myla Lewis?"

"She's a great warrior. That is all." Ghost Devak's smile falters. I've negotiated with this minister for years. I know what it means when Devak stutters while his grin fails.

I speak two more words, slowly and with barely controlled fury. "You're lying."

Ghost Devak grips his hands under his chin. "Please. Name your price to step down. Whatever you want, it's yours. My master must cleanse the after-realms, starting with Heaven."

Not this again. You'd think my people were obsessive cleaners instead of hunters, they way they prattle on about scouring evil from the after-realms. And it's always the bad *outside* Antrum that concerns them. Happily, I have a system for just such occasions.

"I've a scribe who does nothing but field messages from thrax who have ideas on how to cleanse the after-realms. Your friend can address his ideas to Lord Aethelgood." By the way, I had to make the man a lord before he'd accept this particular duty. It really is a horrid job. "What I care about is my original question."

To emphasize the risk here, I reach around my back to pull my baculum from their holster at the base of my spine. These silver rods can be ignited into any sort of fiery blade. I lift the bars high.

Ghost Devak's translucent eyes light up with alarm. *Good.*

"Let's try again," I say slowly. "Why does the Tithe *really* wish to hunt Myla Lewis?"

"My new master erased all my debts," whines Ghost Devak. "Soon he'll turn me into a powerful effigy. After that, I'll live forever in comfort and ease. The Tithe merely asks that I secure your help here. Why won't you just agree? Simply look away while the Tithe hunts one quasi. That's a *demon*, my prince!"

If that's Devak's closing argument, it's downright awful.

"Indeed, I am your Prince," I state. "Before you ever met the Tithe, you vowed to serve *my rule*. Now I command you; share every last detail about the Tithe and Myla Lewis." As I speak a final word, I ignite my baculum into a long sword made of white flame ...

"Now."

*A*ngling my body, I raise my fiery sword. Before me, Ghost Devak shudders, but doesn't say another word.

"Last chance, Devak. Why does the Tithe wish to hunt Myla?"

Ghost Devak hunches over, his face twisted with pain. His gaze focuses on a point behind me. "I hear you, my master," the minster says.

Ghost Devak is speaking to his master, but that's not me. I quickly scan the hallway. There's no sign of the Tithe, but that's no surprise. According to legend, the Tithe only manifests to future effigies. Glad I'm not on the list.

Devak keeps his gaze locked on the point behind me. "I accept the change."

While Ghost Devak speaks, I stay in battle stance, making no other move to attack. By saying he 'accepts the change,' it's likely that Ghost Devak is about to transform into an effigy, which will be a far tougher opponent. Of course, I could attack his spirit-self before he makes the switch to stone, but that's not the thrax way. Devak has a right to a fair fight.

And I wouldn't mind some exercise myself. It's hard to find decent opponents for battle.

Ghost Devak arcs his back in pain. For a moment, I see him.

The Tithe.

He is a dusty figure in a filthy toga. Sandals cover his feet. His grey hair sticks out at odd angles. Scruff lines his chin. In his left fist, the Tithe holds a chisel made of white crystal. A pale, luminous mallet is gripped in his right hand. A thin layer of fire and light encase both tools.

Magic.

The Tithe sets the chisel against Devak's spectral chest. With a swoop of his right arm, the Tithe brings down the mallet, driving the chisel deep into the ghost's body. A flash of white light bursts around the spirit. Tiny pale particles swirl in the brightness. The flare turns more bright, then vanishes altogether.

The spell is cast.

Devak's spectral frame crouches to the ground. A moment later, bits of pale powder rise up from the earth to fill his translucent body. The white specks swirl throughout his ghostly form. Limbs, hair, eyes, tunic—every part of Devak fills with winding tendrils. The dry scent of plaster fills the air as more of Devak changes from translucent ghost into solid rock.

Moments later, Devak slowly rises to his full height once more. By the time he stands completely upright, the minister appears to be made from white marble.

It's official. Devak is an effigy.

This new Effigy Devak appears young and fit, with broad shoulders and limbs that are heavily roped with muscle. He still wears his loose tunic, only now he holds a scimitar and small round shield. The minister's gaze locks with mine.

"I'm sorry, my prince."

Effigy Devak lunges for me, his scimitar angled toward my throat. I block the attack with my fiery long sword. The minister isn't familiar with his new and heavier body, so his movements are jerky and slow. The edge of his blade barely comes within a few feet of my neck.

Out in the arena, the crowd roars, falls silent, and then roars again. That can only mean one thing. Myla's fight has begun. That cheer means someone got in a good hit or two. My pulse speeds.

Who is winning—Myla or her opponent?

I kick Effigy Devak in his chest, sending him falling onto his back. The minister still find his bulky body hard to manage. As Effigy Devak struggles to stand up, I risk a quick glimpse into the arena.

What I see isn't comforting.

A mountain of a human races for Myla, his hefty arms aiming for her throat. His rough cry echoes in from the Arena floor: "I choooooooke you!"

Alarm rattles through my nervous system. *He wants to choke Myla? Not on my watch.* Moving my baculum so I grip one in each hand, I prepare to transform my fiery long sword into a bow and arrow. Just the thing to shoot a few blazing missiles into that human's back.

Unfortunately, Effigy Devak finally figures out how to stand once more. He rushes at me, his scimitar held high.

Myla will have to wait.

I ignite my baculum into a pair of short swords and block his attack. It's quickly clear that speed remains Effigy Devak's weakness. My blades connect with his shoulder and arm. Although Effigy Devak may be slow, his body is almost impermeable. I strike powerfully, yet all I do is send stone chips flying. As each hit connects, Effigy Devak doesn't so much as flinch. Being made of rock, he seems to be beyond pain.

Even so, his stone body gives me an idea. I adjust the grip on my short-swords, ready for a new battle plan. When Effigy Devak next attacks, I block his strike with one of my short-swords. With the other blade, I hack into the growing chip along the minister's shoulder. We continue this cycle.

Attack.

Counter strike.

Soon, there's an inch-long line at the juncture between Effigy Devak's shoulder and neck. A gentle popping sound fills the air.

Perfect.

Effigy Devak notices the pops as well. He steps backward, brushing his fingers along the break on his shoulder line. My opponent knows I'm up to something, he just doesn't know what that might be.

Fortunately, I manage the stone mason's guild, along with many others. Over the years, I've picked up a few tidbits of information.

I know exactly what will happen next.

While Effigy Devak checks his shoulder, I risk another look at the arena floor and grin. Myla got her massive opponent down onto his belly, and she's used her tail to confine him. And by 'confine,' I mean Myla hogtied the human's wrists and ankles behind his back.

Brilliant.

"I beeeeeat you," she calls out.

My smile widens. This woman.

In my own battle, Effigy Devak lowers his hand from his shoulder. Clearly, the minister is giving up on figuring out my plan. Instead, Effigy Devak rushes at me again. Evidently, his idea is to wear me down with attack after attack. Not bad. Eventually, I should tire while Effigy Devak will remain stone. Then once that happens, all the minister needs is one good strike and it could all be over.

Only Effigy Devak doesn't understand stone mason's guild. Big miss.

This time, when Effigy Devak attacks, I allow him to press his blade closer to my neck.

Six inches.

Three inches.

Two.

All Effigy Devak's concentration stays locked on the distance between his scimitar and my throat. What I do next only takes seconds, but each movement is crucial. Fast as a heartbeat, I extinguish my second short sword and setting the doused silver rod into the waistline of my jeans. After that, I pull my dagger from its holster on my thigh and jam the blade into the tiny break on Effigy Devak's shoulder.

Now that blade has become a make-shift splitting wedge.

Using my unlit baculum as a hammer, I slam onto the dagger's hilt, driving the weapon deep into Effigy Devak's stone body.

The minister lurches back a few yards. More popping sounds fill the air. Effigy Devak stares at me, his all-white eyes wide with confusion.

"What's happening?" he asks.

Honest questions deserve accurate replies, even in battle.

"The pops are internal breaks." One might think rock would split with a loud boom. Not always. The strongest material can give out the tiniest noise before shattering.

Sure enough, long cracks fan out from Effigy Devak's shoulder, spreading across his body.

"You're lying," says Effigy Devak. Raising his sword, the minister runs toward me once more. He doesn't get more than a few steps before his body shatters. One moment, there's a stone Effigy Devak. The next, a pile of white rocks line the ground. Perfect.

I nod once to myself, a decision made. I shall increase the wages for the stone mason's guild. They earned it today.

One large rock rolls down from the top of the pile. Effigy Devak's head. The minister's eyes open and focus on me once more.

"The ultimate countdown has begun," intones Effigy Devak. "I am number four. Three more after me, and we are done."

"What do you mean?"

"I must now return to my master. Look for me again."

Did he say to look for him? I'd rather the minister fully answer my questions for once. The pile of rubble trembles in place, including Effigy Devak's head. After that, everything transforms into white particles that cascade into the ground.

Battle over.

With Effigy Devak out of the way, I can return my attention to what's really important.

Namely, Myla Lewis.

Turning, I scan the arena once more. Sadly, Myla's no longer visible. The Great Scala, Maxon Bane, has now appeared. I wonder if my girl has moved to another access passageway like mine. I'd like to think she's still near, even I can't see her directly.

Ah well, it gives me a chance to watch the Great Scala at work. Maxon Bane is the only being who can transfer souls to heaven and Earth. He's also thrax, so my family keeps tabs on him. Not that there's much to do. Maxon Bane's had the same ghoul guards for eight hundred years now. They keep us informed on the Great Scala's health as well as the fact that Maxon Bane also hates visitors. In fact, this is the first time I've seen Great Scala at all, let alone witness his work.

Maxon Bane summons igni, which are tiny lightning bolts of power that move souls. The small streaks of light whirl into a massive column that reaches into the ground. Seconds later, the igni's brightness turns red. That can only mean one thing. The soul of Myla's opponent is being sent to Hell.

Sounds about right.

The evil soul vanishes along with the igni column. More ceremony follows as the Great Scala departs the Arena. I try to focus on the details, but my thoughts keep returning to Effigy Devak. Only three more before the

Tithe does … something? What? And why is Myla Lewis part of this plan? I'm not sure how long I stand there, but eventually my thoughts become broken up by a familiar sound.

Another ghoul portal is opening.

Soon Walker stands beside me again. Like always, he jumps into news without any greetings. "Minister Devak is dead. Your parents had to cut their trip short and request your immediate return. I'm here to offer transport."

"And I'll take you up on that offer. I'd like to see my parents. I've news of my own."

Walker tilts his head. "Anything you want to share?"

"Can you tell me everything you know about Myla Lewis?"

"Regretfully, no."

"I see."

Walker doesn't know it yet, but my friend will share his secrets about Myla. And I'll solve this mystery of the Tithe as well. If it could threaten Myla, then one thing is certain.

I will track it down.

Seconds later, I step out of Walker's portal. Around me stretches a small outdoor clearing that's encircled by sickly trees. The scent of stale rain and moldy grass fills the air. Brown and yellow leaves speckle the earth. *Ah, the Alighieri woods.* From here, it's a short walk to my parent's reception tent.

Walker steps out behind me. "Should I join you?"

"No, this is better on my own."

"Good luck." A moment later, my friend steps back through his portal and disappears.

Time to face my parents.

After a short and muddy march, I stand before the royal tent. As always, it strikes me how this place differs from our reception chambers in Arx Hall. Back at the palace, rooms are all gilded furniture and carved marble. Here the Master of Tents has done what he can, building a sizable square of black tapestry decorated with silver eagles. A guard stands by the entrance flap, his black metal armor gleaming without a single scratch.

Must be the new guy.

"Hello, Nelson," I say.

"Greetings, my prince." His helmet muffles his voice.

"Do I need to be announced?"

"No, your parents are alone and expecting you."

"Thank you."

Pulling back the entrance flap, I march inside. The layout has changed since I last visited. Small oriental rugs now line the floor, a patchwork of rectangles that fan out from the room's center. In the middle of it all, my parents sit on heavy wooden chairs behind a small round table.

As I approach, Mother inclines her head slightly. "My son."

My mother Octavia may be a tiny woman, but she wields a massive personality. Too many thrax get fooled by her prim dress, dainty features, and hair pulled back into a tight bun. In her youth, Octavia was a lethal warrior on the battlefield. Today Mother still fights to the death, only now she uses her mind instead of a sword.

Father rises, crosses the space, and wraps me in a bear hug. He's a mountain of a man with a barrel chest and chin-length white hair. "Lincoln, thanks for rushing over."

I lean into the embrace. "Good to have you back, though I regret the circumstances."

"It was Devak's time." Father sighs. "And your mother and I can reschedule our hunt." He claps me on the shoulders before returning to his chair. Like Mother, my father wears his formal gear today. In this case, that's a tunic, pants and boots. He eyes me carefully. "You're in human clothes."

"I was taking a break with Walker." One thing I learned growing up: I can say just about anything, assuming that statement is followed by the words, 'with Walker.' Some examples ...

I was out all night *with Walker.*

My black eye came from battle practice *with Walker.*

I adopted that lion cub when I was hanging *with Walker.*

You get the idea.

"The nobles of the House of Kamal just left," says Mother. "The Duchess Chaya was devastated about her brother's death. Although, there remains one bright spot in this dismal day." Her mismatched eyes glisten with joy. "Devak was chosen by the Tithe."

I fight the urge to groan. I'd forgotten how Mother and Father adore the Tithe.

"Devak had no head for business," adds Father. "He almost singlehandedly bankrupted the entire House of Kamal. Thanks to the Tithe, Devak's now left behind a sizable fortune." Father looks up to the Heavens. "Great thanks to the Tithe." Lowering his gaze, Father looks to me expectantly. I know well enough what he wants. I'm to dutifully agree that the Tithe is a marvel.

Not about to happen.

I fold my arms over my chest. "The Tithe is a scoundrel who wishes to harm innocents."

Mother and Father stare at me for a long moment. After that, they break into peals of laughter. Mother pats under her eyes. "Oh, that was rather funny."

Father lets out a 'hoo' noise. "You really had us going there."

Mother claps with joy. "We'll need to update the portrait gallery," she gushes.

I fight the urge to wince. In my worry about Myla, I'd forgotten about Mother's portrait galley project. So far, Mother has one hundred and twenty-seven portraits made of thrax that were honored by the Tithe. It's in the east wing of Arx Hall. In the past, I've never seen any harm in the endeavor. It gives our royal artists something to do. But now? The entire concept seems a little sordid. Who else has been fooled by the Tithe?

Mother taps her chin. "Where should we place the portrait of Devak?"

"Right by the entrance," answers Father. He turns to me. "Don't you agree, my boy?"

At this point, here's what I want to say: *Guess what? The Tithe is a bloodthirsty freak who asked my permission to kill Myla Lewis.* And by the passionate way I'd say all this, my parents would know I'm in love with her.

Not the best plan.

Instead, I decide to set aside Tithe for now. Besides, there are other topics which are more pressing.

Like Aldred.

Speeding forward, I take the seat across from my parents. "Place the portrait wherever you see fit." I pause, shifting my gaze between the two of them. "I have other news."

Mother straightens in her chair. "What is it?"

"Aldred wants to hunt the local population," I reply.

My parents exchange another long look, only this one doesn't end in laughter. Once more, I know exactly what that means.

"You were already aware of this," I say. "Weren't you?"

Mother keeps her features steady and unreadable. "Yes," she replies.

Frustration burns through me. Even so, I force myself to keep calm. For an inquest to be approved, I can't seem out of control. "Aldred must be stopped and you know it."

"Hold on!" Father slaps his knees. "We've news for you as well, my boy. Your mother and I had a marvelous demon hunt before it was cut short. We trapped an Arachnoid for the menagerie. Undefeated, that's what those demons are."

This is Father's way of trying to derail the conversation. The fact that Aldred's been mentioned means I'm about to make demands of the House of Acca. Sadly, Father is forever protecting the earl.

"I'm pleased your hunt went well," I say smoothly. "But that doesn't change how Aldred may be targeting innocents. Verus sent us here to make alliances with quasis. We cannot hunt them or allow anyone else to do so. I wish to launch a formal inquest. What do you say?"

My parents stay silent. Not the response I hoped for.

At length, Mother replies. "An inquest will upset our court," she says. "The nobility are already unhappy about visiting Purgatory."

"I'll be discrete," I counter. "Once you sign on, I can ask questions that have serious consequences. That is all."

"Ask one question or a hundred," says Father. "News of your inquest will spread through the camp like wildfire. A panic could start."

Mother nods. "Your father is right. We can't hold an inquest." She fixes me with a serious look. "We need to save our thunder when it comes to Aldred. Don't we have some trade route *treaties* to negotiate soon?"

The way Mother emphasizes the word *treaties*, I wonder if she knows about my anti-Acca project. "Not that I'm aware of," I reply.

"Ah, perhaps it's some other kind of *alliance*." Again, there's the slightest emphasis on that last word. *Alliance.* That settles it. Mother knows exactly what I'm up to. The upside is, she isn't revealing my plan. Mother supports my anti-Acca treaty. The bad side is that she won't extend help for both an inquest and the alliance. I'd press her, but I'm pushing my luck as it is.

I rub my neck as I think things through. An option appears. "We could also try a more positive approach. Our nobles clearly need something to focus on other than hunting innocents. I could establish more rigorous training sessions." I've been meaning to gauge the training level of Horus, Striga, and Kamal as part of my anti-Acca treaty. Two birds, one stone.

Father huffs out a breath. "You have time for that?"

"I'll find capacity." I drum my fingers on the tabletop, my thoughts racing. *There must be more ways to help Myla.* Another inspiration hits me. "We could also reinstate the autumn and winter tournaments."

"But we'd planned to skip the circuit this year," declares Father. "Holding the tourneys in Purgatory would mean building a special battle ground."

Mother nods. "Instead of tournaments, I was planning hold a farewell ball when we left the realm. That only requires the Ryder mansion, not new construction in this muddy bog of a forest."

"You can still hold the ball," I point out. "I'm talking about planning something … extra." Mother loves events.

Mouse, meet cheese.

"True." Mother purses her lips. My heart lightens. Mother only makes this particular face when she's considering something seriously. "I could schedule extra events at the Ryder mansion, if they can spare the space." Her pursed lips move to one side, which is an even better sign. "I'll ask the Great Ladies to help."

With Mother half-way to agreeing, I turn my focus on Father. "And what's wrong with building? It's another way for our people to stay busy. We could assign this to the House of Horus. Their architects are second to none."

"Not a bad notion," says Father slowly. "After all, Horus designed the pyramids."

"Precisely." I return my focus to Mother once more. "How soon can we schedule another event?"

"I almost forgot." Mother snaps her fingers. "There's a ball coming up soon. Where is that parchment?" She pulls a sheet from the pile on the tabletop before her. "Ah, here it is. An invitation to a diplomatic gala. I can no longer attend, but we can certainly force the men from court to be there."

Father's brows pull together. "Why can't you go?"

"The ladies of Kamal are holding a mourning ceremony that evening," Mother explains. "All noblewomen will attend."

"Right, right." Father doesn't seem happy about the fact, but it is a well-known practice for Kamal.

Mother squints at the document. "There will be demons, quasis, and angels in attendance. It's the perfect opportunity for everyone to learn how to interact without killing each other."

I keep up my steady drumming on the tabletop. "This is good. We'll have training, tournaments, and a diplomatic ball. Still, there must be more we can do." Suddenly, I notice that I've been drumming my fingers with such force, the whole table is shaking.

Subtle, Lincoln.

Mother's gaze locks on my hand and the tabletop. "How interesting."

Damn. I force my fingers to relax. It's too late, though. I can almost see the wheels of Mother's mind churning overtime. *Does she suspect why I'm really so passionate about this?* After all, my parents knew about Aldred hunting quasis. Maybe they know about Myla as well.

Father leans forward. "We know why you're *really* upset."

My blood chills. "You do?"

"This is all Verus' doing," grumbles Father. "She claims we're here to meet the quasis, but let's face it. The real reason we're in Purgatory is because of one person..."

Don't say Myla.

"The King of Hell," exclaims father.

"Absolutely!" And if I say that a little too loudly, no one seems to notice.

"You see," continues Father. "If Armageddon controls the Great Scala, then he controls everything. Verus wants us our help somehow to defeat him. Don't see why it requires the entire court, but there it is."

"Agreed," says Mother. "Even if Armageddon invades, it won't be a problem. Maxon Bane's ghoul guard will transport him directly to safety. Beyond making sure that happens, I don't see why Verus wants us here."

My chill of worry disappears. Clearly, my parents have no idea about Myla. "What can I say?" I ask. "I appreciate your understanding."

That's a bit of double-speak—after all, I sound like I agree with their assessment of why I'm upset—but when you're a prince, *tricky replies* go with the job description.

Father pats my hand. "Our people will be back home before you know it. Don't fret about staying here, my son. "

"I won't." *And that's the truth.*

Another idea appears. In all the excitement about the ball and tournaments, I forgot my other big issue—getting answers about the Tithe. And when it comes to unusual information, there's only one source, no matter what the question. It's not my parents, either.

It's the mermaids.

And of all fish folk, everyone knows who's the most connected and informed.

The mermaids of New York.

On top of the training, tournaments, and inquest, I can add another item to my *protect Myla plan*: an unofficial visit to New York Harbor. With that realization, a sense of contentment eases through me. At last, I have a solid scheme to keep Myla safe.

Perhaps.

6

*O*nce my parents agree that I'm only upset about Armageddon, I decide it's time leave the reception tent. No point pressing my luck. After saying my goodbyes to Mother and Father, I head straight back to my cabin.

What I'd like to do is visit Earth. There are two ways I can accomplish that.

First, I can use the temporary transfer platform set up here in camp. Pro: I leave right now. Con: Transfer Central keeps records. Both Mother and Aldred get immediate alerts on unscheduled transports. I'd rather not answer any awkward questions.

Which brings me to item two: making Walker portal me around.

Trouble is, I can't get Walker to show up, no matter how much I yell. Either he's outside Group Think radius (that's how ghouls communicate) or he's avoiding me. One way to find out. Which is why once I'm inside my cabin, I scribble out a quick message for Walker.

Buddy: I need to hit cloud-side without Acca knowing about it. Can you portal me to New York? I'd like to chat up the mermaids. As incentive, I will pay you your weight in cough syrup. — Lincoln

I hand off the parchment to a messenger (unlike Transfer Central, my personal staff are always discrete.)

Three days pass.

No reply.

At this point, I could approach another ghoul for transfer help. For instance Ike, the arena night guard, offered to transport me places. That said,

Walker still has secret info on Myla. My hunter's instinct tells me that he's well within Group Think range; he's probably just avoiding me.

All of which means that I want *Walker* to portal me around, mostly so I can press him with questions about Myla until he cracks. So I write out another message.

Walker: I've sent parchments to your residences in Heaven, the Dark Lands and Purgatory. No word. What's up? — Lincoln

Two more days slog by.

Still nothing.

It's official; Walker's definitely ghosting me. He does this from time to time, mostly when he's called off on some secret mission. But never without a quick note to say he'll be out of touch.

Nope, I'm being avoided.

Which means I'll just have to call in the big guns. Or in this case, send a message to someone else.

From: Prince Lincoln Vidar Osric Aquilus
  To: GSBG-9002, the Honorable Ghoul Minister
  RE: WKR-7
  Hope all is well. When you have a chance, can you please provide me with any alternative addresses you may have for WKR-7 in Purgatory? I've tried the one in Central City but he isn't in residence. The reason for my query is that I'm sending thank-you gifts (deluxe boxes of worms) for your hospitality, and want to be sure he's included. My scribes already have your address.
  Best,
  Lincoln

In diplomatic speak, this letter translates to the following: *give me Walker's real address and I'll send you big worm bribes.* This isn't the first time I've used this trick with GSBG-9002, by the way. Before, it got me information on Myla.

Now we'll see if it works again.

I seal the envelope and hand it off to a royal messenger. Much as I would love to finish off more letters—there's a pile on my desk awaiting replies—I have an event to attend this evening. The Ryder diplomatic gala. Before leaving, I instruct my personal guard to bring any new messages directly to the Ryder Mansion.

With any luck, I'll have the Ghoul Minister's answer—and Walker's help —very soon.

7

*A*n hour later, I stand in an ornate ballroom at the Ryder mansion.
In a tux.

And so, so bored.

Why did I think this was a good idea again?

That's right, it's for Myla. This event will keep my nobles busy and my girl safely away.

I scan the room. It's a human-style chamber with white plaster walls, a glass chandelier, and small balconies overlooking a dance floor. French doors line one wall; they lead to the gardens outside. Attendees from across the after-realms fill the space: ghouls, angels, quasis, demons and, of course, thrax. Even Armageddon, the King of Hell, is here. He's a tall figure with a squat body, long limbs and skin that resembles polished onyx. And considering the hungry way Armageddon scans the room?

The King of Hell's *virtual* rule of Purgatory will soon become *actual*.

There's nothing to worry about now, though. A plan already exists to evacuate Maxon Bane—as well as the entire thrax camp—if Armageddon invades.

I lean lack into the shadows. No one's sought me out, so I can lurk under a balcony and watch. There's a particular person I've been waiting for, and he has yet to arrive. This would be Silvinio, the Minster of Alliances for the House of Striga. Since Devak was targeted by the Tithe, I'm checking in with my other contacts for the anti-Acca treaty, namely Horus and Striga. Both have been tough to pin down. Jali, the Minister from Horus, has been unreachable as his granddaughter is ill. Which is completely understandable.

That only leaves Silvinio, who has no excuse for avoiding me. *Most suspicious.*

I keep up my silent vigil until—*yes!*—the thrax in question steps through the main archway.

Silvinio. Just the man I want to see.

Straightening the lapels of my tuxedo, I circle the outskirts of the chamber, taking care to approach to Silvinio from behind. When being avoided, I find it's best to approach stealthily. Otherwise, my target tends to slip into the crowd. Silvinio doesn't notice a thing until I clear my throat.

"Minister?" I ask.

Silvinio spins around "My Prince."

As always, Silvinio is a round muffin of a man with a greasy comb over and pockmarked skin. He's also as useless with gold as Devak, only the problem for Silvinio isn't a lack of business skill. No, this Minister of Alliances likes betting on Earth's demon fighting circuit. Sadly, he's terrible at it.

Silvinio pulls against his bow tie. "I was just looking for you."

I keep my features carefully unreadable. "Really."

Silvinio guiltily scans the room. "I reviewed the last version of your, uh, parchment."

"And?"

"The Earl has signed it." He lowers his voice. "The anti-Acca treaty."

"Excellent." That makes two houses—Kamal and Striga—that have approved. Now, only one house remains, Horus. I move nearer to Silvinio. "That's not why I wished to speak to you tonight."

"Oh?" Silvinio twists the rings on his hefty fingers. I can't help but notice how those magical bands are the sort created to be used during demon patrol —these particular rings provide protection from magical illusions. Rumor is, Silvinio 'borrows' them and resells for profit. I'd call him on this, but I've bigger issues to deal with today.

Myla's safety.

"There are rumors," I continue. "My nobles may be interested in hunting quasi demons. Heard anything?"

"Devak was asking around about quasi Arena fighters. Aldred overheard him and got the idea for a quasi hunt." Silvinio's gaze lands on Aldred, who stands across the ballroom floor. The Earl of Acca now stares at Silvinio with a glare that says, *you're so dead.* "Did I say Aldred wanted to hunt quasis?"

"You did."

"I got it all mixed up. Aldred would never hunt quasi demons."

"Care to place a wager on that?"

"I don't gamble anymore. Plus I'd never make a deal with the Tithe to lift my debts."

How wonderful. Being aware that Devak asked about quasis? Knowing the earl eavesdropped? Making deals with the Tithe?

Silvinio's been a rather busy boy.

A bead of sweat rolls down the minister's cheek. "You know who's really hunting quasis? Minister Jali."

"You don't say." And I mean this as in, *Silvinio really shouldn't say this.* Jali is one of the finest men I've ever met.

A flush crawls up Silvinio's neck. "Ah, I must leave to comfort my dear wife. She's sick."

"Really? I thought Lilah was attending tonight's mourning ceremony for Devak. That's what she told Octavia."

"Did I say Lilah was ill? It's me." Silvinio grips his stomach. "I've terrible intestinal cramps. You may want to step back."

Of all Silvinio's lies this evening, this one is my absolute favorite. "How specific." Now, I could press Silvinio for more information, but what the minister does next will tell me far more than anything from his mouth.

"May I?" asks Silvinio.

"You're excused from my presence." It's a heavy handed reply, but it's a traditional one.

"Thank you." Silvinio walks away at double speed. No, perhaps that's triple speed. Interesting that Silvinio made no mention of Myla. Devak was the only one with her name, and that was only after he finalized his deal with the Tithe. Once more, everything comes back to that mysterious warlock.

I really must visit the mermaids. If only I could locate Walker.

Silvinio runs directly to Aldred, and the two begin whispering. Silvinio points to me while making a rather pathetic face. If I had to guess, Silvinio just said something along the lines of, *the prince just asked whether thrax are hunting quasis.*

Aldred grips Silvinio by the lapels. Again, I can't hear a word, but knowing the earl? It's most likely, *what did you tell him?*

Silvinio wriggles in Aldred's grip. When the minister speaks, he winces. *I told him you weren't hunting anyone anymore.*

Little by little, the two swivel their heads in my direction. For a long moment, they both stare at me. Aldred is clearly weighing how much trouble he's in with me. Meanwhile, Silvinio's probably wishing he just left the room without talking to the earl. I give them both a friendly wave. This event has gotten downright interesting.

Aldred's jowls turn pink, which is a sure sign he's enraged. The earl then frog-marches Silvinio outside. No doubt, it's the last I've seen of that pair for this evening.

One of my personal guards steps to my side. "A message for you, my prince."

My interest perks up. Perhaps this is the letter I was looking for. *Walker, watch out. I'm coming for you.*

I take the envelope from him. "Thank you." I nod toward the departing minister. "Place a secret watch on Silvinio. Report his conversations, especially if he starts talking to people who aren't there. I want to know every word."

"Yes, my prince."

My guard walks away. I tear open envelope. Inside I find a note written in looping calligraphy.

From: GSBG-9002, the Honorable Ghoul Minister
To: Prince Lincoln Vidar Osric Aquilus
RE: WKR-7
Thank you for your kind letter. Walker's new residence is at 1160 Inferno Avenue in Lower Purgatory. Please let me know if you require anything else as you put together your thank-you shipments!
Best,
GSBG-9002

I grin. The Ghoul Minister is proving to be an excellent source of information, provided I keep him waist-deep in gift baskets of worms. As I slip the note back into my tuxedo pocket, a familiar outline steps into the room. Every nerve ending in my body goes on alert.

It can't be.

It is.

Myla Lewis.

Her lovely form is encased in a brightly colored dress. She smiles at a girl beside her—one with a golden retriever's tail—before her companion leaves for the dance floor. Myla circulates the room, chatting with various quasi diplomats. Every so often, Myla shares a little wave with the girl on the dance floor. Clearly, they're good friends.

My thoughts race. This is exactly what Walker warned me about. At some point, I might run into Myla. At least, Aldred is gone, so there's no worry he'll get interested in Myla as a new target.

Still, I should leave.

Now.

Trouble is, my feet seem locked in place.

Damn.

8

*M*y world has stopped spinning. Or perhaps it's simply whirling too fast. At this point, it's hard to know.

Myla Lewis is here.

Father steps up beside me. "How was the chat with Silvinio, my son?"

"Not too productive. He volunteered that he's no longer gambling." I leave out the tidbits about the Tithe and Aldred, since Father thinks those two can do no wrong.

"Is he gambling the demon fighting circuit again?" asks Father.

"Most likely."

Father then launches into a recap on the latest winners and losers on the circuit. At least, I think that's what he's talking about. It's hard to pay attention.

Myla is crossing the room.

And she's heading in my direction.

At some point, Father stops talking. Myla pauses a few yards away. Her back is toward me, but even so, I'm a hunter. There's no missing the slightest twitch in her ears. No one else stands nearby. Only me and my father.

Myla must be listening to us.

My thoughts race. What did Walker say before? Myla might find me intriguing, and Walker didn't want Myla to turn heartsick. Now, she seems to be paying attention. This is bad. True, I could be imagining her interest. But even if it's one chance on a thousand that I could hurt her, I simply can't risk it. Having Myla in my life will cause her nothing but pain, one way or another.

That leaves only one thing to do. Follow Walker's instructions. His words echo through my mind.

If you ever encounter Miss Lewis, you should play the haughty thrax. Look down on her demonic side. She'll hate it—and you—forever.

Taking in a deep breath, I steel my spine. Here it comes. My anti-demonic tirade. I try to get the words out, but nothing happens.

Oh, Hell.

My mind whirls through more options. Perhaps I should start small and work my way up.

Yes, that could work.

With my new plan in place, I shoot my father a frustrated glance. "I don't understand why we're here, Father."

Perfect. That's testy but not committing to anything horrible.

"More orders from the angels, son. They want closer relations between the realms."

"I understand. What should I do?"

The moment those words leave my lips, I want to punch myself. Hard. That wasn't the horrid statement I'd been working toward.

"Try to socialize," replies Father. "Meet some quasis in particular."

A few yards away, Myla arcs her head ever so slightly. As a hunter, I know what that movement means. She's listening. The realization steels my nerves.

"Quasis aren't people," I declare. "They're demons." To my own amazement, my words sound both smooth and believable. Even so, they seem to burn my tongue like acid.

"Angels say they're different," retorts Father. "Try to keep an open mind." He gestures to the dance floor. "Take that girl, for example. Why don't you ask her to dance? She seems quite, uh, friendly."

My heart sinks. That's Myla's friend. Which means there's no way I can give a kind reply. This is my chance to break things off with Myla before they even begin.

I must take it.

"That quasi has a dog's tail and acts like one in heat." Even if I can almost hear my heart crack as I speak the words. "Besides Father, you know I'm no diplomat."

"Where's my best soldier?" Father punches my upper arm. "I know I can rely on you for this mission."

"Of course."

"That's my boy." Which is his way of saying, *I'm done here.*

As Father walks off, I keep my gaze locked in Myla's outline. She still seems alert, but isn't fidgeting or clenching her fists. A wave of relief moves through me. Maybe I was imagining the connection between us. Every hunter makes mistakes. All this time, I may have been torturing myself over nothing.

Clang. Myla knocks over a can onto the floor.

Now I could leave, but my feet move toward Myla on their own. "Are you alright, Miss?"

She turns to face me and I could cheer for joy. Up close, she's lovelier than I imagined. Life and light glitters in her brown eyes. My arms ache to envelop her. She smells of cinnamon and sunshine.

"I'm fine," she says simply. "I dropped an empty can, that's all."

We pause. Lines of energy and interest flow between us, connecting our hearts. *No, no, no.* This isn't supposed to happen. And it means I should definitely leave.

And I want to.

Yet I can't.

"You look familiar," I say. "You don't visit the Ryder stables, by any chance?"

Her eyes widen. "Nope."

I fight the urge to smile. She remembers the Doxy demons. That's good, considering how I contemplate that night constantly.

"Ah, my error then." I bow slightly. "My name's Lincoln."

Our gazes lock. The energy between us intensifies. The room melts away until only she and I remain. With all my heart, I want to tell her how I admire her … that she transformed every assumption I ever held about what a woman could be … and vow how I'd do anything only for the chance to talk an hour more.

Then thoughts of Aldred appear in my mind, as well as that bloody Vantys demon's head.

All hope burns to ash in my soul. My life isn't a fairy tale. I sacrifice for the greater good. In this case, that means keeping Myla safe from both me and my people. Walker's advice ricochets through my mind once more.

If you ever encounter Miss Lewis, you should play the haughty thrax. Look down on her demonic side. She'll hate it—and you—forever.

When I speak again, it's an effort to keep my features level. "You must be a quasi, um, 'demon.'"

"I'm 'Myla.'"

Her voice goes even lower. That demon line struck home. *Damn.*

"Pleasure to meet you." I need to say something else terrible. *Think.* "Would you … Would you like to dance, Myla?"

Not what I planned to say.

Clearly, I've having some conflicts here.

You can do this, Lincoln.

It's an effort, but I force more disgusting words from my mouth. "It seems to be something *your kind* enjoys."

Myla's eyes flash red with demonic rage. "Do you mean 'our kind' as in my friend with the dog tail?" She juts her thumb toward the pair on the dance floor. "You remember? The one in heat?"

I steel myself. "What I said was true. I can hardly bear to watch."

"So, you find quasis repulsive."

"What do you expect? You're part demon. I'm a demon hunter. Asking you to dance was a kind gesture on behalf of–"

"Kind gesture?!" She purses her lips and it's all I can do not to kiss her. "I've got a gesture for you." She turns and walks away; her tail waves good-bye in my direction.

For a moment, my nervous system is overloaded with elation. *She's safe. I sent her off.* Then follows the inevitable crash. What was I thinking? I just acted like the worst kind of rogue. And I probably ruined my chances with Myla.

Not that I had any to begin with.

Which means this is for the best.

So why is this the worst I've ever felt?

A weight of sorrow settles into my soul. Once Myla is truly gone, I take my leave as well. Myla may hate me, but that doesn't mean I'll stop protecting her. Now that I know Walker's true address, I must track down my friend and convince him to transport me to the mermaids. That way, I can get answers about the Tithe. After all, keeping Myla safe is my only option for bringing something good into her life.

I'm taking it.

9

"*W*ow, you're fast." That's Nelson speaking. He's the new guard and my latest sparring partner today. After last night's disaster at the ball, I've spent all day in battle practice. Nelson's my latest victim. We're both wearing fitted shorts, and I just dodged his attempted *elbow strike* to my chin.

"Focus on the battle, Nelson." To emphasize my point, I deliver a round-house kick to the side of his head. Though I don't use as much force I could. Nelson's a newbie.

"That was even faster." Nelson wobbles a bit, so I give him a few moments to recover. Today, my new guard and I are practicing on what will eventually be the autumn tournament green. It's an open space surrounded by wooden frameworks that will soon become seating pavilions.

"Can you do that kick again?" asks Nelson.

Nothing says *I'm getting punch drunk* more than asking for another round-house to the head. "Let's call it a day."

"Sure, whatever you want." Nelson grins. He's a lanky lad of sixteen with short brown hair that sticks up along the center of his head, Mohawk style. I'd say it's a fashion choice, but I believe it's more of an unfortunate cowlick.

"Do you need another sparring partner?"

To keep my mind off Myla, I've been in non-stop matches with my personal guards. Then my Master at Arms. After that, I moved on to face top contenders for the tournaments. The fact that I'm now practicing with newbies like Nelson shows how much bottled-up energy I still carry. Eighteen fights today and I remain wired. "It's a thought at that." *If there's anyone left to fight.*

"I simply must say something," Nelson gushes.

"Go on."

"What an honor this has been. I mean, you're … you."

I chuckle. "Not sure what that means, but this fight has been my pleasure. We both have warrior mothers. Best for us to stick together." Nelson's father is from Rixa. His mother is a human MMA fighter that his dad met while on demon patrol.

Nelson's smile widens. "I must ask. What's it like?"

"Like?"

"Being prince? Having people hang on your every word. Standing at the center of all ceremonies. I can't imagine."

Now, there are two answers to this question. First, there's the true one. People pay attention to me because I wield power and can change their lives. That's a responsibility, not a job perk. And ceremonies? Painfully boring. But that's not the answer I give. I choose the second option—a generic response that doesn't ruin Nelson's starry-eyed belief in what it means to be royal. "It's my honor to serve."

Nelson steps closer. "What about the ladies? You're so handsome. Power-ful. Everyone loves you."

One thing I've learned about being heartsick. Thrax said such things to me before, and it never resonated. Now, every comment about love feels like a blow. Having someone fawn over your power or looks isn't the same as true intimacy. That only comes after seeing the best and worst in another and still loving them. It's the kind of connection I'll never have. Knowing that shouldn't hurt as much as it does.

I want to give Nelson another *option two style* gentle reply, but it isn't in me. "Thank you again for your time today."

"Did I say something wrong?"

"No, it's almost sundown. I have an appointment this evening." With Walker, although the ghoul doesn't know that yet.

"Sure, thanks so much." Nelson shakes my hand vigorously before rushing off. I imagine him returning to his barracks, telling stories of his fight today with the prince he admires. That person isn't me, however. I'm an illusion.

Chin up, Lincoln. You've work to do.

With Nelson gone, I return to my cabin and change into mortal clothes. With any luck, Walker will take me to Earth tonight, so I must be ready. Once in my jeans, I saddle up Nightshade for a ride to Walker's secret hideout. *1160 Inferno Avenue.* Night soon takes off at a trot. As we move along, scenery consists of sickly thin trees, brown leaves and mud. It's not long before we reach the edge of the Alighieri Woods.

Interesting. Walker's house is not only near the Alighieri woods; he's also set up shop close to Myla's home on Dante Avenue as well. I'd call that an odd coincidence, but it's not.

My friend is keeping an eye on both of us.

I pull gently on Nightshade's reins. "Ho." Night stops. I slide off her barrel and pat her neck. "I can walk from here."

Night swings her head around to face me. With grand movements, she arches her neck up and down. It's her way of saying, *why the Hell are you wearing that?*

None of this is surprising, by the way. My horse has tons of opinions.

"Yes, Night. I'm in casual human clothes again tonight." This time, it's jeans and a *Little Red Corvette* Henley.

In reply, Night does that move where she whinnies while showing her teeth. This means, *thanks for not answering my question.*

"You're such a busybody. I'm dressed casually because I'm on a mission for Myla."

This time, Night tears at the ground with her front hoofs. *She approves.*

"Yes, I know you like her." This isn't our first conversation about Myla. I pat Night's neck again. "Can you get back to the camp on your own?"

Night chuffs—a kind of snorting sound—which is to say, *don't be insulting.* Without waiting for further instruction, she takes off into the forest. I shake my head and grin.

Of all the horses I've raised, Night really is the best.

With Night gone, I march over to Walker's hideout. I soon locate my destination: a one-story ranch house that looks identical to all the others beside it, except for the number. *1160.* The shades are drawn, but lights gleam inside. Someone's home. Excitement streams through me.

Here we go.

After hiking up the short flight of cement steps, I knock on the front door. A nearby curtain rustles. I wave at the window. No doubt, Walker's on the other side of that glass pane, staring at me in shock.

The front door opens a crack. A sliver of Walker's familiar face becomes visible. In classic Walker style, he skips all the greetings. "How many bribes did it take to find me?"

"Only one. GSBG-9002 gave you up for one complimentary shipment of worms."

"Of course." Walker frowns. "Gasbag."

"GSBG-9002 is nicknamed Gasbag? I love it." I hitch my thumbs into the loops on my waistband. "May I come in?"

Walker shakes his head, followed by a dramatic glance toward Heaven. It's his way of saying, *give me patience with my crazy friend.*

"We could also chat out here," I say. "It might get awkward, though. You know how I tend to raise my voice in conversation."

In truth, I can keep a tone low easily. But the statement is a not-so-veiled threat that I could get Walker in trouble with his neighbors. It works like a charm.

"Fine," sighs Walker. "Come in."

Walker fully opens the door and I step inside. The place is what I'd call *generic Purgatory*: chipped walls, cracked ceiling, and dirty carpet. The only difference? This residence looks like a homeless artist decided to turn squatter inside. There's no furniture, unless you count the painter's easel set up in one corner. Scraps of drawings cover the walls. A lone coffee machine sits in one corner, unplugged. It's like Walker meant to make himself some java but never got organized.

I step along the periphery of the room, scanning the drawings as I go. "Here's a Simia demon. And a Limus." I pause before an image of a girl in battle. "Oh, look. A drawing of Myla Lewis. The girl you barely know beyond saying, *hello and goodbye*."

Walker doesn't reply. Instead, he leans against the closed door. My friend is in jeans and a very paint-spattered white t-shirt. The dry look on his face says, *get it out of your system, Lincoln*.

"Did you know Myla lives at Dante Row?" I tap my chin in mock-consideration. "Hey, that's within psychic distance of this very spot. She could scream for you and with your ghoul Group Think, you'd pick it up."

Walker exhales another sigh. "I can't tell you anything about her, Lincoln."

I keep scanning the room. These drawings are a treasure trove of demonic information. Too bad there aren't more images of Myla, though. I pause before the canvas on the easel. It shows two archangels in golden armor, their wings extended as they hover in a cloud-filled sky. Behind them stands the white Citadel of Heaven. It's a massive tower-style castle that serves as the training base of the angelic army. I took my share of classes there over the years.

Which means I can instantly identify this pair.

"You've painted the archangels Aquila and Xavier," I state. "I'd forgotten how they founded the Citadel together." I look to Walker. "Were they both there when you went through training?" Aquila still shows up at random moments, but no one's heard from Xavier in years. "I never saw them when I was at school."

"No comment." Walker crosses the room and places a white sheet over the canvas. "Fine, I will say one thing. This is extraordinarily awkward."

"Clearly, you're uncomfortable with me snooping around your stuff."

Walker fake-gasps. "It's like you can read my mind."

"There's a remedy for this situation. Transport me to New York harbor."

Walker slowly narrows his eyes. That means he's thinking my statement through. "You want to speak with the mermaids, don't you?"

Walker really is clever. "Right."

"And you don't want Aldred to know."

"Right again." I cup my hand by my mouth and speak in a very low and sarcastic voice. "If you'd opened my messages, then you'd know that already."

Walker throws up his hands. "You got me. I'm interested. What's the trouble?"

"Aldred has taken it in his head to hunt quasis. I'm working to squash that effort."

Walker's stance stiffens. "What gave him that idea?"

"It's a bit of a story, but the short answer is the Tithe told Devak to research Myla. After that, Devak asked around, and the earl overheard. Now Aldred is just being Aldred."

"Did you say the Tithe?" Walker frowns. "Isn't that some nice old thrax warlock in a toga?"

"He's a bastard. The Tithe sent Devak to me and in ghost form, no less. Devak then passed along the request that I look away while the Tithe hunts Myla."

A glint of red shines in Walker's eyes. "He *is* a bastard." Ghouls are a bit demonic themselves, it's how they stay alive after death. Walker is seriously enraged for his irises to glow red.

"My feelings exactly. Most thrax wouldn't agree with me, though. Most essentially worship the Tithe, including my parents."

"What do you know about this warlock?"

"Not much. I've had my archivists scour everything. He began mortal life as a sculptor and uses an enchanted mallet and chisel to create his effigies. Beyond that, information is scarce."

Walker rocks on his heels for a moment before answering. He's thinking again. At length, my friend focuses on me once more. "In that case, share every last detail of what's happened with Devak, Aldred, and the Tithe. Afterwards, I'll take you to see the mermaids."

It's unseemly to gloat, which is why I save it for special occasions, like this one. I bob my brows. "I knew you'd see things my way."

"I'm assuming you wish to visit after nightfall?" asks Walker.

"Correct. Mermaids are nocturnal."

Walker winces. "In that case, my portal services will need to wait a bit. I have conflicting evening commitments on Earth."

"That's fine." With my friend, it's always something. What's key is that I pushed him into transporting me at all.

Walker stares at me for a long moment. "You're a bossy pain in my ass."

"It's *Prince* Bossy Pain In My Ass to you, my friend."

And with that, I'm off on the next phase of my plan to protect Myla.

With Walker.

10

*W*alker and I hang out for a time. My friend asks tons of questions. What exactly did Devak say? Why would thrax wish to hunt quasis? How come Aldred gets away with everything?

It takes a while, but I answer all Walker's questions, except that last one about Aldred. Even *I* don't know why Father always gives into the earl. By the time we're done, it's well past midnight. After taking my leave, I return to my cabin on foot. Too much nervous energy thrums through me. With any luck, a walk will be calming.

It isn't.

By the time I reach my cabin, questions still buzz around my brain. In the end, it takes hours for me to fall asleep. When I do, I dream of Myla at the Ryder mansion. Every time I try to approach her, my girl disappears into the crowd.

Even so, I never do give up on her, even in my dreams.

~

Days slip by.

I spend the time in more so-called *battle practice* with my top warriors. They say they appreciate the fact that I'm not holding back anymore, but I wonder. There are a lot of black eyes and stitches at camp these days. Then one morning, I wake up to the sound of a gentle but persistent knock at my cabin door. Only one person raps incessantly without any formal announcement.

"Good morning, Mother," I call.

"Are you decent?" she asks.

Mother knows I loathe wearing pajamas. Nevertheless, I roll out of bed, slip on some loose leathers, and open the door a few inches.

"I am always decent," I say. "Sometimes I just happen to be naked."

"Ha, ha," she deadpans. As I spy her through the crack in the door, I can see that Octavia's already in her full kit as queen, complete with a black velvet dress and silver crown. Mother arches her right brow. "May I come in?"

"Sure." I step back and allow her to enter.

Mother steps around my chamber for a few seconds. "What are your plans for today?"

I yawn and rub my neck. "I've a meeting with the Minister of Alliances from Horus."

"It's been cancelled. Jali's granddaughter remains ill."

That news wakes me up. Considering how we have magic to aid our healing, it's rare for thrax to stay sick. "Anything serious?" I ask.

"I should think not," replies Mother. "Lucas has taken over Rashida's care."

I nod. This is good news. Lucas is the Earl of Striga and a powerful warlock. If anyone can help little Rashida, he can.

"In that case, my day is open. Tonight I visit Earth with Walker."

"How nice," says Mother. And for the thousandth time in my life, the magical words 'with Walker' get me out of an uncomfortable discussion. In this case, it's one about Myla and mermaids.

I lean against the wall. "So, what am I doing today?" Clearly, Mother has a plan for the daylight hours. Otherwise, she wouldn't be here.

"Your father and I have a surprise for you. We're all attending an event."

"One that I'll like?"

"Decidedly not."

This bodes ill. Last time Mother did something like this, I ended up hosting an all-day clown festival for thrax children. It was as terrifying as it sounds.

"May I know where we're going?" I ask.

"Purgatory's Arena."

Those two words send my pulse racing. It takes everything in me to stay calm. "And why would we do that?"

"To help foster quasi-thrax relations. The entire thrax court visits the arena this morning."

"For what purpose?" If Mother says an arena battle, I won't be able to maintain my calm. At the very minimum, I'm going to cheer.

"An awards ceremony."

A mixture of relief and disappointment move through me. I've attended hundreds of awards ceremonies in my life. It's a lot of sitting around and listening to speeches before handing over an honorary sword.

Prince life.

Dull.

I open my mouth, ready to ask specifics on the award in question, when Mother speeds toward the exit.

"Be ready in ten minutes." She slips out the door, almost fully closes it, and then reopens it a crack. "And wear your crown."

Now I could beg off this event. After all, a new pile of demon patrol reports just arrived, ready for review. One of my least favorite demons, the Dissolus, has recently become a full infestation in North America. But I have to admit it. Some small part of me hopes Myla's at the arena for some reason. Perhaps she left her wallet behind … or needs to inspect the grounds?

A man can hope.

*a*n hour later, I stand on Verus's balcony at Purgatory's Arena, along with much of the thrax nobility. Below me, angels and demons stream onto their seats along the tiered benches which surround the battle floor. Across the space, Armageddon settles onto a terrace that matches this one.

Soon the ceremony will begin. *Giving out awards.* Honestly, I'd rather be punctured with quills from a Hystrix demon. And those are tipped in poison.

While we wait, Mother and Father chat up Verus. The Queen of the Angels isn't wearing her crown today. Even so, there's no missing her aura of authority. Somehow, her straight black hair, intelligent eyes, and graceful bearing all scream, *I'm in charge here.* At the moment, no one seems to require my attention. As a result, I've taken to one of my favorite activities at formal events.

Waiting by the back wall, well out of sight.

Over the years, I've perfected the art of appearing interested in a ceremony while I mentally refine battle plans and whatnot. Not as easy as it sounds.

In this case, I internally plan questions for the mermaids. Conversations with sea folk tend to be short. Mermaids can only focus for a minute or two. After that, their urge to drain your life force turns overwhelming. Therefore, I decide to gather information about the Tithe, first and foremost. My royal archivists still have turned up nothing on him.

Down on the Arena floor, Walker opens a ghoul portal. My blood freezes. Could this Myla? A figure steps out from the darkened doorway.

A woman.

With a dragonscale tail.

And she's wearing a skin-tight battle suit that appears to be made from dragonscales.

Yes, the woman wears a hood over her face, but there's no missing the truth.

It's Myla.

My blood heats. I thought this was an awards ceremony, not a battle. My gaze flickers to Mother. Sure enough, Octavia gauges my reaction with interest. Keeping my features level, I mask my shock. It's too late, though. I couldn't have appeared more interested if I'd drooled.

At this point, I'd normally spend some quality time wondering what Mother's up to. Why isn't Octavia worried about my interest in Myla? If anything, Mother wears the starry-eyed expression she gets right before her and Father make out at the dinner table. Yet try as I might, I can't focus on Mother right now.

Instead, all I can see is how Myla practices kicks and leaps on the battle floor. Meanwhile, here I am, essentially trapped on this balcony, unable to do anything but watch her. Desire rockets through me.

Whose idea was it to give her a dragonscale fighting suit? So unfair.

Next Verus sneaks a quick peek in my direction. The Queen of the Angels is almost as conniving as Mother, and I mean that as a complement. Verus gives me the smallest of approving smiles. In other words, Verus likes the fact that I'm riveted by Myla. Once more, this situation should launch some logical thought on my part. How exactly does Verus come into play here? What's her interest in me and Myla?

And I try to contemplate Verus's actual motivations, but...

Dragonscale fighting suit.

Curves.

Hair.

Myla.

In this moment, the higher-functioning parts of my brain don't stand a chance.

While Myla continues her graceful warm-up, Verus and Armageddon begin a formal—and rather loud—conversation across the Arena about the importance of the Scala Heir. Armageddon seems particularly upset that the heir has not yet been found. Our spies say Verus is in fact hiding the heir. Even my people don't know where this person could be.

Which is a wise move.

Being the official Scala Heir hasn't been conducive to a long life span. Not that it's a serious worry, in my opinion. He may be on a stretcher, but Maxon Bane still has centuries before he'll pass away.

While the King of Hell and Queen of the Angels continue their banter, I work hard to contemplate the Scala Heir and inter-realm politics. My thoughts don't go far, though.

That really is a lovely fighting suit.

And Myla's an acrobatic fighter. I've rarely seen a woman lift a sword, let alone twist in the air while practicing kicking someone's face in. It's hypnotic.

At some point, the chatter stops. The arena emcee announces a new match between Myla and some thug named Deacon. Which is fine. It's Myla's job to stop evil souls from entering Heaven. She kicks ass and the *big bads* go to Hell. I look forward to seeing her fight once more.

That's when Armageddon pipes up.

The King of Hell demands that Deacon use a weapon during the battle. My spine stiffens. *That's not acceptable.* I've studied how these fights work. This is hand-to-hand combat, no weapons allowed. The only reason Armageddon's pushing this idea is because he desperately wants a purely evil soul in Heaven, which would give the King of Hell an easy means for causing all sorts of trouble.

As I watch the events on the arena floor, my attention stays locked on the ghoul emcee. That pointy-toothed loser simply can't give Armageddon what he wants. Yet that's exactly what happens. The emcee gives in. Myla must go into the fight without a weapon, while Deacon can bring one.

Protective energy streams through my blood. *This isn't right. Myla could get hurt.*

Before I know it, Mother stands at my side. "Don't worry," she says in a soothing voice.

"About what?" I mean for my tone to sound smooth, but I end up biting off each word.

Mother keeps her voice carefully low, so only I can hear her. "That girl's a fine warrior. She'll defeat Deacon, mark my words."

"And why would you think her fate worries me?"

"You're about to ignite your baculum, my son."

"I am?"

Sure enough, I'd pulled my baculum out from the holster on my spine. Both rods are now gripped on my right hand, ready to be ignited as a long sword. I didn't even realize I'd done it.

Ugh. Caught in the act.

I make a quick scan to see if anyone other than Mother noticed. The answer is *no*, considering how everyone focuses on the fight. I quickly reholster my baculum.

"Thank you, Mother."

"Any time, my son."

What follows are ten of the longest minutes of my entire life. Deacon's weapon turns out to be a long whip made of hellfire. He wraps it about Myla's throat, choking her. No less than three times do I retake my baculum from their holster, but with each instance Mother sets her hand on my arm, calming me.

"She can do this," Mother repeats.

At last, Myla stabs Deacon through the chest with her tail. I join the angels in a hearty cheer. Needless to say, the demons are less than pleased.

Once the battle is over, Father approaches us. "An entertaining fight, don't you think?"

"Exceptional," replies Mother.

I'm glad Mother has the sense to answer. It takes all my strength not to groan. Entertaining? Honestly? Watching that battle took years off my lifespan.

Across the balcony, Verus rises and turns toward our group of thrax. "It's time to visit the Arena floor." Is it my imagination, or is she staring straight at me?

"Of course," says Mother. "Let's begin the awards ceremony." She turns to Father. "Do you have the sword, Connor?"

"I do," replies Father.

All of a sudden, the full panorama of today's nightmare comes into focus. This is both an Arena match *and* an awards ceremony.

Somehow, Mother put this together.

Which means …

I round on Mother. "Am I right to assume I'll be handing out this award?"

"Directly to Miss Lewis," says Mother smoothly.

"What gets me out of this?" I ask. Mother must want something. She always does.

She chuckles. "Nothing."

Ah, Hell.

Father's gaze switches between me and Mother before focusing on Myla down on the Arena floor. *Oh, no.* He's figuring things out at last. Father nods toward Myla. "That's the girl you insulted at the diplomatic ball."

"And who told you that?" I ask.

"Your mother." Father grins. "And how she knows is anyone's guess. Come along, son. If I know your Mother—and that I do—then she wants to you make nice with the quasi girl."

The fact that Father calls her *quasi girl* sets my protective urges spiking again. "Her name is Myla Lewis."

"Perfect." Father claps his hand on my shoulder. "Glad you've got that part down, considering how you're giving her the award and all. You know how I am with names."

My thoughts race through ways to escape this situation. Feign illness like Silvinio? Pretend to receive an emergency message? Not going to happen.

Honestly, there's no way that I'll miss any chance to see Myla, even if I do come up with a fine excuse.

With that, Father and I process down the steps to the Arena floor. I can't help but notice how Mother walks with the nobles, as if she's not part of the royal party proper. It's something she often does when scheming: *hang back and observe*. The court notices, of course. Whispers erupt. No doubt, the nobles will connect Octavia's actions with my handing out the award to Myla.

This is a disaster on so many levels, I've lost count.

Trumpets sound as I step out onto the Arena proper. A herald announces our presence. "King Connor and his son, the High Prince!"

Father and I process forward. As we close in on Myla, my thoughts race. How should I handle this encounter? Certainly, I can't act like I've been obsessing about her. In fact, she can't even know that I recognized her from the moment she stepped into the Arena. And most of all, I must maintain the pretense that I'm an awful fellow.

That's my vow. *Protect Myla from everyone, even myself.*

Before I know it, Father and I stand before Myla and that awful emcee. Walker's still here, which is not surprising since he transported Myla. My friend waits across the Arena floor, standing just inside an exit passageway. That's what you call, *keeping a strategic distance.* Clever.

The emcee rounds on Myla. "Remove your mask, slave."

At those words, my hands curl into fists. Every instinct I have tells me choke the life out of that ghoul. Before I get the chance to move, Myla pulls off her mesh hood. The movement seems to go extra slow, as if charmed by a speed spell. Myla shakes her head, sending her long auburn hair tumbling down her back.

Our gazes lock. Energy and interest zing between us. I imagine reaching forward, brushing my fingertips along her jawline.

My Myla.

She takes in a quick huff of breath, and I realize my mistake. I can't indulge in such fantasies. My people want to hunt Myla Lewis. I can't be with her; I can only protect her. My gaze snaps over to Walker, who now stands with his arms folded over his chest, his face glowering with rage.

I don't blame Walker for being angry. I'm screwing this up.

My plan clicks back into place. I must act as if I didn't know this was Myla all along. With every ounce of princely training, I force on a look of alarm. "You."

Ok, that worked. It sounded both surprised and haughty.

"Yes, me." When Myla speaks, her voice comes out a bit husky. Even worse, we can't seem to look away from each other. In my peripheral vision, I spy Walker over in the access passage, violently shaking his head, *no.*

Walker's right.

I must stop looking at her.

And I will.

In a minute.

While I enjoy my staring contest with Myla, Father turns to the evil emcee. "What is this girl's name?" Not a surprising comment from Father, by the way. He truly is horrible with names.

"It's Myla Lewis, your Majesty." Clearly, this ghoul would rather have his pointed teeth removed than call Myla anything but a slave. The idea of pummeling him in the face returns with a vengeance.

"You fought bravely, Myla Lewis," says Father.

At this point, a great and horrible thing happens. Myla looks away from me to focus on my Father. Our staring contest ends. From his hiding place in a nearby archway, Walker smiles broadly. I'm really starting to hate his involvement in my love life.

Father continues. "Part of our mission here is to build better relationships with quasis such as you. Please accept this sword in congratulation." He holds up the ceremonial sword. Then he stops.

Father turns to me. I know the movement happens in regular time, but it seems to go extra slowly, like we're all trapped under another enchantment. "Perhaps you should give her this, my son. I believe I saw the two of you talking at the ball."

Myla's eyes widen while her mouth contorts into a face one can only describe as 'yuck.' I should be devastated. I'm not. Everything about my girl exudes energy and life, even her hatred for me. I adore every scintilla of her.

Myla raises her hand. "We don't know each other."

I take the weapon from Father. "Let me think." I peruse Myla's form, as if trying to remember if I've seen her before. Big mistake. That dragonscale fighting suit will haunt me until the day I die.

Focus, Lincoln.

A thought hits me. It seems as if fate keeps throwing Myla and I together. Fine. If we're going to hate each other, we might as well lean into it. Setting the sword's point into the ground, I rest my hands rest atop the pummel. "I believe we had one conversation. About pets, as I recall?"

My words are a challenge, and Myla jumps right to it.

She plasters on a false grin. "Now, I remember the conversation. You were a true prince." With a dramatic swoop of her head, she turns to my father. "I am grateful for the sword, your Highness."

Her gaze locks with mine once more. The staring match intensifies. Only this time, we're both sporting smarmy grins.

This is the most fun I've had in weeks.

No, months.

Father clears his throat. "Perhaps if you said a few words, son."

That's right. I'm playing the rogue and handing out an honorary sword. *Back to work.*

"Sure, Father." I inhale a dramatic breath. "This quasi girl–"

"Myla. My name's Myla."

Her smile vanishes. Instead, she looks ready to punch me in the throat. Does it makes me a twisted fellow that I love the defiance in her eyes? Probably. More seconds pass before I realize I've been staring at her, open mouthed.

The award, Lincoln.

"Yes, *Myla*." I make a point of pretending that I'm learning her name. Now, I just need to lean into being a total flaming douchebag. If it gets me more fiery looks from Myla, I can handle it. "You showed some basic ability in the match this morning," I state. "Certainly enough to warrant an honorary sword. Of course, if you fought a true demon hunter then–"

She leans in closer. "Just name the time and place, buddy."

Fresh waves of attraction flow through me. This woman. She'd really pound me in front of everyone. I press my lips together, unsure of what to say next. If I open my mouth now, I'll certainly spout out something revealing like, *I worship you, my goddess.*

That wouldn't land well, on multiple levels.

Fortunately, Myla speaks next. "Okay, how do we end this?"

At this point, Father's trying to hide his grin. And doing a horrible job of it, too. "Perhaps if you set your hands like this?" Father demonstrates how to correctly receive an honorary sword.

"Oh, yeah." Myla sets out her hands, palms up. As I place the sword on her hands, my fingers brush against the bare skin by her wrist. The connection sets my flesh on fire.

Myla pulls the sword—and her touch—far away from me. "Thank you."

I catch her gaze once more. Desire blazes there, same as with me. *This is good. I mean, bad.* Or rather, a catastrophe. After all, I took such care to be an insensitive oaf.

Callous.

Cruel.

Anti-demonic.

And even with all that, Myla and I still have a connection.

Where did I go right?

Father bows low and I follow the motion. *Unfortunately, it's time to leave.*

With the ceremony done, Father and I must turn and march toward an exit archway. Myla's gaze bores into my back as I depart. Not sure how I managed it, but that was another marvelous disaster. I'm supposed to protect Myla, even from me. But between our angry banter and lusty gazes, I'm fairly certain I failed at my task.

Sadly, this can't happen again. I won't allow it.

"Too slow, my lad." That's Nat speaking, although the words are a little slurred with his mouth guard in. Nat's my Master at Arms and latest sparring partner today. Again, we're at the tourney grounds (or what's been built of it so far). We both wear shorts and t-shirts. Nat comes at my chin with a left hook, which I dodge.

Nat scowls. "Don't hold back." He knows I'm not giving him everything. Mostly because I'm not.

Today's another day I've spent in practice matches with all eligible guards and warriors. After Myla's awards ceremony this morning, I've had nothing but excess energy. In fact, Nat insisted on doing a second practice round with me today, even though the man is clearly winded.

I follow up with a quick series of jabs followed by a left hook. I'm not really putting all my fire in it, but I still land a solid hit to Nat's face. Ouch.

"Maybe hold back a little," laughs Nat. He's an older man, barrel-chested and fit. Only at this moment, he's red faced and panting. Meanwhile, I've barely broken a sweat. It's not the thrax way to keep fighting a tired opponent in practice.

I take a quick glance at my surroundings. Before, some young lords were waiting for their turn to spar with me. Now, no one remains. That's a shame.

I lower my arms. "Let's call it quits."

"If you insist."

"Absolutely, just stay alert for what we talked about." In this case, *what we talked about* refers to any chatter regarding Myla from yesterday's Arena award. Mostly, I'm worried about Aldred.

"I will, my Prince," says Nat. He's already assured me there's been no talk about Myla, either good or bad. Which is worrisome. If Aldred were openly planning a hunt, then I could raise the question of an inquest once more. Or if word was that Aldred had sworn off killing quasis—a reasonable change now that he's seen Myla fight—then that would be welcome news. But silence? Evil things hide in the quiet.

Aldred has a plan. I can only wait until he springs it.

A low hum sounds. I grin; Walker's here. At last, he's taking me to visit the mermaids of New York. I hadn't realized it had gotten so late.

Nat steps backward. "I'll be going then."

"Thank you once again."

After waving goodbye to Nat, I keep my senses on high alert. The chances that Walker will try a sneak attack are about one hundred percent.

Sure enough, Walker goes in for the kill. *Now, that's a friend.* He gets me in a choke hold. Breaking free, I slam my fist into his ribs. The good news is that I don't have to hold back here. Walker's fresh for a fight. Even better, he has the power to self-heal. I get into a quick rhythm.

Twist.

Clutch.

Kick out Walker's legs.

Done.

I pin him to the ground with my knee on his chest. For his part, Walker appears unconcerned. He stares at me, his all black eyes filled with sympathy.

"I'm sorry about Myla."

I step away from my friend so quickly, you'd think he just burst into flame. Myla's fierce eyes appear in my mind. *I miss her.* Still, I hold my emotions back.

"Thanks," I say solemnly.

Walker stands. "Just keep doing what you're doing. It's the right thing."

A weight of sorrow settles into my heart. "I will."

"Now, how about we visit those mermaids?"

Walker's question brings the evening's plans back to me. Excitement sparks in my chest. I'm much better with a plan and purpose.

"Let's do this," I reply.

"Do you have everything you need?"

"One moment." Patting down my chest and thighs, I check my pockets for demon patrol charms. *Yes, they're all here.* I'm especially glad I grabbed ones designed specifically for mermaids. My prize find? An anti-glamour ring, which I now slip on my finger. "Ready now." Taking out a matching band, I offer it to Walker. "Here's yours."

Walker shakes his head. "Mermaid glamours don't work on ghouls."

"Have you ever encountered one before?"

"No, but as I said …" He points to his face. "Ghoul."

"You're also part archangel. And these are very powerful mermaids."

Walker sniffs. "I'm in body armor; I'll take the risk."

A low hum sounds, which means Walker isn't open to further discussion. Within seconds, a portal opens. Walker and I step into the darkness and tumble through empty space. Seconds later, we step out onto a long concrete pier on Earth.

Ah, New York.

A clear night sky arches overhead. Since Purgatory is always overcast, I'd forgotten the sight of the moon. Tall buildings loom behind us. Seagulls arch and dive over the harbor. All around us, the other piers are a hive of activity as humans load and unload cargo. A few coast guard boats patrol the nearby shore. A constant rumble of sound and energy surrounds us, even in this relatively desolate spot.

Together, Walker and I march out onto Pier 34. It's a massive affair with heavy cranes bolted to the cement. Piles of metal containers lay stacked nearby. There are no humans around, but that's to be expected. We thrax have charmed this area. Humans either forget to visit this spot or, if they do stop by, they're too frightened to linger for long. It's one of the duties of demon patrols; separate humans and potential trouble-makers like mermaids.

Walker scans the space. "Ike-3 will be so jealous. He loves the city."

And here is yet another example of how Walker knows everyone and everything. "Oh, I know Ike. He sneaks me into Myla's arena matches."

Walker blinks. "You don't say."

I roll my eyes. *No wonder Walker knew I was watching Myla. Ike told him.* "You're so stealthy, they should call you Sneaker instead of Walker." I pause. "That sounded better in my head."

"Let's go, Shakespeare."

Walker and I march out to the pier's edge. Dark water laps against the concrete ledge below. Reaching into my pocket, I pull out what looks like a peppermint.

Another charm from Striga.

Sure, there are already magical protections on this pier, but you never can be too careful. The fact that this is a candy is no surprise. Most demon patrol charms look like common human stuff: coins, paperclips, you get the idea. It's only if you look closely that you see the tiny runes of a spell. I crush the mint in my hand; a puff of purple dust rises from my palm. *Excellent.* Now, Walker and I have extra protection from human eyes.

With the additional magic in place, I summon the mermaids. A rusted steel ladder hangs over the side of the concrete pier. After climbing down enough steps, I can set my bare skin into the water. Icy liquid surrounds my fingers. A moment later, I pull my hand out again, scale back up the ladder, return to the pier, and wait.

Here's what that was all about. Mermaids use kisses to gain energy from your life force. And that energy? It has a particular scent that moves through the water. Evidently my energy smells particularly yummy. I can almost always summon mermaids within a minute or two.

Sure enough, two mermaids pop up from the water, resting their elbows on the edge of the pier while their tails sway below. I know this pair.

Cordelia and Dwyn.

Cordelia has green and scaly skin, gills that layer down her neck, and pointed peaks on her face that remind me of conch shells. Long tresses of seaweed hair fall down to her waist. Meanwhile, Dwyn is similar to her friend, only her coloring is blue.

"Hello ladies," I say smoothly. The trick with mermaids is to let them think their glamour works. In other words, I need to act as if two human super-models just appeared.

Cordelia winds a tendril of seaweed hair around her webbed finger. "We didn't lure those frat boys off their cruise ship, if that's why you're here. They fell over the railing on their own. Total drunks. We put them right back on deck. After a few kisses." She grins, showing off her needle-like teeth.

Dwyn sniffs, a movement that makes her nostril-holes flare. "Nasty kiss-es." Most chats with Cordelia and Dwyn fit this rhythm. Cordelia is the talk-ative one. Dwyn amplifies a few words. Mostly because Dwyn has focus issues. A few words is all she can say before she starts thinking about kissing again.

"Thank you for volunteering that information," I say. "But I'm not here as part of demon patrol."

Cordelia gestures toward Walker. "That explains the ghoul."

My friend sighs dramatically. "We need information from you lovely ladies," he intones. Walker is an excellent liar. Even so, he's doing a better-than-usual job of acting like the mermaids have enchanted him.

At least, I hope it's an act.

I make a mental note to keep an eye on Walker. I don't need him getting kissed and having his life force sucked away. Sure, he can self-heal, but even that ability has its limits. I twist the band on my finger. *This is why we use proper gear on demon patrol.*

"Let me guess." Cordelia drums her webbed fingers on the pier. "You're here about Silvinio?"

"We call him Slimy," adds Dwyn.

"Yup," agrees Cordelia. "Slimy's been asking us to hustle tourists for kisses and jewelry. Demons don't take American Express, you know."

"And do you aid him?" asks Walker.

"We used to, years ago," replies Cordelia. "But that was before he got old and disgusting."

Dwyn sighs. "He was young and tasty once." *Meaning his kisses gave a charge.*

"These days, Silvinio just asks us for help, we tell him no, and then he hits the Bash Bar."

Walker frowns. "What's that?"

"Magical fight club," I explain. "Part of the demon fighting circuit on Earth." I return my attention to the mermaids. "We aren't here about Silvinio. Right now, my friend and I require information about the Tithe."

"The Tithe?" Cordelia bares her needle-like teeth. The waters nearby turn choppy. Senior-level mermaids can control the seas. Clearly, Cordelia is both powerful and pissed off. "We hate that dickhead."

Mermaids also have foul mouths. My theory is that it comes from kissing too many sailors.

"Ocean folk hate him too," adds Dwyn. The waters turn so choppy by the pier, the crests peak with white foam.

Interesting. This is the kind of reaction that happens if humans dump radioactive waste in their grazing grounds. "What did the Tithe do to you?"

"There's an oil rig a few miles offshore." Cordelia lifts her arm. On her command, the waters still. The model of an oil right rises up from the harbor, only one that's made entirely of water. It's a square structure supported by four tall columns. The liquid model rises until it towers yards above our heads. "You know it?"

I shake my head. "It's not on any of our charts." I look to Walker. "What about you?"

"Never seen it before," replies my friend.

"That's no oil rig." Cordelia points at the liquid model. "It's really the Tower of Wonders that's been glamoured up to hide form your sight. It's really a mighty column that's home to all of the Tithe's *little statues.*"

The oil rig then transforms into a tall tower that spins up from the harbor. It reminds me a bit of the human leaning Tower of Pisa, only this version is completely upright.

"All his effigies live within," continues Cordelia. "When they leave, the effigies stomp across the ocean floor, tramping down the seaweeds and frightening our flocks." Mermaids are shepherds of the ocean. They consider schools of fish to be their flocks. Outside of consuming the life force of other beings, mermaids eat tons of raw scaly things.

"I'm sorry to hear that," says Walker solemnly.

Stepping closer to the pier's edge, I examine Cordelia's model more closely. There's never been a location listed for the Tower of Wonders, but that's not what strikes me about this building. Upon closer inspection, I see tall window-holes lining the structure's exterior. Effigies march around inside. All of them wear armor or carry weapons.

"Are all the effigies warriors?" I ask.

"Every last one," answers Cordelia.

"They are?" asks Walker. "I thought he carved dancers."

"That's the story." Cordelia raises her arm, making the water model of the Tower of Wonders flatten with a splash. "The Tithe carved such pretty dancing girls that the archangel Aquila gave him a magical mallet and chisel, so that he could use those tools in order to bring his statues to life."

Something about that watery model of the tower still irks me. "Can you create an aerial view?" I ask.

Cordelia sniffs. "This is an awful lot of asking without any giving."

"Don't I always pay?" I ask.

"Not with kisses."

"That is true." From my pocket, I pull out a necklace created from small purple shells and toss it to Cordelia. *More patrol supplies from Striga.* This jewelry packs an energy punch. Not as strong as a kiss, but it's still something.

"Oh, delicious." Cordelia loops the necklace around her throat and makes a yummy sound. After that, she snaps her fingers. A fresh wall of water rises up, like a chalkboard. On it, I see the coast of Manhattan as well as a small square for the enchanted oil rig.

For a minute, I do nothing but stare at the map.

Walker steps to my side. "What is it?"

"There's something about that spot," I reply. "Maybe it's related to something underground in Antrum ... or above it in Heaven?" I shake my head. "I can't place it now, but my heart tells me that's it's important. I'll have to ask the archivists for more material."

Walker turns to the mermaids. "There's something else we need to check," he says. "A thrax minister, Devak, made a pact with the Tithe. Devak stated that he was the fourth soul. Three souls are left after him. Do you have any idea what that might mean?"

"The Tithe wants a tower full of statues?" asks Cordelia. "Who knows? That warlock is bat shit crazy."

"So crazy," agrees Dwyn.

"Can you guess what he'd want with a quasi demon?" I ask.

"Not a clue," says Cordelia. "The Tithe is obsessed with angels, not demons."

Walker pales, which is something considering how he's already dead. "What kind of angels?"

"Rank and file warriors," says Cordelia. "All his effigies are exceptional in that nothing sets them apart. Know what I mean?"

"Yes." Walker exhales. "That's a relief."

I give Walker the side eye. "What would be different if the Tithe were interested in archangels or seraphim?"

Walker lifts his chin. "Nothing I could tell you about."

Which in a way tells me something. There's something here that involves Myla, but now isn't the time to press for answers. Cordelia and Dwyn are already licking their lips. The two will start demanding kisses soon. I make a mental note to press Walker about it later.

All in all, it's been a rather successful chat with the mermaids. As the saying goes, *discretion is the better part of valor.* Never let it be said that I don't know when it's time to leave.

I bow slightly at the waist. "Thank you so much for your time, dear ladies."

"Hey," calls Dwyn. "I didn't get payment."

I reach into my pocket for another enchanted shell necklace.

"No, I want a kiss," declares Dwyn. "From the tall one."

I take a half-step backward. "I really don't think that's a good—"

But Walker jumps into the harbor and starts making out with Dwyn anyway. *Damn.* He really should have taken the ring. Racing off the pier, I jump in after him.

Splash!

Icy water presses in around me, like a thousand needles piercing my skin at once. Walker has looped his arms around Dwyn's torso. I'd say they're still kissing, but that's not really how it works with mermaids. The motion is more of a mutual lip assault.

I swim over to Walker, pull out the extra anti-glamour ring from my pocket, and jam it on Walker's pinky. He's too far gone, though. Walker pulls off the band and tosses it in the ocean.

Double damn. That really was the easiest way to save him.

"Must … kiss," says Walker, his voice dreamy. Already, his super-pale skin is turning even more colorless. Dwyn is going to town here.

"So tasty," says Dwyn.

"Don't be a greedy bitch," scolds Cordelia. "Give me a turn." The other mermaid has dropped down from the pier. She now bobs in the dark waters nearby.

I grasp Dwyn's shoulder. "Let him go."

"Not yet," she snaps.

"Uhhh," moans Walker. His eyes are rolling back into his head. This is getting serious.

I raise my voice. "Last warning, Dwyn."

This time, the mermaid doesn't even bother to reply as I pull another charm from my pocket. This item may resemble a grimy penny, but it's actually a ricochet spell for ghoul portals. In other words, this coin will force Walker to open a portal to the last place he visited. Technically, I'm only supposed to use it when interrogating ghoul criminals, but we thrax have a saying, *no rules on demon patrol.* In my opinion, these mermaids count as an official mission.

Snapping the penny in two, I jam the broken halves against Walker's neck. His eyes widen. The water around us churns and bubbles.

"Get back, Dwyn!" I call.

"I said, not yet!" Dwyn tries to hold onto Walker as his limp body sinks under the waves.

I round on Cordelia. "Get her out of here or she's dead. I mean it."

Cordelia speeds forward and grabs her friend, pulling Dwyn away. A moment ago, Dwyn and Walker were locked to each other. Now, there's no sign of my friend. Instead, a spinning vortex of liquid swirls in the spot where Walker last kissed Dwyn. I dive underwater, swimming with all my strength until I grasp Walker's arm.

Finally.

Together, Walker and I get sucked down into the vortex. Water whooshes in my ears. Bits of seaweed smack my face. I press my lips together, fighting the urge to breathe.

At last, Walker and I tumble out onto the floor of Walker's squatter's apartment. Gallons of dark water pour through the ghoul portal in the ceiling above us. For a few seconds, the cold liquid cascades like a waterfall. A heavy rumble fills the air.

Then the portal closes.

I sit beside Walker on his living room floor. At least two feet of water surround us. Fish flop around. Old plastic cups, cigarette butts and seaweed bob about. Half of an old bicycle lays in a rusty pile nearby, its front tire spinning. Walker sits nearby, his head sagging forward.

Rising, I slosh-walk over to my friend. "Are you all right?"

Lifting his head, Walker coughs out some dark water. "That was horrible."

"I'd say, *I told you so*, but that's rude."

Walker rolls his eyes. "You're a real pal." He surveys the room and sighs. "This is a disaster. Do you have any charms that can get rid of this water?"

"Absolutely."

Walker picks up a scrap of fabric from the waters nearby. "Is this a thong?"

"Why, yes. Yes, it is." I can't help but smirk. "Maybe we grab some disinfectant spells as well. Portal me back to the camp, and I'll set you up."

"Thank you," says Walker. "And Lincoln?"

I lift my brows. "Yes?"

"Never let me approach another mermaid."

I chuckle. "You have a deal."

Standing up, Walker wrings water from his t-shirt. The droplets cascade to the floor, waterfall style. "Now you know where the Tower of Wonders is hidden. Do you plan to invade the place and confront the Tithe? Get some answers?"

I swipe back my wet hair and think things through. Walker raises a good point. I could certainly invade and interrogate.

Yet I won't.

"Here's the thing," I begin. "I've been running through my first fight with Devak. In retrospect, it wasn't a fight at all."

Walker tilts his head. "Meaning?"

"I've sent out battle scouts before. They give intel on where demonic troops are positioned, weapons, readiness, you get the idea. That's what the fight with Devak was like."

"So it wasn't an attack. It was more of a testing."

"Precisely. And the trouble is, the Tithe is learning about me. Meanwhile I know zero about him. It's unwise to go marching into enemy strongholds without far more detailed information."

Walker rocks on his heels, a motion which makes swishing noises in his new indoor pool. "Until Tithe makes a more aggressive move, your best plan here is to wait and learn."

"Agreed." I wring our water from my own shirt. "Now, let's get you those charms so we can clean up this place."

"You're a true friend, Lincoln." His words drip with sarcasm.

"And?"

"Only you, my true friend, would get me charms to fix my ruined my house ... which you caused get destroyed in the first place. As a favor."

"Anytime, smart guy."

With that, Walker opens a portal and off we go.

13

"*D*on't worry, son." Father nervously scans the open grounds of the Ryder mansion. "She'll be here any minute."

By *she*, Father means Lady Adair. Today's the infamous garden party I discussed with Aldred.

"I'm not worried, Father."

Unfortunately, Mother is off attending another mourning ceremony for Kamal. That means Father believes he needs to keep me company while offering advice.

In a shocking turn of events, Father has been less than helpful.

I scan the scene. Young thrax lords and ladies step around the wide yard behind the mansion. Everyone wears formal garb, meaning gowns for ladies, tunics and mail for men. There's a hedgerow maze, which many try to navigate. Small tables are set out with various drinks and snacks. We thrax love our cheese and mead.

Father bobs on the balls of his feet. It's what he does when he's getting especially anxious. "Many ladies arrive late to formal events. It's their way of saying they're interested."

"You don't say." As in, *you really shouldn't say this*. Being late is just rude.

"Once you two spend time together, you'll see the truth of it." Father lowers his voice to a conspiratorial tone. "Never share power or your heart. Rulers are best off alone."

"So you and Mother have said." *Many, many times.*

"See that?" Father gestures toward Lord Erasmus, a noble from Striga. Lady Chione of Horus strolls along by his side. The two trade stories and laughter. Why is Father pointing this out? The sight only tears at my heart. I'll never have that kind of connection with my wife.

"I see them," I reply.

"That's a lot of lovey-dovey falderal and nincompoopitude."

"Nincompoop-*itude*?" Father tends to make up words. It's one of his more endearing practices.

"You know what I mean." Connor sighs. "Ah, here she is now. Lady Adair."

The crowd still as a newcomer steps into the party. Adair is a dainty girl with blonde hair, mismatched eyes, and a slightly turned-up nose. Aesthetically speaking, she's pretty. I wait to see if that sparks some emotion within me.

Not a bit.

Father takes off while Adair steps up to me. There are no greetings or regular court formalities. Adair immediately launches into an extended soliloquy about her dress. Or perhaps it's her shoes. She might also mention her dead goldfish. I'm having a hard time staying focused. Both Adair and her father have a gift for chatter.

As with the start of the awards ceremony, I slap on an external look of mild interest in Adair's speech. Meanwhile, I internally review the latest information from my researchers in Antrum. They've been hard at work, trying to map out what's below and above the Tower of Wonders. No one's asked for this before, so the maps arrive scraps and bits, like pieces of a puzzle. I even asked for an extra table into my cabin, just for those slips of paper.

Every day, I spend some time placing the pieces into alignment: Heaven, Earth, and Antrum. If there's some correlation between the location of the Tower of Wonders and those three realms, then I'll find it.

I'm still mentally repositioning bits of map when Adair's soliloquy takes a nasty turn. "Did you hear about the angel who was mugged by a quasi girl?" she asks.

"Yes, I received the reports," I reply. "It's a rumor, nothing more. Please don't repeat it."

Undeterred, Adair continues to share stories of quasi lady cruelty. Did I know they roasted children alive? Poisoned their ghoul leaders? Killed their mates after sex?

Each time, I say that is another rumor, and to cease sharing. That doesn't stop Adair. This turns out to be yet another way she's similar to her father: both Adair and Aldred have issues with listening.

"Quasis are really dangerous." Adair shivers dramatically.

"May I be honest with you?" I ask.

Adair steps closer. "Of course." She begins blinking and pursing her lips. I've seen that combination of moves from other ladies. Adair may be expecting some kind of profession of love. If so, she's about to be sorely disappointed.

"I suspect your father suggested you share unflattering tales about the local population. The fact is, there is very little crime in Purgatory, and what happens is mostly caused by the ghouls. The quasi people deserve our respect and support. I trust we can move onto other topics of conversation now."

Adair steps back. Her blinking and lip-pursing stops immediately. "Father thinks you're interested in a quasi girl. The one from the awards ceremony. Were you fighting with her as a demon, or flirting with her as a woman?"

Before, I'd wondered what Aldred was up to after the awards ceremony. Now, this scheme is clear. Aldred has sent his daughter to ask me about Myla, instead of confronting me himself. *Coward.*

For a moment, I debate simply walking away. *Quality time with Adair* is clearly a bust. However, doing so would only confirm my romantic interest in Myla. That might place my girl at risk.

"As of this moment, my only marriage interest is with thrax. Does that answer your question?"

"Oh, yes!" Another too-loud giggle follows. "Guess what?"

"I couldn't."

"I'm the Scala Heir."

The way she stares at me, it seems we won't move on from this topic until I provide a response. The heir is always a thrax, so that part comes as no surprise. But what I know about the current heir doesn't line up with Adair. Verus has been hiding the true heir for years. And honestly? I don't doubt that Verus would bother protecting Adair. The Queen of the Angels loathes the House of Acca.

"Well?" urges Adair.

"How very nice for you."

"You must be wondering how I kept it hidden for so long."

"The thought crossed my mind."

"The truth is, I didn't even know! You see, a demon visited my mother one night, taking the form of my father."

"That's a lot of detail, Adair."

"Nine months later, there's me!"

"Shouldn't there be something unusual about the pregnancy? I thought the current Scala, Maxon Bane, was born rather early."

"No, it's totally and absolutely normal for a Scala Heir to be a nine month pregnancy. The only issue is that Mom was too embarrassed to say anything until now."

"Well, she is a rather quiet woman." In fact, the Duchess Adelaide does little outside of try to blend into the scenery. Considering she has Aldred as her husband, I don't blame her. If married that man, I'd hide behind the drapes.

"Exactly." Adair purses her lips again. "And since I'm the Scala Heir, you have to marry me."

Those words make my stomach churn. "Not following the logic."

"Maxon Bane is near death. Who has two thumbs and will run the after-realms after he's gone?"

"Don't do it."

She does it. "Me!" Adair gives me a double thumbs up.

"What an interesting theory. However, the royal physicians say Maxon Bane will live another two hundred years."

"False. People can die at any time. Look at Devak. He was only 400. Father says Maxon Bane is next."

I narrow my eyes. "Does he?" I wouldn't put it past Aldred to fake that *Adair is the Scala Heir* lie in order to get his damned marriage contract signed. And Aldred's scheme could easily include murder.

"What I said is true." Adair huffs. "The current Scala is totally near death." She sets her hands on her hips. "Father is always right; that's why everyone's afraid of him. Acca nobles can do anything and live anywhere, even Hell. Did you know that?"

"No, that certainly is news." I eye the exits greedily.

"And I'll be the most powerful Great Scala in history. I'll do whatever I want. Wait and see."

One thing I'll say for Adair, she also inherited her father's gift for ignoring facts. "Even if you're the Scala Heir, you're thrax and subject to our laws. That's greater than you, me, or even your father. Have your tutors reviewed the story of Lady Glenna?"

"Who?"

"She was a thrax Great Scala who broke our laws and ended up executed, per orders from the Arbiter." That's our immortal judge in Antrum. She outranks all of us, even royals.

Adair sniffs. "You'll see. Just wait until there's my awakening ceremony. If you're my Angelbound love, then the igni will activate my Scala Heir powers. That'll prove we need to get married. Isn't that right?"

"There hasn't been an awakening ceremony for a Scala Heir in a thousand years. The records on the validity of Angelbound love are rather scarce."

"Which means I'm right." Adair claps. "I win! How about we learn more about me?"

This has officially become a form of torture. "Not following."

"The Ryder mansion has a library here with tons of books. Supposedly there are ones here that you can't find anywhere else in the after-realms. Shall we go there ... alone?"

The *alone* part is not all that interesting. That said, the prospect of finding unique books on the Tithe is rather intriguing. And it's also excellent way to redeem this disaster with Adair. If I get a good book out of the situation, my day won't be completely wasted.

"That's an excellent idea," I say. "Lead on."

∿

It takes a while to find the library itself.

Turns out, Adair is an *act first and ask questions later* kind of person. In this case, that means meandering around the grounds while Adair insists the library was just ahead. At last, we run across the Ryders, a lovely couple who give us quick directions to the spot in question. They even offer us to borrow any book we fancy.

Then we meander even farther off path until we run across the Ghoul Minister. Fortunately, *Gasbag* was able to give us exact directions on where to find books on the Great Scala. After so much wandering to just reach the library, I'm pleased that we may quickly find the book we need.

And it only cost me another basket of worms.

Eventually, we reach the top floor in the mansion, which houses the library itself. The place is a maze of freestanding bookshelves that wind across the floor. Bay windows line the far wall. Everything appears freshly painted and gleaming.

All in all, a lovely spot.

I make a quick scan of the shelves. A section marked Tithe sits by the front door. Sadly, there are no titles there that I haven't already received. There's a shelf for new arrivals, though. Nothing sits there now, but I make a mental note to check it another day. In fact, I'm so absorbed in my thoughts, I don't notice that Adair has snuck up behind me. When I step away from the book-shelf, I almost knock her over.

"Lincoln, don't!" She giggles yet again. "You'll muss my dress."

"Apologies." It really isn't like me to miss someone creeping up on me, so I don't have much experience in these situations. That said, I know it's polite to say something kind. My thoughts race until an idea appears. "It's such a lovely dress too." Adair goes back to blinking and making smooching faces.

Uh, oh. Perhaps that was too kind.

I clear my throat. "The minister said the *Libra Scala* would be over here." With those words, I take off to the shelf in question. Adair follows closely behind.

"Oh, I think I see it." Although the volume sits at shoulder-height, Adair hops up and down, her fingers twiddling toward the book. "Oh my, the shelf's soooo high. Could you please pull the book down for me?"

"Of course, Lady Adair." I remove the volume for her.

"Thank you, your Highness." More giggling. *Is it me, or is her laughter turning more shrill with time?*

"You're welcome."

"While we have a moment, I want to say something. I was so honored that you invited me to join Verus at the Arena match."

Actually, Mother invited all the nobility in my name, but that's beside the point. "My pleasure," I state. "I thought you'd enjoy the battle."

This last statement *might* be wishful thinking. Yet it's worth bringing up the topic. Could Adair possibly enjoy the warrior arts?

"The fighting was fine, I suppose." Adair rolls her eyes.

Correction. My last statement was *definitely* wishful thinking.

"But I really enjoyed seeing you act so graciously afterwards." Adair tilts her head in a movement that says, *anything to add?*

Once more, Adair is acting as a spy for Aldred. She's testing my interest in Myla.

It's enough to make my blood boil.

Much as I want to tell Adair in no uncertain terms to leave Myla alone, that will only paint a target on my girl's back. I've played an anti-demonic douchebag before, I can certainly do so again. Especially if that performance keeps Myla safe.

"You mean when I gave *the demon* an award?" I ask.

"Yes. That demon girl was so lucky you didn't kill her."

"Well, I–"

"Demons don't stand a chance against real thrax warriors."

Adair steps closer to me, and I take a corresponding movement in the opposite direction. "It's not really fair to compare a thrax and a demon girl, Lady Adair."

"I don't know if you'd think me too forward, but–"

"But what?"

"May I feel the muscle of your arm?"

Now, playing a rogue is one thing. Allowing Adair to touch me is another. "I'm not sure, Adair."

"Just for one second? Please."

Steeling my spine, I offer Adair my arm. She grips my biceps and squeezes rapid-fire style, like she's milking a cow.

Awkward, thy name is Adair.

"Oooh! So strong." Adair exhales a dramatic sigh. "How could any girl ask you to 'name the time and place' to fight?"

Now, it's one thing for me to play the rogue. It's another for Adair to critique Myla in any way, shape or form. All rational thought fades from my mind as I level Adair with my most serious gaze. "We need to return to the others now, Milady."

"Oh, I didn't mean ... That is, I didn't think ..."

Without waiting for my so-called companion, I take off for the gardens once more.

Fun time with Adair is officially over. Forever.

14

I'm able to escape the garden party with minimal additional interaction related to Adair. once I leave, my plan is to avoid Adair for all eternity.

My reality becomes somewhat different. Turns out, there's this blasted Scala Heir awakening ceremony I must attend. I try to avoid it. Feign that I'm too busy. Too tired. Hell, I even try out Silvinio's intestinal cramp concept.

Yet there's no avoiding it.

I must attend this blasted ceremony.

All of which is why I now ride Nightshade into the parking lot outside Purgatory Arena. Pausing, I soak in the scene. Beyond the asphalt, there stand rows of industrial buildings made from chipped brick, along with a few warehouses constructed with rusted-out metal. Classic Purgatory.

Night whinnies. It's her way of saying, *stop stalling.*

Leaning forward, I pat her neck. "All right, girl."

Night scrapes at the ground. She's excited about something. "What is it?" I ask. "Show me."

My horse takes off at a gallop, pausing by a back access door. This is the same place she dropped me off when I saw Myla fight.

"We're not here to watch her," I say. "This is another ceremony today." And yes, I asked around to confirm. There are no Arena fights as part of the awakening. All that will happen is Verus performing the ritual to transform lady Adair into the Scala Heir.

Night wags her head from side to side. *You're wrong.*

I slide off Night and step toward the door. "How do you know?"

In reply, Night sniffs. Loudly.

"You smell her?"

In a broad movement, my horse arcs her head up and down. *Yes.*

A jolt of excitement moves through me. *Myla is here.* I pat Night's neck again. "Thanks, girl. Appreciate it." Pulling on the back door, I slip into the access corridor. Once again, I follow a winding path to my chosen passage to the Arena floor.

Garbled voices echo in from up ahead. This could be nothing. Then again, I might learn something useful. Call it a hunter's instinct, but I creep in closer, careful to keep in the shadows.

"You're certain he doesn't know?" I can't see the speaker, but there's no question who's talking right now. *Aldred.*

"Positive," replies another familiar voice. *Adair.*

My brows lift. *Aldred and Adair?* From a reconnaissance perspective, this is a major coup. Someone's getting an extra bucket of oats when I return to camp.

"It was all Verus," continues Adair. "She kept it a secret."

My pulse speeds a bit. *What secret?*

"Nobody knew that demon girl would be here today," adds Adair.

I wind my mouth into a Cheshire Cat grin. *I love this secret.*

"You know how tight-lipped the Queen of the Angels can be," finishes Adair. "Not even Octavia knew about it."

"This can work," says Aldred. "I'm not angry you didn't know the she-demon was coming. What's important is that we found out before Lincoln. Now run through the plan with me."

"I'll be awakened as the Scala Heir." Her voice takes on a dreamy tone. "Lincoln will be confirmed as my Angelbound love. Then he'll be mine, just like you promised."

I shake my head. The Earl of Acca is unhinged. *Who is Aldred to promise me to anyone?* It's true that my father gives Aldred whatever he wants, but that doesn't include me. Father may not have a spine, but mine's more than intact.

"And what else?" asks Aldred.

"We'll walk off the Arena floor and pass the demon girl. I'll make sure she knows that Lincoln is mine."

"I'll be close by," says Aldred. "I've been talking to the major houses. Spreading rumors about Lincoln and the demon girl. If he decides to court a demon, there are some thrax who might just start a hunting party."

Rage zooms through my nervous system. Hunting party? Aldred is still on that? I clutch the wall so hard, I'm surprised I don't pull out a brick.

"Don't say that," warns Adair. "My Prince gets super angry when you talk about hunting quasis."

"That's why we'll keep this a secret, just between us. Trust to me and I'll make things happen. Remember, if Lincoln does anything that hints at caring for this she-demon—anything at all—then you let me know."

"Yes, Father."

"Good girl. We better rejoin the others. It won't do to appear suspicious."

The crunching of footsteps sounds as Adair and Aldred step out from the corridor and onto the Arena floor. Normally, I'd spend a few minutes thinking through the implications of Adair and Aldred's conversation. But the prospect of seeing Myla is just too enticing. The moment those two are out of earshot, I slip up to exit archway and peer out.

Indeed, my girl is here.

In her dragonscale fighting suit.

Playing rock-paper-scissors with her tail.

Marvelous.

And it's such a Myla thing to do. Anyone else might stand around, yawning. But Myla finds ways to stir up activity and excitement, even if it's merely hand gestures against her tail. Watching her, a weight lifts from my soul. Gazing upon my girl today? That's a gift I never expected.

A group of warrior quasis wait near Myla. Verus must have asked them here as an honorary guard from Purgatory. Which makes sense, considering how important the Scala is to sorting souls.

It might be a moment or an hour, but I'm content to simply hide in the shadows while watching Myla goof around. What would it be like to stand beside her and actually join the fun? I picture Erasmus and Chione at the garden party. They strolled along, holding each other's hands and sharing smiles. A band of sadness tightens around my rib cage.

What would I give to have that with Myla, if just for an hour?

I shake my head. That's not something I can consider at this point. Adair and Aldred's conversation returns to mind, the memory pressing in like a vise. Once again, I must play the villain to keep Myla safe. Aldred has determined that Myla may be the biggest impediment to his beloved marriage treaty.

He's not wrong.

I might have signed that horrible document before I met Myla. Still, I definitely would have skipped inking that thing after I met Adair. All in all, that betrothal treaty was always doomed. My parents say that love has no place in a royal marriage.

Well, loathing has no spot, either.

New voices echo in from the arena floor. Most are asking some version of, *Prince Lincoln, where are you?*

Leaning against the passage arch, I soak in my last look at Myla.

Time to play a rogue. Again.

I retrace my steps in the passageway, then navigate through other underground tunnels. Soon I reach the spot where all the thrax are gathered. It's a large stone chamber that's a staging area. Members from all the great houses wait here. In some ways, the awakening ceremony is a lot like the awards ceremony, only in this version, there's a bit where I show off the battle practices of our great houses.

Warrior displays are my thing, so I go through each group and review what they'll do. Before I know it, it's time for us to march onto the Arena floor. A familiar scene greets me there. On one side of the arena, angels fill the tiered stone benches. On the other, there are demons. Verus and Armageddon keep their typical balcony seats.

Only difference? Myla and the other quasi warriors stand by the periphery of the Arena floor. I make a point of *not staring* in her direction. Aldred's words are too clear in my mind.

If he decides to court a demon, there are some thrax who might start a hunting party.

Once the warrior display is over, there's a painful section where Adair makes a great show of swooning and claiming our never-ending love for each other.

Not feeling it, personally.

Adair then claims to wield igni, the magical power of the Great Scala. I recently saw Maxon Bane wield true igni—he summoned thousands of tiny lightning bolts into a whirling column. What Adair calls look more like sparkles than igni, but what so I know? Verus seems convinced.

At last, it's time to process off the Arena floor. Sure enough, Adair makes a beeline for the archway next to Myla because, *of course she does.* Aldred's other command echoes through my mind.

If Lincoln does anything that hints at caring for this she-demon—anything at all— then you let me know.

All of which means one thing. Adair is performing this march as some kind of love test. *Is there any kind of deeper hatred than loathing someone?* When it comes to Adair I'm really starting to explore that question.

As I close in on Myla, fresh tendrils of energy ricochet between us. This time, the sensation flares between interest, connection, and pure rage.

Walker was right. She's learning to hate me. Only the process isn't complete.

Yet.

While Adair walks at my side, she wrap her arm around mine. Normally, I'd gently brush her off. Not this time. It's better if Myla thinks my heart is promised to another, even if that person is Adair.

This isn't about me. It's to keep Myla safe.

Maybe if I keep thinking that, this won't hurt so badly.

As we walk past Myla, Adair gives my arm a squeeze. "What do they call these lesser demons again? Partials? Semis?"

It's a reflex reaction for my gaze to land on Myla. The pure fury in her face feels as painful as a punch. It's an effort, but I keep my features unread-able. "I'm not sure."

"Whatever they're called, I'm glad they saw *real warriors* in action today." Adair does that move where she speed-squeezes my bicep. Not my favorite.

For a moment, I debate telling Adair that a real warrior stands before her. *Myla Lewis.* But then, I think back to the alternating waves of interest and hatred I felt from Myla. My caring for her places her at risk, either from attack or heartbreak. I recall that Vantys demon, steel my soul, and do the right thing.

"Yes," I say in a loud voice. "I'm sure it was quite an education for the poor creatures."

The look of pain on Myla's face strikes me through. The last thing I ever wanted was to hurt her, and yet, it seems as if that's what I must do, time and again.

15

*A*fter this morning's encounter with Adair, I spend the remainder of the day leading battle training. The autumn tourney ground is getting reseeded with grass, so our practice has moved to a nearby clearing.

Right now, four young lords stand before me: Acton from Acca, Husani from Horus, Francesco from Striga, and Birju from Kamal. Of all these houses, it's Acca that still needs the most help. The Dissolus outbreak in their territory is skyrocketing. Sure, Dissolus are invisible to the human eye. But if enough of them merge, that might change ... And humans don't react well when confronted with proof of the demonic world.

Which brings me back to battle training. These lords need to learn how to hold a sword before they can master the nuances of fighting a goop monster.

I hold a wooden practice sword before me. "You each hold a practice sword."

"Why not a real one?" whines Acton. Of course, it's Acca that wants to start off deadly.

"Prove yourself with this first." The way I say that statement, there isn't an opening for further argument. "We begin with stance. Don't face your opponent straight on—that creates too large of a target. Instead, present yourself at an angle." They all stare at me, open mouthed. "Why don't you all try? Assume I'm the opponent."

The four lords angle themselves. Essentially, they shift their shoulders a little and that's it. Based on the nervous glances to the sidelines, I can see the problem.

It's Adair.

The Scala Heir and her ladies now stand beside the practice field, whispering and giggling. That's no distraction to a seasoned warrior, but these four have never been cloud-side on demon patrol. They've no idea what they're doing, so every movement feels like it's under a microscope. I know. I remember the sensation well. Only I was five when I started battle training, so girls were still yucky in my mind.

Behind Adair and her friends, Mother also waits on the sidelines. She has her *scheming face* on today, which involves narrowing her eyes while thinning her mouth.

Well, Mother can plot away. I have battle training to finish.

I go from lord to lord, grasping their shoulders and moving them into better position. "That's it," I say at last. "Again, I'm the opponent. Now you present a far smaller target."

Once more, the laughter strikes up from Adair and company. Tension moves through the bodies of the four warriors. It's as if someone exploded a bomb nearby, not a bunch of giggles. Leaning in, I lower my voice. "I realize our audience may be distracting, but it'll be worse when your spectator is a ten-foot tall demon."

The lords all nod and refocus. *Excellent.* Practice is back.

I swipe the air with my sword. "Your practice weapons are weighted to match their metal counterparts. There are six key slicing motions you must master. Learn these until they're deep in your muscle memory." I scan the lord's faces. Unfortunately, they're all distracted again. Only this time, they aren't looking over at Adair and her ladies. I follow the line of their gazes, and there she is.

Myla Lewis.

I'd think this a curse, but that would be lying. Part of my soul soars to know that Myla has arrived. The last time I saw my girl, she seemed almost crushed with sorrow. *What a disaster that Scala ceremony proved to be.* Yet now? Her eyes are alight with deviousness while her tail slowly flicks behind it. No question about it. Myla is here to wreak her revenge on me.

How this woman steals my breath.

And did I mention she's wearing that dragonscale fighting suit again? She is.

"Is that the one Aldred wants to hunt?" murmurs Acton.

"No one is targeting the local population," I state. "Stay here and let me handle this."

"Hello, there!" calls Myla. "I have a message for the–"

Acton leaps forward. "A demon! I shall protect you, my Prince!" He races at Myla with his arms reaching forward.

I wince. That's might be the worst attack approach I've ever seen. And as is typical for his House, Acton has trouble listening to basic commands. I asked them all to *stay put.*

Once Acton gets within arm's length of Myla, my girl leaps into the air, her tail streaming behind her. While still airborne, Myla crouches, heaves up her knees, and then kicks Acton squarely in the chest. She follows up with a backwards somersault, lands upright, and keeps going.

At this point, I want to cheer. Seeing Myla kick ass is a beautiful sight.

Unfortunately, any celebration would place Myla in danger. Two reasons why. First, Adair's watching all this with interest. Second, there's Walker's advice. I can't break Myla's heart. Playing the rogue now will only make it easier for Myla later.

Meanwhile, Myla maintains her steady march in my direction. Everyone watches her in stunned silence. That is, until Husani decides to help.

"Stop now, foul demon!" cries the Horus warrior.

I'd grab and pull Husani back, but the man needs to learn a lesson: *Disobey your commander at your own peril.* Plus, I can't wait to see what Myla does next.

Husani runs at Myla. Unlike Acton, Husani leads with his shoulders versus his very breakable hands. His plan is to knock Myla out of the way, line-backer-style. At least, he has a better plan.

It still won't work.

Myla keeps walking. Her casual gait says she isn't fretting the new attacker. Sure enough, a second before Husani slams his shoulder into Myla's chest, my girl bends over at the waist, creating a kind of fulcrum for Husani's bulk. While the warrior slams into Myla's side, her tail wraps around Husani's neck, whipping him around in a perfect arc.

Husani lands on his back with a combination *thud and crunch* that will definitely require medical treatment.

Myla cracks her neck and continues her march.

Now, Birju and Francesco are the only two left. Noting how Husani is moaning in pain, I decide to repeat my command.

"Do not—"

But I never get the chance to finish. Birju's already taken off toward Myla while swinging his wooden sword about wildly. I wince. *This won't end well.* As Birju closes in on Myla, he takes up a cry.

"Die, you demon sc–"

Her tail punches him right in the dick. I'd feel sorry for the man, but he'll be magically healed and—most importantly—this may be a learning moment for him. Acca's *do whatever you want* attitude is starting to take hold in my nobility. I can't allow that to fester. And yes, my girl looks great as her tail punches some guy's nuts.

Myla steps up to Francesco. "Are you gonna try anything?"

Francesco shakes his head with such vigor, I'm fairly certain he injures his neck. "No, your ladyship."

"Good."

Myla rounds on me. Her eyes flash with pure hatred. With every corner of my soul, I want to sweep her into my arms and whisper how amazing that display was.

Not possible.

Instead, I pull on my years of royal practice and keep my features unreadable.

Myla lifts her hand and starts to slowly unzip the top of her fighting suit. I have to admit, I did not see this as a possibility. Adair and the other ladies give out chirps of distress. Myla grins. She's absolutely enjoying this. Reaching inside her suit, Myla pulls out an envelope and hands it over.

While keeping my face neutral, I take the letter from her palm. Not sure how I manage that feat, but I do.

"Message for you from the Ghoul Minister," reports Myla. "It's urgent."

It's an effort not to grin. I know the Ghoul Minister. Unless something involves free worms, the man has no interest whatsoever. Which means that whatever this letter is, it's not critical. Myla is here for revenge, not to play delivery girl. How stellar.

Myla bows. "If you'll excuse me, I'll leave you *real warriors* to fight it out." With that, she turns and departs. And am I imagining things, or is she shaking her ass a little extra as she goes?

Why, yes. Yes, she is.

A little scary that I can quickly categorize the level of shake in Myla's ass within any given situation. But there you have it. I can.

Adair and her ladies still stand on the sidelines. I forgot all about them. Not surprisingly, they launch into exclamations of outage.

"How dare this quasi girl attack our warriors?"

"Evil she-demon!"

"Foul killer!"

You get the idea.

But Adair isn't what concerns me now. No, what worries me is the fact that Mother is grinning. That's both interesting and ominous, considering how Mother's smile is combined with the narrow-eyed look that means she's still actively scheming.

No doubt, whatever Mother is working on, it will be a plan of mythical proportions.

Ah, well. Octavia will *reveal all* when she's ready.

In the meantime, I get to watch Myla leave. Her tail waves goodbye to Mother as she goes. That's the perfect touch. Of all the people in this clearing, Mother is the one to build bridges with.

At this point, the young lords begin recovering their senses. And along with consciousness comes a new round of whining.

"She attacked me."

"The demon girl is a menace."

"I think my dick will fall off."

That last statement comes from Birju. I move to stand in the center of the four lords and speak in a loud voice. "Let this be a lesson to you all," I announce. "Listen to your commanding officer. I ordered you not to engage in battle. Next time, pay attention. Now, get to the medical cabin for treatment. We'll meet at the mead hall in twenty minutes."

Husani rubs his head. "But I may be permanently damaged."

"I've been on demon patrols since I was six," I state. "I've seen truly horrific injuries. None of you have any hurt that can't be fixed." I point toward the medical cabin. "See the royal physicians. Then hit the mead hall. That's all."

Without giving Adair another glance, I rush off to follow Myla. The last thing I need is someone from Acca following her home. It only takes seconds for me to catch her trail in forest. What I discover is a surprise.

Myla has taken off on horseback. And not on any horse, mind you.

Nightshade. My own mare.

I smile. This is great news. My own horse has taken over Myla's care. And since Night can cast minor spells, no one will follow my girl's trail unless my horse specifically wills it. *How wonderful.*

Knowing Myla is safe, I take off for the mead hall. After all, my people are rather worked up now.

Best to wear my crown.

16

*B*efore hitting the mead hall, I stop by my cabin, change into my formalwear, and—most importantly—examine Myla's message. Sure enough, it concerns some minor scheduling incident with the Ghoul Minster. Myla was after revenge, not a chance to play delivery girl. I think through my calendar. I've a meeting with the Ghoul Minister coming up. I can confirm if anything in this message is an actual problem.

Right now, I must face my court.

By the time I open the door to the mead hall, all the young lords wait around, breathless. Beside them stand all the earls from the great houses. Even Adair has decided to join. Mother stands in the back, half hidden in shadows. Father is nowhere to be seen, but that's expected, considering how Aldred is here and looking for blood.

In terms of layout, the hall is a long wooden structure with an arched roof. Long tables line the floor. A single fireplace sits at one short end of the rectangular structure. It's unlit now, leaving the air chilly. Still, whether lit or not, it's where our speakers or minstrels present. Once I enter the hall, I head toward that fireplace. As I cross the packed room, a new round of shouts ricochet through the air.

"That demon girl attacked my son!"

"She's a menace!"

"We'll never be safe here!"

Pausing before the fireplace, I scan the crowd. As a leader, I've learned how to read a group in a heartbeat. The tension here isn't terror. My people had their pride hurt, that's all. If I allow the thrax to show their true skills, then I think they'll calm down quickly. The four lords I trained this morning aren't exactly our finest warriors.

An idea appears. I know exactly how to smooth this situation over. I raise my arms. The room goes silent. "My thrax," I begin.

Adair steps forward, grabbing my elbow. I pointedly step away from her grip. "I have something to say, my love. It's *really* important."

"Do tell," I say.

"I am the injured party here."

My brows lift. "Really."

In a stance that says, *woe is me*, Adair moves to stand in profile, resting the back of her hand against her forehead. "There I was, the Scala Heir, with my angelbound love fighting nearby." Dropping her hand from her forehead, Adair turns to address the room. "Did you all see today how the igni confirmed that Lincoln and I share true and undying affection?"

This girl is certifiably bonkers. I need to end this, now.

I tap her shoulder. "Adair."

"What, my love?" she asks.

"Whatever happened with your igni, it does not prove my affection."

"I didn't fake my igni display," she snaps.

"What a very odd thing to volunteer."

I scan the room again. Adair's speech didn't land well with the thrax. My people value honesty, almost to a fault.

Adair waves to Aldred. "Explain this, Papa. My intense adoration for Lincoln has me completely flummoxed."

Aldred speeds to Adair's side. "The essential facts are this," announces the earl. "A demon girl has viciously attacked our people, and now I demand the right to hunt her!"

Hunt her ... those two words echo through my consciousness. *Not good.*

The room erupts.

"Hear! Hear!"

"Huzzah!"

"Thrax must hunt the demon threat!"

Rage corkscrews up my spine. "Silence!" I bellow. The room falls quiet once more. "Verus summoned us here to build alliances with quasis. No thrax is to hunt the local population. Is any part of that unclear?"

Aldred lifts his chin. "Verus spoke before our people were attacked."

"I could have been hurt, too." Adair sniffles. "And here, my own angelbound love shows more interest in my demon attacker than me." Once again, she rests the back of her hand against her forehead.

I pinch the bridge of my nose. Meanwhile, Mother keeps up her silent vigil in the back of the room. Father is still nowhere to be seen. His absence is getting on my nerves.

"Acton, Husani, Francesco, and Birju," I call. "Step forward."

The lords in question move to stand apart from the crowd. Once they're visible by everyone, I continue. "Did you or did you not attack ..." I stop myself, as I almost say Myla's name. "Attack the girl *first*, and explicitly against my commands?"

All the lords lower and their heads and mumble.

"In full voices, please." I swear, sometimes being prince is like running a kindergarten.

The lords speak more clearly, and all in some variation of "I attacked first."

"Thank you," I say. "Does anyone here doubt the truth? The young lords defied a command from their commander and prince."

Silence. That means the people agree. Perfect.

I glare at each of the young lords in turn. "I could bring you up on charges of treason." The lords hang their heads. "You're all extraordinarily lucky. Past thrax rulers haven't been as kind as I am."

I allow another long pause to hang in the air. This is for the crowd's benefit. I wish them to think through my meaning of *past thrax rulers.* That would be the House of Acca. Vicious. If soldiers didn't follow orders, Acca would cut off their ears. And that was on a good day. On a bad ones, the warriors would lose tehir lives.

A chill fills the room. *That's a good sign.* Everyone realizes where mindless support of Acca ends. I return my focus to the four lords. "And are the four of you healing from your injuries?"

Another chorus of *yes-es* erupts, this one more loud than the first.

Lifting my voice, I make sure to address every corner of the hall. "My people. The correct response to today's happenings is not a murderous rampage. We thrax are known for our battle prowess. Let's show our skills in a way that *builds* alliances with other realms, just as Verus wishes."

Many nods follow from the crowd. *Yes!* I'm getting to them.

"Here is my suggestion," I continue to the crowd. "You may all display your battle prowess to this quasi girl, and do so with all the pomp and glamour of the upcoming Autumn Tournament. Let's invite her to the tourney and show our true abilities! That is the thrax way." I switch my focus to the young lords again. "What say you four?"

The lords exchange looks, and then nods. A buzz of excitement fills the room. *I was right.* My nobles crave respect more than blood.

I allow myself the smallest of smiles. My plan is working. Myla will stay safe. I address the young lords once more. "Can I get a huzzah?"

"Huzzah."

"That's rather low energy for such powerful warriors. Give me a big huzzah."

"Huzzah!"

Raising my arms, I address the entire room. "And now, my court, what say you? Do you wish to show off the true might and dignity of the thrax?"

"HUZZAH!" This time, the cry is so loud, bits of dust sift down from the rafters.

"I agree. Therefore I shall speak to this quasi girl—"

"No," interrupts Aldred. "Adair and I must confront the she-demon. After all, it's only right after what my sweet daughter suffered at her hands."

The muscles in my neck tighten with frustration. There's only reason why

Aldred wants to talk to Myla: he'd like to fake up some excuse to cause trouble. "No. I am the High Prince. I will handle this."

Adair's pretty features crumple into tears. "But what about *me?*"

At this point, Mother steps forward. One of Octavia's most impressive skills is how she can transform from blending into shadows into full queen mode, all within a second flat.

"What about you?" asks the queen. "You're a thrax woman, not a sniveling coward. You'll conduct yourself properly when our quasi guests arrive." Mother's voice lowers to such an ominous level, it could darken sunshine. "I'll spend some time with you so you understand what that means."

I stifle the urge to chuckle. Mother's etiquette lessons are legendary. No one gets through them without crying at least once.

Adair slumps her shoulders. If the girl were a balloon, there would be a soft hissing noise as all the air left. "As you command, Your Highness."

Mother shoots me the barest of winks. I return the gesture. What can I say? I am absolutely a Momma's boy, but when the mother in question is Queen Octavia, that makes one rather badass.

With that, the majority of drama settles down. In no time, everyone returns to their respective cabins, myself included. As I walk back, I notice a translucent figure in the woods.

A ghost.

I follow the wispy apparition until we're far away from the camp. In the center of a muddy clearing, I finally get a good look at the ghost I've been trailing.

Silvinio.

Huh. I was wondering when his spirit would show up.

As ordered, my guards have been trailing Silvinio for days. Seems the minister regularly chats with someone who remains invisible. *That would be the Tithe.* Although my warriors can only hear one side of the conversation, the words *in exchange for my death* came up quite a lot. It was only a matter of time.

I grin from ear to ear. "Minister Silvinio," I say smoothly. Rubbing my palms together, I add one final thought.

"Just the man I wanted to see."

17

*T*he ghostly Silvinio looks as he did when alive: a hefty and balding fellow in a tunic with chain mail and boots. For a long moment, the minister scans the clearing. After that, he float-walks toward a massive oak. I eye his movements carefully. Supposedly, Silvinio buried caches of magical rings that he then dug up and sold to the highest bidder. I never got solid evidence of the practice, though.

Did Silvinio hide some valuables beneath that tree?

Once he reaches his chosen spot, the ghost of Silvinio turns toward me. "Greetings, my Prince. Lovely day, isn't it?"

I can't believe this. "You didn't return from the afterlife to discuss the weather."

"No, my Prince." Silvinio puffs out his chest. "I'm here because I made a deal with the Tithe."

"How shocking." My tone says the news is anything but a surprise. "Does this deal change my treaty against Acca?"

"No, of course not," states Silvinio. "My new master has a question for you."

"I have some for him first," I counter. "If your visit is like Devak's, then the Tithe is lurking nearby, listening yet invisible. There a few things I'd like to ask him. "

"What do you want to know?" Silvinio glances to a specific point across the clearing.

"To begin with, I wished to pinpoint where the Tithe is standing." I follow the line of Silvinio's gaze. "Greetings, Tithe."

Silence is my only reply. Yet as a hunter, I can sense hidden eyes upon me. *The Tithe is watching.*

Once more, I address the invisible warlock. "Devak said he was the forth soul in some a kind of countdown. Silvinio here must be the third. Which means there are two more to go until … what, exactly? You've every right to make deals with my people, but you're picking on my minsters." I lower my voice to a menacing tone. "I can't help but take that personally."

Silvinio's ghostly gaze flips between me and the invisible Tithe. "My master wants to know if you'll allow him to hunt Myla Lewis."

"That answer remains, *no*."

A prickle of awareness creep over my skin. Whatever is happening, it's not about whether I'll allow the Tithe to hunt Myla Lewis. There's some larger plan at play, only I can't see it. Questions tumble through my mind.

Why doesn't the Tithe appear or fight?

How come he's so focused on my minsters?

What's the connection to Myla?

Silvinio rubs his palms together. "Since you say no, my master demands that I fight you."

Interesting. The Tithe keeps asking for what amounts to exhibition battles. I know what those are; I do them almost every day. When I'm assessing a warrior, I'll often watch him fight another opponent. The Tithe wants to know how I might attack his effigies.

Which means Silvinio has a short time left to remain a ghost.

Sure enough, Silvinio hunches over in pain. "I accept the change, my master," whispers the ghostly minister.

As with Devak, there's a flash of the Tithe appearing. The warlock strikes Silvinio in the chest with his mallet and chisel. White mist surrounds Silvinio. When the maze clears, the ghostly minister stands on the clearing. White particles rise up from the ground, filling his spectral form. Pale tendrils swirl through the minster's transparent body. With every passing second, Silvinio becomes less a ghost and more an effigy. I've seen this show before.

Time to get ready for battle.

I pull out my baculum from their holster at the base of my spine. My dagger remains hidden at my thigh. Can I use that blade to defeat Silvinio the way I did Devak?

I'll find out soon enough.

Silvinio's body fills out. Soon he's a solid figure that seems carved from white granite. The minister still wears his tunic. Only now, he carries a wooden stick with a barbed metal ball at the end of a chain. A flail. So far, everything has happened as did with Devak.

"My master demands that I fight you," intones Silvinio.

"I thought as much."

Silvinio raises the flail high. "My master gave me this, but I've made extra preparations."

I casually toss my baculum between my hands. Clearly, Silvinio is the sort who talks before fighting. Baculum-tossing kills some time. "Get what you need," I say. "I won't fight until you attack."

Silvinio stares at me, dumbfounded. "You won't?"

"Thrax battle code."

"Thank you, my Prince." Silvinio nods quickly.

I shake my head. *How can he not know thrax code?* Like so many of my nobility, Silvinio believes that battle prowess is all about weaponry and armor … rather than practice and codes of conduct. Just another sign of how the great houses desperately need more training.

Kneeling, Silvinio scrapes at the ground. When his hands are visible again, two silver bands gleam on his palm. The first ring is hefty and holds the insignia of a dragon. *That's for armor.* The second is thin and covered in tiny markings. The band could expand into any number of weapons. Without seeing the runes, I can't be certain.

Even so, it's clear why Silvinio has first ring. With armor, I can't chip away at key body points as I did with Devak.

A new plan of attack is needed.

Narrowing my eyes, I think things through. Facts and options spin through my mind. I scan the clearing. The oak trees here have solid lower branches. Good. These oaks are more than strong enough to carry Silvinio's weight, even as an effigy.

A new battle plan takes shape. I nod once to myself. *Yes, that will work.*

Silvinio slips the bands on his stone fingers. Now there isn't time for further contemplation. A puff of purple smoke rises from Silvinio's hand. The ring's spell is now live. A second later, the effigy version of Silvinio becomes encased in silver armor. He turns to me, his all white eyes visible through the slits in his helm.

"See this?" asks Silvinio. "Devak warned me about your tricks."

"And why isn't Devak here himself to fight me?"

"This is my master's plan. I merely do his bidding."

"That, I believe." I ignite my baculum. In my left hand there appears a small round shield made of angel fire. In my right, I grip a short sword made of white flame.

Silvinio rushes toward me, swiping at my head with his flail. I block his strikes with my shield, and make defensive moves with my short sword. All the while, I take care to slowly back toward the best and lowest-hanging tree branch. Silvinio follows my movements like a dog toward a bone.

It really is sad, the state of battle training with my nobility. Silvinio doesn't have a clue here.

Once I'm under the ideal branch, I re-ignite my baculum into a massive net. Once the fiery cords crisscross under Silvinio's feet, I toss the silver baculum over the branch. The entire sequence only takes a few seconds to complete. Silvinio looks from left to right, wondering what's happening.

He's about to find out.

Silvinio makes another swipe at my head with his flail. Dodging the strike, I race over to the other side of the branch. The fiery net still sits beneath

Silvinio's feet. Meanwhile, there's also a cord I created; it will loop up the webbing into a sack.

My fiery rope is the key to it all, and that cord now dangles from the other side of the tree branch.

I grab the line of fire and heave. My net loops up, hoisting Silvinio off the ground. The effigy tries to break loose, but only manages to entangle himself more deeply in the fiery net.

As Silvinio struggles, I step around him. The Tithe may still be nearby; it's best to stay on alert. Even so, Silvinio is one of my people. He deserves a fighting chance to understand what's about to happen here.

"Did you know that I oversee the Stone Mason's Guild?" I ask.

"Let me down from here!"

Now, I *could* go into a long explanation of how I created this net with white-hot angelfire, and why that level of heat always weakens stone. I could also add that since Silvinio chose to wear metal armor, he's basically created the perfect oven for his rock body.

But I won't. Monologuing with opponents isn't my thing.

Yet as predicted, Silvinio's armor starts to light up pink. This doesn't cause the effigy any pain, but it *does* mean that his stone-body turns more brittle by the second.

"I'll make this easy for you," I say. "Stay there. Talk to me. I'll let you down. All will be well."

"I serve the Tithe now."

"Then answer my question. What's the Tithe's interest in Myla Lewis?"

"That I cannot tell." Silvinio fidgets in the net. He's up to something.

"Stay still. This is dangerous for you." Based on the bright red shade of his armor, the makeshift oven is working perfectly. "Let's try another question. Why does the Tithe need two more souls?"

"To end all the angels and perfect the after-realms … and to enact his revenge."

Another puff of purple smoke rises from Silvinio's hand. The magic of his second ring comes to life. A second later, Silvinio holds a diamond dagger in his fist. Those are powerful enough to slick through almost anything, including angel fire. A jolt of alarm moves through me.

"No, Silvinio!" I cry. "Don't!"

He does.

Silvinio slices through the fiery net that holds him. His bulky form tumbles to the ground. With it hits the earth, the super-heated stone instantly smashes like chalk. Bits of rock tumble out of the armor to sizzle in the mud.

"Tithe?" I scan the clearing. "Tithe! Stop hiding and face me!"

The little bits of Silvinio seep into the ground. Like Devak, he's not dead. And although I know a little more about the Tithe's plans—the revenge part is new—there are still far too many questions.

"TITHE!"

The clearing remains quiet. Unlike before, the silence does not come with the charged sense of hidden watchers in the forest. The Tithe is gone. And I still have so many questions.

Even so, I won't give up. In the end, my own actions are all I truly control. This mystery of the Tithe involves Myla, and it will be solved.

he next afternoon, I march up the front stairs to the Ryder mansion. My goal? Convince Myla Lewis to attend the Autumn Tournament. I've no illusions this will be easy. If anything, convincing Myla to watch the tourney will be more of a siege warfare than a hot battle. Some folks require time and patience.

When it comes to Myla, I have plenty of both.

The mansion's front door opens before I even reach the top step. A tall woman with pale skin and a monkey tail stands on the threshold. Her appearance is remarkable in being perfectly average: not too tall or short, fat or thin, pretty or plain.

"Madeline Ryder," I say. "So good to see you again."

"Please, call me Maddy." She smiles, and the grin transforms her appearance from average to astounding. Maddy is a perfect fit for a diplomat. Her enthusiasm makes you want to do anything for her.

We shake hands, and I step into he reception area. Maddy and I have been in almost constant contact since yesterday's meeting at the mead hall.

"Thank you for helping with this business," I say.

And by *business*, I mean plotting to corner Myla so I can invite her to the Autumn Tournament.

And by *invite*, I mean coerce.

It's been a very chatty time for me and Maddy.

"My husband and I are just glad to help," says Maddy. "Please let the Ghoul Minister know that we didn't plot to misdirect his message." She twists her hands in a nervous rhythm. "GSBG-9002 is still rather peeved, I'm afraid."

"Have you sent him a thank-you gift for his patience?"

"No. Should I have?"

"I always send him gift baskets of worms. In fact, I met with him this morning and he mentioned a particularly ugly incident that was far worse than mis-delivering a message. More worms and it's all smoothed over." Specifically, the incident involved the Ghoul Minister's wife and Aldred. What a scumbag that earl is.

Maddy flashes her smile once more. "Perfect! I'll do that right away." She starts to leave, then pauses. "Oh, you'll find what you're looking for in the library. You know the way?"

"I do. Thank you."

"And remember, feel free to borrow any books."

"I won't forget."

After Maddy goes off to ship the Ghoul Minister some worms, I trek to the Ryder library. While I step along, I think through my most recent interactions with Myla. A certain kind of rhythm has developed between us. It's a lot like fighting, but also a little like flirting. My pulse speeds. I can't avoid the truth; I'm rather excited to verbally spar with her again.

I can't spend my life with Myla. Therefore—for as long as this lasts—I'll enjoy our fights.

No one said that the heart was a logical organ.

Soon I reach the familiar labyrinth of bookcases that make up the library. My hunter's hearing tells me someone's flipping pages on the other side of the room.

That's my girl.

I cross the space to find her perched on a window seat, her tail slowly moving in arcs behind her. A heavy leather tome sits on her lap. Instantly, I'm disappointed to see she's back to wearing grey sweats. That dragonscale fighting suit is my absolute favorite.

Myla looks up as I approach. Like always, she radiates energy and excitement. A lively sense of malice shines in her large brown eyes. She knows why I'm here and she's ready.

Time to play my role. And if I enjoy it just a little? That's something I'll keep to my grave.

I slap on my most stony demeanor. "Hello, Miss Lewis."

"Hello, Mister The Prince."

Inside, that line cracks me up. I've never been called Mister The Prince before. On the outside, I maintain my air of quiet menace. "I had an official audience with the Ghoul Minister today. It seems he didn't approve your delivering his message."

The look on her lovely face says, *this is me, not caring.* "And?"

"So, you admit you raided the thrax compound without authorization?"

She taps her cheek in mock-contemplation. "So, you admit that a lowly quasi girl successfully raided your super-awesome demon-hunter compound?"

"Your actions were rude and startling. The lords were not prepared." *And you have delicious-looking lips.*

I cough into my hand and try to regain some composure. *Careful with the internal monologue, Lincoln.* You could slip up and say that out loud, and then where would you be?

Myla rolls her eyes. "They were wearing chain mail, carrying weapons, and in the middle of battle training. I call that a fair fight."

No question about it. Myla is correct. The battle was completely fair. I should know, I watched it with interest and rooted for Myla every step of the way. Even so, I can't reveal that here. It's imperative I continue playing the part of an absolute butthead.

When I speak again, I keep my voice carefully calm. "My men don't expect strange girls in unitards to appear out of nowhere."

I'm rather proud of the use of the word *unitard.* She'll loathe that.

Sure enough, Myla's eyes flash with fresh anger. "One, it's a dragonscale fighting suit, not a unitard."

In my heart, I can't help but grin just a little bit. *Unitard line? Winner.*

"Two," continues Myla. "What exactly do they expect girls to do when they're attacked? Half the best Arena fighters are women."

Now this is something I also know quite well. After all, I've already snuck into Myla's Arena matches. But again, the truth isn't helpful here.

And yes, I'm still enjoying this.

"That's not how it is in Antrum," I counter.

"What's an Antrum?"

"Where I live, where all thrax live. Back on Earth, deep underground."

"That makes sense. Not knowing girls fight; it figures you all live under a rock."

If I slammed Myla with my *unitard* line, the *living under a rock* comment hits me with a wallop. Mostly because it's hilarious. A belly laugh threatens to break free from my mouth, so I close my eyes and take a deep breath instead.

Get organized, Lincoln. Think. What would a regal dickhead say?

In a flash, my reply appears to me.

"No one speaks to me like that." I'm glad that came out sounding serious, because it's still rather tempting to laugh my royal ass off.

Myla narrows her eyes. "Welcome to Purgatory."

In my head, I'm cheering my lungs out. *Well said, Myla!* Yet as much as I enjoy this, we can't banter forever. I'm here for a purpose.

"The earls demand you attend a tournament of demon fighting prowess to celebrate the autumnal equinox. As senior members of the thrax nobility, they will battle on the field of honor."

"Humph." As grunts go, Myla makes that single sound pack in a ton of commentary, all of it unflattering to the thrax. And in this case, I once again agree one hundred percent. That said, it wasn't easy to get my court to agree to this plan. For her own safety, Myla must attend.

"Sounds like a *we'll show her* kind of thing," she adds.

"The lords have a right to display their skills under traditional circumstances."

"Well, there's one thing they need to do first."

I fold my arms over my chest, thinking, *this will be epic.* "And what's that, in your experience?"

"Say. Please."

I look down to hide the grin that's now spreading across my face. To make the movement seem more natural, I rake my hand through my hair. All of which beings me back to the question of the day.

What would a dickhead do?

I snap out one word. "Disrespectful."

"Funny, I was about to say the same thing to you."

Myla's verbal sparring reminds me of her work on the battlefield. She's sublime. I want to toss this ruse aside and take her in my arms. Without realizing it, I've been clenching and loosening my fists. That's a surprise. I rarely lose mastery of anything, especially my own body.

If I'm not careful, I'll soon spoil my act, and that won't help Myla. And there's still time before the Autumn Tournament. This is a siege I will win. Myla must be there.

Sometimes, the best move is a tactful retreat, so that's exactly what I do—head for the exit. With every step away from Myla, my thinking clears. In fact, by the time I reach the door, I have the sense to scan the bookshelf for new arrivals. Sure enough, there's a fresh title waiting for me. Even better, it's one I've never seen before, *Secrets of The Tithe.*

Scooping up the book, I head out the exit. The Ryders watch me stomp out the front door. Unfortunately, I can't stop to chat. If I do, the Ryders could tell in seconds the truth of my situation.

When it comes to Myla, I'm more fanboy than upset prince.

19

*I*n the days that follow, I juggle my moving my anti-Acca treaty forward, continuing my battle training, and finishing the inter-realm map for the Tower of Wonders. Mother has taken the lead on the tournaments. Clearly, she's still scheming. I've been too busy to focus on it. Plus I've been tinkering with the Tithe book from the Ryder library. Why?

No matter what I do, the pages appear blank. It is incredibly irritating.

As a result, I've given the book to Lucas. If anyone can figure out how to make the volume reveal its secrets, it's the Earl of Striga.

Being exceptionally busy helps to distract me from thoughts of my girl. There's one bright spot: I've gotten word from the Ryders—who in turn were told by Myla's friend Cissy—that indeed, Myla is attending the Autumn Tournament.

I can't wait.

The days move slowly until at last, the Autumn Tournament is ready to begin. The wooden pavilions now surround a neat battle ground. Within that, that fighting space is surrounded by a waist-high wooden face. Horus did well when designing this space.

Thrax nobles meander around the tourney area. There are representatives from all the great houses: Acca, Rixa, Kamal, Striga and Horus. The parade of different colored dresses and tunics move around, reminding me of spring blossoms on Earth.

I shake my head. Spring petals? Me? Most of my days are focused on maps and killing demons. Just the prospect of seeing Myla transforms me.

It's not a bad thing, actually.

Feels excellent, as a matter of fact.

I step around the grounds, checking on the battle schedule. And yes, looking for Myla. She's supposed to attend with her friend, Cissy. Mother even chose a particular dress for Myla to wear. Red. Unmistakable in the palette of house colors. Yet there's no sign of a red dress or Myla. *Yet.*

Nat soon finds me. There's a wild look in his eyes. "My Prince."

"What's wrong?"

"Aldred changed his battle schedule."

The muscles in my neck lock. This could be trouble. Of all the earls, Aldred was the most upset by Myla's so-called *battle with the young lords*. Since then, Aldred has insisted on introducing the event as well as leading the first battle. Mother planned the day, but I made the demon fighting assignments. Aldred is slated to battle an Insectile. This variety of demon looks like a massive locust, always goes on the attack, and dies at the slightest scratch. Ideal for an untalented windbag.

"I'll check into it," I say. The final schedule is held in the Rixa preparation tent. "Thank you for letting me know."

Soon, I stand outside our house's tent. "I am a warrior for the House of Rixa," I call. "May I enter?"

The entrance flap opens a crack. Bera, my mother's handmaiden, peeps through the break in the fabric. "Just one moment, your Highness. A few maidens need to leave first."

I nod, grip my hands behind my back, and wait. A moment later, my world turns upside down. A particular voice echoes out from the tent.

Myla's.

I kick at the ground with my boot, my thoughts racing. What could Myla possibly be doing with Bera in my house tent? Mother sent her a gown. Myla is here as a spectator, so she shouldn't be looking for any weaponry.

It's a puzzle.

Minutes later, the tent flap whip open. Mystery solved. Myla wears what we call a *gown of welcome*, which is a horrid affair with tons of flounce. Evidently, Myla didn't wear the dress that was sent to her. Of course. My girl isn't the type to do as told. And that dress? It's not Myla's style at all.

Still, my girl steps out of the tent with the flair of a runway model. She smiles, an expression that lights up her features. I admire her bravado. Not many can pull off a dress like that one, yet Myla looks transcendent. I can't help it, I look her over from head to toe. Instead of a puff ball, my girl resembles a warrior ballerina.

All the while, I work hard to keep my features unreadable. After so much effort to hold this tournament—and then get Myla to attend—I can't ruin things by overtly drooling before her presence.

I bow slightly. "Miss Lewis."

"Your Highness."

We're only a few inches apart now. Fresh lines of connection and interest crackle through the air between us. This is insane. I have to get out of here, fast.

"Excuse me." I speed into the tent, closing the flap behind me. The interior is lined with weapons of various kinds, as well as trunks which overflow with various supplies. Best of all, Bera is here.

My mother's handmaiden waddles toward me. She's all round cheeks and loving smiles. Seeing me, she throws open her arms. "Ah, my Little Lincoln!"

"My Big Bera." That was my nickname for her as a child. I thought Bera to be all things lovely, soft, and feminine. Even as a toddler, I'd always reach for her and want to cuddle in her lap. She became my Big Bera. I like that I'm still her Little Lincoln. We share a short hug.

"So," I say slowly. "A gown of welcome? I didn't realize we even carried those anymore in Antrum, let alone in Purgatory."

"Octavia warned me to pack some in a chest, just in case. Shoes, too."

"Mother is scheming."

"Verily. She wants Myla at the tourney."

"And Mother gets what she wants." I tilt my head. "How did the manners training with Adair go, by the way? Did Mother hold those sessions?"

"Did she?" Bera's apple cheeks redden as she giggles. "Peek outside and see for yourself."

Curious, I peer out a side flap. Sure enough, Myla sits next to Adair and the Great Ladies, meaning the leading single women from each of the great houses.

"That seating arrangement," I scan the precise order. "Was that part of Octavia's manners training?"

"Oh, yes."

I can't help but grin. "What else did Mother do?"

Bera rocks on her heels. "First, Adair had to invite Myla to sit beside her. Second, she can only call her Miss Lewis. And third, the Great Lady of Acca must comport herself politely at all times."

"I hate to ask this. How many times did Adair, you know…"

"Cry? Constantly. All crocodile tears. A fake display to get out of manners training."

I shake my head. "What did Mother do?"

"Kept her longer. And assigned a new Mistress of the Tissues to dab her eyes."

I shake my head. "That's a classic. How did I miss all this?"

"You've been rather busy." Bera stares at me a moment too long. Does she suspect my true area of interest, which is protecting Myla?

Best to change the subject.

"Do you have the demon fighting schedule handy?" I ask.

"Sure do." Bera waddles over to a table, picks up a parchment, and hands it over.

I scan the sheet. "Aldred is fighting a Limus?" Those are similar to a Dissolus in that if you don't know how to kill them, they're nearly indestructible. I exhale a frustrated breath. "I better get out there."

A voice sounds outside the tent. "I am a warlock for the House of Striga. May I enter?"

My blood speeds with interest. Lucas has already signed my anti-Acca treaty, so if he's here with news, it's regarding the Tithe book.

Cupping my hand by my mouth, I call toward the entrance. "One moment, Lucas." I then turn to Bera. "Would you mind giving us some time?"

"Not at all, Little Lincoln." She goes on tiptoe and pinches my cheek before leaving. *Love Bera.*

Lucas steps inside. He's a tall and lean fellow wearing the long purple robes of his house. His long grey dreadlocks are decorated with beads of spell achievement. "Greetings, my Prince."

We clasp hands. "Good to see you. I appreciate your support on the treaty."

"Not a problem. You know we have an old rivalry with Acca." Even so, the words come out as more of a question.

"But?" I prompt.

"You also know Aldred. He's always making deals. Lord Gilberto promised some kind of arrangement with his daughter, Gianna."

I narrow my eyes. "What's the nature of that deal?"

"I don't yet know, but I wanted to be honest. That may effect things."

"Your honesty is most appreciated." While other earls try to hide problems from me, Lucas is fearless in letting me know when things aren't going well. It's why I trust him so thoroughly.

Lucas continues. "If anything does change—and by *change* I mean it would affect the treaty—then I will certainly let you know."

"Thank you. Are there any updates on that book I sent you?"

Lucas pulls the volume out from the folds of his robes. "I've checked this out magically. The pages are blank." He taps the leather cover with his pointer finger. "There's an impasse spell on it. Only certain viewers can scan what's inside."

I pick up the small volume and turn it over in my hands. "Who can see it?"

Lucas shrugs. "I don't know. It's very old. The magic is deep. I'll keep at it."

"Do you need the actual book to continue? There are some other experts I'd like to bring in."

"No, I've already built up a magical research matrix. I can keep casting without the actual book."

"Thank you." I set the volume into a nearby chest for safe keeping.

All of a sudden, a roar sounds from the tournament crowd. Angry voices ricochet through the air.

"An insult to the House of Acca!"

"Evil she-demon!"

"Such a humiliation!"

I suck in a shocked breath. *Aldred!* With the news about the treaty and Tithe book, I'd forgotten about the fight with the Limus demon. I race out of the Rixa tent and speed to the tourney ground. Immediately, it's obvious what's happened.

Aldred sits in the center of the tourney ground, his body covered in green slime. An extinguished lantern lies broken beside him. The earl still grips a crossbow in his hands.

I shake my head. Aldred used a crossbow against a Limus demon? That's useless. Fire is the only solution. Someone chucked the lantern at Aldred and saved his life.

Across the stands, members of the House of Acca point at Myla. They keep yelling horrid things about her being a she-demon, throwing fire at their earl, and humiliating their house. Even so, Myla remains the only person in the viewer pavilions who stands tall.

Oh, damn. Myla did the right thing, but for the worst person possible.

Cissy rushes to the pavilion, grasps Myla's hand, and guides my girl away. As she leaves, a fresh round of cries rise up from the stands.

"Foul demon!"

"Scum fighter!"

"Quasi whore!"

Protective energy spins through my nervous system. Myla hears these foul words. *Outrageous!* I take off through the crowd, one thought on my mind.

Find Myla.

I soon discover my girl sitting in the mud behind the Striga tent. Her large and soulful eyes are lined with tears. I pause before her. Every instinct I have screams for me to kiss away her sorrow.

She lifts up her hands. Mud drips from her fingers. "Look, buddy. If you're here to complain, I've already heard it. The House of Acca yells much better than they fight."

Her words strike me through. My people are mandated to protect the innocent. Here, I find the worst kind of cruelty, and against someone who—despite being in a strange situation—did the right thing. My chest tightens with grief. *What can I say here?* I clear my throat and do my best. "On behalf of myself and my people, thank you for saving the earl's life."

Myla's eyes widen with disbelief. "You're welcome."

In my heart, I want to kneel down and console her. Yet I know what's best for her. So I turn and march away.

My destination? The royal stables. There, I find Nightshade. "Find Myla. Take her away from here."

Night rears on her hind legs. Purple smoke surrounds her. *Another spell.* When Night returns to all fours, she's fully saddled up and ready to go. My horse takes off for Myla. I watch from a safe distance as Night approaches my girl.

Upon seeing Night, Myla smiles. Warmth fills my soul. My girl mounts Night and together, they take off into the woods.

I watch her leave and shake my head. My girl is demonic. And yet she acted closer to thrax warrior code than Aldred. Even so, my people wanted to hurt her. With words, yes ... but can knives be fear behind?

Things are going too far, too fast, and at the crux of it all is that damned marriage treaty. It places Myla at unacceptable risk.

With a flash of realization, I know exactly what I must do. There's only one way I can ensure Myla always stays safe. I steel my shoulders. *Anything for my girl.*

Footsteps slosh up behind me.

"My Prince," huffs Bera. "So glad I found you."

"Let me guess," I state. "I'm needed at the mead hall."

"Sorry for the last minute request. They're all rather rowdy. Someone needs to talk to them. You wouldn't have any ideas?"

"As a matter of fact, I know exactly what to say."

And so I head off.

*M*inutes later, I step into the mead hall. Dying light streams through the small window holes atop the peaked roof. A thin layer of hearth smoke lurks by the ceiling. The floor is packed with nobles. After the battle of the young lords, my people were more humiliated than angry. This time, all the faces contort with rage. Angry energy ricochets through the air.

The situation hangs by a thread. If I do the wrong thing here; it could be a disaster for Myla.

Pushing through the crowd, I find Mother and pull her aside. "Is Father coming?"

Mother winces. "He's gotten an emergency communiqué and—"

"That's fine. I'd rather he not be present." I scan the crowd once more. My gaze lands on Cissy, Myla's friend. I nod toward her. "I need that girl to leave."

"Cissy Frederickson?" Mother frowns. "Why would we do that? It's good she's here. The girl's taking an interest in inter-realm relations."

There's a lot that's worrisome about what Mother just said, not the least of which is the fact that she knows Cissy's last name. I didn't even know that fact, and I pride myself as a master of Myla trivia.

"I must say things to protect Myla, and Cissy can't hear them."

Mother arches her right brow. A long pause follows. This is the first time I've addressed Myla by her first name, which reveals my level of interest. And using the word protect? It's clear that interest runs deep.

At this point, there are two things Mother could do. One, she could grill me for details on my true feelings for Myla. Two, she could tacitly agree that we both know damned well that I care for my girl. If the latter option, Mother will simply jump in to help me get what I want.

"Consider it done," states Mother simply.

All of which proves yet again that I truly have the best mother.

Meanwhile, Aldred marches up to the fireplace. The hearth is lit now, so the earl's outline becomes framed by flickering light. "My fellow thrax!" Aldred cries. "You all know what happened today. That she-demon humiliated me!" He slams his fist against his open palm. "We must track her down. Make her pay!"

Raising my arm, I bellow across the room. "If you bring up the topic of hun—"

Aldred cuts me off. "We must file an official diplomatic complaint."

Acca nobles yell. "Hear hear!"

All the color fades from Cissy's face. That's not a good sign. Ghouls rule the quasi people. A complaint could cause serious trouble.

I march to the fireplace and round on Aldred. "Let's discuss the facts. The Limus was not on your battle schedule. You added that fight without knowing how to properly defeat your opponent." I turn to the crowd. "The bottom line is simple. Miss Lewis saved the earl's life. We owe her thanks, not a complaint."

Mother makes her way through the crowd, closing in on Cissy.

"She's a demon," howls Aldred. "A demon!"

Cissy's still here, so I can't yet launch into my true speech for today. "It's not the thrax way to repay kindness with cruelty, even if this girl is a demon."

Octavia reaches Cissy and escorts her to the exit. I exhale. Ever since Myla saved Aldred from the Limus, a plan has been forming in my mind. Once Cissy is well and truly gone, I raise my arms. The room falls silent.

"My thrax," I announce. "We need to discuss Myla Lewis. Some of you wanted to hunt her. Now, Aldred wishes to file a complaint against her." I scan the room, ensuring I have everyone's attention. "I'll make one thing very clear, right in this moment. I respect Myla Lewis, both as a warrior and a person of integrity. The words I'm about to say are to protect all quasis, but they especially focus on her."

Part of being prince means reading a room. Right now? That sense is total shock. At least, that's not rage. I consider it an improvement.

"We've been called to Purgatory," I continue. "There's one reason why. Our spies say Armageddon will invade soon. When that happens, it's our responsibly to ensure the Great Scala and Scala Heir are safe in Antrum. Should an invasion take place, we shall all leave this realm. I will too."

"But my daughter is the Scala Heir," cries Aldred. "Will you sign the betrothal contract?"

I stifle the urge to smile. This is exactly what I'd hoped Aldred would say. "No, I will not sign."

"We all know why!" Aldred's jowls flush pink with frustration. "You've fallen for this demon girl."

"Her name is Myla Lewis," I correct. "I'm not signing because I have made a decision. Listen carefully, my people. I shall never marry. If I'm fortunate enough to become king, I'll adopt my heir based on their suitability for the role, as is my right by thrax law."

Silence and shock take over the room. A chill fills the air. Mother stands by the wall, her features stony and blank.

Aldred's face turns red with fury. "And you'll adopt from the House of Acca?"

I round on Aldred. "There are four major houses. *Four.* And hundreds of minor houses, such as Gurith." I gesture toward Mother, who's from that house. "I will not favor your house above all others." I allow a long pause to follow. The shock in the room turns to something else. Some nobles nod. Others relax their postures.

This is what I'd hoped for. No one wants to see Acca get more power.

"Every house deserves consideration," I declare. "My choice will be based on suitability. The king and queen are young. This decision won't be made for hundreds of years."

Aldred folds his arms over his chest. "We'll see what the king has to say about this."

"I suppose we will." I return my focus to the crowd. "Are there any *other* questions about my decision?"

No one says a word. Some excitement ricochets through the crowd. Many houses don't have eligible ladies for marriage, but they do have sons that could be adopted. This announcement appeals to them, as I'd hoped.

"Then I wish you a good evening." I turn to the fireplace, set my hand on the mantle, and stare into the hearth. Somewhere, I know the thrax are leaving the chamber. Mother wishes them smooth goodbyes. I watch the logs burn down to embers. The realization strikes me.

Walker was right from the start. I never should have gotten anywhere near Myla. Every time we see each other, I only make things worse for her … and myself. A weight of sorrow presses onto my shoulders.

I can't see Myla again. Ever.

I'm not sure how much time passes, but when I look up, the mead hall is empty. Mother stands beside me. She practically invented the unreadable look, and she's wearing one now.

"Mother," I begin. "I apologize that you had to learn of my decision this way. I must protect Myla. That means removing the question of marriage from the equation."

"You wish to protect her? Why?"

"Aldred. He's wanted to hunt her, one way or another."

"You care for her." It's not a question.

I pick up an iron and poke at the embers. "This life, my crown. It's what I truly care about. Marrying a quasi demon isn't an option for me, no matter what my heart says. I must do my duty." Looking up, I meet Mother's gaze once more. "That's what you taught me."

"I did teach you." Mother lifts her chin. "To be a better man than this."

My brows lift with surprise. "What do you mean?"

"If Myla were thrax, what would you be doing right now?"

"Not talking to you," I say with a chuckle.

"Right. You'd be at Myla's side. So what's stopping you now?" Mother steps closer. "Follow your heart."

A combination of rage and disbelief churn through me. "I have followed my heart. These past months, everything I have done has been for Myla. The extra trainings. The autumn and winter tournaments. All the messages at the Ryder mansion. And face to face, I've been nothing but a rogue to Myla, and it's all torn through my soul, but it's served one purpose: I must keep Myla safe from my own people."

"We're thrax, not monsters."

"It's true that we have a thrax code, but it's as much *hope* as it is *reality*. I've seen what our people can do." I shiver, recalling the Vantys demon. "And especially what Aldred can is capable of. Walker has concerns as well, although he can't tell me specifics. Myla is better off without me."

Mother tilts her head. "But you want to be with her.""

"You're such a hidden a romantic." I sigh. "You want to believe that being a quasi doesn't matter. Yet that's not reality. I won't take risks when it comes to Myla's safety."

"That's a choice you should let Myla make. You take too much on yourself."

I shake my head. "Myla doesn't know what it means to be royalty. It isn't a fair choice to ask." I scrub my hands over my face. "This is something I've thought through a thousand times. I've made my decision. Today is the last time I see Myla Lewis."

Mother frowns. "Your father and I were wrong. We should never have taught you that love has no place in a royal marriage. Love is what makes the rigors of ruling worthwhile."

"And where is Father right now? Hiding away out of respect for Aldred, that's where. You see my feelings for Myla and you want to make your son happy. That makes you a fine mother. But that original advice? The one you gave me every day growing up? Those words were ones you gave me to me as queen, and *that's* when you were right. Love has no place in royal marriage."

"Oh, my son. How I wish I could fix this for you."

I force a smile. "That is definitely not your job."

She sets her hand on my arm. "I understand why you've made this choice. You have my blessing."

"Thank you." My voice cracks. I wasn't sure if Mother would support me, but it means the world that she does. I kiss Mother gently on the cheek and leave the mead hall. It's all settled now.

I'll live my life alone.

21

*I*n the days that follow, I maintain my schedule.

Train nobles.

Keep an eye on Aldred.

Work on my map of the Tower of Wonders.

Yet whatever I do, my every word and movement feels sluggish. It's as if I'm out of my body, watching someone else experience my life. Even the anti-Acca treaty has lost its lure. Now that I've announced I won't marry, that alliance isn't as necessary to protect Myla. Still, only one house has yet to sign. *Horus.*

Before I know it, the day of the Winter Tournament arrives. This time, it's held at another and larger green. More pavilions encircle the battle area. Extra tents dot the landscape, since minor houses are coming in from Antrum for the day. I go through the motions.

Wake up.

Get on my body armor.

Visit the tourney grounds.

Greet my nobles.

I'm having that *out of body experience* again when a familiar face moves through the crowd. With a mental crack of lightning, I feel my body once more. I stop, blink and look around again. Energy streams through my veins. No, my eyes aren't wrong.

Myla's here.

And there's only one person who could have gotten Myla invited back after the incident with Aldred and the Limus. *Mother.* I can't have Myla here without understanding exactly what Octavia is up to, so I speed back to camp and the royal reception tent. This time, I don't even bother asking the guard for entry. I simply march inside. Sure enough, Mother waits for me. She's alone, sitting in a high back chair as if it were a throne.

"Greetings, my son."

"Mother." I sigh. "What are you up to?"

"I want *a woman* to win the tourney's title." There's no question what title she's referring to, either: the winner of today's tournament is named the Greatest Warrior in Antrum. The award is given out at every winter tourney. "You keep winning this event, over and over. It's rather a bore, that's all. I brought Myla here to compete."

"You're meddling in my personal life."

"That as well."

I pinch the bridge of my nose. "This isn't going to work."

"Please try to enjoy this day." Mother's voice cracks with emotion. "I just want to see you smile again."

Closing my eyes, I search my soul. Is there any scrap of happiness left in there? I find nothing. The electric sense in my body fades into numbness once more. "I promised myself I wouldn't see Myla again. I'm holding to that vow."

"Why not just once more? All I ask is a last look and smile."

I shake my head. I've always known that Mother has a romantic streak, but this is beyond belief. A look. A smile. It may please Mother, but it only prolongs my agony … while placing Myla's heart at risk.

Mother means well, but no.

Simply no.

I'm about to explain all this when Father steps into the tent. "There you are, my sweet!" He steps to Octavia's side and kisses her cheek. "The tourney's about to begin. Aldred holds the first match of the day. I promised we'd be in the pavilion to watch."

Mother smiles. "Of course, Connor."

Father rounds on me. "What about you?"

"I'll be a long shortly." I try to put on my most unreadable demeanor. Sadly, my words sound hollow and lifeless, even to me.

"Why not follow now?" asks Father. "We really should all be—"

"Lincoln will join us when he's ready," interrupts Mother. My parents exchange a long look, and I have a feeling they've both discussed about my feelings for Myla. At one point, that might have worried me. Now, I simply feel burned out. Hollow.

"Take whatever time you need," says Father. "I'll send a messenger along when it's time for your exhibition battle. You're fighting a shadow dragon, you know?"

"Yes, I know."

My parents exit the tent. I sit on the chair Mother vacated and stare out at nothing in particular. Minutes tick by. I'd gotten so used to looking forward to my next stolen glimpse of Myla. Now emptiness gnaws inside me. I want to see her again. Yet I know it will only make the pain worse later on. Time heals everything, or the saying goes.

Perhaps I just need to be patient.

A messenger calls me for my exhibition battle with the shadow dragon. I head back to the tourney area, ready for my fight. When approaching the actual battle ground, I avoid looking directly at Myla. That isn't easy. Myla's been seated next to Mother—meaning above the crowd and on an elevated platform—so it's rather a feat to keep my attention elsewhere.

The shadow dragon is released onto the battle field, and that locks in my attention. I take a few turns around the creature, sizing up my opponent. In less than a minute, it's clear that I will never make a single strike. The reason? The creature isn't yet a full grown dragon. My insides churn with outrage. I've been asked to fight a child. Not acceptable.

Even worse, my Master of Creatures hurt the youngster with stinging nettle. The pain was so intense, it forced the dragon to attack. After a quick chat with Nat, I call off the match. Then I find Lucas. If anyone can help the little dragon feel better, it's the Earl of Striga. Once I locate the master wizard, we take off for the stables, which is where the dragon's been placed for recovery.

As I walk away, I try not to think about the fact that, chances are, I'll never see Myla again. It helps that I can focus curing the little dragon. Lucas and I step up to the final stall in the long stables. There the dragon lays on its side. The poor thing's eyes are filmy, while its breaths come in rough gasps. Leaning down, I touch the dragon's flank. The skin is cold.

Lucas steps pauses behind me. "The beast doesn't look good. What do you suggest I try?"

"Cast a health status spell. Check for poison. Boost the child's strength."

Kneeling beside me, Lucas completes casting after casting. With each spell, bursts of purple light flare from his palms. As the sparks near the Furor's skin, they die out to embers. At length, the earl tosses his hands up into the air. "It appears immune. I'm sorry."

"*It* is actually a little boy," I correct.

Lucas sighs. "And the child is suffering. Wish I could do more. "

I scan the little dragon. Since Lucas began, the child's breathing has turned more shallow. A white film now covers his scales. Worry tightens up my spine.

"Feel free to return to the tournament," I state. "I'll watch over our friend here." I scan a nearby shelf. "Hopefully, the stinging nettle is the problem. I've a full set of ointments here for when horses are injured on demon patrol. I'll test these out. Perhaps one can help."

"That sounds wise, Lincoln." He pauses.

"What is it?"

"None of the great houses won any awards this year."

I know what he means. When it comes to battle, the great houses have been on the decline for a while, even Rixa. It's never been so bad that they didn't win anything, though. "And?"

"Do you *really* think we have what it takes to defeat Acca?"

"They didn't win, either."

"But they don't mind death the way our soldiers do. Aldred has them under his thrall. We can't win against men who don't value their own lives."

"Let's hope it doesn't come to that. Most alliances work due to the threat of retaliation, not actual war."

"It's a hope at that." After bowing, Lucas leaves the stables.

The little dragon opens his eyes half-way. Tears spill down his leathery cheeks. The gaze is almost human. A thought hits me.

I can't repair things with Myla, but I can help this boy. Somehow, that makes it even more important to save this child.

Stepping over to the shelves, I pull down a jar of ointment. It's a white and sweet-smelling paste. With gentle motions, I rub the crème onto the dragon's wounds.

Minutes pass.

Nothing changes.

With careful movements, I wipe away the first ointment. *Time to try the second option.*

Next I select an anti-poison crème. This is foul-smelling stuff that stings like Hell. I gently dab it on the wounds and massage it in. The shadow dragon perks up, sipping a bit from his water bowl.

My pulse speeds. He's better.

Finally I grab a green liquid that's for rapid healing. This jar comes with a small brush which I use to apply the medicine. The child's breathing evens out. His color improves.

I lean back on my haunches and exhale. *This little guy will live.* Some of the weight in my heart lightens. I even feel good enough to straighten up the stall a bit. In all the rush to save the dragon, his muzzle and reins were left laying about.

All of a sudden, Nightshade prances into the stables. She stops beside me, staring at me with her large and knowing eyes. I know this particular gaze from her. My mare has news.

"What is it, Night?" I ask.

My horse whinnies. Puffs of purple smoke waft from her nostrils and settle on the ground. *Another spell.* Scraps of straw magically lift up from the floor. The bits form into a small scene. It's Myla, and she's fighting a massive spider demon. The arachnoid. In all the excitement about the shadow dragon, I'd forgotten about the tournament.

"Myla won?" I ask.

Night shakes her head.

"She hasn't fought yet."

Night nods. The sculpture spell changes once more. The arachnoid demon balloons in size until it towers over me. The straw jaws snap. Night whinnies.

"You're worried about her," I state.

Night nods again. Another puff of smoke fills the stables. When the air clears, all the bits of straw float down to the floor. The spell is over. Night canters to the stable door, pauses, and stares in my direction. The implication is clear. *Are you coming or what?*

I look down at my little dragon. He's much better, so I can certainly step away for a few minutes. And Night is correct. If anything went wrong at Myla's match, I'd never forgive myself.

Leaning over, I give the dragon's flank a gentle pat. "I'll return shortly." Rising, I brush the bits of straw from my body armor and then stride out the door. Soon I stand at the end of the tourney grounds. Myla strides onto the field. She's dazzling in a golden breastplate over leather body armor. Tall boots reach up to her thighs. The look on her face mixes confidence and fierce joy.

Magnificent.

The arachnoid lumbers onto the field. It's a massive spider monster, seven feet tall with legs as solid as iron. A few grey marks line the bottom half of its limbs. No question what that means. Other warriors have already tried to defeat the arachnoid, and they went after its limbs. Big mistake. Then again, there are thousands of demon types. Few have studied enough lore to know that the only way to kill an arachnoid, and that's to get atop its body. A pang of worry moves through me.

Will Myla know what to do?

When I was cleaning up, I'd grabbed the dragon's muzzle. I meant to put it away, but somehow it remained in my grip. I now clutch it in my fists like I could snap the thing in two.

Myla approaches the demon, trying to hoist herself atop the round body. Our gazes meet. She stumbles, catches herself and refocuses. What happens next is more ballet than battle. Myla's irises flare red. Her demon power comes to the fore. With graceful movements, Myla glides about the spider's body. Every twist of her limbs is an act of natural grace. No one taught Myla how to fight. It's just part of her soul. Within minutes, Myla's wrapped her tail about the demon's legs, capturing it in place.

Myla's safe. More than that, she won. A sense of pride balloons inside my chest.

My girl. What a warrior.

Smiling, I head back to the stables. I spend more time with the little dragon. Before long, Night joins me once more. Her prancing steps means she's happy.

"What boon did Myla request?" I ask

Night looks away. *You won't like this.*

"What's that face for?" Little by little, my horse swings her head back in my direction. "Did Myla request you?"

With broad motions, my horse nods.

"And do you want to go with her?" I ask.

Night nods even faster.

"Traitor." But even as I say the word, I'm grinning. I raised Night. It's good to know some part of my world will stay with Myla. And I am glad I saw her one last time and smiled. I'll have to tell Mother. As always, she was right. And it was thoughtful of Octavia to go through so much trouble just to see her son happy.

I return to tending the dragon. Time passes. I test out different ointments. The young dragon continues to improve. At some point, I hear a familiar rhythm of footsteps approach the stables. My eyes widen.

Myla.

My pulse speeds. Myla is taking Nightshade right this second?

Night nudges my back with her nose, which is her way of saying, *Myla is coming right now! Yay!*

With a long creak, Myla opens the stable doors. Part of me wants to leap to my feet and call to her. *I can't.* The shadow dragon still needs my attention. Plus, Myla may just take Nightshade and leave. And I made my vows. Seeing my girl will only makes things harder.

Night nudges me again; I pat her cheek. "I know you're there, Night. I'm happy to see you too."

Myla sounds from across the stables. "Hi, there."

In reply, I suppose I should want to grumble.

Or sigh.

Instead, all I feel is bone-deep satisfaction. Rising, I stand to face Myla. "Oh, hello."

"I'm here for Nightshade."

"She knows." I pat Night's neck. "We've been saying good-bye."

"Is she your horse?"

"One of them. The House of Striga breeds them; I raised her from a foal. Every Striga horse is enchanted, but Night takes it to a new level."

Myla grins; the sight makes my heart soar. "I know, she keeps me on her back without a saddle. I don't even have to ask, she takes me where I need to go. Or she's waiting for me when I get there. I think she does magic."

I sift my fingers through Night's mane. "The House of Striga specializes in witchcraft. Nightshade casts spells for everything you described. She also has the power to make small things appear and disappear. Oh, and she loves to send fireballs at enemies during battle. We've gotten out of some close scrapes that way."

"Look, I never would've asked for her if I knew–"

"It was a fair request. You fought well today. My mother comes from the House of Gurith. It's a lesser house, but one of the few that allow women warriors. She's wanted a female tournament champion for years. You've made her very happy." I tilt my head. "Besides, Nightshade chose you, didn't she?"

"Yes. At the Ryder stables."

"I rode her there to meet the minister. Normally, she comes back on her own." Night tosses her head and snorts. "I don't take it personally, girl."

Reaching into my pocket, I pull out a few small biscuits. Night nibbles them from my palm while scenes from Myla's battle flicker through my mind.

"I've never seen anyone fight the way you did today. Your eyes turned red."

"That's my demon side. All quasis have a power with one of the seven deadly sins. Mine's wrath."

"Have you any battle training?"

"Nope. I started fighting death matches in the Arena when I was twelve. I sorta learned on my feet."

A low whine sounds from the stall behind me. Considering how quiet my little friend was before, some noise is a good thing.

Myla steps forward. "What's in there?"

"The shadow dragon. He was too sick to haul back to the menagerie." I open a white jar, sniff the contents, and wince. "This may smell bad, little man, but it'll help." Crouching down, I apply more of the ointment.

Myla steps closer. Her tail strokes along the dragon's back. "This isn't a shadow dragon," she declares. "He's Furor."

"How do you know? It's never changed into human form."

She gives me the side eye. "One guess." Her tail gives me a friendly wave.

I chuckle. "Okay, I'll take your word for it." I scan the little dragon once more. "Why do you think he hasn't changed form?"

"I think he's too frightened." She gently examines the dragon's back leg. "His first talons haven't come in yet. He can't be five years old. Poor little thing."

"I'll send a message to the Furor ambassador tonight." I pat the dragon's back with long strokes. "Are you absolutely certain?"

"Yes. By now, a shadow dragon would have tried to spear us with its tail. That's how they consume your soul." She smiles. "Or try to."

I grin back. How is it that we're here, having a normal conversation? Then I remember. I've given up on having any kind of wife and family. Plus, I'll return to Antrum soon. I can chat with Myla one last time and not play the creep.

"You know a lot about demons," I say.

"Arena fighters like me see all the matches they want. Last month, I saw a horde of Cellula."

"Really? I haven't seen that breed in years." Narrowing my eyes, I review all Myla's battles in succession. "So that's how you knew."

"Knew what?"

"How to save Earl of Acca from the Limus. He's a pompous blowhard, but he is one of our most important earls." Our gazes meet again. That familiar buzz of connection moves between us. This time, I allow it. After all, this is our last conversation. How much can happen in a few minutes?

"Thanks again for saving his life," I add.

Myla shifts her weight from foot to foot. "You're, uh, welcome." She looks back to the dragon. "Poor little guy."

A flare of anger moves through my soul. "Shadow dragons are rare; the

Master of Creatures wanted something to dazzle the crowd. But any creature this young, it's not–" The dragon flinches, I pat his side. "Calm down, boy."

Myla finishes my thought. "Honorable."

"Yes."

It happens again. Our connection, only deeper this time.

"It's late," says Myla. "I better head out."

I nod. What a perfect way to end my acquaintance with Myla. I'll never stop protecting her from afar, but face-to-face is simply too intense for us both.

Myla reaches for Nightshade. My horse whinnies and prances away. Myla follows the mare down the stable's main aisle. "Come on, girl."

I scan Myla's form. A jolt of surprise moves up my rib cage. "Myla, what did you do to your back?" A line of infected scratches wind down her spine. Those could be deadly.

Myla glances over her shoulder. "Oh, that was the arachnoid. I forgot it got one good lick in."

I rise. "Come over here."

"It's fine, really."

I march in for a closer look. "That looks bad. Arachnoids are poisonous. Wait one minute." I rush over to the shelves on the far wall, pull down a white towel, and jog back to her side. "I'm going to pat the wound, all right?"

And with any luck, prove to you that this is serious.

"Okay."

I gently press the towel against the wound, step before Myla, and show her the fabric. It's covered with green and yellow pus. "See what I mean? Bad."

"Hells bells! But I don't feel anything."

"It's the neurotoxin." I jog back to the shelf of ointments. "By the time you feel the pain, it's too late." I remove a yellow jar and check the label. *Anti-Noxus Crème.* "Don't worry, this one'll do it."

"How do you know that?"

"I've hunted demons since I was six years old. I've seen every injury you can imagine. That's an arachnoid cut, and this ointment's the cure." A green horse blanket hangs from a peg on a nearby wall. I pull it down with my free hand. "You'll need to take your upper armor off. Cover up with this."

I toss Myla the blanket; she catches it easily. "Give me a minute." Myla steps into a nearby stall. When she walks out again, she holding the blanket to her chest. Her back is bare.

I move closer. "You better sit."

Myla kneels; I crouch behind her. I lean forward and whisper. "This is going to hurt at first." I open the jar, scoop out some ointment, and pat it onto her wounds.

"I don't feel anything," says Myla.

"Give it a few seconds."

All of a sudden, Myla hisses in a pained breath. "Son of a bitch!" She jams the blanket into her mouth and bites down. On her back, the wounds lose their yellow color. Her skin begins to scab over.

"You're doing great," I say. "Just a bit longer."

The cuts close completely. Some red lines are the only outward sign she was hurt. That said, some of the poison could have gotten into her bloodstream. The next hour will tell if that's the case. Even so, Myla seems much better. A sense of pride swells in my chest.

I protected her again. It's what I do.

Myla pulls the blanket from her mouth. "Okay, it's better now."

I lean in closer. "Good." I rub more of the ointment onto the reddened lines of her wound. If any poison did enter her bloodstream, this will help fight the infection. I rub my palms across her shoulders, down her sides, and against the small of her back. Myla shivers.

She's enjoying this.

I am, too.

Myla tries to stand. "I'm totally fine now."

I grasp her waist, pulling her back to the floor. The barest moan escapes Myla's lips. It's the most erotic sound I've ever heard.

"You're not fine. Stay still."

"I think I can–" She tries to stand again, wobbles on her feet, and topples onto her back. The blanket lays askew across her chest. Her eyes are closed. She breathes in a slow rhythm.

Kneeling beside her, I scoop my girl onto my arms. In all my life, nothing has felt better than holding Myla Lewis. I'm completely unprepared for the rush of protection, desire and affection. Deep within me, something snaps. A truth ricochets through every cell in my body, settling into my bones.

I may lose my throne, but losing Myla? That could cost me my very soul. In light of that, being prince doesn't seem so important. Nothing is worth risking this. But could she ever care for me?

The arrowhead end of Myla's tail slides up my arm and throat. Against my skin, the brush of her tail is all things cool and soothing. At length, the arrowhead end presses against my cheek. I lean into the touch. There's no reason for me to have a psychic connection with Myla's tail, but in this moment? That's exactly how I feel. And I know one thing.

Myla wants me too.

One by one, the cords that held me back break. I make a new vow.

No longer will I battle against this.

I will fight *for* this.

With everything I am, I will trust to this connection. The rest of my life can turn to dust. So long as Myla is beside me, I will be happy. Pulling my girl closer against my chest, I march out of the stables and into a new world. One where no matter what, I will battle for this love.

22

*C*arrying Myla, I march out of the stables. Outside, a starless night sky arches overhead. Pausing, I soak up the moment: a quiet night by the forest and Myla in my arms. Her scent surrounds me. *Cinnamon and sunshine.*

My hunter's sense kicks in. The hairs on my neck stand on end. I'm not alone here. Sure enough, Bera steps out of the shadows. She does a good job of pretending to have been walking by. "Why, Lincoln. Fancy seeing you here."

I shake my head. "Mother should let you sleep."

"I'm not here as a spy for Octavia. I helped Myla get on her armor, you know. Is she all right?"

"She should be fine. Just sleeping off a scratch from the arachnoid." It seems I got all the poison out of her system. I'll know for certain within the next hour.

Myla's tail pops up. The arrowhead end points at Bera.

"Oh, my. What's that?" asks Bera.

"A tail," I deadpan.

"I know that part." Bera tilts her head. "What's it doing?"

Perhaps when it comforted me back at the stables, Myla's tail and I forged some kid of bond. But whatever the reason, I'm absolutely certain what her tail wants.

"It would like to shake your hand," I explain. "Isn't that right?" The arrowhead end swoops to point at me. It then arcs up and down in a nodding motion. "See? It agrees."

The arrowhead end points back at Bera. "Go on," I suggest. "Shake it."

Bera reaches forward, shaking the tail with her fingertips. "Pleasure to meet you again." She curtsies.

"Well done, Bera. Is the Rixa guest cabin still empty?"

"It is."

"I'm taking Myla and her tail there. Send the royal physicians please." My eyes widen as I recall another task. " And will you gather up her armor? I'm sure Myla wouldn't want to lose that lovely breastplate."

"Of course, my Prince." Bera waddles away, then pauses. "And Lincoln?"

"Yes, Bera?"

"Most of the people like her."

My heart lightens. "In what way?"

"They admire her fire. We thrax can be a rather saggy bunch, if you catch my meaning."

"That I do." Myla's strength is what drew me to her as well. Glad my people and I have that in common. "If they feel this way, why not say anything? I've had two mead hall encounters where I'm the only one speaking up for Myla."

"Most are simply too afraid of Aldred. Yet things will change." Bera grips her hands tightly at her waist. It's something she does when screwing up her courage. "Myla and I had such a sweet time getting ready today. Don't let Aldred ruin it." Her voice takes on a pleading tone. "Give us a chance with her, too? She could be good for our people."

If my heart felt light before, now I have the sense I could fly. "Thank you, Bera. And yes, I'm working on a plan."

"That news makes your Big Bera smile." She twiddles her fingers, which is a Bera motion for, *move along.* "Now off with you both."

I wink. "As you command."

In my arms, Myla curls closer to my chest. Leaning in, I kiss the top of her head.

My precious Myla.

Adjusting my grip, I move Myla so I can hear her gentle breathing more clearly. After that, I march through a maze of wooden structures until I reach the Rixa guest cabin. In the least surprising revelation of all time, someone already stands outside.

Mother.

As always, my mother wears a simple black gown and an unreadable look on her face. Now, I'd ask how she knew I was heading this way with Myla, but that would be a waste of breath. Knowing things is what Mother does.

I step into the cabin. It's a snug space with a wide bed and some simple furniture. A trio of serving ladies bustle about, getting things ready. I gently lay Myla atop the coverlet. After enjoying the touch of her skin against mine, it almost hurts to set her down.

"That's quite enough," declares Mother. "You can wait outside now."

I fold my arms over my chest. "I'm not going anywhere. She was poisoned by an arachnoid scratch and isn't out of danger yet."

Mother points to the door. "She also needs to wear a nightie. Cool your heels outside. Five minutes."

I step closer to Myla. Her skin looks far more pale than it did before. Although, that could also be a trick of the light.

"The longer you wait to leave, the longer before you can return," says Mother.

"Five minutes."

I step outside once more. The door closes so quickly behind me, there's a soft whoosh of air. The royal physicians approach. They're a trio of older ladies with pinched features, gray hair, and simple black gowns.

"What do you know about quasi health? " I ask.

The lead physician, Lady Kinborough, speaks. "Queen Octavia already sent us some books on her physiology, just in case anything went wrong at the battle. We're excited to help."

"Let me ensure I understand," I state. "You knew Myla was fighting today?" *Because it was a shock to me.*

"Of course, all the physicians were made aware." Lady Kinborough beams. "We're so excited to have a lady be our champion. She fights exceedingly well, don't you think?"

"That she does."

For a moment, I allow myself a spark of hope. It feels like years have passed since I first confronted my parents about the Tithe and Aldred. All my ideas to help protect Myla—balls, tournaments, and even battle practices— they didn't always go as I expected, but perhaps they worked in a different way. I'd simply wanted my thrax not to hunt Myla. Have things fared better than I planned? Can my people really be warming to my girl?

The cabin door swings open. Mother stands in the frame. "Come in. I fear she has a fever."

I speed through the door and take up vigil at Myla's side. The process involves dragging a large chair beside her mattress and staring. Then worrying. Then staring some more. In moments like these, I wish I were in battle. Too much energy zooms through my system.

Octavia and her ladies leave. The physicians get to work. Lady Kinborough rests the back of her palm on Myla's forehead. "She does have a fever."

I nod. "Do whatever you need to do."

Lady Kinborough now shows why she's such an excellent physician. She administers a series of tonics to Myla, spooning them onto my girl's lips, drop by drop. Myla's temperature lowers. In the end, this was far from the worst fever I'd ever witnessed. Even so, I worry at least a month off my lifespan.

At last, Lady Kinborough makes her announcement. "She's fully recovered."

"Thank you all," I say. "You may all leave now."

The physicians head toward the door. An idea appears. "Lady Kinborough, how long before Myla can return home?"

"She's healing quickly. I suspect she'll be awake and ready to go by morning."

More of my plan takes shape. "I think she looks ill," I counter. "She can't return for at least a few days, wouldn't you say?"

Lady Kinborough lowers her voice to a whisper. "If you don't mind my asking, why do you wish to keep her here? She's perfectly well."

"Why, I intend to court her and turn her into your future queen, of course."

Lady Kinborough laughs. "No, seriously."

"I'm deadly serious. Not all the specifics are worked out yet, but I've decided to—*how do the humans say?*—wing it."

"Apologies, my Prince, but aren't you set to marry Lady Adair?"

"Never signed that betrothal document." Leaning back in my chair, I kick my kegs forward. "And I've decided to marry for love. Myla Lewis, the Greatest Warrior of Antrum, will be my bride. She just needs to adjust to the idea, mostly because I've been rather horrible to her. Which is why she must stay here for a few days. Courting first, then crowning."

Lady Kinborough pales. "Oh, thank you for clarifying."

"You're welcome. You may leave, my good ladies."

The physicians speed out the door. Normally, I'd spend some time contemplating my next move on the chess board of this romance. But that's not part of my new *winging it* program. So instead of scheming, I spend time contemplating a sleeping Myla. Her skin holds a healthy amber glow. Locks of auburn hair fan out across her white pillow. Strength and energy surround her, even as she sleeps.

My thoughts whir through the next few days. I've some precious hours I can spend with Myla. It isn't much time, yet I need her to see who I really am. That will be far easier if I get rid of Aldred for a while. Fortunately, I'm enough of my mother's son that I have back-up plans in place for just such occasions. I'll head back to my cabin, write a few messages, and get rid of Aldred.

Rising, I kiss Myla's forehead. She grins in her sleep. I can't help but smile as well. Turning, I head back to my cabin and to scheme and stall out Aldred.

I plan to enjoy this. A lot.

few hours later, I stroll up to Myla's cabin door. It's now early morning. I haven't slept much, but my excitement in seeing Myla has me wired anyway. Glancing across the front window of the cabin, I see movement within. My pulse speeds.

She's awake.

I gently rap on the door. "May I come in?"

"Sure."

I press the handle and walk inside. There she is. My Myla. Standing like a goddess in a white cotton sheath. Affection warms my soul. "Hello, Miss Lewis."

"Hi." She scans me from head to toe. "Wow. You know about the twenty-first century."

"That's right, you've only seen me at official court events." I gesture across my black T-shirt, jeans, and boots. "Welcome to my day off."

"I like it." She mimics my movement, highlighting her white nightgown. "Welcome to this random nightgown someone put on me." She winces. "That wasn't you, was it?"

I can't help but smile. "I'll never tell."

Myla starts to return my grin but pauses. Her gaze locks on the open window once more. Anger pours off her in waves. The reply is there if unspoken; *whatever you're doing, Mister the Prince, it won't fix things.*

Not that I blame her.

My girl needs time; that makes perfect sense.

I take a half step toward the door. "I wanted to check that you're okay. Things were a little touch-and-go last night." I exhale, thinking about time before her fever broke. "And you look fine."

Myla stands in profile, her stare still locked out the open window. A heavy weight of worry settles onto my shoulders. *Have I ruined things with Myla?*

"I'll take my leave now." I reach the door.

"Hey." Myla twists around to face me. I freeze, my palm gripping the handle. Her eyes meet mine. "Thanks for ... you know."

"Saving your life?" I offer.

"Yes, that."

A thin cord of connection winds out between us. I could shout for joy.

"No problem," I say. "We're running a special this month on magical horses and lifesaving."

She smiles and, damn, her face lights up with that expression. "You have a sense of humor. Somehow I didn't expect that."

I give her the side-eye. "Well, it's not like I wowed you with my dazzling personality when we met."

"No, you didn't." Myla chuckles, and I love that sound.

The moment freezes in my mind. This is it. A crossroads in my history with Myla. It's on the tip of my tongue to explain everything. What I want to say is this: *the tournaments, the trainings, my playing the rogue ... it's all been to protect you. Myla Lewis, you exploded my world and I couldn't be happier. I'd do anything to keep you safe. My heart is yours.*

Speaking that out loud might feel good, but it would lead to questions about why she needed protection in the first place. I want Myla to be my queen. My people are finally moving away from their fear of quasis. Telling Myla that my nobles wanted to hunt her? That won't help matters any, either for Myla or my people. I recall what Bera said last night.

Give us a chance with her, too.

And in the end, I can't pretend this was my people's doing. It was my decision—*and mine alone*—about how I chose to protect her. I'm no fan of long excuses. I made choices, and I will own them. When I next speak, I try to express all the emotion and honesty locked in my soul. Whatever I did, I hurt her. That was wrong.

I take in a deep breath. "In fact, I was closed-minded and awful for far too long. I'm very sorry."

Myla scrunches up her mouth that says, *I believe you. Maybe.* "No more nasty 'demon girl' comments?"

I set my palm hand over my heart. "Never again." I wink. "I got a stern talking to from my mother about that." I grin, thinking about my conversation with Octavia in the mead hall. Mother was dead set on making me smile again. And here I am, grinning. "And you know how she can be."

"Yes, I do." Myla laughs and it's a ringing sound that echoes through my soul. With every corner of my being, I want to begin again.

No Aldred.

No fear.

No duty.

An idea hits me. Why not do just that?

I move closer to Myla. "How about we start over?" I bow slightly. "Hello, I'm Lincoln."

She gives me the mother of all side-eyes before replying. "Myla Lewis."

I offer her my hand. "Friends?"

"Friends." She sets her palm on mine. Everywhere we touch, there's a current of excitement and desire. The connection turns intense, fast. Myla drops her hand. "I guess I'm stuck here for the next few days." She shrugs. "I don't feel all that sick though."

Leave it to Myla to figure out that something's off here. I give her a mischievous grin. "I have a very over-protective court physician."

She pokes my shoulder. "Hey, now. Did you get me out of school?"

"If I did, it would be justified as an extra tournament reward."

"So, what's there to do around here, *friend*?"

No question what to do first. I've only spent hours fantasizing about it. "Want to take Nightshade for a ride?"

She nods. "Sure."

"Good." *If I died now, I'd be a happy man.* "I'll have some riding togs sent over."

"Pants, please."

Of course, my girl would want to avoid heavy gowns. "I'll make sure they offer you a wide selection."

"Great." Myla yawns and stretches. "See you at the stables in an hour?"

I frown. "You don't need more time to get ready?" Mother is one of the fastest ladies I know, and it takes her two hours to *put her face on*, as she calls it.

Myla sniffs. "Do I look like that girl to you?"

I can't help but chuckle. "No, you don't." I swing open the door. "In an hour, then."

I'm not ten yards from the door when Lady Adair steps into my path. "Oh, my angelbound love! There you are."

"Good morning." I pointedly sidestep around her and continue toward my own cabin. Adair must jog to keep in sync with me. It's an impressive feat, considering how she's wearing a heavy gown and fancy shoes.

"There seems to be a problem with Fortes Pointe." That's their main castle in Antrum.

"You don't say."

"The water main just burst."

I already knew this, considering how I sent an urgent message to my hidden contact at Acca, asking for some non-lethal sabotage. A broken water main is brilliant. My contact will be paid well.

"Are the royal engineers there?" I ask.

"Of course."

"Then you are in good hands."

Adair grabs my wrist. "It's just that Father's not here now, and I need to talk to you."

It's with a not-so-small sense of satisfaction that I feign complete ignorance. "Whatever would we need to discuss?"

"Our future, dummy."

"Interesting statement." I pry Adair's fingers off my wrist. "Here's the thing." I look Adair straight in the eyes for this next part. "There is no future for us. I'm marrying Myla Lewis; she just doesn't know it yet."

"The demon girl? Father will kill her."

"He can try, but he'll have to get through me first. And let's not forget Myla's skills, either." This is turning into one of my favorite conversations with Adair, ever. "Myla's the Greatest Warrior of Antrum. My girl can squash Aldred like a bug." I purse my lips. "On second thought, encourage your father to attack Myla. It could be entertaining."

Adair stomps her foot, which causes a loud slurping sound in the mud. "You're just saying this because you want better terms on the betrothal contract."

"No, I'm saying this because we ..." I slowly gesture my hand between us. "Are never getting married."

Adair gasps. "This isn't over. Father will fight this."

"I wouldn't expect anything else. Excuse me."

As I step away, a small voice in the back of my head states that when it comes to Myla, there's still too much to worry about, from Armageddon's inevitable invasion ... to Aldred's scheming ... and to the sketchy motivations of the mysterious Tithe. But I decide to ignore that voice for now.

I'm off for a ride with my girl. Nothing in the after-realms can distract me.

24

*A*fter ditching Adair, I head back to my cabin and change into my own version of riding gear. Perhaps it's the elation of spending a day with Myla, but my mind has never felt sharper. I step over to my puzzle table and —BOOM—that's when I see it. The correct way to position the pieces. My fingers move swiftly to realign the little scraps of map.

And there it is.

Alignment between the after-realms.

Turns out, the Tower of Wonders sits directly above a particular spot in Antrum called the Echo Vortex.

Time to see that place first-hand.

The Echo Vortex is the equivalent of a magical powerhouse for Antrum. Without the vortex's energy, my people wouldn't have regular air pumped through our caves. Even the Incaenda river, the fiery waterway that connects our houses, would cease to flow. Elaborately built-out caverns would collapse. But like any powerhouse, running it is a sensitive business. Surprise visits from royalty are both rude and unwise.

All of which means I must send a letter to schedule my visit.

But I'll pen that missive only after riding with Myla because MYLA.

With the Echo Vortex plan in place, I change my clothes and head out. By the time I reach the stables, Nightshade has already gotten herself saddled up. It's one of her best spells, by the way.

Although Night's ready to go, my horse Bastion needs more care. I just finish saddling up when Myla strolls into view. She looks lovely in a mortal-style blouse and pants. My girl grins as she approaches and, damn, that smile sends warmth right through me.

I gesture toward my steed. "I'd like you to meet Bastion."

"He's a beauty." Myla pats the horse's neck. "Another from the House of Striga?" She runs her fingers through Bastion's mane.

"Yes. I didn't raise him, but we're still very close." At this point, it's simply too tempting that Myla's hand is so close to mine. I run my fingers through Bastion's mane, making sure that I brush against Myla. Once again, a connection ignites wherever our skin meets. It's glorious.

Does she have any idea what she does to me?

Myla pulls her hand away and our gazes lock. Those cords of attraction wind between us ever more tightly. Myla clears her throat and looks away. Her cheeks redden.

With that blush, I know the answer to my question. *No, Myla has no idea how magnetic she is.* Somehow, this phenomenal woman has moved through life without being worshipped.

That's about to change.

Myla clears her throat. The intensity of the moment cools. "How's the Furor?" she asks.

"Much better. He still hasn't changed form, but we moved him to the palace infirmary all the same."

A thought occurs to me: once Myla is my queen, we can regularly share details of our days and realms. The thought makes me giddy. Hell, everything about Myla makes me smile.

"I'm glad," says Myla.

Nightshade trots up to us and stomps on the ground with her front hoof. I'm about to tell Myla that means Night want to go, but there's no need. In one fluid movement, Myla hauls herself onto Nightshade's saddle. I shake my head. Most people find Night foreign and unreadable. Leave it to Myla to decipher the mare right away.

In turn, I hoist myself onto Bastion and focus on Myla. "Ready?" I ask.

The flush on Myla's cheeks deepen, and it's nothing less than adorable. "Sure," she replies. "Where to?"

"Follow me." I click my tongue and both horses take off at a gallop.

Now, Night will follow wherever I lead. And certainly, I could guide both our horses along the outskirts of camp, far away from prying eyes. But my people need to start adjusting to the idea of me and Myla together. Am I getting ahead of myself? Probably. That said, I've already missed too many chances to show off Myla.

Plus, for once, I'm trusting to what I feel.

In short order, Myla and I ride past the main row of cabins for upper nobility. The Great Ladies peep out of the windows. We don't have a strict speed limit here, but most riders slow their horses when passing the cabins.

Not this time.

Myla and I rush by at a gallop. It's all things heady and marvelous, especially when I see how every inch of my girl lights up with speed and freedom. This is how Myla is meant to be—barreling along on horseback, her auburn locks streaming, and her brown eyes flaring with delight. The only way she'd look better is leaping through the air.

Which gives me an idea.

Within minutes, we leave the camp, pass the forest and hit some open ground. I click my tongue once more, which signals the horses to slow down. I scan the landscape. Somewhere around here there's a line of hedges that are perfect for jumping. Now, one of Night's many spells is keeping any rider safe. That said, it doesn't mean that Myla will *want* to leap over anything while on horseback.

The line of hedges appears on our right. Glancing over my shoulder, I call out to Myla. "Do you think it's too dangerous to–"

My girl doesn't seem worried. "Hyah!" She calls, her voice loud and confident. Night leaps into action, racing for the hedge at full gallop.

This woman. How could I even wonder if she'd want to jump?

I click my tongue and Bastion takes off for the hedges as well. It's a close race, but Myla and Night definitely finish first. Once we're both past the barrier, Myla rounds me. "And that is me kicking your butt!"

I can't help but laugh at my own folly. Here I was, wondering if Myla would feel comfortable simply jumping the hedge and she takes it to the next level. I lock gazes with her again. "I didn't realize it was a competition."

Our stare turns heated. When Myla speaks again, her voice has a husky edge. "To a warrior, everything's a competition."

"Are you really prepared to all-out compete with me?" In my heart, the question takes another turn. Competing means challenging each other, side by side. Can she really want that? It seems too fantastic to be true.

Myla sticks out her tongue. "Do your worst."

It's a simple answer, and like all things with Myla, there's no artifice here. My girl enjoys a challenge. And since she used the words, *do your worst*, I fully intend to fight a little dirty, should the opportunity arise.

"Good," I state. "I will."

There's no question about where I'll take Myla next. This is one of my favorite spots in Purgatory, and I can't wait to share it with her. Clicking my tongue, I command our horses in a new direction. A short ride later, we reach the top of a cliff overlooking a massive desert made from charcoal-colored sand.

The Grey Sea.

Together, Myla and I dismount and step up to the cliff's edge. The way Myla scans the place, it's clear she's seen it before. Which makes sense, considering how this is her homeland.

Myla sits on the cliff's edge, her feet dangling below her. "How often do you come here?" she asks.

I take a seat beside her. "Whenever I need a break from court. Maybe once a week."

"The Grey Sea is lovely in a ..." Myla pauses, searching for the words.

"Bleak desert kind of way?"

"Exactly." Myla grins, and I decide that I'd do anything in the world to keep her smiling.

"So, what's it like to hunt demons on earth?" she asks.

I wince. "A bit grisly. Most of the ladies in court ask that I skip the more gruesome bits, so I usually cut the description short and simply say that—"

"Well, if one of those ladies shows up, you can stop talking." Myla gives me a dry look. "It's *me* here, Lincoln."

"Right." I stand again. "Let's say I'm the demon. I'm on Earth's surface causing all sorts of trouble, only humans think I'm a storm or an illness breaking out or whatever."

Myla gasps. "Humans can't see demons?"

"Nope." I point to my blue eye. "Thrax only see them as part of our angel nature, and you probably see them from the demon part in yours. You be the thrax."

She rises as well, holding up her hands our as claws. "Grr."

There's no stopping my chuckle. Myla's really getting into things— meaning she's enjoying this side of my world—and it's wonderful.

"And a 'grr' to you, too." I gesture toward her. "So you find out demons are causing trouble somewhere. Let's say it's a forest. You get your team together and suit up for demon patrol."

"Do you wear those tunics to fight demons?"

"Nope. The one place thrax go high-tech is on demon patrol. We have the latest in body armor, night vision goggles, that kind of thing. The Rixa bring one traditional piece of equipment." I pulls two silver rods from their holster on my jeans. I'm casual today, but that doesn't mean I'm unarmed.

Myla beams. "I was hoping we'd get to this part."

"They're called baculum." I toss them to her.

"This I know." She proceeds to ignite the baculum. I blink hard, not believing what I'm seeing. Most thrax would love to wield baculum, but it's only the House of Rixa who can. But here's Myla, igniting the rods into any number of weapons.

"These things are amazing." She leaps for me, wagging a fiery trident at my chest. "Taste death, evil demon!"

Do I love how she's getting into this? Why yes, yes I do.

I shoot her a sly look. "Did you just ask me to *taste death*?"

Her cheeks redden. "I might have gotten carried away."

"No need to blush," I say in a deep voice. "Although it looks good on you."

Goofing around isn't something that royal princes do. As a child, other kids were too scared to play with me. They either feared that they'd hurt me, or that I'd hurt them. Which wasn't an unfounded worry. For years, I didn't know my own strength. Now in this moment, it's great to play-act with Myla. There's no worry about peerage, royalty, or strength. All I know if that we're enjoying each other.

I tap my chin as I mock-contemplate my next move. "Taste death. I can work with that." Staggering about, I clutch my heart. Then I tumble onto my back, twitch dramatically, and play dead.

"Excellent performance, your Highness." Myla extinguishes her trident. Leaning over me, my girl places the baculum onto my stomach. "Thanks."

I open my right eye. "You're welcome." Sitting up, my thoughts return to the fact that Myla actually ignited baculum. "How'd you do that? Only Rixa can use baculum."

"I don't know." She shrugs. "Did you ever test these with quasis? Maybe we've always been able to."

Nodding, I think things through. Myla has a point. My people know next to nothing about quasis. "Sure." The moment the word leaves my mouth, I try to figure out how anyone demonic could possibly ignite a baculum. That power comes from being an angel. And not just any rank and file angel, either. An archangel. Another comment tumbles from my lips. "Maybe."

Myla sits down beside me. Her body warmth radiates against my own. That heat makes all other thoughts melt away. *Myla is with me.* She goofs around with the grass a bit before lying down at my side. The thought hits me. If I shifted my weight, I could press my body against hers.

Myla breaks the quiet. "So, what are you doing tonight?"

"Official state dinner. Prince stuff. Boring."

"You got me out of school. The least I can do is return the favor." We turn our heads to share another gaze. Our mouths are only inches apart now.

I lift my brows. "What exactly will you do?"

She gives me the mother of all sneaky grins. "I have some ideas ... But I want it to be a surprise."

"Fine," I agree. "Just get us both in *big trouble.*"

"You got it." For a long moment, Myla's gaze roves over my face. After that, she shakes her head. "I can't believe you're the same guy I met before."

"I'm not." There are so many things I want to tell her now, but in this moment, all I can do is grin. Trusting to this bond between us is both crazy and exhilarating. I lower my voice to a whisper. "I saw you once before the Ryder ball, you know."

She rolls her eyes. "Sure you did."

"You were chasing a pack of Doxy demons through the woods by the mansion's stables, as I recall."

A long moment passes while a host of emotions flicker across her face. It's like watching one work of art after another. There's surprise, recognition, and then, a gloating kind of joy. Myla speaks again. "I killed the demons first, didn't I?"

I mock-frown. *Leave it to Myla to focus on the battle side.* "Yes."

That gloat turns into something like a glow. It really works on her. "Let's see, now. That means I beat you in jumping the hedge and killing the doxies. That makes not once, but twice."

I quirk my brow. "Is that a challenge, Myla?"

"With you? Always."

A memory appears—the last time Myla and I discussed challenges. My girl specifically told me to do my worst. And in this particular moment? No question what that means. Fast as a heartbeat, I roll my body atop hers. She feels perfect beneath me, all soft curves against my hard planes of muscle. Her breathing quickens. I can sense her heart pulsing under my own. There will be time for us. But not yet.

I lean in until my mouth hovers just above hers. "Are you sure?"

She keeps staring at my mouth. "Sure, I'm sure."

Raising my hand, I slide my finger down the smooth skin of Myla's cheek. Her breath catches. "I don't mind the thought of you beating me, Myla." I brace my arms on either side of her head, my knees straddling her hips. "Not at all." Her gaze stays locked on my mouth, and I can't help but grin. "Want to know why that doesn't bother me?"

Thunder rolls, which is no surprise. It's constantly raining in Purgatory. And that fact is nowhere near as interesting as the woman laying beneath me.

Myla nods.

Leaning in closer, I lick my lips. "I don't care because ..." She's ready for my kiss, but it won't happen just yet. Anticipation makes everything so much sweeter.

Myla nods again.

"Because I'm about to beat your ass back to the stables." Leaping to my feet, I race over to Bastion and mount up.

Myla rises and shakes her fist. I'm happy to see her skin is still flush from our almost-kiss.

Soon, Myla. I want more than a kiss from you.

"You bastard!" she yells. "You lying sneaky evil sonuvabitch bastard!"

Before replying, I make sure Bastion rears up on his hind legs. "Catch you later." And then, I take off for the stables at a gallop.

And Myla being Myla, she quickly recovers and mounts Nightshade. We race to the stables, but I've got a mighty lead. By the time Myla catches up, I've dismounted. As she approaches the stables, I stand beside Bastion, taking care to shoot Myla a smarmy grin.

"Hey, loser," I say.

"Hey, cheater." She points directly at me. "Besides, if I were you, I wouldn't poke fun at someone who's about to get you out of an evening of suck."

"True. And you're still one up on me, after all." I bow slightly.

"That's better." She tosses her head, sending her hair flowing down her back. "Now, if you'll excuse me, I have a lot of prep work to do for tonight."

Once again, I've a smile on my lips. My face hurts, I've grinned so much today. "Have fun."

"I will." She pats Nightshade's neck. "Girl, take me to–" Night gallops away before Myla's done speaking. What a horse. I'm sure Night already cast a spell to detect Myla's plans.

As the two race away, a rare thought crosses my mind.

This will be fun.

*a*fter Myla left for her secret mission, I make my rounds at camp, checking in on all my ministers. Jali still isn't taking any visitors, which concerns me.

I worry for little Rashida.

Setting Jali aside for now, I make my first stop: the House of Kamal. Or rather, the *cabin* of Kamal. Here I find the Duchess has already invested in new furnishings, saying that Devak would have wanted her to go shopping. Who am I to disagree?

Next I drop by the Striga cabins. No one seems particularly upset at Silvinio's passing, except perhaps those he once placed bets with. It's sad to have lived for six-hundred-plus years, and yet in the end, your closest relationship is with your bookie.

Before I know it, the time has come for my official court dinner.

And Myla's surprise, whatever that is.

After changing into my princely best, I head off for the mead hall. It's a packed event tonight. All the upper nobles are here, including Aldred and Adair. The Earl of Acca must have rushed in order to return from Antrum in time for dinner. No doubt, Aldred has already heard about my day with Myla. He'll have something planned for the evening, of course.

After making my greetings, I take my chair beside my parents. Mother raises her right brow. "Busy day, eh Lincoln?"

"Quite," I say simply. There's no point recounting additional details. Doubtless, Mother's spies already told her about my riding off with Myla.

Father leans forward. "Damnest thing! The House of Acca had a water break. No permanent damage, but it took up most of Aldred's day." Father cups his hand beside his mouth. "To tell the truth, it was pleasant to have him gone."

Mother beams at Father. "I got you all to myself today," she declares. Not sure how she doesn't stab Aldred; the Earl of Acca follows Father around like a lost puppy. It's amazing my parents get anything done at all.

Mother sips from her mead goblet, then pats the corners of her mouth with a white napkin. "Aldred has something special planned for the evening." She shoots me a dry look. "Whatever could it be."

The way Mother says those words, one thing is clear. Octavia knows exactly what Aldred is up to, and she thinks it a terrible idea.

Sure enough, the Earl of Acca stands up. "Perhaps the Scala Heir will honor us with a song?"

Mother and I exchange a dry look. *So that's what he's up to.*

Adair's musical stylings are notorious. Typically, she sings traditional thrax ditties like *Lady Mine*, *Thrax in Love*, and *Hearts of Acca*. All the tunes have one thing in common: they wax poetic about an irresistible thrax woman. Adair's parents forced her to sing tunes of self-love from an early age. Yet although Adair has years of practice, she's still a horrible songstress.

Honestly. There are goats in our royal flock who carry a better tune.

"Of course, Father," says Adair, who then speeds over to the minstrel. Lately, Adair has taken to wearing a white cloak, like the Great Scala. It's an unflattering choice, but it's for political reasons instead of fashion. Wherever Adair goes, she makes it clear that she now wields a new power.

Maybe.

I'm still not convinced Adair conjured actual igni. That said, Verus did proclaim Lady Adair the Scala Heir. No doubt, Aldred wants to emphasize how Scala power means I must marry his daughter. My guess? This song will segue to a betrothal discussion in some way or another.

Adair scans the room; the place falls silent. She opens her mouth, inhales a deep breath, and pauses. With that, I know what's coming next. *A speech.* Adair often gives one before her songs. At least, she isn't singing yet.

"I know you're all wondering what it's like to be the Scala Heir," begins Adair. "Of course, it represents a massive power shift for the House of Acca." She gestures to her father.

The earl wears what can only be described as a grimace. My guess? Aldred is angry about being called off to Antrum. The earl knows I spent the day with Myla. With the water break, Aldred had no time to engineer perfect counter play for this evening. Adair's song is a last minute effort.

It's rather un-princely of me to admit this, but I do love seeing Aldred uncomfortable.

"I'm now more than a thrax," continues Adair. "Maybe even more than a mortal."

These speeches take time, so I spear a few leaves of lettuce onto my fork. That's when the hair on the back of my neck stands on end. I set the utensil down. My hunter's sense tells me someone's overhead. My pulse speeds. *Myla.* I won't do something so obvious as lean back and gawk, though.

The mead hall layout appears in my mind. This building's a long wooden structure with an arched roof. The only windows are two high vent-holes, one on either side. A network of heavy wooden beams crisscross under the arched ceiling. Gentle scraping sounds echo down from the rafters. No one else seems to notice but me.

Perfect.

Chances are, Myla's crawling across the main beam.

Excitement sparks through me. Lifting my goblet, I sip at my mead. The movement gives me a chance to scope things out without being obvious. Indeed, Myla is above. A case is gripped in her left hand. And my girl wears her dragonscale fighting suit.

I adore this plan already.

Adair scans the room. "Tonight, I wanted to share my personal Scala journey with you all."

All focus stays fixed on Adair. Myla uses the distraction to her benefit, creeping along the dining room's main ceiling beam, still gripping the handle to her questionable cargo. An electric jolt of anticipation moves through my limbs.

This will be epic.

"I've written a song to the tune of, *Are you going to Scarborough Fair?*" Adair gestures to the lute player who plinks out a quiet melody. Attention stays locked on Adair as she sings with a warbling old-lady voice:

> *Who will worship the Scala Adair?*
> *All the thrax if given the time*
> *My powers are great, my face is so fair*
> *Who won't want the love that is mine?*

She stares directly at me when she sings the 'love that is mine' part. There's no way I want Myla getting the wrong idea here. Wincing, I shoot my girl a subtle glance. Myla catches my gaze and grins. And with that, it's official. This is the finest meal I've ever had, despite the fact that Adair keeps singing.

> *My powers are great, my face is so fair*
> *Who won't want the love that is miiiiiiiiiiiiiiiiiiiiine?*

I mouth two words at Myla. *No way.*

My girl grins so broadly, her teeth glint in the shadows. I think myself rather suave until she mimes showing off her arm muscle while whispering, *can I touch you?*

Oh, no.

That day at the garden party. Up in the library. Myla must have been there. Which makes sense, considering how I met Myla at that exact spot later on. My girl wears a shit-eating grin. In a spirit of healthy competition, I simply must respond.

I angle my forehead in her direction. Then I smooth over my brows with my middle finger. Myla laughs so hard, she must jam her free fist into her mouth to stay silent. Questions appear.

Must I continue to be a prince?

Is there a world where Myla and I just hang out and make each other laugh?

It's something to contemplate in my free time.

Adair raises her arms. "Thank you, my people!" The room breaks into enthusiastic applause, no one more than the Earl of Acca. I clap politely, make small talk with Adair's sister Avery, and wait for Myla to release whatever she's hiding in that case of hers.

I'm not disappointed.

Seconds later, a troop of Reperio demons come skittering down the walls. These are harmless little monsters who possess trash in order to create miniature men and women. Reperio are tricksters who love to cause all sorts of trouble.

Genius move.

Before me, a pair of spoon-men make lewd hand gestures at the Duchess of Acca. Napkin-ladies do the backstroke through our soup. A broccoli boy jumps onto my plate and begins kicking my salad's ass. I find it all extremely entertaining.

My nobles don't.

As I've learned over the past weeks, what my court doesn't know about demons is a lot. That said, they still imagine themselves demon hunters extraordinaire. Which means the nobles all go into action, stabbing at the little creatures. The Reperio take this as an excuse for a food fight. I laugh so hard, tears stream down my face.

Meanwhile, Myla scooches across the beam above. She's heading toward one of the exit holes at the ceiling. No question what to do next.

Meet Myla outside.

I slip through the crowd. Along the way, I'm especially happy to see Aldred get a face full of cranberry sauce. The white gown of the so-called Scala Heir is covered in so many different foods, it resembles abstract art. Beside Adair, a pair of fork-ladies imitate her singing skills. Reperio are clever mimics, and these two have the warble down perfectly as they belt out:

Love that is miiiiiiine!

Adair's face pinches with rage. "How dare you?" she cries.

Lifting her right foot, Adair stomps down on the pair of mimic Reperio. Obviously, that's a bad idea. Those two demon-ettes are currently made from forks. Adair screeches, gripping her injured foot in her hands while hopping.

Now, there aren't many times I wish we thrax had modern conveniences like cell phone cameras. But now is one of those moments. Especially considering the look on Aldred's face as he watches Adair hop about. *Bewildered,* that's the perfect term for it. Couldn't happen to a better fellow, in my opinion.

Still, amusing as this is, it's time to leave. I slip out the front door. Myla stands outside, every inch of her overflowing with energy and life. She grabs my hand and together, we run for it. I love the touch of her skin against mine. We don't have to race anywhere in particular. As long as her hand is in mine, that's more than enough for me.

Once we reach the stables, Myla stops rushing. Instead, she bursts into a bout of belly laughs. "Did you see the look on Adair's face?"

"Adair? I was watching the Earl of Acca. I think he was going to cry."

"Do you need to go back and help?"

My mouth falls open with surprise. "Absolutely not. I've been sprung. Is there a part two for this plan?"

"Of course." Myla points to Nightshade and Bastion. Both are saddled and ready to ride. "We're going to break into the Ryder botanical gardens."

That's a massive greenhouse behind the mansion proper. Now, I must be honest. Of all the things I expected Myla to say, *let's break into the botanical gardens* wasn't on the list.

I love it.

Myla tilts her head. I can imagine words hanging above her head in a thought bubble. *Too much?*

I speak one word. "Nice." And in that single declaration, I pack all the excitement in the world.

Myla doesn't wait for more chatter. She races over and hoists herself onto Nightshade's barrel. Soon we're both galloping over the darkened country-side to a massive glass building that towers over the landscape. A huge tree extends through the building's ceiling, ending in an arch of branches and green leaves. Myla slows Night to a walk, pausing once we reach the back door.

"Here we are." Myla slide off Nightshade and yanks on the door handle. It doesn't move. "Well, I should've seen that coming."

I address Nightshade. "Do you mind helping us out, girl?"

The horse whinnies; the handle vanishes. Night really is the best horse.

With the impediment gone, Myla pushes open the door and steps inside.

We've many greenhouses in Antrum. It's amazing how much you crave green things when you live miles underground. This Ryder version is rather small by our standards. Still, the trees, vines, and shrubs are all healthy and glowing. For Purgatory, that's rare. Everything here seems in a perpetual state of decay.

Myla strides around the greenhouse floor, stopping before the massive tree at the building's center. "And here we are." Myla bows. "The very rare and beautiful Tumtum tree." She sets her palms against the rough bark. "You only find them in Purgatory."

Her full plan comes into focus. Myla sprang me from a court dinner to come see a tree. How unexpected and marvelous, all at once.

I steal closer. "You're trouble, Myla Lewis."

My girl mock-frowns. "I am not trouble. We're here on a mission of mercy."

"Really now?"

She point to a nearby sign. "See? This poor thing has a huge *do not climb me* sign, and that's just not right. If anything ever screamed, *climb me now*, it's this particular tree."

I rub my chin in an exaggerated display of consideration. "You have a point."

"Of course, I do." She grips the trunk and starts to climb.

Moving to the other side of the tree, I begin scaling up as well.

Beside me, Myla anchors her tail on a nearby branch. Then she allows herself to swing upside down, giving the illusion that she's standing underneath the branch itself. It's a feat of extreme balance and skill, but Myla acts as if she does this kind of thing every day.

Come to think of it, she just might.

"First one to touch the ceiling wins," announces Myla.

I firm my hold to the trunk and scale up more quickly. "You're on."

We climb for a time and if I'm not mistaken, Myla purposely ogles my butt. *I'm being treated as a sex object and honestly? It's rather grand.*

Too often, being prince means being treated as either a serial killer or a newborn babe. I like that Myla is comfortable with both herself and me. Plus, I'm about to win this race to the ceiling, which will make us *even* in the contest department.

I actively ignore the rustling noises from the outside woods. There's also telltale thump of footsteps and horses. I know what's happening.

A thrax search party.

With any luck, my people will give up and go home. It's never happened before, but the new Lincoln is all about hope.

"Prince Lincoln!" Thrax voices echo in from a distance. Spots of torchlight glisten in the trees.

How disappointing.

Still, they are my people and they worry. I leap down, landing at the base of the tree. Turning to my girl, I reach up. "Do you need a hand, Myla?"

"Sure." She steps off the trunk and into my arms. Little by little, her body slowly slides down mine. Each soft contour of her frame moves against me. Once her boots reach the ground, my arms remain tightly wrapped around her. Desire burns through my veins.

Myla licks her lips. "Thanks, Lincoln."

"You're welcome." I rest my palms at her waist. "I meant what I said today, Myla."

She blushes again. "You mean when we were talking about beating?"

I slide my hands up her back, setting my palms at the base of her neck. "About beating as challenging. My subjects complain, but no one pushes me to be better. You did that, even when you hated me." I grin. "Especially when you hated me." I lace my fingers through her hair. "Does that make sense?"

Her features turn slack. "Yes, it does. Very much."

My every nerve ending is alight with wanting her. "I like this. Feeling like I have a peer, a partner." I cup her sweet face in my hands. "I like *you*, Myla."

I guide her mouth onto mine. Our kiss quickly turns tough and demanding. Every flick of her tongue tears through my soul. Somewhere in the distance, lightning strikes the earth, followed by a low roll of thunder. Myla breaks the kiss, her gaze locking on the place where the bolt struck. We step apart.

"That's weird," says Myla. "It's not supposed to storm tonight."

"Prince Lincoln!" Those are my helpful subjects. Again. Based on how loud they sound, it seems as if they're closing in.

Damn.

"We better go," I say gently.

Hand in hand, Myla and I leave the greenhouse. After remounting our horses, we ride back to camp. All the while, more voices call for me. I make sure to lead our steeds on the fastest path to Myla's cabin. Once we're close, I ride up beside Myla and grip Night's reins. "Your cottage is past those trees. You should go; I'll take care of Night."

She gives me a silent thumbs-up, slides off Night, and tiptoes off. I watch until she's safely inside and smile.

That was perfection.

26

*O*nce the horses are settled, I head for my cabin. By this point, Aldred's had enough time to create a counter-move for tonight's dinner with Reperio demons. After all, he's still pushing for that betrothal contract and I haven't signed.

The man does not give up.

Once I arrive home, I fully expect to find a messenger waiting for me with a summons to my parent's tent. *More quality time with Aldred.* That's not exactly what happens.

Instead, none other than Minister Jali waits by my door.

Interesting.

As the Minister of Alliances for Horus, Jali is the my last step in finalizing my anti-Acca treaty. So far, Jali's been unavailable. His granddaughter Rashida remains ill. With any luck, the fact that he's here means the little girl is feeling better.

I open my mouth, ready to wish Jali good evening. The minister places his pointer finger across his lips in a gesture for silence. I nod, open my door, and usher Jali inside.

Minister Jali is an older man with ebony skin. His white hair is worn closely clipped to his skull. He has a long face with deep laugh lines and a whip-fast, wiry body. Even at four hundred years old, Jali remains a formidable warrior. Tonight he wears a kaftan of bronze fabric.

"Apologies, my Prince," says Jali. His basso voice echoes around the cabin. "I hope this isn't too late."

"Not a problem at all. Would you like to sit?" I gesture toward the larger table in the corner of my cabin. The smaller one is still covered in map puzzle pieces.

Jali stares at the big table for a moment too long. "Yes, that would work well."

Once we take our seats, Jali launches into the reason for his visit. Not a surprise. This minister is never one to waste time. "I've come to see you tonight because I've been visited by the Tithe."

Concern sharpens my senses. "I've been meaning to chat with you about that."

Jali's eyes take on an intense look. "It's like that old saying. You know the one? About attack plan omicron delta?"

In truth, there's no old saying about attack plan omicron delta. Jali has years of demon patrol experience. When fighting on Earth, thrax warriors have different pre-set battle plans, each one defined with Greek letters. Omicron delta calls for me to mimic whatever Jali does next.

"Of course." I say the words casually, but the meaning is clear. *I accept this battle plan.*

Jali stares at his hands, which he pointedly slides off the tabletop and rests on his knees. After that, the minister leans forward. I copy the movement.

Under the table, Jali grips my hand. The moment his fingers touch mine, a figure appears behind the minister. No, *appears* isn't exactly the right word. It's more that he becomes visible. Most likely, this person was always lurking behind Jali's shoulder.

It's the Tithe.

The sight sends a jolt of alarm through my nervous system. This is the warlock who keeps asking my permission to attack Myla. From my peripheral vision, I scan him carefully. He's an older man with leathery skin, unkempt gray hair, and a few day's growth of beard. He's dressed in a simple white toga and has the mismatched eyes of a thrax. A leather satchel is slung over his shoulder; the white crystal mallet and chisel peep out the top. White dust covers him from head to toe.

No question about it. Something about touching Jali makes it possible for me to see the Tithe. Which makes sense. After all, the Tithe has a book that's only viewable to those he's recruiting. It's logical he'd use the same approach in other ways as well. It's also why Jali wanted to sit at the table and called for attack plan omicron delta. That was so the minister could grab my hand without being seen by the Tithe.

"What troubles you, Jali?" As I speak, I take care to keep my features level. Jali went to great lengths to hide the fact that the Tithe was near. I must maintain the illusion.

"It's my granddaughter, Rashida. No matter what we do, her illness worsens."

Bands of sadness tighten across my rib cage. Rashida is a sweet child with bright eyes and a sharp mind. "I thought Lucas was healing her."

"He's tried." Jali huffs out an exasperated breath. "Nothing works."

"I'm sorry, brother."

"That's why I'm so happy that the Tithe has visited me." At the mention of his name, the Tithe's glares at the back of Jali's head. The look on the warlock's face is a unique mixture of hunger, hatred, and greed.

"I've been blessed," continues Jali. "The Tithe will grant my dearest wish. He will cure my granddaughter in exchange for my eternal service. I said I could not possibly accept until I had spoken to you."

"You haven't told my parents?"

"You and I are working on a rather sensitive treaty. If I take this deal from the Tithe, I must leave your service before that particular document is signed."

With my free hand, I scrub my palm over my face. Intuition tells me that Jali is saying this for show. Still, I need to act as if my world imploded. Or at the very least, my anti-Acca treaty. "I cannot pretend to be happy about this, but you have my permission. Rashida's life is what's most important."

"Thank you," says Jali.

Behind the minister, the Tithe steps backward. I don't look at the warlock directly, but even so, I can make out enough of what happens. A swirl of white dust surrounds the Tithe. Pale light flashes around his form. Then the cloud of magical particles disappears. With it, the Tithe is gone as well.

Jali releases my hand. "He's left, hasn't he?"

"Yes." I lean back in my chair and kick my legs forward. "Talk to me."

"The Tithe visited me yesterday. I was holding Rashida's hand when he appeared. Afterwards, she asked about what she called, *the funny ghost man.* That's how I found out my touch can help others see him. I'm chosen by the Tithe. It seems that gives me certain abilities."

"So you know, the Tithe already visited Devak and Silvio. I was aware he was targeting my ministers, but I didn't want to bother you, considering your plight with Rashida."

Jali shrugs. "It wouldn't have changed things, one way or another. The Tithe announced that he wants to scuttle the anti-Acca treaty."

"And will he?"

Jali grins. "Funny thing, that. The anti-Acca treaty is not signed. But the Earl of Horus already approved a trade route document which includes an addendum with the same provisions as your treaty, so ..."

I chuckle. "There's a reason why you're Minister of Alliances. Brilliantly played. You get the deal with the Tithe and keep your word to me as well."

"Thank you."

"Have you and the Tithe finalized your deal?"

"No, I'm supposed to sign a document in blood tomorrow." Jali rolls his eyes. "He's a rather dramatic one, this warlock."

"It's no laughing matter." I sit up straight and meet Jali's gaze dead on. "Know this. The Tithe is a liar. He may cure Rashida, but most likely? You won't spend a happy eternity in some tower. That warlock has evil plans, and it concerns both me and my future queen. Something about revenge."

Jali shoots me a sly look. "I heard all about her. Myla Lewis."

I frown. "You must take this seriously. Both Devak and Silvinio were sent to fight me. And the Tithe has said things about cleansing Heaven."

"I do know the import of this situation," retorts Jali. "I don't worry about fighting you. And you shouldn't, either. As for the rest, I'll simply have to risk it. Whatever you say about the Tithe, he always keeps his side of the bargain. Both Silvinio and Devak died wealthy men. I seek fortune of a different kind. Rashida must get better."

Most times, I'm on the receiving end of the *you're being too noble* speeches. This time, it's my turn. "Your loyalty is admirable. But at what cost, Jali?"

All signs of lightheartedness disappear. When Jali next speaks, all the seriousness in his soul is written on his face. "At what cost, you ask? A far smaller one than doing nothing." He exhales a long breath. "You understand, don't you?"

"I do." There's nothing more to say on the topic, really. Whatever tortures the Tithe could hand out to Jali, it wouldn't be any worse than the minister watching his granddaughter die, knowing he could have saved her. "How much longer do you have before you become an effigy?"

"Weeks at most."

"Has the Tithe told you anything about his plans?"

"Beyond the deal being contingent on burying the anti-Acca treaty? Nothing." Jali snaps his fingers. "He did say there was one more effigy after me, whatever that means."

"Devak and Silvinio said the same. The Tithe is working on some kind of countdown." A memory appears. *The Ryder mansion.* My eyes widen. "I have a book." Rising, I cross the room and grab the blank volume I got from the library. I hand it over to Jali. "This volume appears blank to me. Lucas thought someone who was in a deal with the Tithe might be able to read it."

Jali opens the book. "Indeed, I can see writing here."

My pulse speeds. "What does it say?"

"*The Story of the Tithe,*" reads Jali. "*Also known as Pygmalion.*" Jali looks up. "You know the tale?"

"Yes," I reply. "In ancient times, Pygmalion was a sculptor. He created a statue of such beauty, a goddess took pity on him and made the statue real."

Jali turns the pages. "This is mostly pictures. It shows the same sort of story." Jali flips forward. "Only here, Pygmalion is the Tithe and the goddess … that's the archangel Aquila. She granted him the power to create effigies through the gift of an enchanted mallet and chisel. Over the centuries, the Tithe has used this power to gather other magic to him. That's how you can know he'll keep his promises."

"Let me get this straight." I point to the leather-bound book. "That's basically a recruiting brochure?"

"You are correct, my Prince." Jali flips through to the end. "The rest of the pictures are what the Tithe delivers. Health, wealth, that sort of thing."

"Is there anything in there about warriors? I saw a model of the Tower of Wonders. Inside all the effigies were in battle armor."

Jali scans the pages again. "There's nothing in here about fighting."

I rake my hands through my hair. "I'm missing the bigger picture, I know it."

"Well, if anyone will figure it out, you will." Jali sets the book onto the tabletop and rises to stand. "Now, if you'll excuse me, Rashida can't sleep unless her Jaja is near."

"That's what she calls you? Jaja? It's perfect."

"So is she." With his head held high, Jali marches out of the room and my cabin. Once the minister is gone, I change into some loose flannel bottoms. After that, I return to my smaller table and the inter-realm puzzle map. Sure, I now know the Tower of Wonders is located far above the Echo Vortex. Even better, the House of Mulciber (who oversees the vortex) has confirmed my official visit. I'll inspect in a few days' time.

So I know the vortex lies below the tower.

That said, what's above it? What in Heaven is the Tithe interested in? How could he possibly cleanse there when no one has breached the gates of Heaven before?

Not for the first time, I consider marching into the Tower to confront the Tithe, once and for all. It's tempting, but until I know more—or have a compelling reason to risk my life—I'll keep up my research.

Something in this map holds the key.

Time seeps away as I tinker with my puzzle. In the end, I work through until dawn. At some point, an unfamiliar voice breaks the early morning silence. "This way, Myla. You're in deep trouble, young lady."

Uh oh.

That kind of speech is standard for mothers around the globe. I head over to my window. Myla steps out from her cabin. How can a woman make sweatpants look gorgeous? Somehow, Myla manages.

Beside Myla, there walks an older version my future queen. Myla's mother. As the pair march on, all the nobles peep out their doors and windows. I stride over to my own door, throw it open, lean against the frame, and watch my girl stroll by.

We share a smile, then a wink. Warmth and affection spreads through my chest.

Ah, Myla.

While my girl trudges off to her car, her tail waves good-bye to me. I return the gesture. After everything that happened in the stables, Myla's tail and I still have a special relationship.

As Myla and her mother drive away, I make a decision. In the end, it doesn't matter what Aldred plots, Armageddon schemes, or the Tithe wants.

I'll keep trusting to my heart. It's already working out stupendously.

27

*O*nce Myla's out of sight, a royal messenger approaches my cabin. I memorize the messenger rotation schedule. You'd be amazed how useful such information can be. In this case, the messenger for the day is Odelinda. She's who my parents use when they require both discretion and speed.

In other words, *I'm in trouble.*

Odelinda stops before me. She's a tall woman, athletic and lean with long brown hair pulled back into a neat bun. As a messenger, she wears a simple black gown with the Rixa eagle emblazoned on her shoulder. "Greetings."

"Good morning, Odelinda."

"Your presence is requested at the reception tent."

"I'll be along shortly."

"Yes, my Prince." She bows and strolls away. Despite the heavy gown, Odelinda can sure hustle. I have messengers in tunics and short pants who can't beat her stride.

Stepping back into my cabin, I change into my princely garb: tunic, pants, and boots. This meeting is undoubtedly Aldred's doing; I refuse to give him the satisfaction of seeing me wear my crown. That's an honor I reserve for the full court.

After crossing the camp, I approach the royal reception tent. This time, the guard's armor is rather scratched. That's Toland, one of my parent's oldest and most trusted guards. I pause before him.

"Greetings, Toland."

Toland raises his ceremonial spear, a motion that causes his armor to squeak. "My Prince." He lowers his voice. "They're waiting for you."

"Who?"

"Your parents. Aldred. No one else."

"Thank you. Please announce me."

Toland coughs a few times before starting. "Hear ye! Hear ye! The High Prince Lincoln Vidar Osric Aquilus requests permission to enter the royal reception tent."

"Granted." That's Father's voice.

In my mind, I focus on my marvelous time yesterday with Myla. Riding horses. Sharing kisses. Frightening the court half to death. Confronting Aldred will be nothing less than ghastly. To keep my cool, I'll need to hold my thoughts of Myla close.

After taking a deep breath, I open the entrance flap and step inside. My parents sit at their regular table. Both are done up in their royal best, including crowns. Aldred stalks the floor nearby. Food stains still cover his tunic. The man must be peeved indeed. Since the reperio dinner, he's neither slept nor changed.

"Greetings." I step forward and take my seat at the table.

Aldred pauses. His entire frame shivers with rage. "You said you would never marry."

"Funny thing, that." I grin. "I've had a change of heart."

Aldred and Father gasp. "You have?"

Mother stays perfectly serene. "He has."

"You see," I continue. "What I'm planning to do is—"

"Marry Adair!" Again, Father and Aldred speak in unison.

I inhale a long breath. "Perhaps I've been unclear. Allow me to explain." I focus on Aldred. "I shall never, ever marry Adair. Not if the angel Verus herself ordered it. Not if the future of the thrax people depended on our nuptials. Not even if every other female in the after-realms disappeared and only Adair remained. Me, Adair, no. Is that clear?"

Aldred trembles with rage. "Then I'm taking my house cloud-side."

I sniff. Cloud-side means living on the Earth's surface. "You won't last a month."

"Not true," snaps Aldred.

"Let's see." I count off on my fingers. "You've promised me no less than six times to end the Dissolus infestation in New York. You've yet to kill *one* of those demons. What makes you think you can live cloud-side permanently?"

Aldred lifts his chin. "My house will join Ethan's thrax colony. He's been surviving well for years."

Ethan was a childhood friend of mine. Then tragedy struck. After his family died, Ethan relocated to the Earth's surface. It's true that his cloud-side settlement is surviving, but I suspect that's because my parents send him a steady stream of thrax warriors to protect his compound.

"Your house now includes the Scala Heir," I point out. "Moving cloud-side will place her in danger."

"Adair will be safe," says Aldred.

"That's false and you know it," counters Mother. "You're placing your own flesh and blood at risk because of a bruised ego."

"Ego?" Aldred's jowls turn pink. He's getting worked up and fast. "Your son promised to marry my daughter."

"Never happened," I say coolly.

Aldred rounds on me. "You misled her."

This thread of accusations could go on all night. Best to speed to the negotiating bit. "What do you want, Aldred?"

Aldred leans over the table, resting his fists on the top. "Acca will remain in Antrum, so long as you remain open to a marriage alliance."

"Absolutely not," I state. "Any other options?"

"My house will stay in Antrum," replies Aldred. "But *you* must stay away from the demon girl."

Now, it's interesting that Aldred returned so quickly with a counter-offer. That means one thing. Aldred knows he'll be at risk in Ethan's compound. He wants a way to save face, not get a marriage treaty inked at this very moment.

Aldred truly is an awful negotiator. I let a long pause go by before replying. His jowls turn an even deeper shade of red. "Well, what do you say?" asks Aldred.

"To staying away from the so-called demon girl? Another no. And her name is Myla Lewis."

Aldred balls his fists so tightly, his knuckles flare white. "I'll go cloud-side. Don't think I won't!"

"Believe me, I don't think you won't not go." There, let's see who understands the concept of double-negatives.

Father pipes in. "Come along now. We must see some way to reach an agreement." He slaps the tabletop with him palm. "I have it. How about only chaperoned access to Miss Lewis?"

"That could be interesting." Aldred's tiny eyes narrow. "But I must approve any meetings beforehand."

In Aldred's mind, the fact that he can pre-approve Myla access means *no access at all*. With forewarning, Aldred can transform any Myla-time into disaster.

Fortunately for me, I'm a rather sneaky fellow. With Walker's help, I can get around this easily.

Mother focuses on me. "What do you say?"

"Agreed," I reply.

"Excellent!" Aldred rubs his palms together. His hands must be sweaty, since a gentle slurping noise sounds in tandem with his movements.

Honestly, the man is just disgusting in every way imaginable.

I motion to the exit. "If there's nothing else, I'd ask you to depart, Aldred."

"But, I…" Aldred stammers.

"Please leave us," says Father. "I'll be along shortly."

Once Aldred is well and gone, I remain in my chair, waiting. There's more to come from my parents. It will be interesting who launches the opening volley. No doubt, Father will press for a marriage commitment.

In a negotiation, it's not that, *whoever speaks first loses.*

But whoever speaks first, *absolutely* loses.

In this case, the first to pipe up is Father.

"This is a fine mess," he grumbles. "How can we stop Aldred from leaving?" Father looks to me as if to say, *you know what needs to be done. Marry Adair.*

"As a matter of fact, I already have a plan." My pulse speeds. This is the moment I've been working months toward. "I've finalized a treaty with the Houses of Kamal, Horus and Striga. We will combine warriors at the command of the House of Rixa."

"They already do that," says Father. "Every house under our rule will serve at the crown's command."

"Only for non-thrax enemies," I explain. "The new treaty states they'll fight with us against Acca."

All the color drains from Father's face. "You did what?"

"I love this idea," says Mother quickly. "Brilliant." She looks to Father. "Going cloud-side risks none other than the Scala Heir, so I'm sure you agree. We must support Lincoln here."

Father drums his fingers on the tabletop. I know that move, he's considering how to sidestep my alliance. There's no way around it.

How I love it when my plans succeed.

"And all the earls have signed?" asks Father.

"Every last one," I reply.

Father's eyes narrow. "Funny I didn't know about it."

I'd planned for this statement, of course. "I sent you copies of everything. You know our arrangement. If I don't hear from you in a week, I move forward." Every once in a while, Father decides he needs to look at things. Within days, the machinery of state grinds to a halt. Then we reinstate the one-week review rule. In Father's defense, it's not as if he wastes his days dancing or playing the lute. Managing Aldred's whining is a full-time job.

"Thank you, son." Mother waves to the exit. "Excellent work. You're free to leave."

Not for the first time, I decide that my mommy is the best mommy ever. I know when I'm being given a quick exit, and I'm wise enough to take it. With a fast bow to my parents, I depart the tent.

Once outside, I could shout, I'm so excited. My Anti-Acca treaty is working. There's no signed marriage contract with Adair. And there's also no way Aldred can leave Antrum without a massive army blocking his path.

A memory appears. My warm mood chills over.

There is one way this could all be derailed.

It has to do with the House of Striga. Lucas once stated that one of his nobles has gone rogue … Something about Lord Gilberto making a deal with Aldred that involved Lady Gianna. If my guess is right, then Aldred's next stop will be a visit to Gilberto. If Striga pulls out of my alliance, that could ruin everything.

For a moment, I consider pushing on Lucas to resign a stricter document.

I could try pressuring him to commit to the treaty forever, no matter what the circumstances.

Still, that won't work.

Lucas is a good man. He already gave me a heads-up that the treaty is at risk. No matter what pressure I place on him, he won't commit farther than he can manage. I just have to trust that when it comes to the treaty, Lucas will tell me if he must back out. And if Lucas *does* leave the group, then that isn't the end of the world, either. After all, I've faced worse. If anything, this situation gives me time to brainstorm some contingency plans.

My future with Myla is too important to leave to chance.

Or to Lucas.

*N*ow, I certainly promised Aldred that I wouldn't have any meetings with Myla without the earl's pre-approval. That said, when dealing with Aldred, I've found that it's best to save outright confrontation for special occasions. Otherwise, I could easily turn into a burned-out hulk like my father. Instead, I plan to use a bit of subterfuge in order to see my girl.

When it comes to *all things Aldred*, being sneaky is my way of life. It is also rather enjoyable.

But in order to see Myla on the sly, I must recruit Walker's help. My scheme is simple: get a message to Myla that defines a time and place to meet. Unfortunately, my thrax messengers will be seen leaving camp for Purgatory. If that happened, my plan would be uncovered in a heartbeat. So when it comes to getting secret notes to Myla, it's Walker or nothing.

Once I'm done with my parents, I head back to my cabin and scribble out a fast parchment.

Walker, I need to get a message to Myla. You around? — Lincoln

The reply follows quickly.

Just called to Earth for water elementals. Big rush. Will portal to your cabin when possible. — Walker

Now, I've always known my friend was involved in unusual stuff. But elementals rarely interact with any outsiders. Based on the tone of Walker's note, my friend has no idea when he'll be returning.

Which is a major letdown.

When you miss someone—and that someone is Myla Lewis—you really want to know when you'll see her again.

One week passes.

Two.

I contemplate reaching out to Ike. Maybe he can connect with Walker on Group Think. In the end, I dismiss that idea. Knowing Walker, he could be in any number of risky situations. Best not to bother him until he resurfaces.

Yet I do miss my Myla.

To stay busy, I deploy troops from Horus, Striga and Kamal in a unified defense of Antrum's exit stations. Horus and Kamal send their soldiers. Striga does not. Lucas isn't officially backing out of the treaty, but not deploying warriors? A serious problem.

I develop a back-up plan: recruit some minor houses as back-up in case Striga folds. I've sent a few letters. Gotten some sketchy replies. No one wants to agree to fight Acca by mail. To get lesser houses to sign up, I must visit Antrum directly. Trouble is, touring hundreds of houses will be a real time-suck.

I'd rather Lucas just deploy his troops already.

In addition to my anti-Acca military movements, I focus on battle training and my inter-realm map. In fact, I'm working on that very puzzle when Walker finally portals into my cabin. My friend looks even paler than usual. His cheeks seem hollowed out. In typical Walker fashion, he launches right into things.

"I won't talk about the elementals."

"Understood," I say. Although based on how awful Walker looks, the story must be a whopper.

My friend plunks down onto a chair beside mine. He scans the table for a moment, then starts rearranging bits of the map. Hundreds of scraps line the surface. Many are tiny pieces of Heaven and Earth, outlined with quill and ink on parchment.

Walker moves a few bits around. "I saw your note about Myla."

"And? Will you deliver a message for me?"

He shifts a few more pieces. "This is maddening."

"The message or the puzzle?"

"Both."

"Here's the thing." I purse my lips, trying to think of a good way to say what happened with the Earl of Acca. *And there really isn't.* "I made a deal with Aldred. I can't see Myla unless he approves. I'd push him into backing down, but there are snags with my anti-Acca treaty."

Walker sniffs. "Treaties." The way he says the word *treaties*, it's clear Walker places little faith in them.

"Say what you like, they work. I'll grant you, it's not as dramatic as battle.

Yet it's what a true ruler does. Create strong alliances. Forge compromises. Kick ass."

My *true ruler* speech always helps with Walker. He hates that I'm doing so much at eighteen. It's not my joy either, but there isn't anyone else who's up for the job.

"Fine," grumbles Walker. "Let me see it."

One wall of my cabin is lined with bookshelves. Rising, I pull a small envelope out from its hiding place inside a particular volume. I then hand the message to Walker. "Please deliver this to Myla. It invites her to come to a battle practice that Nat is holding at the Ryder mansion. I'll be there as well. Unofficially."

Walker plucks the envelope from my fingers. "You'll just stop by."

"That's the story."

Walker taps the envelope on the tabletop. "I thought you'd sworn Myla off. You're placing her at incredible risk. I made promises." Walker huffs while staring at the ceiling. It's his *I'm exasperated* face. "I can't say more, except that you are a very real and specific danger to Myla Lewis."

"Armageddon is worse," I counter. " The King of Hell is a danger to all of Purgatory. Plus, the old demon's been rather quiet lately. I preferred him blustering about and causing trouble."

Walker waves his hand dismissively. "If Armie does anything, I'll portal Myla to safety. We've discussed this already." *Which we have, numerous times.* "No, I'm talking about *you*, Lincoln. You could place Myla at far greater risk than you know."

Standing behind my chair, I grasp of the back panel tightly. "You've made your point, Walker. Clear, concise."

"Good." Walker offers me the envelope back.

I raise my hand, palm forward, in what I trust is a very clear motion for, *keep that envelope right where it is, buddy.* "That doesn't change the facts. I wish to marry Myla Lewis. If she refuses me, that's her choice, not yours."

Walker's mouth falls open. "You're kidding."

"Would I joke about my queen?" I ask.

"What does she know about this concept?"

I bob my head from side to side, thinking. "She's warming to it."

Walker sighs. "Come now. I know you've been miserable missing her, but marrying Myla? This is rash."

"Allow me to explain. Hers is the face I wish to see when I awaken, the hand I plan to hold all day long, and the touch I need beside me as I drift off to sleep. What's more, I believe the same is true for her. We're one soul in different bodies. The same vibrancies and passion within, yet with different outward expressions. Together, we will make each other stronger. More alive."

Walker stares at me, open mouthed.

I grip the wooden chair so tightly, it starts to creak. "And if you think for one moment that I'll do anything but fight for her with everything in me, then you're sorely mistaken. Deliver the message or don't. When it comes to Myla Lewis, I *will* find a way."

Walker sighs. I fight a grin. *I'm getting to him.*

"How fares your anti-Acca treaty?" asks my friend.

"Striga, Horus, and Kamal have signed. Lucas won't actually deploy soldiers, though. If Striga backs out, I'll need a lot of lesser houses to take his place. That will be months of travel through Antrum. My message?" I gesture toward the envelope. "It could be one of the last times I see Myla for quite some time."

Walker slips the envelope into the folds of his ghoul robes. "Fine. I'll deliver it. But I have one condition."

"Go on." Unlike Aldred, Walker knows how to drive a bargain.

"I told you I made some promises in relation to Myla, and I've pushed the limits of those vows and for your benefit."

That perks my interest. "How so?"

"To begin with, you shouldn't even know that I deliver Myla to her Arena fights. If her mother found out ..." He shudders.

"Fair enough. So what is my *official* understanding of your role in Myla's life?"

Walker pats the spot where he stowed the envelope. "I delivered this message to Myla for you."

"And that's it? Seriously?"

"Is it too much to ask?" There's an edge to Walker's voice.

"Not at all." I hold my hands palms forward in a gesture for, *whatever you want.* "You are officially the delivery boy. You can be an exotic dancer for all I care, so long as you get Myla the envelope. Only, I leave soon for Antrum, so please deliver it right away."

"And so I will." Walker points at the empty seat across from him. "But for now, I need you to work on this puzzle with me. And call in the servants. Cough syrup for me and mead for you. We both need a break."

It must certainly have been a rough time with elementals for Walker to actually want a break and cough syrup. The man is a worse workaholic than I am.

"Consider it done." I head to the cabin door, ready to call for a personal guard. They always remain within shouting distance and are happy to pass on messages to the servants. As I cross the room, I hear Walker muttering under his breath.

"Exotic dancer," he grumbles.

Uh oh. Walker sounds especially grouchy tonight. I'll make sure to order him some extra cough syrup for all his trouble, both for me and the elementals.

After all, how would any of us get by without Walker?

ays slog by. At last, it's time for my secret meet-up with Myla. Nat and I set up a battle practice area in the Ryder ballroom. Both of us sport human-style workout sweats for the occasion. And so we wait: me, my Master at Arms, and a lot of practice mats on the wooden floor.

"I'm sure she'll be here soon," says Nat.

"She will."

Walker swore it would happen.

And my friend is never wrong.

While we wait for Myla, I throw punches with Nat. Energy streams through my limbs. My girl will be here soon. I can't wait.

Myla's voice echoes through the ballroom. "Hello!"

Nat stops and waves. "Hello there!"

Now, I could pause and wave as well. But Nat spent years training me, starting at the ripe old age of four. One of his favorite practices was to get into battle position, call a start, and then have someone release an animal from the royal menagerie, usually my cat, Perkins. When I'd inevitably yell, *kitty,* then Nat would then flatten me. It taught me a valuable lesson. *Stay alert.* Even so, did I mention I was four at the time? Which means that in this moment, I shall show no mercy.

While Nat happily waves at Myla, I drop to my knee, swoop my free leg, and slam it against Nat's shins. My Master at Arms tumbles forward, hitting the mat face first. WHAM.

That was for you, Perkins.

I rise. "Always stay mindful of the battle, Nat. You taught me that." I jog to the edge of the mats, pull on a white t-shirt and wave at my girl. "Hello, Myla!"

Today, she wears grey sweats and a moth-eaten T-shirt. It truly is amazing how Myla can make that look work for her. Although, considering how she mastered the white puffball dress that is our *gown of welcome*, sweats should really be no problem.

"Hi. Sorry I'm late." Myla scans the practice area, her eyes wide.

"No problem. It gave me and Nat a chance to practice." I gesture toward Nat, who's now standing and grinning. "I don't believe you two have officially met. Myla, I'd like to present Nathaniel Archer, my Master at Arms."

"Master at Arms?" asks Myla.

"That means I teach the young prince how to fight demons, milady." Nat bows.

"And stay alive in the process," I add.

Her gaze meets mine. Tendrils of connection loop between us. And now? There's no reason to worry about that energy. I can simply soak it in. Allow it to grow. A slow smile rounds my lips. Myla's mouth curls up as well.

At last.

Nat moves to stand between me and Myla. "I'm also here as royal chaperone." He clears his throat. "In case any ladies should stop by what's officially a boys-only work out."

Myla tilts her head. "You've never had a chaperone before, Lincoln."

My smile melts away. "We'll get to that in a bit."

Myla shoots me a thumbs up. "Good."

It's a single word reply, but I can guess the many pages of thought that lie behind it. Both Myla and I have waited too long to spend time together. There are numerous dark clouds of news hanging over our heads. But forget that. In this moment, we'll enjoy our time.

Which brings me to the day's activity.

I rub my palms together and smile. "I've a surprise for you first. Nat here will teach you how to fight with something besides your tail."

Myla's beams. It's one of those smiles that envelops you, charging your soul with hope and light. Every cell of this woman's body seems to vibrate with energy. I could look upon her forever.

It's a thought at that.

"Really?" Myla races to the edge of the mats. "I've never had actual combat training."

"Now, be fair, my Prince." Nat shoots me a worried look. "I never agreed to attack the young miss."

"I told you, Nat. She's not like the ladies of the court." I pick up a wooden practice sword by the hilt and point it toward Myla. Nat gasps. It's a big reaction, considering how the weapon is a full six yards away from my girl.

Nat hasn't seen anything yet.

I flick the wooden blade straight at Myla's head.

All the blood drains from Nat's face. His body starts to shake. I know how my Master at Arms thinks. He believes that Myla is certain to lose an eye, and that's at a minimum.

For her part, Myla barely flinches. When the wooden point is barely an inch away from her nose, Myla grasps the blade, holding it in place. If it were a painting, it might be called *Woman About To Be Speared In Eye*, except for the part where said woman holds the weapon stationary. Nat starts breathing again, which is good. I was starting to worry there.

Nat gives me a shocked look at that says, *what in the world is this?*

I shoot back a smarmy one that replies, *told you so.*

"It's a shame that you missed her at the tournament," I add. "She was amazing."

Myla blushes, which is one of my favorite looks on her. "Thanks." She turns to Nat. "I fought in the arena since I was twelve." She then proceeds to set the blunt point of the sword on her fingertip, balancing it there. I don't think Nat could be more shocked if she'd swallowed the blade while it was on fire.

"Hand-to-hand combat," adds Myla. "To the death."

Even so, Nat still isn't completely convinced. I don't like how his heavy brows pull together. That's his face which means, *this is still a bad idea.*

Myla grins, bobs her brows, and peels off her sneakers. My girl isn't taking *no* for an answer. She strides onto the practice mat, the wooden sword remaining in her grip. Myla's gaze locks with mine once more. A different kind of energy moves through her now.

Battle power.

It's the coiled strength of a lioness about to pounce, and I love it. Myla gives me the barest of nods. Her words are there if unspoken. *Attack me.*

Happy to oblige.

I give my Master at Arms a sideways glance. "Here's what I know, Nat." Then I raise my sword and race straight for Myla.

Now, I've fought many opponents. Angels. Demons. Thrax. Each has their own set of unique skills. Demons are fast. Angels are strong. Thrax are clever. Myla combines all three of these into a single force that's beyond anything I've ever witnessed. Her sword stays raised and ready, as if she'll repel my strike with a counter-thrust.

Then, at the last possible second, Myla does something completely different.

With supernatural speed, Myla leans over just as I close in on her. My body slams against her side, shoving me off balance. At the same time, Myla's tail loops around my neck. There's a sensation of weightlessness as I'm flipped though the air. After that, a heavy thud slams against my spine as I land back-first onto the mat.

That was brilliant.

But Myla and I compete. And in the spirit of competition as urging the other person to be better, I simply must add some commentary here. I raise my right brow.

"You're using wrestling moves in a sword fight, Myla."

She sniffs. "Says the guy on the mat."

Touché. In this situation, most courtiers would bow, scrape, and slink away. Not my Myla.

Arching my back, I spring onto my feet. Before, I wasn't aware of how quickly Myla could move. Or how well she masked her true intentions. Now, I now better. No matter what strike I make, I need to be ready for anything.

Fair enough.

Lunging forward, I strike at an angle, top right to bottom left. Then I slice my blade from slide to side. My weapon goes for different targets. Hips. Arms. Neck. Myla keeps up, blow for blow. Her full mouth thins to a determined line.

My girl is an ace at blocking and defense. That said, I know she's hating every second of this. The tight set of her shoulders says it all. My girl wants to crush me already and can't.

I decide to give her an opening; see if she'll take the bait. Spinning about, I prepare for a moving strike.

Extra force.

Extra impact.

Extra tempting for Myla to try and kick my head in.

Sure enough, my girl leaps into the air, jutting her out her feet to where my skull should be.

Yet I was expecting it this time, so I dodge before she can connect.

Without my face to stop her kick, Myla flies through nothingness before falling onto the mat like a stone. As her back slams against the floor, she lets out a little *'oof.'* Adorable.

But not so cute that I won't go for the close.

Leaping forward, I pin Myla to the mat, holding her wrists above her head.

"I warned you about wrestling moves, Myla."

"And I should have warned you about my tail." The way Myla says the word *tail,* I know what she expects. The arrowhead should take me down, as it did to poor Husani. Even with the healing charms, that young lord still walked funny for days.

But Myla's tail and I have a special relationship. Instead of punching me in the dick, the arrowhead end slides up my arm and musses my hair. I can't help it; I fix Myla with a gloating grin.

"Some secret weapon you've got there," I say.

She groans. "My inner demon and I don't always see eye-to-eye."

It's the groan that does it. All sense of playful competition evaporates. All of a sudden, I'm extremely aware of the swell of her breasts against my chest. She writhes her wrists under my grip and smiles. Myla's gaze locks onto my mouth. *So tempting.*

Nat steps up. His outline sits just outside my peripheral vision. "You've proved your point, my Prince. I'll fight the young miss." His voice takes on a nervous edge. "The pair of you need to be getting up."

Myla licks her lips. "No," she whispers. "Just one." She shifts her hips just so, causing her leg to move between my thighs.

That does it.

Little by little, I lean in until our mouths meet. *There it is.* Sunshine and cinnamon, bursting through my senses. I press my tongue against her lips, she opens for me. Our kiss deepens.

Off in the distance, a bolt of lightning strikes, sending a flash of brightness through the ballroom. Low thunder rolls. Now, that's definitely odd. Every time Myla and I kiss, there seems to be a lightning strike. Then again, who cares about weather when MYLA.

Nat's meaty hand yanks on my shoulder. "That's quite enough, you two."

I frown. The weather may not stop me, but Nat certainly can. I roll to the side. The sensation is like stepping away from a blazing fireplace and into an arctic blast. I miss Myla's touch already.

Nat ushers me off the practice mats. I stand nearby, my arms folded over my chest. Meanwhile, Nat waves Myla to the center mat. "Let's begin the lesson."

Myla beams once more.

A warm sense of satisfaction seeps through my limbs. Myla's smiling her face off. Clearly, my girl is excited to get formal training. And here, I can give her this. I can provide.

Nat picks up a wooden sword from the floor, pauses, and eyes Myla. "You're a little bit of hellfire, aren't you, young miss?"

She shoots him a combination grin and wink. "I hope so."

That's when something happens that I've never seen before. Nat blushes. I've known the man my entire life, and I've never seen so much as a hint of pink on his skin. In fact, I wasn't even sure if the man had actual capillaries. Yet here Nat is, blushing something fierce. Myla just made a friend for life.

A spark of hope lightens in my chest. *Another ally for my future queen.* One by one, we can win over the thrax. I just need to win over Myla first. While Nat runs through moves and practice sequences, my thoughts segue to sadder topic. I must leave soon. But at least, I can see her once before I go.

At length, Nat announces the end of the session. "That's all the time we have, little miss. You done well."

"Thanks, Nat." Myla glistens with sweat, and yes, that's an incredibly hot look on her. "That was great."

Nat points at her nose. "Don't forget to practice. An hour with the sword, every day."

"I won't." Stepping across the floor, Myla sits with her back against the ballroom wall. I won't lie. I can't miss that she's panting a little bit while sweating. All that *pinning my girl and kissing* got me a tad overheated.

Nat drags the practice mats about, stacking them for cleanup. I grab a water bottle, cross the room, and take a seat beside Myla. That was the fun part of the day. Now comes the Aldred stuff.

I offer her the plastic bottle. "Want some water?"

"Yes, please." Myla's tail slides the water from my hand. "And thanks for setting up training with Nat. He's amazing."

"I'm glad." I drum my fingers on his knees. "I asked you here for another reason as well." It may be me, but it feels like the tendrils of connection between us are transmitting nothing but sorrow now. Seconds pass. I don't want this to end.

"I know what you're about to say, Lincoln." Myla takes a long sip from the bottle. "Walker told me about the Earl of Acca. About Adair. It's pretty obvious why Nat's playing chaperone today."

"Walker told you?" The muscles along my jaw tighten. What a pain in my royal backside.

Walker won't tell me anything ... but he blabs my secrets to Myla?

"I'm gonna kill that guy." I open my mouth, ready to complain about a lifetime of Walker quirkiness, when I remember my vow. "I told him to deliver a message, that's it. He doesn't even know you."

"He was only trying to help," Myla offers.

Turning, I face Myla directly. "And you still came here today?"

"Of course, I did." She elbows me in the arm. "Besides, Walker said you had a master plan to defeat the earl."

My anger at Walker fades. It seems he did more than tell Myla about my need for a chaperone. He also shared his confidence in my expanded anti-Acca treaty. I wink. "That I do."

"See? Nothing to worry about."

Myla shrugs, and it's a movement that combines supreme confidence with something I haven't felt in years. Hope. My life was supposed to be a never-ending list of duties. Protect my people. Prevent harm to humans. Lock away my heart. But to Myla? Life is a challenge that's fun to attack. Lioness that she is, Myla can't wait to sink in her teeth to anything. Her strength awakens something in me.

"Most people crumble in front of the earl, my parents included." I angle my head, soaking her in from a different perspective. *Still beautiful.* "How are you possible?"

"I've wondered the same thing about you." She curls her finger toward me and with that, I'm a goner. I lean in for another kiss.

Right before our mouths connect, Nat clears his throat. "Come on, you two."

I can't help but chuckle. "Nat's taking his role as chaperone rather seriously." I take in a deep breath. "There's one more thing you need to know. For my plan to work, my people must return to Antrum immediately."

Myla's shoulders droop. "When do you leave?"

"Next Saturday."

She nods slowly before straightening her spine. "If these are our last days together, then I want to have fun." She wags her brows again. "Maybe get into some more deep trouble."

I all-out laugh. "More Reperio demons?"

"No way. That's so two weeks ago."

"I have it." I rise to full height. "There's a party Thursday night, a kind of official send-off. We could be troublesome there." I offer her my hand.

Myla slowly slides her fingers across my palm. Her touch sends a charge through me. "Sounds like a plan." I pull Myla to standing.

Our bodies are so close. Almost touching, yet not. Our fingers remain laced together. I can't let go. It seems that she can't, either.

"Excellent," I say at last. "I'll have you added to the guest list."

"Can you add my friends Cissy and Zeke, too?"

"Of course." Nat keeps glaring in my direction, so I release Myla's hand. My only comfort here is the fact that, if my extended treaty works, I'll never have to release Myla again. "The Great Ladies of the court are organizing this event." *Meaning Mother is pulling their strings like marionettes.* "It'll be wearing traditional thrax attire. Someone will be in touch about making you another gown."

Myla winces. "I went through all that with the tournaments. I'm not really Ball Gown Girl. Maybe we can break-in somewhere again?"

At that memory, I can't help but chuckle once more. "With the scrutiny I'm under, I'm afraid that won't be possible. But I'd really like to see you at the ball." I look into her eyes, trying to convey all that I feel, but cannot name. Little by little, I run my pointer finger alone my girl's jaw-line. "Say yes, Myla."

She flushes and it's beyond lovely. "Yes."

I've lived a life of emptiness and duty. With that *yes*, I'll keep fighting for hope and Myla Lewis.

I stand outside the main doors to the Ryder mansion. Since tonight is the farewell ball, I'm wearing my royal formals: crown, tunic, boots, the works. Trumpets sound. The herald, a stooped and wary fellow named Woodrow, announces me.

"His Royal Highness, the High Prince Lincoln Vidar Osric Aquilus."

That's my cue. I march inside the main doors and enter the mansion's reception. It's a tall and round space that's all fancy woodwork and marble floors. My pulse speeds. Everywhere I look, there are thrax. I quickly scan the faces, my nerves on edge.

None of these folks are Myla Lewis.

It's disappointing, but perhaps she's in the ballroom proper. I march about the space, greeting different nobles and searching for my girl.

Still, no sign of her.

Adair approaches. "Don't I look pretty?" she asks.

I frown. I didn't believe anyone could actually start a conversation that way. *Oh, wait. I'm fairly certain Adair did so at the garden party.* Correction.

"Well?" asks Adair.

"I see you, and you're you, and that's that." Not my best verbal sidestepping, but I'm in a hurry. "If you'll excuse me, I'm heading back to reception."

"Why? They aren't letting people in anymore. The prince is always the last one announced. If you're late, you must go home. And it doesn't matter if you got your dress at the last minute or anything. That's thrax tradition." A smug look lights up her mismatched eyes.

Lady Adair has many faults. Fortunately, over-sharing is one of them. "Excuse me anyway."

Adair grips my elbow and rapid-fire squeezes. "What will you do at reception?"

"We've talked about the touching, Adair." I remove her grasp from my person. "And you know very well that I'm off to see Woodrow. I'll make certain he announces Myla, even if you did somehow cause her to be late."

"Who told you I made her late?"

"You did. Just now."

"Well, that's just … and I … while you're … I have to go." Adair stomps off to talk with her friends. No doubt, she's planning her next move.

Like father, like daughter.

I catch Woodrow out back. He's hanging solo by the mansion's dumpster, having a smoke. He almost chokes on his cigarette as I approach. "My Prince."

"I'd like you to return to your post. More guests are due to arrive."

Woodrow stubs out his cigarette on the asphalt. "But Lady Adair was so insistent. She got these rules from Queen Octavia." He shivers. "I don't want to break protocol or cause trouble."

An idea appears. When it comes to Myla, that happens quite often. "I have great news for you, then. There's been a new protocol called the Purgatory Prerogative. It states that when the prince allows it, anyone named Myla Lewis or her guests may arrive whenever they damned well please."

Woodrow gives me a sly look. "You don't say."

"I'll even put it in writing for you."

He chuckles. "All right, my Prince. I'll keep an eye out at reception."

"And I'll see you there."

With Woodrow in line, I march back to reception. The place is packed. Woodrow arrives a minute later, still smelling of cigarette smoke. He scans the room. "I wonder why everyone's still here? You've already been announced."

"It's the new protocol, obviously."

In truth, it's probably because my people waiting for Myla to get turned away. I wouldn't be surprised if Adair sold tickets. I wait by the back wall, my pulse speeding.

Any minute now.

Adair steps up and grips my elbow. *Again, with the grabbing.* "I have such an interesting thing to show you, my love. But not here. It's across the ballroom."

In other words, she wants me away from the reception room and Myla.

One by one, I pluck Adair's fingers off my elbow. Again. "No."

Adair stomps away. But then a steady stream of her friends approach me instead. All seem to have very interesting things to show me *somewhere else.* I decide to politely ignore them.

"My prince, did you know there's a rabid gnome at the other side of the ballroom? Let's go see him!" That's Gianna. To her credit, the girl looks terrified.

And I keep staring at the door. There's no such thing as gnomes, rabid or otherwise. *Still, points for creativity.*

"Ouch, I broke my ankle. Can you escort me to the physician's cabin?" That's Lady Keisha, another friend of Adair's.

I don't reply.

"My Prince, did you know there might be a ghost in the ladies bathroom?" It's Lady Nita's turn. One guess who she hangs out with.

Sometimes, being royal means ignoring people who are exceptionally irritating. So that's what I continue to do. This is the last time I'll see Myla, possibly for months.

No way I am missing this.

At last, a trumpet sounds. Woodrow steps forward. "Miss Cecilia Frederickson, escort to Mister Ezekiel Ryder."

Myla's friend sashays into the reception room, meets up with Zeke and leaves for the ballroom.

Another trumpet blast follows. Adrenaline speeds through me. Woodrow calls out again. "Miss Myla Lewis without escort."

And finally, she's here. Myla steps through the doorway, looking stunning in a red gown. It hugs her hourglass figure and sets off the natural color of her lips. I ache to taste her. Our gazes meet. Her brown eyes are nothing less than hypnotic. We must stare for a while, because the next thing I know, the trumpet blares once again.

"Miss Myla Lewis without escort."

The words finally register. *Without escort?* Woodrow expects her to walk into the ballroom on her own. That is tradition, after all. However, considering my new Purgatory Prerogative, old traditions simply won't suffice. I step forward and offer Myla my arm.

Everyone gasps in shock. It's a most satisfying sound.

My girl grins while she takes my arm. Feeling her touch again is grounding. A part of me that was lost now returns. Together, we step into the ballroom.

"I think we shocked your nobility," whispers Myla.

"They need to be shocked every so often; keeps them on their toes." I nod toward the dance floor. "Speaking of which ..."

Myla scans the dancing nobles and pales. Everyone is performing one of our traditional jigs. I don't blame her for finding it less than attractive. I've always thought this song should be entitled, *The Get-This-Spider-Out-Of-My-Shirt Polka.*

"I don't know that dance, Lincoln. I'll sit this one out."

"Let's see what we can do about that." I snap my fingers at the violinist. The musician glances in my direction. I make a slicing motion across my throat. The polka transforms into a seductive pulse of violins.

"Ah, a slow dance." I lead Myla toward the floor. "Anyone can do that."

She smirks. "That's a neat little trick."

I arch my brows. "It's good to be the Prince." We reach the center of the dance floor. "Shall we?" Bit by bit, I guide her hands around my neck. The weight of her touch makes me shiver. Myla weaves her fingers through my hair. I glide my fingertips down her spine, then rest my hands at her waist.

We're now an arm's length apart, our bodies swaying to the slow tune. The rest of the room fades away. In all the after-realms, there's only me and Myla.

Leaning in, I brush my nose by her ear. "I have a secret for you," I say in a low voice.

"Really? What is it?"

"I can't whisper it when you're all the way over there. Come closer."

Myla steps closer. Only a few inches separate us.

"How's this?" she asks.

"Closer."

At last, Myla fully presses her body against mine. We freeze. Energy ricochets between us. I stroke the small of Myla's back. Once more, we sway to the music.

Myla tilts her head. "And now?"

I lean in once again and whisper. "A girl like you ... In a dress like that ... Should always dance this close."

Myla blushes. "I'm not sure the thrax agree, Lincoln."

I inspect the nearby faces. Adair and her friends are all dance a few yards away while taking care to glare at my girl. It's making Myla uncomfortable.

Not acceptable.

Options to get rid of them all appear in my mind. Most involve finding another set of Reperio demons. I lean in and whisper once more. "Time to start causing trouble, don't you–"

"Prince Lincoln!" It's Gianna again. "It's urgent! A demon patrol's under ambush!" Gianna grabs my hand, trying to yank me from the dance floor. I make a mental note to have some proper training given on *How To Respect The Royal Personal Space.*

Even worse, it's clear that Adair and her friends are trying to ruin my night with Myla. Again. Demon patrols under ambush are supported by a back-up team in the field. The High Prince doesn't get pulled from a gala ballroom. The patrol would be dead before I hit the Earth's surface. Still, this could be an opportunity.

An idea appears. I can use this situation as an excuse to leave. After that, I shall find a way to spring Myla from the ball, and then?

It's time to start causing trouble.

Gianna's dancing partner, Aldo, steps up to our group. "If it pleases your Highness, I'll keep the young lady company tonight."

"Thank you, Aldo." I turn to Myla. "If the patrol's under attack, I'll be unable to return. Making the trip to Earth takes some time."

"I understand," says Myla solemnly. "Protect your people, of course."

I leave the room with Gianna, excited for my new plan.

Trouble, here we come.

*O*nce I leave the ballroom, I take care to stash my crown behind an obliging bookcase. I plan on spending a fun evening with Myla. Crowns are far too much hassle. After sneaking out a side door, I make the long trek to the back of the mansion. My thoughts segue to *scheming mode*.

To begin with, there's Myla.

Then I have myself, newly sprung from an evening that was the definition of *claustrophobic*.

So the question becomes, how do I separate one gorgeous future queen from a ballroom of nincompoops ... and still have an evening of joy left over?

There's only one solution.

A diversion.

As I close in on the hedgerow maze, I brainstorm different distractions that could allow me to spring Myla from the ballroom. Clearly, Myla's best exit is via the French doors lining the back wall. I could knock on the window and wave her over, but that lacks a certain level of romance, not to mention that it's dead obvious. I want to lose Adair, not have her trail me all evening.

No, far better would be to fetch Nightshade. Once here, Night can perform her trick with doorknobs, break into the Ryder mansion, and cause a general ruckus. At that point, luring Myla out a back door will be far more successful.

I close in on the line of French doors from outside the Ryder mansion. My plans are for nothing.

Myla's already here.

For some reason, she's sitting alone on a bench, mumbling to herself. Moonlight plays off her lovely profile, making her seem more a faerie apparition than a regular girl.

Then Myla stands up, frowns, and stomps the bench into kindling.

What a woman.

I step closer. "Nice kick," I proclaim.

Myla stares at me and gasps.

"Hello, Myla."

Myla still wears her *gasping in shock* face. I wonder if I've interrupted something important. Perhaps she needs to smash more benches.

Then Myla's surprise morphs into a wide smile. *Lovely.*

"Shouldn't you be on Earth right now?" she asks.

"Why ever would I do that?" I meet her grin with one of my own. "That was the worst fake emergency I've ever seen."

Leaning back, I scan her appearance. Closer up, it's clear that my girl's missing a huge swath of gown. No doubt, this is the work of Adair and her pals. Mother asked them to care for Myla specifically so they could make my girl feel welcome. Clearly, they failed in flying colors. It will be manners lessons for the group of them, I'll wager. Those girls better stock up on tissues.

"Looks like there was more to their master plan, though," I declare. "I'll be honest. I didn't see that coming. Rather elaborate scheme, don't you think?" The way Myla stands, I can make out the profile of her bare legs in the moonlight. "Not that I'm complaining."

"No fair peeking." Myla reaches behind her, pulling the open back of her dress together. She has nothing to be ashamed of, however. I hate that Adair has made her uncomfortable.

"They did us a favor, you know." I tap my temple. "That's why I played along."

She rolls her eyes. "I'm so sure."

"Think about it. We could have spent a few hours at the ball, irritating certain people. But this way, we can be alone." I step closer. "It'll be some time before they figure out I'm not on Earth." I can't help the mischievous grin that crosses my face. "Want to get in trouble?"

For a moment, I'm sure Myla's about to say *yes*. Energy and life pour off her in waves. Then she stares at the ground. "I'm not going anywhere dressed like this, except home."

Perhaps it's the dress that bothers her? I purse my lips, thinking. This doesn't have to be a problem.

"So, if you had something to wear, you'd be interested in a little stroll?" I ask.

"I would." She gives me a look that says, *but that's impossible.*

Leaning forward, I pull my velvet tunic over my head. *Problem solved.* "This should work fine."

"What?" She pokes at the garment. "You want me to wear that?"

"Why not? You'll be covered." I wink. "Mostly." I waggle the tunic.

Take this. You know you want to.

Myla screws up her mouth onto one side of her face. I'm wearing her down and it's glorious. "Where would I change?" she asks.

"How about behind the hedges?" I toss her the tunic; she catches it with ease. Using baby steps, I then slowly turn around. Once my back is to her, I speak again. "I promise not to peek."

What follows are the soft sounds of footsteps on grass as Myla jogs into the hedgerow maze. The rustle of fabric comes next as she changes. I can't help but notice how she isn't leaving the maze yet. At last, she calls out.

"I'm feeling a bit exposed, Lincoln."

"Don't worry, you'll be fine." *Mostly because I'll ensure you aren't the only one who's exposed.* I whip off my chain mail and jerkin. Now I'll be bare chested, just as Myla shows her bare legs.

My girl tiptoes past the line of hedges. She eyes my new appearance and freezes. Her gaze slowly rakes across my chest and lingers by my waistline. Not many men can pull off wearing black leather pants and nothing else. Fortunately, that happens to be one of my superpowers.

"Now we're both a bit exposed," I say.

Myla shifts her weight from foot to foot. "Are you sure that's a good idea?"

"Why not? I won't return to the ball." To emphasize the point, I kick at the pile of chain mail with my bare foot. "Plus, this stuff weighs a ton." I fold my arms across my chest. "And I was promised some trouble, remember?"

Myla performs an exaggerated bow. "Alright, you got me. Where to?"

"I have a specific spot in mind." Stepping forward, I lace my fingers with hers. It feels beyond wonderful to touch her again. "Let's go."

There's no question where we're off to. I've spent many hours contemplating the night Myla leaped out of the lake, covered in Doxy demons and laughing. How many times have I worshiped that vision of my lovely queen framed by water? Now is my chance to see it live once more. Guiding Myla through the paths, I quickly lead us to the maze's center. Here stands a fountain which will suit my purpose perfectly, especially since the water's shut off. Since the liquid is calm, it resembles the lake that still haunts me.

With gentle movements, I lead Myla to sit onto the fountain's edge. Then I step back. Before me is nothing less than a dream come to life.

"There." I hook my thumbs into the waistband of my leather pants. "That's how you looked when I first saw you by the lake."

Myla scratches her cheek. "So, that's why you brought me here?" The way she asks the question, it's not a ringing endorsement. And yes, this isn't exactly classic first date activity. It's just ... when it comes to Myla, none of the rules seem to apply.

"Well, I think about that night all the time," I explain. "Maybe too much." I shoot her a shy smile. "That sounds kind of crazy, doesn't it?"

"Depends." She tilts her head. "What's the interest?"

"It's a bit of a story, actually. I was chasing down some Doxy demons at the Ryder stables. I thought you were another thrax, tracking the same pack."

She mock-frowns. "Another guy, of course."

I set my hand on my chest. "Guilty as charged." I move nearer. Myla's scent surrounds me. "You disappeared into the water. I thought you'd be drowned, but you came out fighting." I stand before her, setting my palms onto her bare knees. We've never been this intimate before. Even so, it feels natural. Right.

With soft pressure, I guide her legs apart. Myla lets out a low moan. "You were fighting like a demon yourself, eyes glowing red in the darkness. And you were laughing." I press my firm body against her softness. My heart stutters. Myla's breath hitches.

"I saw you were a woman, a warrior." I lean in until our lips almost touch. "A force of nature. From that day on, I've thought of you, that night, and the water."

She takes in a long and shaky breath. Then she speaks two words in a low alto. "I understand." And in that short statement, I know what she means. We've both changed each other in deep ways.

I speak from my soul. "Good."

Our mouths meet in a slow kiss. As I taste her, Myla loops her arms about my bare shoulders. I trace my fingertips along the hem of her tunic. She shivers.

A thin bolt of lightning hits the ground nearby. Thunder rumbles. Myla breaks the kiss. "Did you see that?"

I follow her gaze and indeed, lightning hit not far from this very spot. This is now the third hit while Myla and I have kissed to the backdrop of a flash storm. Definitely odd.

Tilting my head, I consider the situation. Perhaps we should stop kissing and step apart. The moment the thought crosses my mind, I crush it with a vengeance.

"No." I kiss a line up Myla's neck. She moans again. I set my teeth onto her earlobe, just a bit.

"But Lincoln, aren't you worried about the—"

Leaning back, I frame her beloved face with my fingertips. "No." I lock with her gaze, trying to find the words for this moment. A dozen bolts of lightning could strike and I still wouldn't want us to stop. Instead, I move my mouth closer to hers once more. "Kiss me, Myla."

Sure enough, Myla leans in. We kiss, deep and fierce. Her body rocks against mine. The connection between is feels natural. Inevitable. Desire fires through me.

Myla slips off the fountain, looks down, and starts pulling off her tunic.

Then she pauses, trembling. That sense of fire between us cools to something else.

Looking more closely, I can see what's changed. Myla's eyes now flare red. As a self-taught expert on all things Myla, that means her demonic side is active, either lust or wrath. In this case, it's lust. Myla's so confident on the battlefield, it never occurred to me that she wouldn't be as comfortable with intimacy.

Myla drops her grip on the tunic and stares at the ground.

I'm fairly certain what's going on, but I want Myla to tell me in her own words. Moving slowly, I set my hand on her arm. "What's wrong, Myla?"

Myla nibbles on her lower lip while keeping her gaze locked on the earth. Avoiding my gaze? This isn't my girl. She's feeling overwhelmed. But she doesn't need to experience that alone.

I'm here now.

Setting my knuckle under her chin, I try lifting her gaze to mine. My girl won't budge.

"That's not a good idea, Lincoln."

Twisting, I look directly into Myla's sweet face. "Your eyes are changing. It's beautiful."

"It's my Furor lust side." Her voice shakes. "I've only ever felt wrath before."

I link my fingers with hers once more. "Let's take it slowly, then. We have all the time in the world."

She exhales. "Yeah, that would be good."

Tilting my head, I listen for any sign of intruders. We're still alone. "Especially since they haven't sent out a search party yet." I grin. "Shall we find another way to cause trouble?"

"Sure." She gives my fingers a squeeze. "How about exploring more of the maze?"

I kiss the tip of her nose, just because I can. "That is a great idea."

Fortunately for me, there's a long list of things I wish to know about Myla. Now, I finally have a chance to ask them. The evening just keeps getting better and better.

*M*yla and I stroll through the hedgerow maze, our arms swinging between us in time with our steps. There are so many questions I wish to ask her, so I launch right in. "What kind of music do you like?"

"Oh, we don't get much music in Purgatory. Only ghoul anthems."

My brows lift. "Ghoul anthems?"

"You know, *A Mighty Fortress Is Our Ghoul … Love Is An Undead Pasty Ghoul … Save the Ghoul, Grab Me Instead* … that last one is new, by the way. The ghoul government trying to make it a hit, considering how everyone believes Armageddon will invade soon."

I can't believe what I'm hearing. "As in, they want you to throw you to Hell in order to save their own skins?"

"Sure." Myla gives me the side eye. "Our ghoul rulers are a bag of dicks. Seriously. I hate them."

"And with good reason, it seems."

"What about you?" she asks. "What kind of music do you like?"

"Human jazz mostly. Modern stuff."

"Oh." She presses her lips together, hard.

I pause. "Come on. You have an opinion."

"No, I don't." She mimes whistling while looking around. *Sure, she doesn't have an opinion.*

I tilt my head. "Myla, please tell me."

"I'll put it this way. What do you find interesting about jazz?"

"It's *not* the notes they *do play*, it's the ones they *don't*."

She punches my upper arm. "My point exactly. There's a song. So sing the sucking song!" She makes her voice go all over the place. "Iiiiiii geeeeeet no kiiiiiiiiiiiicks from champaaaaaaaaaagne!" She stops, eyes me again. "They know the song right?"

"That they do."

"So just sing the fucking song. Don't *not-sing* it."

I nod sagely. "You have a point."

"Of course, I do."

"Next question," I say. "Where'd you learn to fight?"

"Self taught."

"One hundred percent?"

"Sure. You?"

"Nat. The Citadel."

"In Heaven?" Myla lets out a low whistle. "That's intimidating."

I roll my eyes. "Did I hear the word intimidating from your lips? You're an amazing fighter without any training." Stopping, I pull her closer. "You have no idea how attractive that is."

"Really?"

"Oh yes."

Her irises flash red. She grins.

"There, now." I wink. "That got your eyes to spark."

She pushes my shoulder again. "You suck, you know that?"

"Only when called for." Myla's eyes flare again, and I decide to change the subject before things get out of control. I've another question on my list. This one is less fun, though. "Have you ever heard of the Tithe?"

"Nope."

"He's a thrax warlock. Is there any reason he might be interested in you?"

Myla shrugs. "Ugh, I don't know. I get weird followers from the Arena. Last month, this quasi found gum on his seat and sent me a pile of hate mail. People are weird."

I laugh. "So true. In fact, I have a scribe dedicated to nothing but random death threats over trivia."

Thinking about the Tithe makes me recall Walker's warning—how I may be placing Myla at risk. "Another question for you."

"Wow. You're using your *I'm such a badass prince* tone."

I grin a little. It's nice that Myla can already tell my moods "I've been sworn to secrecy, but someone has warned me that my relationship with you places you at serious risk."

Myla pauses, her face blank. "So?"

"Are you concerned?"

"I don't know. What's the risk? Are my arms about to fall off or something?"

I shake my head. *Arms about to fall off?* Only Myla. "I doubt that, but possibly."

"Let me tell you one thing." Myla wags her finger in my face. "All my life, people have tiptoed around me. Don't fight evil demons to the death … Beware of making new friends … Avoid the angels! And I'll tell you one thing, mister."

I can't wait to hear this. "What?"

Myla glances around. "Oops, I got so carried away, I lost my train of thought there."

If I didn't love Myla before, I adore her now.

Myla snaps her fingers. "Oh, I've got it. I am so done with all this *let's make decisions for Myla* bullshit. I don't know who is feeding you a pile of crapola that you'll hurt me, but that is not happening. I like you. I'm not going anywhere. Sheesh." She grips my hand, marches forward a few paces and then pauses. "You'd think I didn't kick ass like it's my job. Oh, wait. It *is* my job."

"And you do your work so very well."

"Damn right, I do. And another thing." She tosses her head, making her hair cascade down her back. Fresh rage and energy fill the air around her. "I'm so not worried about some dude named … what was it again?"

"The Tithe."

"He's a thrax, right?"

"Thrax warlock."

Myla gives her eyes a half-roll this time. "No offense, but outside of you, all the thrax kinda suck in battle. I mean, I'm the greatest warrior in Antrum and it really wasn't all that hard."

"You have a point. I've won the last ten years or so, and the competition has never been that stiff."

"Sha." Myla sighs. "If anyone, it's Armageddon that keeps me up at night."

I already know the answer to this question, but I can't help but double-check. "If Armageddon invaded, do you know anyone who could get you out of town quickly?"

"Oh, sure, there's this one ghoul. He'd do anything for me."

That would be Walker. I try not to feel jealous about the *he'd do anything for me* line. It doesn't work.

"Long story short," continues Myla. "I know one ghoul who is awesome. But the rest of the undeadlies? I hate them with the fire of a thousand suns. Quasis like me, we're basically slaves to them. Did you know that?"

"No, I'm sorry. I should."

Myla stops. This seems to be her default move when she's about to make a big proclamation. *Can't wait.*

"Let me get this straight," says Myla. "You've been here months and … what have you been up to, exactly? How come you know dick about my people?"

"In truth, I've been researching one particular quasi versus their entire population."

Myla's brows lift. "So you're a stalker."

"Only to ensure your safety. And never when you were alone or doing personal things. Unless when you say *personal things*, you count the night in the stables, but you were absolutely aware of my rubbing your back."

Myla smacks her lips, hard. "You know what?"

"Hmm?" I blush something fierce. My obsession with Myla really isn't very princely.

"You're very cute when you're embarrassed," says Myla. This time, her eyes flicker blue. Another curious item to add to the *List Of Awesome Things Done By Myla Lewis.*

I bow slightly. "I'd hoped to impress you."

"You have."

I huff out a breath. "I wonder sometimes."

And I mean it. With this woman, I have no idea what I'm doing.

"If it's any help, you have my full permission to protect-stalk me any time."

"That's comforting to know, especially since I've already assigned myself the job."

Myla slowly licks her lips. Her irises flicker red again.

I pull her against me. "You like that, don't you?"

"Hmm?"

"Me, being protective. Taking charge."

"Mmmmmaybe."

"I got your eyes to spark again." I brush the gentlest of kisses across her lips, then pull away. Anticipation makes everything better.

And with Myla, I plan for lots of time to enjoy each other.

33

*M*yla and I walk through the maze for hours, talking about all sorts of topics and nothing at all. Being with her is a jolt of color in an otherwise grey life. It's close to midnight before we part. Although the hour is late, there's no way I can sleep. Fortunately, it happens that Lady Babylon is just starting work at the Echo Vortex. She said I could visit any time during her shift.

Hands down, Lady Babylon is one of my favorite thrax. Even though I last met her at the ripe old age of eight, she made a lasting impression. I look forward to the visit immensely.

Which brings me to the present moment. I stand outside a large round tent made of black tapestry that's woven through with images of concentric circles. The round pattern is the emblem of Transfer Central—the folks who manage our transport platforms. This tent marks our temporary Pulpitum station while in Purgatory. Officially, this place is for demon patrols. In reality, it's our evacuation plan in case Armageddon invades. After all, although I respect Verus' wishes, that doesn't mean placing my entire court at risk of immediate annihilation.

As I step inside the tent, a series of candelabras flare to life. Lucas enchanted these; it's a nice touch. I step into the center of the space. My footsteps clank as I go along. That's because the floor here is not earth at all, but a large round metal platform that will transport me deep underground into Antrum.

I stand in the center of the metal circle, gripping my hands behind my back. "Activating temporary sta—"

The entrance flap to the tent shifts. The Earl of Striga steps inside. "Excuse me, my Prince. May I have a word?"

With a sweeping glance, I scan Lucas from head to toe. His shoulders are slumped. Meanwhile, his normally neat dreads are knotted and askew. Even his long purple robes look rumpled. I know the Earl of Striga. He's rarely anything but careful in his appearance.

The warlock is not here with good news.

"Of course, Lucas. What is it?"

"I don't know how to say this." Lucas's olive skin looks pale. He hasn't been sleeping.

"Allow me. Things have gone poorly with your lord and his deal with Aldred."

"Yes. Gianna, the Great Lady of my house..." Lucas inhales a long breath. "She could die."

The title Great Lady means Gianna is not only an eligible woman. It also comes with a long list of duties for her people. Gianna is a great favorite with Striga in general and the earl in particular. She's dedicated her life to helping young warlocks and witches who have challenges controlling their magic.

I lift my chin. "And so, you can't send troops to guard the exits of Antrum." *Please, let it just be that.*

"It's more. I must take the out-clause in the contract. I can no longer participate."

"I'd say it's a surprise, but you've been honest. I have contingency plans in place." It's a big point with me that my nobles share bad news, early and often. It makes things easier on us all. And I'm far less likely to be angry if they've given me an honest warning. There's almost always a contingency plan that's possible, if given enough time.

Lucas hangs his head. "It's worse."

A pang of worry moves inside me. "How so?"

"Kamal and Horus may also back out."

"Lucas." My voice takes on a warning tone. "How do they know you're leaving the treaty?"

"Aldred told them. He's the one who got me to back out. Your scribes will receive the necessary paperwork today to confirm the change."

This could be helpful. "My scribes?" I ask. "Only them?"

"Yes, I shall leave it to you to tell your parents. I can contain Aldred for a few days. Keep him away from your father." He hugs his elbows. "I wish I could do more."

"You know my rules. Honesty deserves patience. We'll work through this. What's important is that the bond between Rixa and Striga remains strong."

Lucas shakes his head. "I must take my leave now."

In other words, whatever is happening with Aldred, it could change the basic alliances of our people. Striga might work more closely with Acca. That's serious stuff. There are a number of trade routes and royal offices that Striga holds, all thanks to my sponsorship. I make the house rather wealthy. That said, there are other houses of magic that could be elevated.

"Wait," I command. Lucas pauses. "Don't risk your entire house for one member. If you're relying on my fondness for you to prevent me from favoring another house of magic, *don't*. I leave for Antrum soon. Permanently. My goal is to build up an alliance of lower houses to match the warrior power of Kamal, Striga, and Horus. None of you are irreplaceable."

Lucas looks up, his mismatched eyes wide with worry. "You wouldn't."

"You lived through the rule of Acca. Thousands of thrax died in irresponsible attacks on Hell. There was hunger. Cruelty. Death. And those were just the thrax. Up on Earth? They went through two world wars thanks to unchecked demonic activity. Do you honestly think the same wouldn't happen again if Acca gets the throne?" I step closer. "I have my role as ruler. I will do my duty."

Lucas stares at me for a long moment, his jaw hanging open. "Yes, my Prince."

"You may go."

The Earl of Striga shuffles out of the tent. I hate to be so hard on Lucas, but I also know Aldred. The earl's a blowhard. If Lucas stands up to him, Gianna will be safe. Even so, I have other tasks ahead of me. Once Lucas is well and gone, I retake my spot on the center of the platform.

"Activating temporary station. Lincoln Vidar Osric Aquilus." From the top center of the tent, a grid of white laser beams crisscross the tent, scanning me.

A woman's voice echoes through the chamber. "Identity confirmed. Nice to have you back, my Prince."

"Good to be back, Cassandra." As with guards, it's important to know *who's who* at Transfer Central.

"We have you confirmed for a visit to the House of Mulciber. Is that still your destination?"

"It is."

"Confirmed and ready at your signal."

"Launch transfer on my mark." I start the countdown. "3, 2, 1."

The massive disc hurtles into the ground. Mineral deposits, soil, magma … they all flash past as I speed by. As a child, I'd try to touch them. Father would always pull me back at the last moment with a laugh.

You'll lose your hands that way, my boy, he'd say. *And you need those to kill demons.*

I'd still try the odd reach toward the show of minerals and light. In those days, my heart brimmed over with wonder and passion. Somewhere along the way, I buried all that deep down. Memories appear: Myla and I, walking through the hedgerow maze.

With my girl, that part of me is alive again.

All the more reason to visit the House of Mulciber and inspect the Echo Vortex. If there's any threat to my girl from the Tithe, I will discover the risks. And after that, I will end them.

*I*t's an especially long journey from Purgatory to Antrum. As I speed along, the Pulpitum platform shimmies beneath my feet. I firm up my stance. Transfers can be rickety, especially when the final destination station is old.

Like the House of Mulciber.

The platform jolts to a stop. I now find myself in a square chamber of rough-hewn rock. Before me stands a woman with cocoa skin and long grey braids. Her body and movements all have a ballerina's grace. She straightens the folds of her pink gown. The emblem of white flames is emblazoned on her front; the symbol of Mulciber.

"Greetings, Lady Babylon."

She rolls her eyes. "Call me Babs." She rushes forward with her arms thrown wide. "And give me a hug. It's been too long."

I accept the embrace. The House of Mulciber are big into hugging. I find it one of their best practices. "Agreed."

She steps back and eyes me. "Last time I saw you, the top of your messy brown head came only to here." She taps her right shoulder.

"I was but eight at the time."

Specifically, I'd visited the House of Mulciber for the last igniting of the Echo Vortex. Normally it's a big court affair, considering how the vortex only lights up once a decade.

"And we looked for you last month." She sets her fists on her hips. "And where were you, eh?"

"In Purgatory, along with the rest of the court."

"Well, I can't show the vortex while it's lighting up. That's another nine and some years away now."

"I'd still like a tour, if I may."

"Anything in particular?"

"The basics of how the system works. When I last came here, my attention span wasn't yet at its best." I wink. "Eight years old and all."

"Of course." Babs takes off down a thin corridor. Like everything else here, it's all rough grey stone and not much else. Still, the place is clean and dry. Mulciber marks an early settlement for Antrum. We didn't figure out how to get fancy with stone until much later.

At the end of the corridor, there's what looks like a stone wall. Babs taps the corner and the rock panel swings about, allowing us through. Once past the entrance, there's a short walkway that juts out a few yards into what looks like empty space. It takes a moment for my eyes adjust to the low light. Soon, I see that we stand inside a massive cylinder made of blue granite. All the smooth stone is woven through with threads of sparkling white.

Babs steps beside me. She points to the darkened pit below us. "Angel fire gets ignited at the base of the vortex." Bab's gentle voice echoes through the massive tunnel. "It burns right up through the column, straight up to the top. As it goes, it activates all the white conductor threads in the blue stone. In turn, those crystals transfer power throughout Antrum."

I rub my chin. "We also have systems to regulate those things." I get regular reports on the devices and magic that manage air circulation, for instance.

"Think of the Echo Vortex as a powerhouse. Once the energy gets to a particular structure, there are plugs and so forth to further control and regu-late things." As Babs speaks, she waves her arms about in an animated rhythm. Its clear how much she loves this place.

"That makes sense." I step to the edge and peer down. "Why only once every ten years?"

"The balance of power is very fragile. Too much and it overloads our systems. To use the electricity analogy, it burns out our circuits. Everyone in Antrum would die."

"I had no idea." My skin erupt sin gooseflesh. "How do you control when the vortex goes off?"

"Not sure what you mean." But Babs says those words far too quickly to be believable. She knows exactly what I mean.

"How does the angel fire ignite?"

"Oh." Babs looks away. "That's a mystery."

Now, I play around with double-meanings for a living. She kids no one. "It's not a mystery to *you*, though. Is it?"

Bab's levels me with a serious look. "Whatever do you mean?"

"When we first walked out here, you stated that angel fire gets ignited at the base of the vortex. That implies someone's doing the igniting."

Babs sighs. "I heard you were clever."

"Does that mean you'll reply?"

"Can you keep it a secret?"

I set my hand on my heart. "Absolutely."

"Once a decade, an archangel flies down to the base of the vortex. It's their power that ignites everything. The specifics aren't something that even I know about."

"Who visits?"

"It's different each time. Aquila comes most often."

I rock on my heels. "Aquila. She's the one who gave the Tithe his powers." I focus on Babs again. "A series of effigies have attacked me, claiming they are part of some kind of countdown for the Tithe. Can you see any connection between the vortex and the Tithe?"

Bab sniffs. "Many people have tried to access the vortex. Light it up. Burn it down. That kind of thing. They never get in." She hitches her thumb toward the tunnel behind us. "That's the only way into the vortex proper, and we have that magically booby trapped. No one has ever entered the vortex without our approval."

I scan the tunnel behind us. Now that I'm looking for it, I can see the lines of spells carved into the rough stone. Well done.

"That's it." Her face brightens once more. "Would you like to inspect our living areas? We've upgraded things since you last visited. We've even planned a feast in your honor."

"I'm dreadfully sorry, but Verus wants me in Purgatory as much as possible. This visit was approved only because it would be limited." Bab's entire demeanor becomes the definition of deflated. "That said, once the court returns to Purgatory, how about I return and bring my parents with me? We'll make it a real celebration, considering how we missed the last lighting of the vortex."

Babs grins. "That would be lovely."

As I head to the transport platform, we discuss some basics on when that visit might take place. After a short walk, I stand on the round metal transfer disc once more. "Thank you for your time today, Babs."

"You're most welcome." She stands before me, tapping her chin. "Aw, screw it." Leaning forward. She wraps me in another big hug.

"And thanks for that," I say.

A minute later, I'm hurting back to Purgatory, my mind racing through all I learned in the Echo Vortex. If anything, the visit convinced me that there is some kind of link between the vortex and the Tower of Wonders. The Tithe keeps saying something about cleansing Heaven. That might explain the soldiers. With the power of the vortex behind him, he could attack virtually anyone. But how would Myla come into play?

Trouble is, I still have no idea what the true threat against her could be.

Another jolt strikes me as the platform comes to a halt in Purgatory. The round tent stands empty, save for the flickering candles.

Then it isn't deserted anymore. Another ghost stands before me.

Jali.

My heart sinks. Jail looks as he always does: tall, lean, and strong. Close-clipped hair. Deep laugh lines.

Only now he's a ghost.

When I speak, my voice comes out hoarse. "So, it is done."

"The contract is signed."

"And the Tithe has sent you to me."

The ghost of Jali nods. "I'm to ask you to renounce the demon, Myla Lewis. The Tithe still wishes to hunt her."

A mixture of rage and sorrow pulses through my veins. "If this is anything like what happened with Silvinio and Devak, then the Tithe is lurking nearby, ready to turn you into an effigy for the battle." I whirl about, scanning the empty shadows. "Show yourself. Stop sending my own people after me. Fight like a thrax."

"It wouldn't be a fair battle," says Ghost Jali simply. "The Tithe can not be killed by anyone who lives."

I rest my fingertips against my forehead, trying to think through my next steps. An idea appears; it's a way to get the Tithe to fight or leave. Nodding, I move to stand at the edge of the transfer platform. "Come closer, Jali," I command.

The minister float-walks to the other side of the metal disc. "What is it?"

"There have already been two attempts on my life." I scan the tent once more. "If the Tithe is about to make a third, then know this. I don't appreciate being treated as a test subject for effigy battle practice. You strike me, I strike back." I turn to Jali. "The Tithe must renounce his plans, whatever they are, and leave my realms forever. If he doesn't, I will make him pay."

"My Prince, you cannot stop this. The Tithe is too powerful." Ghost Jali grits his teeth. "I am fighting the change." He hunches over. "It hurts."

I kneel so I can be eye to eye with Ghost Jali. "This is between me and the Tithe. Do not suffer on my account. Accept the change."

Ghost Jali moans. "He says I can't stop it, only slow it."

When I speak again, my voice is gentle. "So let it happen. You have my blessing." I lower my voice to a whisper only Jali can hear. "Just keep your eyes on his feet. That's all I ask."

Ghost Jali nods, then speaks in a loud voice. "I accept the change."

There's the flash again as the Tithe appears. He stands just off the platform, his magical mallet and chisel in hand. The Tithe strikes the chisel deep into Ghost Jali's chest. A burst of light follows. The Tithe disappears.

And the ghost of Jali changes.

White bits of white stone float up from the ground, filling in the spectral Jali with granite. As with Devak and Silvinio, the tendrils of white grow heavier until Jali is no longer a ghost, but a solid figure made from white stone. He appears young once more, although with Jali, that doesn't mean too much a difference in his appearance. There are fewer laugh lines and that's about it. Jali's wiry strength remains.

Another flare of white light surrounds the effigy version of Jali. My brows lift. That's new. The Tithe just cast an extra spell after creating the effigy version of Jali. When the light fades, the stone version of Jali now wears the scaled metal armor of ancient Egypt. He also grips a long dagger in each hand.

But it's not Effigy Jali's new stone body or weapons that lock my attention.

It's his gaze.

Effigy Jali stares at a spot by the tent's periphery.

That won't do at all. If I'm to get rid of the Tithe, I need him much closer to the platform.

If there's one thing I learned at the Echo Vortex, it's that Aquila and angel fire are somehow interesting to the Tithe. That's information I can use.

Stepping backward, I move to stand in the center of the platform. I pull out my baculum, igniting the two bars into a single sword made of white flame. Holding the weapon before me, I move into battle stance.

"Want to see how I wield angel fire?" I swipe my sword in a few broad strokes. "I am the grandson of none other than Aquila, and it is her power that drives me in battle."

Effigy Jali gets into battle stance, with both his daggers pointed downward. He doesn't move closer, through. Instead I track Effigy Jali's gaze as he follows the invisible Tithe closer to the Pulpitum platform.

Six feet.

Three feet.

Two.

One.

"Cassandra, emergency ricochet!" I call.

The entire Pulpitum goes berserk. Lights flash. The Pulpitum rattles beneath my feet. With all my energy, I rush off the metal platform. What happens next seems to go in slow motion, although in reality, what takes place lasts for less than a second.

The platform bursts into the Heavens, moving at a rate so fast, the change becomes little more than a blur. A scream breaks the air. The Tithe. Once the platform is gone, I race over and grab the hand of Effigy Jali. We share magick. Sure enough, I can now see the Tithe.

He writhes on the ground, gripping the bloody stump where his left arm once lay. He tried to step closer to me on the platform, and got his arm whacked off in the process.

When I next speak, I take care to glare directly at the Tithe. "I warned you. Leave my people alone. Back off Myla Lewis. You think I can't touch you because I'm alive?" I raise my fire sword high. "Think again. I know things about battle you can't even guess at. Go back to your tower and carve effigies. Otherwise, it will be all out war, and you'll lose more than your arm."

The Tithe looks directly at me, his face wild with rage. "Citadel bastard." Another flare of white light surrounds him, and he is gone.

I release Effigy Jali's chilly stone hand. The stone version of him remains majestic, just as the living one was. "Thank you," I say simply.

"You'll watch over Rashida?"

"You have my word."

"The instructions from my Master were to fight you until one of us was downed. Either you die, or I am defeated and return to the tower."

I extinguish my baculum. "I won't fight you, my friend."

"I know." Effigy Jali takes his daggers, points the blades at his chest, and plunges in the knives.

"Jali!" I gasp. "No!"

Long cracks form along Effigy Jali's stone body. "Don't worry, my prince. It doesn't hurt." Low pops sound as the fissures spread throughout his form. The minister gives me a sad smile. "One more after me, and it is done."

A moment later, Effigy Jali's body shatters into a thousand small bits of white granite that tumble to the earth. The shards of stone disintegrate and merge into the ground. And my friend is gone. My eyes sting with held-in tears. One so noble shouldn't have to die.

I barely notice the tent flap open once more. Lucas has returned.

"I know," I say in a low voice. "You've come to me with news. Jali is dead."

"I've had no word of that," says Lucas. "I came here hoping to find you again. Since we last spoke, the Earls of Horus and Kamal have approached me. They wish to leave the alliance. I've done what I can to stall them, but they need to speak to you."

Rising, I reset my baculum into the holster. "Where are they?"

"The mead hall, my rince."

"I'll be right there."

Lucas leaves and I try to regroup my thoughts. That comment from the Tithe; he called me a *Citadel bastard*. What was that about? I suppose most warriors are trained there, but it feels significant. Unfortunately, with the Earls of Striga and Kamal waiting for me …. The loss of my dear friend is still fresh… And with my anti-Acca alliance on the line … I can't put the pieces together right now.

Straightening my royal tunic, I head off for the meal hall and yet another battle, only one that will use words instead of knives.

Yet it's one I still need to win.

*A*fter leaving Lucas, I step through the muddy pathways that lace through our camp. With every passing moment, more shadows disappear. The low caws of ravens announce the time. Early morning has arrived.

Soon the wooden mead hall looms before me. Two men stand outside. First there is Zosar, the Earl of Horus. He's an older man with ebony skin, long dread locks, and the crest of an Egyptian eye on his chest. Beside him stands Kian, the Earl of Kamal. He's a middle aged man with cocoa skin, high cheekbones, and short gray hair. Both wear tunics with the emblazoned with the symbols of their houses.

"Greetings, Zosar and Kian." I focus on Zosar. "The loss of Jali is deeply felt."

"He was blessed by the Tithe," replies Zosar. The earl has a low and gentle voice. "Rashida is well now. There is nothing to mourn."

Thinking of my friend sets an ache in my chest. "Even so, I'll be there for the ceremonies. You'll hold them when we return to Antrum, yes?"

"Correct." Zosar gives me a sad smile. "It will be good to have you there."

"Let's go inside," I say. "We've much to discuss."

I pull open the mead hall door and step inside. The moment I enter the hall, I notice a number of things. The gentle scent of cinnamon and sunshine. A soft rustling from the shadows. It all adds up to one realization.

Myla is here.

The earls enter behind me. The question appears. Will they sense Myla?

Probably not. Zosar and Kian aren't hunters.

The room still hides in the semi-darkness of early morning. Zosar rustles around the feasting table. "Curses, where are those blasted candles?" he asks.

Needless to say, there's no way I'll allow Zosar to add any light. That would expose Myla, and my protective instincts for her are stronger than ever.

"Never mind that," I say. "You said your need was urgent."

"We heard the House of Striga backed out of the alliance," says Kian.

I nod. "Striga has some questions, but I still have their seal on the alliance parchment." Which is still true as of this moment. In two days? Not so much. "If they back out—if any of you back out—it will mean the king's wrath." I lower my voice to a menacing level. "You gave your seal. You gave your word."

Zosar waves his hand. "This alliance isn't worth the parchment it's written on. Even with Horus, Kamal, Striga, and Rixa together, we don't have enough strength of arms to face down the Earl of Acca."

I'd point out that we have the men in terms of raw numbers, but he raises a good point. Over the last weeks, I've seen first-hand how weak the warriors are in our major houses. I won't throw bodies around to get killed if they aren't properly trained. That's what Aldred does, and it's a waste of life.

Kian snaps his fingers. His falcon, Ka, swoops from the rafters to land on his shoulder. "Take my advice." Kian runs his pinky down the falcon's head. "Give Acca what he wants."

I chuckle, but there's no humor in it. "Really? Is that what he wants this week? You've seen what happened with my father. Give in once and there's no end." I point between the two men. "We all know what's happening here. Acca sees my father as toothless, so now he's coming after my canines." I slams my fist against my palm. "I must stand my ground or I no longer deserve my crown."

The earls say nothing. *Good. That means I'm winning them over.*

"You speak of the great houses," I continue. "But are they the only ones in Antrum? The Houses Gurith, Zerihun, and Alura are all loyal to the king, perhaps many more." I don't need to add the obvious. Those three houses all out-performed the so-called great ones at the Winter Tournament.

Zosar points at me, the hint of a smile on his wide mouth. "You're a crafty one, I'll grant you. So much like Octavia."

I nod. "We leave for Antrum tomorrow. I'll reach out to the lesser Houses the moment I return." I point between them once more. "Don't forget why you signed this alliance in the first place. Once Acca takes down my house, he'll come for you next. All I'm asking for is a little time."

Kian frowns. "And your father supports this? Word is he bows lower to Acca each day."

A steely sense of resolve ricochets through my soul. "Have you ever seen me bow?"

Kian steps to my side. "No, my Prince. Never."

"Nor will you." My gaze shifts between the earls. "We leave for Antrum in the morning. There's much work to do. If you'll excuse me." I gesture toward the door.

The earls pause, share a long look, and then nod. I open the door. The scent of cinnamon and sunshine turns overwhelming. That means one thing. Myla stands only a few inches away from me now.

Unfortunately, so do the earls.

Kian steps toward the exit; then he pauses at the threshold. "I'll give you a month. I can risk no more with Acca."

Myla's scent turns downright overwhelming. My pulse speeds. After everything that's happened with Lucas, Jali, and now the earls, I need her so much, it hurts.

Zosar steps up and grips my forearm. "You're the last chance we have."

I grin. "And have I ever failed you?"

Kian scowls. "Not yet."

The two earls leave; the door slams shut behind them. *At last.* Twisting, I pin Myla against the wall, hungry to feel her body against mine. We share a kiss that's wild with need. I press her more fully against the wall. She's everything soft and iron at once. Desire heats my blood.

Leaning in, I whisper by her ear. "You're lucky those earls can't hunt worth a damn. I could hear you breathing from across the room."

She licks her lips and smiles. "Lucky me."

For a long moment, all I can do is soak in the sight for her. She's here and wearing ghoul robes for some reason. Who cares? She's present, none the less. My world pauses. The last few hours feel like a chaos of revelations. Now, with my girl before me, life makes sense again.

It's all Myla.

I take in a deep breath, centering myself. "That was the part where I lose control because I didn't expect to see you." I shoot her a shy smile. "Next is the part where I say we take things slowly."

"Thank you." Although, the way she says the words, she doesn't seem entirely happy not to be kissing my face off.

I link my fingers with hers. "To what do I owe the pleasure of this visit?" I swing our arms in a happy motion.

"Lincoln, what did my eyes look like yesterday?" She stays flush against the wall, careful to pull her hood down.

"Oh that." I frown, thinking things through. "They were changing colors. Brown, blue, red. You said it was from your lust demon awakening." Leaning in, I nuzzle her neck. Damn, I adore her scent. "Did I mention how much I liked red?"

Myla laughs. "That you did. No less than six times, as I recall."

"As long as I'm consistent, that's what matters." I give her a sideways glance. "Is that why you came here, to ask me that?"

Myla fidgets. "No, I came here to show you something."

Concern tightens my features. "Okay. What is it?"

Myla's hand trembles in mine, and I hate that she's upset. "What if I were different from who you thought I was?"

A jolt of worry moves up my back. Of all the things I've faced in the last day, the idea of Myla being at immediate risk? That sends my protective instincts into overdrive. Every cell in my body goes on alert.

"Like how, different?" I ask.

"What if I became someone who was a target?" Her voice quivers. "Someone who needs to disappear for a very long time."

My poor girl. I envelop her in my arms. "And you're afraid of what, exactly?"

Myla leans into my shoulder. "We've already got a lot stacked against us, Lincoln. Maybe you're better off with someone like Adair."

"Really?" I kiss the top of her head, gently. "Did you know Adair thinks Simia demons are cute?"

"You're lying."

"I wish." I slide my hand up Myla's side. "You're hiding your eyes again, Myla." I lift my fingers to the edge of Myla's hood, and bit by bit, I pull it away from her face. "I already told you. I like it when your eyes turn red." I tilt my head. "Your eyes are blue." Last night, Myla's irises flashed blue, but it wasn't permanent. Is this what has my girl upset? Whoever changed her will pay. "Did someone from the House of Striga cast a spell on you? So help me, I'll—"

"No, it's not that."

I cup her face in my hands. "Are you sick?"

"No, nothing like that either." Myla winces. "My father is an angel named Xavier."

"The *archangel* Xavier? I studied him at the Citadel. Greatest warrior in history. Legend says he never loved anything but battle."

Myla lets out one of her sarcastic *humph* noises. "Until he met my mother."

"I can see that. If she's anything like you." The revelation moves through me. Myla's definitely part human and demon. Now, she's half angel as well. "I don't understand. That would make you—"

The Scala Heir.

"That's impossible," I add.

"I thought so too." Closing her eyes, Myla raises her right arm to shoulder-height. An electric sense of power fills the air. When Myla opens her eyes once more, her irises glow blue. A dozen tiny lightning bolts of power swirl around her palm. The brightness is vibrant. Dazzling. The tiny bolts dance around her hand for a moment longer. After that, they spout into the air like a geyser. I know what those are.

Igni. Myla commands the power to move souls.

My breath catches. *It's true.* These igni aren't the piddle of sparkles that Adair summoned. This is true angelic energy.

Overwhelming.

Supernatural.

Breathtaking.

And unquestionable. Myla *is* the Scala heir.

A memory appears. Back at the awakening ceremony, Adair had to become angelbound to me in order for her powers to appear. Igni power *is* angel power. It's also the energy behind love. And for the true Scala Heir, igni are activated when a deep love is shared equally between two people.

Can it be?

For months, I've followed Myla. Protected her. Obsessed over her. Only recently, I'd hoped that somehow, Myla might slowly grow to care for me. And now? Her powers became active when we kissed in the hedgerow maze. We're angelbound. That makes me the happiest man imaginable.

I love and am loved.

"Myla, I—"

Myla raises both hands at me, palms forward. "No, I need to say something first. Now that my Scala powers are active, I must go into hiding. I don't know when I'll resurface, if ever. Walker told me about all the things stacked up against us ... How the Earl wants you to marry Adair. And I heard what you said to Kamal and Horus before. Unifying the lesser houses? You've got enough to worry about without adding me to the list." She hugs her elbows. "What I'm saying is, if you want to see someone else, that's okay with me." She rolls her eyes. "Not that we're really dating in the first place."

I can't believe this. *There is no one for me but Myla.* But before going forward, I need to ensure there isn't something else I'm missing here, so I keep my features carefully blank. "May I ask a question?"

Myla picks at non-existent lint on her ghoul robe disguise. "Sure."

"Do you love me?"

Myla gasps. "Um, well, I..."

"Alright, I'll ask a different question." I keep my face unreadable. "When did this happen?"

"It's been happening for a while, but I didn't know it. The ceremony at the Arena actually awakened me, not Adair. Then, I was angelbound last night when we—" She bites her lower lip.

And my world explodes into all kinds of happy.

I beam with joy. Wrapping my arms around Myla's waist, I pull her flush against me. "That's wonderful."

Myla freezes. "So, you're not worried about what I just said?"

"No. Should I be?" On the *list of trouble*, it isn't an item. At all. In fact, it clears things up immensely. Myla being the Scala Heir means power— as in serious leverage to get her whatever she wants. And if I'm on that list, then I just need to position her abilities all to my parents, that's all.

Myla's mouth falls open. "But I must go into hiding. Who knows when I'll resurface? Don't you want to, you know, move on?"

Oh, my sweet girl.

Gripping Myla's waist more tightly, I spin her around. My girl laughs —*fully and freely*—and damn, I crave that sound. I kiss her once and softly. "Of course, not. You've made me very happy."

At those words, Myla's eyes widen. "You just heard blah-blah-blah *getting angelbound means Myla loves me like crazy* blah-blah-blah. Am I right?"

"Yes." I pull her so close, I can feel both our hearts beating in tandem. "And

I love you too, Myla. Like crazy." I brush my mouth along her jawline. "Now you say it back to me."

Her voice sounds low and sweet. "I love you, Lincoln."

"There now. The rest of it doesn't matter." I cup the back of her head, gently guiding her lips to mine. Our mouths meet in a slow kiss. A set of rather distinct rustling sounds echo in from the shadows.

Oh, Hell.

"Ahem." A voice sounds from across the room.

I frown. "That would be Mother."

Myla gasps. "I didn't hear anyone come in." She pulls down her hood and steps away from me. "Does she always sneak around like that?"

"Pretty much." In fact, I'm lucky I heard her at all.

Mother stands by the closed door, her body stiff and tall in a black velvet gown. "It seems we've much to discuss. This way."

Even from a distance, I see how Myla trembles. Mother has that affect on people. I step up behind my girl, firmly resting my hands on her shoulders. Leaning in, I brush my mouth against the shell of Myla's ear. "We can do this."

In fact, the revelation that Octavia's here is a good thing. In her own stoic way, Mother's trying to help. I'd explain that, but Myla seems edgy enough as it is. We can cover to the parental management part of things in a bit.

When it comes to my parents, the motto here must be, *baby steps.*

Myla wraps her fingers with mine. She smiles, and that's all I need to know.

Yes, we can do this.

*M*yla, Octavia and I leave the mead hall. It's a short but muddy walk through the early morning camp. Soon, we're at the royal reception tent. Octavia enters first, which gives Myla and me a chance to chat. Namely, I give Myla a heads-up about Father. There are three key facts.

First, Father wants me to marry Adair.

Second, he'll likely be a bit gruff with Myla.

And third, for whatever reason, Father kowtows to Acca.

Myla's not thrilled about any of these items, but my girl's a fighter. Plus we kiss a little bit, and that seems to help. In short order, Myla and I stride into the reception tent. My parents stand on the other side of the space.

"Hello, hello!" calls Father. He lumbers over, wrapping me in a bear hug. After that, he turns to Myla. "What's this? I wasn't informed of any strangers coming to visit."

My back teeth lock with frustration. *Sure, Father wasn't informed.* Like Mother hadn't sped into the tent first. We all know why she rushed inside. Octavia warned Connor that Myla was on her way.

Undoubtedly, Mother also asked Connor to play nicely with others—and by *others* I mean *Myla*—which is an order he's already ignoring.

And all because my own father can't say *no* to one of our earls.

For years, I've put up with Father's preferences for Acca. After all, it isn't easy to rule. Anyone can have a blind spot. Or in some cases, a blind canyon. For Father, the canyon in question is Acca. For Mother, it's Father. Overall, I've never been one to judge him too harshly.

Until now.

Outside the tent, I prepared Myla, letting her know that Father may act gruffly. I suppose I should have prepped myself far better. Because seeing Father's inhospitality in action? Anger streams through my nervous system, more fierce than anything I've ever felt before. Gripping Myla's hand, I meet Connor's gaze. "This is Myla, father. She's the girl I've been telling you about."

From the corner of my eye, Myla's false smile turns into a real one. *Good.*

"Yes, I remember." Father scans Myla from head to toe. "You're the quasi-demon."

"Her name is Myla." Fury rumbles through my tone. *How dare he?*

Father crosses the room, taking his favorite seat at the table. Mother takes the chair beside his.

I stand with Myla, not moving. It's one thing to be gruff, but then there is outright unacceptable behavior.

Father exhales a long breath. "If you're here, I assume the two of you are in *trouble.*"

There's no question what Father means here. He thinks Myla's pregnant.

Something happens next which is rare indeed. I'm in shock. Speechless. Father and I don't discuss sex. Sure, I've had my relationships, but every girl I've been with knows what I'm looking for, which is nothing more than one encounter. And I always use protection. Father has never said a single word about my dalliances. And yet, here is the woman I wish to marry, and he's randomly accusing her of carrying my child. Bands of outrage tighten around my throat. There aren't even words for how low this is.

Mother gasps. "Connor!"

Connor slaps the tabletop with him palms. "Well, they *are* in trouble, aren't they?" He turns to Myla. "Aren't you?"

"That would be no, your disgustingness," says Myla. "Keep your dirty mind to yourself."

Now, I was ready to tell Father off, but I'm his son. "Myla, what are you doing?" I lower my voice to a whisper. "No one speaks to my father that way."

Myla sniffs. "Don't worry. I got this."

Closing her eyes, Myla pulls back her hood and raises her hand. Hundreds of igni whirl around her palm. Fast as a whip, the igni churn into a tornado of power that dances before her before breaking free. The tiny pieces of energy then whip around the tent, knocking over knick knacks and a candelabra or two. They end by forming a great whirlpool in the center of the room that speeds faster and faster.

Then, with a burst of light, all of them disappear.

Myla shoots me a look that says something like, *and that was me, getting this.*

I never thought I could love Myla more. Yet in this moment, I do.

Myla then shifts her focus to Father. "I'm the Scala Heir, Connor. I'm not in trouble." Her irises glow so blue, the entire room gets washed in turquoise brightness. "I *am* trouble."

Myla lowers her hands. Her eyes return to their non-glowing shade. The universe seems to pause while I stare at the woman I love. What just happened was nothing less than amazing. I felt too beaten down to fight, so this fierce woman battled for us both. How did I get this fortunate?

Father slams his hand onto the tabletop. This is his motion for, *I might change my attitude.*

About time.

"Well, well." Father shakes his head. "I'll be damned." He breaks out into deep peals of laughter. Combined with the tabletop slam it means, *one attitude change coming up!*

Myla frowns. "Are we good here?"

"Oh, yeah. He's loving this." I lean in closer. "Well played, Myla." Smiling, I gently kiss her cheek.

Father's laughter slows. "Lincoln, my boy. What a treasure you are." He points to Myla. "And you! A spitfire." He gestures to the empty chairs at the table. "Have a seat, both of you. Let's talk a bit, see what we can do here." He looks to his left. "Octavia, I'm sure you're behind this. At least in part?"

Mother half-smiles. "Always, Connor." She slips onto the chair beside Father. Myla and I seat ourselves at the other side of the table.

"It seems we have the Scala Heir with us today," says Father. "What does that make Lady Adair?"

"A fraud," replies Mother. "I can't believe I didn't see it before. Adair only showed Scala powers when Gianna was whispering nearby; such spells are nothing for the House of Striga." Mother clicks her tongue. "Gianna's witch-craft could have changed Adair's eyes as well."

"The Houses of Acca and Striga have quarreled for centuries. Now they team up." Father sighs. "Dark news."

Darker than he knows, as a matter of fact.

"Their treachery has worsened," I say, my voice stony. "Striga asked to abandon the alliance against Acca."

Father scowls. "And when did they make this request?"

It's hard to keep track of time, considering how I haven't slept. I make my best guess. "Two days ago."

Connor grits his teeth. "Interesting that you waited until now to tell me, boy."

"You know why I waited, Father." I make sure to stay perfectly calm. "If I told you two days ago, you'd have done *something rash.*"

I pause, allowing that phase—*something rash*—to sink in. No doubt, that would have been Father running to Aldred and ruining everything.

"Now," I continue. "We can consider the news about Striga in the context of what's really important." Myla's fingers are still linked with mine. I give her palm a gentle squeeze and then—THUNK—set our entwined hands onto the tabletop. My meaning is clear.

This is happening, Father.

"I thought you wanted to talk about me and Myla?" I ask.

"Perhaps." Father's using his growly and petulant tone. Normally, that gets him what he wants.

Not this time.

Father meets my gaze. In his eyes, I see all the concern about Aldred. Their warriors. Our people. Peace. A thousand worries battle it out in his mind, and that conflict is clear. I know the sensation well. After all, I carried a similar battle in my own skull for weeks.

But I've moved on.

I'm trusting to love. To Myla. To Us. Nothing else matters. This love is what I'll fight for, whatever the cost. Because, at the end of all things, I know the world will be better if Myla and I are together in it.

My stare with Father never wavers. If anything, the intensity in my gaze only grows more fiery.

At last, Father looks away.

I'd say there's a sense of triumph in winning this war of wills—and there is, to a certain extent—but there's also a heavy sense of sorrow. My future with Myla is so important to me. I'm heading along a new path, and although Father may seem to follow, I know he never will.

I'm losing him.

No, that's not it.

I lost Father a long time ago. Myla just makes the truth unavoidable.

When Father turns to Myla, his manner becomes gentle. "The Scala Heir must excuse my temper." He clears his throat. "Now that your powers are active, do you wish asylum with the thrax?"

"I came here to see Lincoln," explains Myla. "Mom and I have other plans for what happens next."

Mother focuses on Father. "You remember Senator Lewis from the era of quasi rule?"

"Absolutely," replies father. "Very capable. The only one who predicted Armageddon's rise, as I recall."

Mother gestures toward Myla. "This is her daughter."

"Interesting," says Father. "Very interesting."

Mother turns to Myla and grins. "Do you know how Connor and I met, Myla?"

"Not this story, Octavia." Father half-rolls his eyes.

I focus on Myla. "It was at the ball to celebrate the spring equinox."

"That's the official story," says Mother. "It was actually at the winter tournament. I used to fight in those, you know."

"Yes," says Myla. "Bera told me."

Mother mimes shooting an arrow. "My skill lay with the bow. The tournament beast that year was a Manus demon. I shot it full of arrows—and was within seconds of winning—when I ran out of time. Connor waltzed onto the field of battle, ran the monster through with his sword, and won the tournament."

"It was quite a bit more than that, Octavia." Father chuckles. "This was two hundred years ago and she still carries a grudge."

Myla does a double take. "Two hundred years?"

I nod. "Thrax live a long time."

Myla's gaze meets mine, her eyes lighting up with interest and excitement.

I can almost see her thinking, *the Great Scala lives a long time, too*. And she likes the idea of a full lifetime together.

So I do, for that matter.

Under the table, I rub my foot against hers. Myla smiles.

Meanwhile, Father continues with his story. "Never was there a worse tournament beast, and never a greater warrior to fight it than Octavia." He pauses for dramatic effect. This happens a lot in my life. "Afterwards, I went to visit my lady in her family's tent. I wanted to commend her valor on the battlefield, but I failed to announce myself formally."

Mother smirks. "He walked in while I was alone and half-dressed. Appeared behind me out of nowhere."

"What did he get?" asks Myla. "Elbow to the gut?"

Mother arches her right brow. "Knee to the groin."

Myla winces. "Yowch."

I try to hold in my laughter. "You never told me that, Father."

Father chuckles once more. "It's not a memory I like to recall." He takes Mother's hand. "But after that moment, no one else would do. You see Myla, for the thrax, everything is about strength in battle."

Myla gives me a sideways glance. "I've noticed."

In reply, I start another game of footsie with her under the table. She blushes. It's lovely.

Father nods, his decision made. "This, my dear, is why I'm willing to take a chance on you. You've some strength in your heart." He leans back on his chair. "But I get ahead of myself. If you're the Scala Heir, you need angel blood. Who's your father then?"

How I'll love dropping this particular bomb.

"The archangel Xavier," I declare.

Mother and Father pause. Then both their mouths fall open. That's an absolute first.

"You're first-generation archangel, then." Father lets out a low whistle. "And not just any archangel, Xavier!"

Myla frowns. "Why is first generation important?"

"More angel blood, more power," I explain. "The current Scala is fifth-generation common angel. I'm third-generation archangel. Father's second. We descended from the archangel Aquila. Have you heard the story?"

"Yes," Myla replies. "Mom told me how she founded the House of Rixa."

Father grins. "I've heard of the Archangel Xavier. Amazing warrior turned diplomat. Led the final battle to drive demons from Heaven."

Mother narrows her eyes. "But he disappeared after the Ghoul Wars, I believe."

Beside me, Myla stiffens. "I don't want to talk about that."

I tilt my head, wondering. When we were walking through the hedgerow maze, Myla spoke at length about her mother. But whenever I asked about her father, Myla changed the subject. She wouldn't say much beyond the fact that he wasn't around. Once I learned her father was Xavier, I figured that was because archangels are always off on Heavenly business. Now, it seems something darker happened to him.

What became of Xavier, anyway?

"Of course, of course." Father folds his arms over his chest. "Now, what are your plans exactly?"

Myla tosses her head. In typical warrior style, she sets aside the pain of her father and moves on with the challenge at hand.

"I have an Arena match tomorrow morning," explains Myla. "Right after that, I go to a safe house until we hear from the angels."

"I see." Father drums his fingers on the tabletop, his face lost in thought. Mother and I exchange a worried look. No question what Father is considering here. Does he stand up to Aldred? Do I have time to salvage my treaty?

Myla isn't impressed. "You're clearly debating something, Connor. What is it?"

Did I mention how my girl is amazing? She is.

"If you must know," replies Father. "It's whether to endorse Lincoln's plan to gather together the lesser houses."

Myla shrugs. "I'll help him."

Father huffs out a breath. "And how will you do that from hiding?"

"I'll find a way." Myla glares at him, Arena warrior-style. "Strength in battle, your Highness. If the earl doesn't like it, I'll pull some strings and send him to Hell."

Father nods slowly. "I believe you'd do it, too."

Myla snaps her fingers. "In a heartbeat."

I beam with pride. *My future queen.*

"Fine, we'll wait." Father points at my nose. "You've got a month, boy. Bring together the minor houses." His face droops. "I'll stall the earl."

I can't help but grin. "Thank you, Father." I give Myla's hand an especially long squeeze. We've been together for less than a day, and already, my girl's taking on Aldred. She'll be a queen for the ages.

Mother taps the tabletop with her fingernail. "We have other matters to discuss." She turns to Myla. "This match tomorrow morning. How will you compete without exposing your identity?"

"My fighting suit has a face-mask that hides my eyes," answers Myla.

"Very good." Mother turns to me. "And you'll be there as well?"

"It's not an official thrax event, but I'll contact the minister. I'm sure I can watch from an archway." *After all, I have before.*

Myla looks at me with wonder. "You'll be there?"

I wink. "Nowhere else."

"Will you bring extra soldiers with you?" asks Father.

We're now in the *detailed planning phase* of the operation. I lean back in my chair, swinging my joined hand with Myla between us. "No, that would only attract unnecessary attention."

Octavia wags a finger at me. "Be sure to wear full demon patrol gear: body armor, baculum, daggers ..."

"I'll be safe, Mother."

Father rubs his chin. "And stay with her tonight."

Mother gasps. "Connor!"

"Whoa!" cries Myla.

"I mean in a separate rooms," says Father quickly. "But ready for trouble."

Mother clears her throat, clearly trying to re-steer the conversation onto safer ground. "After the match, Lincoln will join our procession to Antrum."

A chill creeps into my soul. After tomorrow, Myla and I will part.

"That's the plan." Myla's voice quivers.

I give her hand a squeeze. "Let's get you back home. Did you ride Night-shade here?"

"Yes."

"Good. She's probably outside waiting for you now, along with Bastion." I gently kiss her cheek.

In less than twenty-four hours we'll be apart, but the more importantly, Myla will be somewhere safe.

That's what's truly matters.

Myla and I leave the reception tent, gather our horses, and ride back to her home. It's dark by the time Myla and I near her house. It's a standard Purga-tory one-story ranch. I already know the area and style, having visited Walk-er's residence. As we ride along on Nightshade and Bastion, our horses' hooves beat out a silent rhythm on the quiet streets. I'm glad for our future, but I'm anxious about getting Myla safely into hiding.

Plus, there's Armageddon's silence.

Not to mention Aldred's constant scheming.

And the Tithe is forever lurking somewhere.

There's so much to worry about. But later. Right now, there's the fact that I haven't slept in a rather long time. Myla and I dismount our horses. Yet again, I'm happy Nightshade can cast magic to keep both herself and Bastion safe. With the horses set, Myla and I then march up to her front door. Camilla greets us. Myla's mother seems rather pleased I'm bringing weapons, which makes sense. She also dictates that I should sleep on the couch. Again, I understand the logic.

Yet there's no way I'm leaving Myla alone tonight.

My girl is ferocious in her bravery, but sometimes, even the strongest of us need to be held. So I slip into my girl's room, sit with my back against her headboard, and hold my Myla all night. In my dreams, I keep searching for an important parchment. There's something written on it about Myla being part angelic and why that's important to the Tithe. My dream-self won't stop searching for it. Yet every time I get close to the document, it vanishes.

And for some reason, that makes me frantic with worry.

*I*t's just past dawn when I awaken with a gasp. No surprise that I'd have a nightmare. Myla still sleeps by my side, which is instantly comforting. Amazing the things you notice when in love. For instance, Myla makes these adorable little 'ah-poo' breathing noises in her sleep. I run my fingers through her hair and cherish this moment for the gift it is.

With the slightest of movements, I shift myself out of bed, careful to allow Myla to keep resting. I write her a quick note.

Off to rumple the couch before your mom wakes up. See you at breakfast. L.

I leave Myla's bedroom and head into the house proper. I was too exhausted last night to really soak in my new surroundings. That said, Myla's house is classic Purgatory: chipped walls, frayed couch, and small kitchen. Everything is run-down yet clean. It reminds me of Walker's place, only with actual furnishings. After messing up the couch, I get ready and change into my battle armor.

At some point, my stomach growls. When did I last eat again?

Too long ago, clearly.

Heading into the kitchen, I rummage through the cabinets and find a breathtaking assortment of candy disguised as food. Honestly, it's a wonder Myla has all her teeth. There are even things called demon bars which should be billed a *pro-diabetes treatment*. Eventually, I find an untouched jar of peanut better. *Protein, such a concept.* I'm spooning it from the container when Myla's mother shuffles into the room.

"Good morning," I say.

"Humph," replies Camilla. She looks bedraggled in her threadbare robe. Her auburn hair stands up at odd angles while she fiddles with the coffeemaker.

Damn. I should have done that for her. Brewing some coffee would have been a nice touch.

Then I realize that I have no idea how to use machinery to make any kind of food. My life is rather bizarre that way. For instance, there's Minister of Ice who keeps cubes at the ready for me. If there were servants here, I could order them around with precision. Other than that, not too helpful.

So it's probably best that I left the coffee to Camilla.

I scoop more peanut butter onto my spoon while Camilla sips her coffee. After drinking half-way down, Camilla looks at me over the rim of her mug. I'm reminded that this is a legendary senator as well as Myla's mother. In this moment, she's inspecting me with an experienced eye. What is she thinking? One way to find out.

"Are you angry?" I ask.

"Should I be?"

Now, that's the sign of an expert politician. Answering a question with a question.

"The fact that Myla and I fell in love ... that's what activated her Scala powers. You could very well blame me."

"I don't blame you," says Camilla softly.

A realization hits me. That's what Walker had been warning me about. Camilla didn't want Myla to be the Scala Heir, and for obvious reasons. The mortality rate is through the roof. But falling for me would make it happen. And yet, even though I lived in a different realm, it happened anyway. What are the chances?

My eyes widen. *Verus.* The chances are rather good when you have an oracle angel setting things up. Verus didn't invite my people here to protect Maxon Bane. She wanted Myla to become the Scala Heir instead. A line of worry wriggles through my belly. There's an obvious question here.

Why did Verus want Myla to become the Scala Heir?

There's a likely answer as well, and it involves Myla fighting Armageddon.

My spine stiffens. If that's Verus's plan, it won't happen. I'll get Myla to her safe house, and that's the end of things.

Camilla stares into her mug. "I'll tell you who I do hold responsible. Verus." She sighs. "Although, the Queen of the Angels wouldn't do something if it didn't protect us all." She looks up and meets my gaze. "You've no need to worry. You've done nothing wrong."

Many men would move on from this point. But if I'm to have an honest relationship with Myla's mother, I need to start now. "You should know. I was warned away from Myla."

Camilla nods. "And you tried to run her off. For a while."

"But eventually, I ignored those warnings." It's on the tip of my tongue to say the warnings in question came from Walker. After all, it's logical that Camilla would have gotten Walker's help. Half the after-realms seem to have Walker secretly aiding them. But I vowed to Walker that I'd keep his secret. So I try another route.

"You know I tried to avoid romantic entanglements with Myla," I prompt.

"Sure."

"Who told you that?"

Camilla takes an extra-long sip from her coffee. If she says *Walker*, it opens things up.

"A mother knows these things. That's all." She accents that last statement with a glare so powerful, I'm surprised the paint doesn't peel off the walls.

Point made. We can cover Walker another day.

Dreams from last night appear in my head. *Something about Myla's father is important, I know it.* I take the seat across from Camilla's. "I've been tracking different threats toward Myla. Trying to proactively protect her."

Camilla swigs down the rest of her coffee. "Xavier tried to do the same thing with me."

"Meaning?"

"*Proactively protect*, as you call it. I can tell you this. Don't go too far. Myla would take torture in Hell, so long as you're together." Her voice cracks with rage and grief. "Does that make sense?"

I rub my neck, trying to understand. "I'm afraid I don't get it." I shake my head. "There's no way I'd never allow Myla to face that kind of pain."

Camilla sighs. "And that's why my daughter adores you. Vicious cycle, right?"

It strikes me that Camilla is having a conversation about something else here. Most likely, that something is Xavier. Wherever Myla's father is, it's not here. I can't imagine how hard that must be.

Even so, I have some precious time with Camilla right now. There are so many threats against Myla. My dreams last night rattle in the back of my head. There was something about the Tithe, wasn't there? I try to grasp the thread of the night's vision, but it snaps before I can take hold. All I can recall is one name. *The Tithe.* Perhaps that's enough.

I focus on Camilla once more. "Look, Myla is the Scala Heir now. There are threats against her. In particular, there's this fellow called the Tithe. Does that name sound familiar?"

Camilla rises so fast, it's like I pulled a weapon on her. "I don't know that name."

"It's important. The Tithe. Can you think of any reason why he'd want to hurt Myla?"

"Let's get through today first. Once my daughter is settled in exile, we can chat." Her eyes take on a wild and cornered look. "We're not talking about threats any more, right?"

"Of course."

Camilla rubs her eyes with her fingertips. "Try not to worry too much. Your kind have such protective instincts."

More half-talk and riddles. "My kind, meaning thrax?"

"Meaning a nobleman. Noble and a man." She shivers. "Experts at breaking hearts."

She isn't speaking to me again. This is about Xavier. Even so, something tells me Camilla deserves an answer here. Clearly, Myla's father hurt Camilla deeply. And for whatever reason, Camilla sees me as a stand-in for Xavier's so-called type. If there's any comfort I can give Camilla on this, I must try.

"About breaking hearts." I take care to speak in my most gentle voice. "My kind would never mean to do so."

Camilla's eyes glisten with tears. "And that's the deadliest part of your appeal." The wild look is gone from her eyes, though. I take that as an improvement.

The doorbell rings. Camilla rises and tightens the sash on her robe. "I'll get it."

A small troop of visitors pile into the kitchen. There are Cissy and Zeke, who are two of Myla's friends from school. Walker then joins and I must admit, it isn't easy to pretend I don't know the fellow. There's also an odd ghoul along for some reason. His name is Tim. When there's a quiet moment, I glance at the new ghoul, then shoot a pointed stare at Walker.

Having known Walker for so long, he realizes what I'm asking. *Who is this guy?*

Walker shakes his head slightly. *Not now.*

I nod. This is Walker's world. If my friend thinks it should wait, then I'll wait. For the moment.

Still, my hunter's instincts tell me this guy is not reliable.

Myla marches into the kitchen, looking indomitable in her dragonscale fighting suit. As she steps closer, I pull her into a deep hug. "Good morning, Myla."

She presses her cheek against my shoulder. "I'm glad you're here."

I whisper in her ear. "You'll kick ass today."

Myla grins. "Hells, yeah." She breaks our hug. Stepping back, my girl scans me from head to toe. I can imagine what she sees: black body armor, daggers holstered on my outer thighs, and baculum strapped to the base of my spine.

"You look ready to kick ass, too," declares Myla.

I shrug. "Another day at the office."

Across the kitchen, Walker pulls an array of maps from the folds of his ghoul robes. He's like one of those clown cars that humans have at circuses— it's amazing how much he can hide in one place. I watch over his shoulder as Walker preps his mission briefing on the tabletop. This is standard practice we both learned at the Citadel.

Now, I'm glad Walker has this all planned out, but I can't help but feel a little irritated. All this secrecy between Walker, Myla, Camilla, and me. It isn't

LINCOLN 193

efficient. All of us should have been reviewing these plans last night as a team. We could have discussed weak points then, like this Tim character.

Cracking my neck, I force myself to focus on the present moment. No point crying over missed battle planning sessions. While I watch Walker over his shoulder, Myla chats with Cissy and Zeke. *Tim the ghoul* seems overly interested in Myla's blue eyes.

Did I mention I don't like this guy? I don't.

With the opening chatter over, Walker launches into the mission review. Walker, Myla, and I will go to her Arena match this morning. It's important to keep with official ghoul government responsibilities for as long as possible. If Myla skips out, that will cause both alarm bells and trouble. Meanwhile, Camilla, Cissy, Zeke, and Tim will go to a desert bunker and await our arrival. After Myla's match, we'll meet up in the bunker until the angels can arrive and take Myla to a safe house.

It's a good plan.

I still don't like Tim's involvement in it, though. What can I say? After years of leading all my own demon patrols—and even a few demonic wars—I have strong opinions. A few times, I open my mouth, ready to question Walker. But the glare I get from my best friend tells me to stay silent.

And perhaps he's right. Part of being a good leader is knowing when to hang back.

"I believe that covers everything," states Walker at length. "Any questions?"

Myla shifts her weight. Clearly, she's uncomfortable. And I don't blame her. The Arena was her life. Now, she's stepping into an entirely new existence.

Walker clears his throat. "Myla?"

Myla's head snaps up. "Yeah?" She has the distinct look of someone awakening from a long sleep. "I mean, what was the question again?"

"Are we ready to go?" asks Camilla.

My mind soaks in this moment. Myla's experiencing I what I call *the vise*. It's the jaws of power snapping in around her. I remember the moment I realized *the vise* had me. It happened on demon patrol. My unit was tracking a pack of humanoid maggot monsters called Vermis. All the thrax warriors had their blades out, ready to taken down the Vermis before they struck a Siberian village. But no one moved to fight. Then I realized all eyes were on me. Stiffening my spine, I called out one word, *attack!* All the warriors went into action.

I was nine years old.

Power presses in around you with metal jaws. From now on, Myla will be expected to give her guidance on everything. I was raised to this responsibility. Myla wasn't. I'm torn between feeling this is isn't fair … and relief that if nothing else, Myla has me. I can help her adjust.

For her part, Myla takes the change in stride. She slaps on a convincing smile. "Yes, absolutely. Let's go. Cissy, Zeke, Tim, and Mom open the bunker.

Walker, Lincoln, and I go the Arena. Then Walker takes me to the bunker. Yeah."

For a first speech, it was a solid effort. Still, Myla nibbles her thumbnail in an anxious rhythm. I lace my fingers with hers. "Together, we can do anything," I say softly.

She takes in a shaky breath. Myla doesn't believe that yet.

That's fine, I have enough faith for both of us. We can beat this. That said, I wish I knew more about what this day holds. Between Armageddon and the Tithe, I can't shake the feeling that more surprises are definitely coming our way.

*W*ith the briefing over, Tim portals Camilla, Cissy, and Zeke off to the bunker. After that, Walker opens a portal of his own. Destination: the Arena. Soon Walker, Myla and I stand in one of the Arena's darkened archways. The place is familiar; it's the same blocked off corridor I've used before. There's no one here but us three.

For weeks, I've wanted to get more information from Walker about his true relationship to Myla. Who knows what could help in keeping my girl safe? Before, I kept waiting for the right time.

That moment is now.

I round on Walker. "Before we go further, I want to thank you for taking such good care of Myla and her mother. I only asked you to *deliver a few messages...*" I let that phrase hang out there. Walker knows what I'm really saying. I promised to pretend that Walker was only a delivery boy.

Now I'm not so happy about that arrangement.

To be absolutely clear, I add an extra verbal kick. "And you've gone *above and beyond.*"

Above my head.

Beyond my knowledge.

Meaning: you better talk, brother.

If Myla catches my sarcasm, she doesn't show it. Instead, my girl approaches Walker and kisses him. It's only on the cheek, but my reaction is both immediate and overwhelming. I've heard about 'seeing red,' but I've never had it happen to me. Yet right now, Walker's entire visage is painted in shades of crimson.

If he weren't already dead, I'd kill him.

"I can't believe it," Myla says to Walker. "This could be our last Arena match together." She glances to the ceiling, her lips whispering silent calculations. "The first time you snuck me in here was, what, eight years ago?"

My red mood instantly turns dark. Walker's known Myla since she was a child? How have I not known this? It's been a long time since I wondered Walker's real motivations here. In fact, I'd dropped the whole idea of him wanting anything but her safety. But seeing that kiss? Hearing their history? It sets off an avalanche of jealousy inside me.

She kissed him.

Kissed.

Him.

I glare at Walker with every ounce of malice I can conjure. It takes all my years of training not to punch my so-called friend in the throat. Myla glances between us for us time. Then her eyes widen.

"I forgot, you know each other too. How did that happen?" She asks.

How did that happen indeed? I keep glaring at Walker.

For his part, Walker turns to Myla. "You remember how my great-grandmother was an archangel?" he asks.

My girl nods. "Mom told me about it ages ago."

"She's the archangel Aquila," explains Walker. "She also founded the House of Rixa. Lincoln and I are both members of the Aquilinea, a society for the descendants of Aquila."

Myla chuckles. "I should start a society for the descendants of Xavier. It'll give me something to do when I'm alone." She glances between me and Walker some more. Finally, her gaze lands on Walker with a silent entreaty. *What?*

Walker exhales a long suffering sigh. "Your mother forbade me to mention my personal history, so I've respected her wishes. Now, however, it's time you knew about the Aquilinea."

"Thanks," replies Myla.

Did I mention my future bride has no business kissing Walker? I'm still stuck on that part.

"That explains why Octavia and Lincoln trusted you with their messages," continues Myla.

All this time, I haven't broken my stare at Walker. "That explains you and me," I say. "How about you and Myla?"

Myla's mouth contracts into an 'o'. "You didn't know that Walker knew me?"

"Not beyond the few messages I gave him." *Not officially, anyway.*

"I'm under an unbreakable oath," explains Walker. "Myla's mother must approve anything I say about her."

"How about I act as proxy for my mother?" Myla twiddles her fingers in Walker's direction. "I release thee from thy oath."

"That should work." I lower my voice and keep right on glaring at Walker. "Speak."

Walker shrugs. "Xavier was my instructor ages ago, in the Citadel. He became like a father to me. When he left Purgatory, he asked me to watch over Camilla. I took an unbreakable oath. When Myla was born, I watched over her, too."

This isn't helping. I now have a pretty good idea who my girl is to Walker now. "So, Myla's the mystery girl you've been visiting all these years?"

How many times does Walker sneak off for his mystery girl? Countless.

How often have I assumed they were romantically entangled? Constantly.

My hands ball into fists. I just want to punch Walker once. Couldn't he have found some sneaky way to give the heartsick prince a heads-up here? The whole time, he's been blocking me and Myla ... and it's all for his own purposes.

Walker lifts his chin. "Yes."

In my peripheral vision, I see Myla make her 'o' face once more. I'd soak in the full sight of her but that would mean no more glaring at Walker.

In this moment, that's not an option.

Myla moves to stand before me. She cups my face in her hands, forcing me to meet her gaze straight on. "It's not like that between us. Walker's basically my brother."

You'd think that would stop my jealous rage. It doesn't. "So, you two never?"

"Sha!" Myla rolls her eyes. "I appreciate the jealousy, but we're burning up valuable *goodbye kiss time.*"

And with that, my anger cools to something else. Grinning, I lean in and kiss her, hard. Our mouths move in a intense dance. It's my way of saying, *this can't be our last kiss.*

I press my forehead against hers. "Be safe."

Myla's tail musses my hair. "I will," she says. And she brushes her lips against mine again. Turning to Walker, Myla pulls her body armor mask over her face. "Let's do this."

Walker nods, then twists to face me. He sets his fist on his chest, the appropriate farewell for an Aquilinean. "Goodbye, Shield Brother."

I exhale, regroup, and do the same motion. "Until we meet again." Walker winks. He knows he totally got out of a throat-punch that time.

Myla and Walker stride out onto the arena floor. Some part of my heart goes with them.

Please, let this work out. Keep my loved ones safe.

39

*T*here are moments that sear into visual postcards for your mind. Right now is one of those for me. It's the vision of Myla and Walker stepping away as they cross the Arena floor. It's the kind of image that I'll go back to later on, thinking one of two things:

Here was the golden moment before we triumphed, or ...

Right after this, everything fell apart.

I lean against the corridor wall, my gaze locked on their departure. Myla steps over to a group of quasi warriors. Alert and silent, Walker waits near Myla's side. Up in the stands, angels and demons take their seats. Now, I'm no expert in Arena battles. In fact, when I came here it was mainly to watch Myla, not everyone else. That said, Myla knows her stuff. As she scans the Arena, her brows draw together until there's a small furrow between them.

Something is wrong.

I inspect the stadium once more, even more closely this time. Verus has extra guards today. *That's strange.* Adrenaline kicks through my bloodstream. Extra guards means the Queen of the Angels expects trouble.

The emcee thumps his staff. "Angels, ghouls, and demons, I bring you—"

From his balcony perch, Armageddon cries out. "I request the presence of the Scala and Scala Heir." The King of Hell stares daggers at the four ghouls who rule both Purgatory and the Dark Lands. *The Oligarchy.* "Do you agree?"

The Oligarchy speak in unison. "Call the bearers."

Anxious energy streams through my limbs. Verus called my people here to protect Maxon Bane. The Great Scala has no business on the Arena floor. It's far too exposed. And bringing along the Scala Heir here as well? They must mean Adair, and I can only hope the lady of Acca has the sense to ignore the summons.

Within a few minutes, a large portal opens. Out of it steps six ghouls carrying a stretcher. Maxon Bane lies atop, deep in sleep. Next Adair saunters out in her white robes. She lifts her chin, scanning the crowd with the same look she wears before launching into one of her mead hall songs. Not helpful.

Adair raises her hand. "I'd like to say something, if I may?"

The emcee bows. "Of course, oh, Scala Heir."

"I was so touched when this random ghoul visited me and asked if I could join you people today. It really shows you've come to revere me. Thank you. Really."

From across the Arena floor, Myla's gaze locks with mine. I look between Myla and Adair; then shake my head. My intent is obvious: *Adair should not be here.*

Myla nods and half-rolls her eyes. Her meaning is also clear: *No kidding.*

The emcee pounds his staff onto the stadium floor. "Now we shall—"

Armageddon raises his voice again. "I was not finished."

Alarm courses through my nervous system. It's the same adrenaline kick I get when a fight is about to begin.

The emcee stammers. "Ye...Yes?"

Rising, Armageddon lifts his arms. "ATTACK!"

A quick inventory speeds through my head. It's all part of my training. Never run into a fight before thinking through the three W's.

Who is there.

What threat they represent.

Where is your objective.

Who. I count quasi warriors, angels, demons, Verus, the Oligarchy, ghoul workers, Walker, Adair, Maxon Bane, and the Great Scala's Guard.

What threat. The demons and Armageddon are the enemy.

Where is my objective. The way I see things, most people here can fend for themselves. Verus is a warrior. Maxon Bane and Adair can exit with their ghoul guards. That leaves one goal for this mission. Get Myla, get Walker ... and *get out.*

I race out of the stone hallway, heading straight toward Myla. The Arena floor becomes overrun with Manus demons, their bulky forms block my path. These are the thugs of Hell; massive furry creatures who literally pound their enemies into the dirt. I dodge them and run on.

I'm not here for a battle; I'm after Myla.

Above me, Verus takes to the skies, along with her angelic warriors. The Oligarchy open portals for themselves and disappear. The Manus head for the exits. They punch through anyone blocking their path.

Clearly, this is an invading army. I'll deal with that later. For now, only question matters.

What happened to Myla?

Pulling out my baculum, I ignite them into a long sword and keep heading for where I last saw my girl. My senses sharpen. I catch the trace of her. *Cinnamon and sunshine.* I'm getting closer. I dodge more Manus demons. One decides to attack, so I slice it straight through from shoulder to hip. Another comes for me, I take off its head.

I roar with rage as the black demonic blood spatters my body armor.

"Myla, where are you?"

Overhead, more angels and demons swoop and dive through the air. Demons bite and claw. Angels cut and dodge. A Murena demon swoops in toward me, ready to attack. This is a long eel-like monster with wings, long fangs, and venom galore. As the monster speeds toward my head, I raise my sword. My blade bites into the creature's belly. I brace my legs, keeping my stance steady as my fiery blade cuts through the Murena's long body. The monster glides past me and crashes onto the Arena floor, dead.

At last, I reach the spot where Myla had been. There's no sign of her. Walker swore to Camilla that he would always keep Myla safe. Did my friend speed her to safety already? I can only hope my girl is healthy and well.

Manus demons race across the grounds, taking down angels, quasis, and ghouls.

Wait, ghouls?

Ghoul-kind should portal away from this battle. Something must be wrong with Group Think. Or perhaps a block spell has been cast. At this point, it's too hard to tell. Only one thing is for certain. The Oligarchy took off, but no other ghouls are leaving. Apart from Walker, most ghouls are easy to kill. This is becoming a massacre.

A groan echoes through the air. It's a familiar voice, and it's close.

Walker.

A Manus demon leaps toward me. I kneel, brace my stance, and point my blade at the creature's heart. The trick with a Manus is to use their weight and momentum against them. The monster plunges at me, a massive humanoid with long arms and deadly intent. My blade pierces the demon's rib cage. With my legs in position, I slice up, cutting the demon's head in two.

Then I see Walker.

My friend is wrapped in the long appendages of a Crini demon. These are massive octopi whose central body includes wide black eyes and a massive beak-like mouth. Rushing over to Walker, I slice off one wriggling leg of the demon who's trying to crush my friend.

Then I cut off another.

That only angers the Crini. But now I can reach its massive head mound much more easily. Lunging forward, I jut my blade in through the side of its skull. The creature falls over, lifeless. I kneel beside Walker.

"Are you all right?"

My friend can self-heal, but even that has its limits. Walker grips his stomach, the very spot where the Crini had been crushing him. Terror lights up his all-black eyes as Walker speaks one word: "Myla." He nods behind me.

That's all I need to know.

Rising, I spin about. Before me, there's a sight I never want to see.

A Crini attacks Myla.

The monster's slimy appendages hold back Myla's legs and tail. Other slimy arms wrap around Myla's middle as the monster pulls Myla toward its razor-sharp teeth. My girl grips either side of the beak-like mouth, stopping the creature from eating her whole.

"Myla!" I let loose a battle cry as I leap toward my woman.

With supernatural speed, I cut the monster's head into sections. The crini hovers in place for a moment before collapsing into pieces on the arena floor.

Myla tumbles out of the demon's grip. She lands on her feet because, *of course she does*. My girl scans the dead bits of Crini and grins.

"I owe you one," she says.

I return her smile with one of my own. "I know." "

Turning, I check out Walker once again. He's still clutching his belly. A portal stands open beside him. The rectangular shape wavers. I scan the floor. No other portals are visible. The other ghouls are still here, but unable to leave. Whatever is happening, Walker's powerful enough to work past what's stopping the others. That said, how much longer can he hold out?

I grasp Myla's hand. "Walker's free, let's get out of here."

A high-pitched cry ricochets through the air. I wince. "I know that voice," I state. And it's someone who didn't portal away with Maxon Bane.

"I do too," says Myla. "It's Adair."

My hunter's sense picks up something else as well. Gentle vibrations move up through my limbs. Kneeling, I touch the ground. Another predator has arrived. And it's worse than the others.

My world collapses as I focus the earth's rumbling. I'm vaguely aware of Myla as she talks to Walker. My girl's asking to close the portal since Adair needs to be saved. Walker shares that he was hurt by the Crini but will recover enough to open the portal once more. The trembling in the earth takes on a certain rhythm.

Unmistakable.

Deadly.

A Tinea demon.

I snap out of my hunter's haze to find Myla kneeling beside Walker. His portal is closed. The Arena floor is clearing out. Most demons have moved out across Purgatory. The skies overhead are empty. I can see no sign of Armageddon. This is always the most dangerous part of war. The main battle is over, so you lower your guard. It's the easiest time to get killed.

And that's why Armageddon set loose the Tinea. *Clever.*

Approaching Myla, I point across the arena floor. "Tinea demon. And it's heading straight for Adair."

Myla frowns. "Of course, it is."

Tineas are hunter-seekers of the demonic world. Set them on a scent and they'll never stop until their quarry is dead. Doubtless, Armageddon set the Tinea after Adair, thinking she's the next Great Scala. Trouble is, Tineas have an excellent sense of smell. If this one gets near Myla, it will scent igni on her.

Even *I* can catch the electric undertone she now carries. It's like lightning before a storm. Unmistakable.

"I'll stall the demon." I reignite my baculum. "Make sure *she* doesn't move or make any noise." There's no question who *she* is in this scenario. Adair.

Myla nods. My girl knows that Tinea demons are masters at detecting motion and sound. As long as Adair stays in place and quiet, the Tinea won't kill her.

After bumping fists with Myla, I race off toward the opposite side of the arena floor. With all my focus, I will my boots to thud the ground with extra force. Rhythmic pounding like a dinner bell to a Tinea. I'm almost to the opposite wall when the ground before me starts to crack.

Something is surfacing.

The Tinea hauls itself out of the earth. A humanoid worm, the Tinea stands about five feet tall with a sinewy body, greasy brown skin, and a great gaping hole of a mouth. Its head is an eyeless lump covered with fine, hair-like quills. Diamond-sharp claws shaped like rotors spin at the end of its rope-like arms and legs.

The only way to kill a Tinea is to cut off all its arms and legs at once.

No one's done that yet.

That said, people have fought it and lived. For a little while, anyway. Tinea never give up.

The demon swipes a wormlike arm in my direction. Its diamond claws aim for my eyes. I firm up my stance, block, lunge, and dodge. The demon is incredibly fast. We quickly get into a dance of battle moves. Sweat beads down my spine. My arms ache from such quick movement. I fought thrax for eight hours straight and never had to dodge this quickly.

A piercing voice echoes across the Arena. "You're pretending to be the Scala Heir, aren't you?" *That would be Adair.* "Well, you're not. I'm the Scala Heir. I'M THE SCALA HEEEEEEIR!"

Damn.

The Tinea stops. Angling its lumpy head, it sniffs through two jagged nose-holes. "Scala Heir."

Oh no, it caught the scent of igni on Myla.

A new burst of adrenaline courses through me. I hack onto the Tinea's limbs with fresh vigor. Slices appear on its worm-like skin, but the wounds close almost as soon as I open them. Nevertheless, I still cut away at the demon while it burrows back into the earth.

No question where it's heading.

Myla.

Turning, I rush back toward my girl. "Don't move!" I cry.

Adair stands beside Myla. My girl is still and quiet, while Adair chatters away while moving so much, you'd think she'd been asked to start dance lessons.

As I close in, Adair wraps her arms around me. "Lincoln! I knew you'd come for me." She jumps up and down. Again.

I sigh. "Adair, you need to work on your listening skills." No doubt, Myla told her a million times to be silent and not move.

Adair cuddles into my chest. "Oh, my Prince! I was so frightened."

"Everything will be fine, Adair." I focus on my girl. "Myla, you said you'd keep her still."

Myla sets her fists on her hips. "I tried. She's kind-of a bitch."

I try not to laugh. That said, I don't try too hard. Adair really does have listening issues. It runs in the family.

Adair rounds on Myla. "No one speaks to the Scala Heir in that manner!"

Myla raises her hand to shoulder height. It's what I've learned is her move for, *I'm about to call down a lot of pain and igni on your head*. But there isn't time for my girl to summon her powers.

Beneath our feet, the earth rumbles once more. Rotor-like hands break through the ground. A lumpy head and wormy body peep up from the broken earth. Up close, the leathery skin shimmers with mucus.

The Tinea is resurfacing.

Adair screams her head off.

The quills on the Tinea vibrate, then fall still. The creature sniffs through its thin nose-holes. Its lumpy head turns in Myla's direction. "Scala Heir."

Myla goes into battle stance, tail arched over her shoulder. Adair steps between my girl and the demon.

"No, no, no!" whines Adair. "I'm the Scala Heir."

I grab Adair's arm, trying to pull her out of the way. She won't budge.

This is officially irritating.

Myla does a few more moves to both protect Adair and stall out the Tinea. The protecting bit is entertaining, considering how Myla had to trip Adair in order to do so. Another moment where I wish I had a camera. I've never seen anyone kick Adair. It isn't very princely of me to admit, but it wasn't too terrible.

In terms of stalling out the Tinea, Myla jams her tail into the ground, spears the monster through the head, and flings it against the opposite wall of the Arena. I saw this move once before, when Myla was fighting the arachnoid at the winter tournament. It involves her swishing her hips while sending something zooming from her tail, whip-style.

It's one of my favorite sights, actually.

With the Tinea safely across the arena floor, we have a precious few minutes before it rounds back for another attack. A battle plan appears. My eyes widen.

I turn to Myla. "I've got an idea." To demonstrate, I split my baculum from a long sword into a pair of short swords. Right away, my girl knows what I'm thinking. She smiles and tilts her head. The question is there, although silent (this is a Tinea after all). My girl's asking, *What next?*

"Get behind me," I say.

Myla gets right into position. It's like we've fought together our entire lives, and I love it. I sense the rumble of the Tinea through my legs as is closes back in.

"Now?" whispers Myla.

I keep my voice calm and low. "Not yet."

Then, it happens.

The Tinea's greasy head-lump breaks through the Arena floor.

Next, the demon's wormy torso follows.

Finally, ropy legs pop out of the dirt and lock onto the ground.

"Now, Myla!" I bend over at the waist. There's pressure as Myla sets her foot on my back. She launches herself into the air, somersault-twists over the Tinea's head, and lands behind the demon in a crouch. I raise my short-swords high.

That's it.

We're in position.

As I bring my blades down through the demon's arms, Myla swipes her tail through the monster's legs. The creature pauses, shivers, and then disintegrates into a puddle of brownish goop.

We did it.

The first Tinea has now been taken down.

"You killed it," whispers Adair. "Together."

I'd think she was being kind, but Adair's wearing her *plotting face*. Clearly, she'd planned this visit to the Arena to end far differently than Myla and I fighting side-by-side. If history is any indicator, Adair will now find Aldred, whine, and come up with another plan.

Something to deal with later.

Myla and I bump fists. She wiggles her bottom. "We are a lean, mean demon killing machine."

I laugh. Is there anything better than fighting with Myla? Actually, I can think of a few things, but we're taking it slowly.

"How'd you know how to fight like that?" asks Adair.

"Lincoln broke the baculum in two," explains Myla. "So, obviously he's going for the demon's arms. And if he's taking out the arms, then I need to get the legs. That's the only way to kill a Tinea."

I wrap my hands about Myla's waist. "Nicely done."

She kisses the tip of my nose. "Back at ya."

Suddenly, the air around us pulses with energy. There's nothing like battle to make you realize how much you want to get naked with someone else. Myla's eyes flare red.

"Later, Myla."

"Got anything more specific for me on that?"

I frame her beloved face with my fingertips. "There will be time for us. I swear it." I lean in to whisper in her ear. "I think that's a record for fastest time from zero to sparkling."

"You're such a competitive little creep," Myla retorts. But there's no mistaking the smile in her voice. Exhaling, she steps away. "I need to find Walker. I'm late to the bunker as it is."

I arch my brows. "*I* need? Do you think you're going alone?"

Myla blinks. "I thought that was the plan."

"When Armageddon invaded Purgatory, the plans changed. I'm not going anywhere until I'm certain you're safe."

"I'd tell you to join your people, but you won't listen to me anyway."

I shoot her a sly grin. "And secretly, you totally want me around."

She blushes. "That too."

"Knew it." I wink at Myla, then turn to Adair. "Can you walk?"

Adair turns up her nose. "I'm fine."

"Very good," I say. "I'm afraid you must travel with us until we can get you home."

"That's okay," says Adair. If you didn't know her and her family, you'd think Adair was being a normal person right now. Unfortunately, I know the House of Acca. The plotting continues.

"Hello, there!" Walker limps toward us, his arm raised in welcome. He looks far better. *Which is amazing.* That ghoul's ability to self-heal is nothing less than phenomenal. "I can portal everyone to the bunker now."

I take Myla's hand in mine, ready for the next phase of our adventure. The definition of *staying with Myla until she is safe* could certainly be open to interpretation.

I'm hoping for a century, minimum.

40

*M*inutes later, I step out of Walker's portal and into the bunker. Walker, Adair, and Myla are with me. In terms of space, the bunker is a large square space made of smooth concrete. There are shelves overflowing with supplies. Metal folding chairs lay stacked against one wall. Reminds me of the houses of Liten and Rena. Those clans still don't allow electronics, but they keep their homes more cost-effective and modern.

Speaking of electronics, the communications wall was supposed to be lit up by now. I frown. It's still dark. Camilla, Cissy, and Zeke all lurk in a corner, looking wide eyed and silent. Tim appears jittery and pale.

Fresh adrenaline courses through me.

I don't like this.

Myla waves across the room. "Hey, guys."

No response.

"Don't all say hello at once," adds Myla.

Both Myla and Walker try to get folks talking. It soon becomes clear what the problem is.

Tim, the oddball ghoul.

"I know who this one *really* is." Tim points his bony finger toward Camilla. "*You* would never accept being a seamstress, Senator. You're plotting against the ghoul government, you and that witch you call a daughter. I chose to side against my people *once* when I decided to work for you. I won't make that mistake *twice*."

Oh no. There's so much unhinged in that speech, I don't know where to begin. Tim seems to have worked for Camilla and carried a massive torch for her. The experience has somehow rotted out his logic. In a strange way, I can understand. I know how the heart can fool with the mind; I just experienced it myself. After all, who would think that I'd give up a kingdom for a girl? Is what Tim's doing that much different?

Tim spins around, showing that he holds a short spear against Cissy's back. "This weapon's covered in poison. Make no mistake; one scratch will kill her. None of you move."

I take it back. *What Tim is doing is far different. We don't threaten women.*

My fingers itch to grab my baculum and strike Tim through, but the young ghoul looks far too twitchy for that. Cissy could end up dead. Instead, I bring out my diplomatic skills and approach Tim.

"We came from the Arena," I explain. "The demons attacked everyone, ghouls included. The Oligarchy barely escaped with their lives. We're on the same side, friend."

"The demons attacked, eh?" Tim scowls. "And whose fault is that? You forget, I worked with the Senator for years. She'd never give up on the republic. She's still scheming and fighting, mark my words."

Camilla steps forward. "Please understand, Tim. I'm not the same–"

"Spare me." He turns to Camilla, eyes blazing. "I'm not sure how you've angered Armageddon, but you'll pay for it. The Oligarchy are coming."

A new portal opens; through it steps the Oligarchy in their deep red robes. The Scala lies on a stretcher between them; the old thrax's eyes closed in deep sleep. The portal disappears. Now we're all trapped in here together. Not good.

My thoughts race through this new development. The Great Scala is here. Maxon Bane disappeared from the Arena floor. At the time, I assumed his guards followed their *protection plan* and evacuated the Great Scala to Antrum. So what happened to the guards? Faint arcs of shiny black liquid mark the edge of Maxon Bane's stretcher. If I could lean in, I'm sure it would have the scent of charcoal.

That's ghoul blood.

Maxon Bane's true guards are gone. The Oligarchy have taken over transporting him around.

This has Armageddon written all over it.

And Myla is the Scala Heir, so now she's a pawn in their games as well.

Damn, we were so certain things would be fine with Maxon Bane as the Great Scala. We didn't suspect his guards would fail. You can't plan for every turn of fate, but somehow, I wish I'd seen this coming.

Tim's sneer melts into a look of awe. "Mighty Oligarchy, I bring you a prisoner to appease our invaders." He gestures to Camilla. "Senator Lewis." Next, he points directly at Myla. "And *that one* may pretend to have special powers. Don't be fooled."

The Oligarchy set down the Scala's stretcher. "Excellent work." These ghouls always speak in unison. "And this place is safe from demons?"

"Yes, it's surrounded in angel fire," answers Tim. "It's the perfect place to conduct your negotiations."

"And you're certain this plan will work?" ask the Oligarchy.

Tim's huge black eyes beam with pride. "Yes, it's like I told you. Senator Lewis would never really become a seamstress. She's been planning to restore the old republic. Believe me, this is why Armageddon invaded. Get rid of the Senator, you'll get rid of him too."

Not sure what Tim sees, but Myla's mother does not strike me as a viper planning to return to power. To me, Camilla seems all *mother bear*. Obviously, Tim's thinking with his injured heart. And the Oligarchy? They are well-known cowards. It's how they ended up being puppets for Armageddon in the first place. They'll be happy with any reason not to fight.

Well, I won't allow them to hand over women to Armageddon.

The Oligarchy let out a low hiss, then speak in unison. "The King of Hell arrives any moment." Their heads turn in a single motion, scanning the room. "Let us hope that handing over the senator is enough to appease him."

A pang of realization hits me. Armageddon is coming here? Now? I thought I was leading Myla to safety. Instead, I took her to the absolute worst spot in the after-realms. Now we're trapped underground with none other than Armageddon coming after us.

Myla's mother comes to the same conclusion. "You told Armageddon where we're all hiding?" Camilla rolls her eyes. "He'll come here all right, but not just for us."

The Oligarchy glare at the Great Scala and then Adair. "We see the Scala Heir is here as well."

Tim rushes to Adair's side, pulling her up from the floor. "Yes, mighty Oligarchy. She'll be useful to you. If the senator isn't enough, you can negotiate with her as well."

The Oligarchy's eyes flare bright. "Yes, most suitable."

Adair struggles under Tim's grip. "I'm not the Scala Heir. It was all a fake." She points directly at Myla. "She's the one. She's the heir."

Pure rage swells within me, but I keep it contained. Reacting to Adair's words will only validate them. I look to Walker. There must be something he can do. I catch his eye and whisper the word, *upsilon*. Walker knows thrax battle codes. That one is for a quick exit. In this case, I'm thinking a ghoul portal is the obvious choice.

Walker nods. He agrees. My friend closes his eyes, but no portal appears. I think through the charms I have on my person. Perhaps Walker is still ill and needs some healing? I want to speed things along, but I can't risk attracting more attention.

The Oligarchy continue addressing Adair. "You're whatever Armageddon believes you to be, little girl."

Adair staggers backward until her back hits the concrete wall. "But I'm not the heir, really." All the color drains from her face.

"It won't come to that," say the Oligarchy. "Armageddon will take the senator and leave."

With those words, the Oligarchy's plan becomes clear. Appease Armageddon. They'll hand over Camilla, Adair, Maxon Bane … anyone. I scan the old thrax on the stretcher. That poor soul is Armageddon's son. The King of Hell has sent us many royal missives, demanding we help deliver Maxon Bane to his father. Those letters contained overly-long descriptions of the tortures Armageddon had planned for his child. I can't stand by while one of my people is sent off to agony.

"Don't worry, Scala Heir." The Oligarchy bow slightly to Adair. "The plan is perfect. Handing over the senator will work."

Walker's eyes blaze red. "Time to change the plan." At last, a portal starts to take shape by the far wall.

I contain my urge to cheer. *Yes!*

The Oligarchy's gaze snaps in Walker's direction. "Don't try to circumvent us, traitor."

The portal vanishes.

Maybe Walker wasn't strong enough to keep the portal open. Perhaps the oligarchy blocked him. Either way, the end is the same. No exit portal.

There must be something else we can do. Handing over Camilla and Maxon Bane is madness.

Myla must be thinking the same thing. Beside me, she closes her eyes and raises her hand. It's her classic pose for summoning igni. Knowing my girl, she wants to help everyone escape, but it will only paint a large target on her back.

I grab Myla's wrist, pulling it down.

"Myla, please." I keep my voice to the lowest of whispers. "He'll know." She knows who *he* is here. Armageddon. If the Oligarchy see her power, Myla will be the first tosser out to the King of Hell.

Myla pauses. I know her heart; she wants to protect her family.

"Hiding you," I say in a low voice. "It's the reason we're all here. What if Armageddon got both the Scala and the Scala Heir? With that kind of power, he could control all the five realms. This is bigger than any of us, Myla."

My girl nods.

It's another *vise moment* for her. Like mine with the Vantys demon. The weight of power. People think leading is all about dressing in fancy clothes or having people bow to you. That's what failing rulers enjoy. If you really want to help your people, it's all duty and sacrifice. Even when, like Myla, what you're giving up is your family. She must stand by as they risk everything for her.

Across the room, the Oligarchy gesture to the Great Scala. "Maxon Bane." The old man half-opens his eyes. In Latin, the Oligarchy whisper the words for "Imprison them." Igni rise from Maxon Bane's hands and fly about the room. Electric cords bind my hands and feet. I check the room. Everyone is tied up except the Oligarchy and Tim.

The Oligarchy's eyes blaze bright red. "Every Scala develops a special skill with igni beyond the soul column. Maxon Bane creates ropes and cages." Their four mouths coil into satisfied grins. "Don't bother trying to escape. Nothing can break your bonds." They turn to Tim. "Go outside to Armageddon. Tell him we await his orders."

Nodding, Tim creates a portal and disappears.

The Oligarchy inspect our faces. "There's no need for all of you to suffer for the senator's crimes." Their voices come out syrupy and low. "Help us. We'll keep you safe from Armageddon."

"And how will you manage that, exactly?" asks Camilla. "You can't protect *yourselves* from him."

I can see why Camilla was such an excellent Senator. She's able to look uncomfortable truths in the eyes and name them. When it comes to ruling, that's half the battle.

The portal reopens. Tim steps through, his chest slashed wide open, a mass of purple organs wriggling inside. "Lord Armageddon says thank you for the offer, but he's here to kill us all."

Tim crumbles to the floor, dead.

I wish there could be some pleasure in saying, *I called this one.* But I did predict this and Tim still got us imprisoned underground.

Boom... boom...

The walls shake as something tries to break through the sands and into our bunker. Armageddon. The King of Hell isn't waiting for an invitation. He's coming to meet us here.

The news scares both the Oligarchy and Maxon Bane. The old thrax sits upright, his crinkled face trembling in terror. "Armageddon is here!"

A plan quickly takes shape. Every thrax promises to protect their prince. Silvinio and Devak were one of the few who broke it. Most respect the vow as sacred, just as Jali did. Lifting my voice, I call to the awakened Scala in Latin. "Thrax! Brother!"

Hearing his native tongue, the Scala turns to me. He says two words in a reverent tone: "My Prince."

Instantly, the electric bonds around my hands and feet disappear. The Scala collapses back onto his stretcher. "Come here, my Prince."

"Maxon!" cry the Oligarchy. "Imprison him!" They point all point in unison to me. But it's a wasted effort. By calling me his Prince, Maxon Bane acknowledged his vow.

"I cannot harm my Prince." The Great Scala reaches out a withered hand in my direction. "Come sit beside me, brother."

The Oligarchy put up some additional fuss, but it's a token effort at best. Stepping past them, I approach Maxon Bane and kneel beside his stretcher. My first order of business is to free Myla and her friends.

"I am Lincoln Vidar Osric Aquilus from the House of Rixa, High Prince of the Thrax. Release them all. Now."

Maxon Bane flicks his hand. "I obey my Prince." All the igni bindings disappear. I scan Myla, ensuring she's well. She gives me an approving nod, and that means everything.

We're now trapped but together, we can break free.

Maxon Bane grips my arm. "They say Armageddon is coming. I must escape!"

"Yes, Armageddon attacks," I say gently. I turn to the Oligarchy. "I wish him portaled to safety. What do you want in exchange?"

The Oligarchy lower their heads and close their eyes. "Group Think is a jumble. It isn't safe to portal anywhere."

I don't believe them. Tim just opened a portal a minute ago. "So," I state. "You still think to trade the Great Scala to Armageddon." I return my attention to Maxon Bane. "We'll keep trying, brother. But we must stay here for now."

Maxon Bane's tightens his grip on my arm. "Ignite your baculum. Give me an honest death, my Prince."

"No, brother."

If the Oligarchy can't open a portal, perhaps Walker can. After all, he got close a few minutes ago. I turn to address Walker, but I should never have taken my focus away from the old Scala. Maxon Bane grabs my dagger its holster. Fast as a heartbeat, the ancient thrax buries the blade deep into his own chest, stabbing himself through the heart. His white cloak blooms red with blood.

"No, brother!" The old man's chest heaves and falls silent. His wrinkled hand tumbles off the stretcher. I set my fingertips on the old man's neck. "He's gone."

The Oligarchy's eyes blaze blood-red. "Traitors! Murderers! You've killed our–" The dead Scala moves. The Oligarchy shut their mouths.

One by one, the igni seep from the Scala's lifeless form and swirl around his body. Maxon Bane begins to breathe again. The dead man opens his eyes; both glow bright blue. Around him, the tiny igni multiply into a wide column of light.

I don't need a hunter's intuition to know this is very, very bad. The dead man points to Myla. His movements are jerky and odd. "I give my powers to the new Scala."

What happens next takes only a matter of seconds. Each moment burns into my brain as if hours passed. Thousands of igni burst out of the old Scala's body, forming a swirling column of brightness. That small tornado of power swirls across the bunker floor, heading straight for Myla. After that, thousands of tiny lightning bolts attach to my girl's skin before sliding inside. She gasps in pain.

Myla! I try to run to her. My mind goes swiftly, but my body and the world are simply too slow.

The dead thrax leans back on his stretcher. His eyes close. "Esme. I come to you. At last. Esme." He smiles and falls silent. His chest ceases to move. This time, he really is gone.

More igni slip under Myla's skin. The column of Scala power dims and thins until the last of the igni enter her body. The room becomes perfectly silent.

I pause a few yards before Myla. She positively glows with power and beauty. The pain, whatever that was, has ended. She offers me a smile and I return it.

My girl survived. And she's the Great Scala.

The Oligarchy bow so low, their foreheads hit the floor. "The new Scala."

Myla rounds on them. "Yes, I'm the new Scala. And now we'll discuss how to drive the demons from my homeland." I turn to Walker. "Bring me the angel Verus."

The Oligarchy keep speaking with their heads seemingly stuck to the floor. It would be comical if Armageddon weren't outside and trying to kill us. Once again, they speak in unison. "We cannot allow unauthorized portals at this time, Great Scala. There's some kind of interference in Group Think. It's not safe."

"Really? How'd you like a quick trip to Hell?" Myla raises her hand, hundreds of igni encircle her palm.

The Oligarchy stay prone to the floor. "We can allow portals for you, Great Scala."

"That's more like it." Myla snaps her fingers. "Walker, go get Verus."

Walker nods. A portal opens. Its edges blur and waver. Gritting his teeth, Walker steps into the black emptiness and disappears.

Myla points to the folding chairs. "Grab a chair, boys. We've lots to talk about."

The Oligarchy finally stand. "As you wish, Great Scala." The Oligarchy pick up the metal folding chairs and drag them across the concrete floor.

In some ways, this is heading into familiar territory for me. Negotiations and treaties are what I do. But in another sense, this is all upside down. Myla just became the Great Scala. That was an awesome sight, but also frightening. I simply must be certain that she's all right.

I step up behind Myla. "May I have a minute, Great Scala?"

"I'm Myla."

So, she's having issues adjusting to her new role. No judgment here. When I was twelve, I wouldn't let anyone call me prince for an entire year.

"I see. Follow me, please." I slip Myla's hand in mine, guiding her into the small antechamber off the main room. It's a snug space with dark walls that are lined with supplies. Once inside, I shut the door, drag out a cot and sit down. I pat the space beside me. "Let's talk."

A wild look overtakes Myla's blue eyes. "This is no time for chit chat. Hell's about to break loose. For real."

If she thinks that's convincing me she needs to go back out there, it won't work. I lock gazes with my girl. "A few minutes ago, you sucked in enough supernatural electricity to power a universe. We're not doing anything until I'm sure you're okay."

Her bottom lip quivers. "I'm fine. Maybe."

Rising, I wrap her in a deep hug. *My poor, sweet, and supernatural girl.*

She leans into my shoulder. "This whole thing began because, like a dumb-ass, I wanted to know who my father really was. Now it turns out that my dad's an archangel who's in Hell, getting tortured for all eternity."

I pull her more closely against me. Which answers the question: what happened to Xavier? Hard enough to lose a father. Worse to know he's being tortured.

My poor Myla.

"So that sucks," continues my girl. "Then I meet you, get all lovey and—BOOM—I'm the Scala Heir. Which was weird, but hey, the old Scala could have lived another thousand years, so no big deal, right?" She pokes me softly in the belly. "Am I right or am I right?"

I smile. "You're right."

"Well, he didn't last a week. Now I'm the Great Scala, which is a very sketchy job description that involves everyone trying to control me." She snif-fles into my body armor. "If I'd just listened to Mom, I'd still be fighting Arena matches, skipping school, and living what now looks like a pretty sweet life before I mucked it up."

I rub her back in long strokes until her sniffles end. "I'm so sorry this happened to you, Myla."

Myla loops her arms around my waist. "Maybe after this is all over, we can see if *someone else* can be the Scala? An heir must be running around some-place. Or, I've heard of some pretty amazing magic users. Maybe one of them can zap the igni into someone else." She groans. "I want to get today over with, kick Armageddon's ass out of Purgatory, and forget any of this ever happened." She nuzzles into my shoulder once more. "Except for the *you* part, of course."

I kiss the top of her head. "Let's get through today. We can discuss every-thing else later."

A long moment passes before she speaks again. "You're right."

I cup her face in my hands. "Are you ready to go back now?"

"Nope." She points to her lips and grins.

I know what she needs.

I kiss her once, gently. "And now?"

"Yup."

We link hands and step toward the door.

"Oh, Lincoln?"

I pause. "Yes, Myla?"

"Thank you." Myla blushes. "No one else thought to ask me how I was after, *you know*."

I give her palm a little squeeze. "We're a team, right?"

"Absolutely right."

Once again, I consider telling her about the Tithe. There's something I'm missing regarding with her father, angelic blood, and the Tower of Wonders.

Yet as soon as the thought occurs to me, I push it aside. My girl has too much on her shoulders right now. Once the situation with Armageddon is well and truly over, we can talk then.

For now, there's still the King of Hell to handle.

I've lived my life negotiating treaties. In terms of this one, the setting is a little odd, considering how it's in a bunker and on metal chairs. Yet beside that, it's rather regular stuff. Walker has returned and with Verus and her guard, but it does seem as if opening portals isn't easy for anyone right now. The Oligarchy may not have been lying before.

Even so, I don't trust those four ghouls.

Cissy, Zeke, and Adair wait in a side room. Myla's friends are making sure Adair stays out of trouble, which is greatly appreciated. This situation is tough enough without the House of Acca getting added into the mix.

The negotiations start off poorly with the Oligarchy suggesting we hand over Myla. I'm ready to rip their bony heads off, but Myla threatens to send them to Hell and that makes the ghouls back off.

Did I mention how I hate the Oligarchy? *They are evil. And a spineless variety of bad, which is even worse.*

In the end, Myla negotiates that Purgatory will return to quasi rule. The Oligarchy will depart the realm; the angels shall ensure they stay gone.

My heart warms. This is a brilliant plan; my girl will indeed be an excellent queen one day.

The only negative is, of course, the constant pounding over our heads from Armageddon. The agreement to oust the Oligarchy from Purgatory—and free Myla's people—is contingent on us figuring out a way to inspire Armageddon to leave here as well.

As always with the Oligarchy, it all about what's easiest for them.

That's a sticking point. How does one get rid of the King of Hell? It looks as if negotiations will crumble. Then Myla volunteers to use her igni powers and send Armageddon to Hell.

The thought of my girl risking herself is nothing less than terrifying. Even so, it's a solid plan.

I volunteer to stand beside her, obviously. Camilla, Zeke, and Cissy offer to act as a distraction. Turns out, there's a back exit to the bunker. Myla and I can sneak through that hidden path and crawl up onto the ridge. The ledge overlooks both the main door and Armageddon. From there, we'll figure it out as we go.

I've gone into major demonic wars with worse plans.

And my Myla? She's clearly anxious about wielding her powers. But I believe in her. She's got this.

Walker, however, disagrees. He makes one last plea to Myla. "You saw the old Scala at the iconigration. He almost collapsed sending a few dozen icons to Heaven. Even at his best, he could only move a few hundred at a time in one place. You're talking about five thousand demons across all of Purgatory."

Myla rounds on him. "You're being a downer, Walker. I'm a first-generation archangel, whatever that is. Plus, I'm an Arena fighter, a Lewis, and someone with a lot to lose. I can do this." She forces on a confident face, and I love her for it.

In this moment, my woman embodies everything that's fierce. She's like a statue labelled, *strength*. If we get through this, I'll have to commission one for the royal feasting hall. I ignore the small voice that says there will be no feasting hall, no queen. This is a long shot at best. Yet I push those thoughts aside. In this moment, I say, *we will kick ass*.

I choose Myla.

Verus runs off to write up the treaty terms. Myla turns to me. "Time to face my demons," she says.

Camilla points to a spot along the back of the room. "There's a secret exit behind those shelves. It opens to the great dune behind the rock wall. We've checked the periscope. Armageddon's troops are deployed on the low sands in front of the wall. If you stay behind the dune, you'll be hidden."

At this point, we discuss some concerns about the Oligarchy. Specifically, I'm worried about leaving them alone in the bunker. In the end, Verus volunteers to babysit the four ghouls. After that, Camilla heads to the bunker's exit with Cissy and Zeke behind her. Myla's mother has changed, so she's now dressed as a senator. Cissy wears the robes of a junior senator and Zeke is dressed their guard. By marching out the front door, they'll grab Armageddon's attention ... and hopefully, serve as a diversion for me and Myla.

Meanwhile, Myla and I explore the shelves along the back wall. It doesn't take us long to find the panel that Camilla told us about. With a light shove, the shelves easily slide away, revealing a low and dark tunnel in the concrete wall.

We're off.

Myla and I crawl through the tunnel. As promised, it empties out onto back side of the hill outside the bunker. I've been on my share of demon patrols. Crawling up to a sniper's spot isn't anything new to me. But Myla's only been in Arena fights. She should be overwhelmed and testy, but she isn't. I'm more than proud.

Together, we belly-crawl to the peak of the hill and take up position. At this point, it's like we're snipers without a rifle, looking down on the enemy below. That thought is comforting, somehow. Familiar.

I quickly catalog the body position of all our enemies. A legion of troops surround the bunker's door, which s a round portal set into the sand. A massive Manus demon stands at the center of the crowd. This gorilla-like monster is the largest creature I've ever seen. Hoisting its long arms high above its head, the Manus slams its fists onto the desert floor, scooping up piles of sand and throwing them off to one side. With each throw, he gets a little closer to the bunker door.

Boom, boom...

That's what's been rattling over our heads. The Manus has been trying to break in, or scare us into coming out.

The circular door springs to life, igniting into a ring of white flame. The Manus demon leaps out of the fire's path. Camilla, Cissy, and Zeke step outside.

Straightening her shoulders, Camilla speaks in a calm voice that echoes through the desert. "I come here today on behalf of angels, ghouls, thrax, and quasis. This unwarranted invasion of our–"

I gently tap Myla's upper arm. "We're on."

Myla nods, takes in a long breath, and closes her eyes. As she's done before, she raises her hand. Sure enough, a handful of tiny lightning bolts swim around her palm. It's breathtaking.

"Great, Myla. You're doing it."

Armageddon's voice echoes through the air. "I have a surprise for you, Camilla."

"What could you possibly do to surprise me?" asks Myla's mother.

The King of Hell snaps his fingers.

In the back of my mind, I'm aware that something is flying toward us. A pair of large flying demons drop off a massive metal box by the bunker's door. But I set those thoughts aside, only focusing on Myla. So far, she's done a great job summoning a few dozen igni.

That's all that have appeared, though.

More noises sound from the enemy below. A thud sounds as the box opens, followed by the flap of wings. Armageddon tells Camilla, "This is for you."

Myla's igni decrease, from about twenty to ten.

Then five.

Then none.

I grip Myla's shoulder. "What's going on? The igni are gone."

"That's my father."

It's part of warrior training to hyper-focus on your task when needed. I'd been so attuned to Myla and her powers, I didn't really notice what happened below. Now, I really see what Armageddon has done.

Someone was chained inside the box. That person has been revealed. Scars and bruises cover his body. Blood seeps down his shoulders. *The archangel Xavier.* Armageddon must have ripped the man's wings off. Excruciating.

Back in the bunker, Myla said her father went to Hell. Now it's one thing to know someone's been tortured, but it's another matter to see so much blood and pain. I wouldn't blame Myla if she gave up and went back to the bunker.

That's not what happens.

Before me, Myla's features harden. Anger pours off her soul. She turns to me, ready to explain what she's about to do. But I'm already there with her. Armageddon must be stopped. Xavier will be freed.

Myla rises, her tail flicking in a predatory rhythm. I stand by her side.

Armageddon's head snaps in our direction. "Look, who we have here. The little arena girl and the thrax High Prince." His eyes sparkle. "You're King Connor's boy." He rounds on Myla's mother. "And that girl's your daughter, isn't she, Camilla?"

Xavier slowly lifts his ragged head. His blue eyes glow with a soft light. He looks to Camilla and rasps out one word: "Daughter?"

Camilla offers him a gentle nod.

Xavier swallows. "Is she–"

"Yes, Xavier." Camilla's eyes brim with tears. "She's yours."

The archangel strains to twist his head and look upon Myla. "She's lovely, Camilla." He forces his broken voice louder. "You're lovely."

"That's not all I am, father." Myla raises her hand and calls to igni. A hundred whirl up and down her arm.

Perfect.

"So, you're the true Scala Heir." Armageddon's long face twists into a sneer. "Interesting."

Myla summons even more igni. "You almost have that right." Soon a white column of power stands beside her. "I'm not the Scala Heir. I'm the Great Scala."

I ignite my baculum. *That revelation won't go over well.*

Armageddon's eyes flare bright red. "What are you saying? Where's my son? WHERE IS MY SON?"

"Killed by his own hand," I declare. "He died a true thrax warrior." I toss my blade from hand to hand, sizing up Armageddon. I can't let him touch me, but that shouldn't be too hard. It's all a matter of how fast the demon moves and how long I have to keep him away from Myla.

King of Hell throws back his head and howls. "My son is dead? MY SON IS DEAD?!" He crouches to Xavier's side, grips his hair and yanks up his skull. "I want to you watch your daughter closely now, because I'm going to break her bones and drag her to Hell. She will fulfill my vow to torture Maxon Bane."

If Armageddon thought that would upset Myla, he was sorely mistaken.

"Try this on for size." Myla blasts her column of white lightning straight into the sky, pumping the storm clouds with bright flashes. "How about you get your goddamn hands off my father?" The clouds roll with an ear-splitting peal of thunder. "NOW."

With a great leap, Armageddon jumps up onto our ridge. His greater demon aura slams into me, but I keep my focus. This isn't my first time fighting this demonic class. Armageddon goes to attack my girl; I block each strike.

Myla pumps more power into the clouds. Below us, small columns of igni appear around each demon. Soul columns. Every swirl of igni flare with brightness and then vanish, taking the monster inside along with it to Hell. Myla conducts all the action from inside her own column of igni.

What a marvel.

Within minutes, all the monsters on the grey desert are gone. Only Armageddon remains. He's preternaturally fast, but not the worst I've ever fought. A sneaking suspicion appears: the King of Hell is saving his energy.

Then, Armageddon makes his move.

The King of Hell leaps inside Myla's column of igni. Panic spreads through me, burning my every nerve ending like fire. Inside the column, I can barely see Myla move. Armageddon looms above her. The color of the column changes from white to red.

Angel fire to Hellfire.

Armageddon is winning.

I slam on the column with my blade. I simply must break through and grab my girl. "Myla!" I scream. "Myla!"

A great boom shakes the air. It's thunder clap like none I've never heard before. Suddenly, Myla's column turns white again. Images are visible through the swirling igni. A pit opens before my girl's feet. Armageddon tumbles into that hole, falling down to Hell. The ground closes up before her. The soul column vanishes. One by one, all the igni blink out of existence.

From below, Camilla calls out. "Word just came from Verus! The demons are gone!"

Myla stands before me, wobbling and yet grinning. She wavers a moment before collapsing into my arms. I hold her tightly against me.

One woman who saved an entire realm.

A true warrior queen.

*H*ours later, Myla's still unconscious. I keep vigil by my girl's bedside in Purgatory. After the battle with Armageddon, we consulted a long roster of doctors. All agree it's best for her to be here, sleeping in familiar surroundings with those who love her nearby. Camilla spends much of her time in the master bedroom where Xavier recovers. I've made Myla my top priority. Mostly, my role involves watching my girl sleep while experts troop in and out.

Lucas.

The royal physicians.

Quasi doctors.

Each time, it's a similar routine. The experts check Myla's pulse. Run a few tests. They conclude they've never seen anything like this before, as there are no records on the Great Scala. Then they grab a brownie from the kitchen and take off.

Which brings me to Myla's friend Cissy, who keeps the house well stocked with sugary sweets for when Myla wakes up. I had one of my stewards bring up some patrol rations for me. Bland stuff, but healthy. I keep the tins in a pack under my chair. Demon bars are out of the question. I can't eat that much sugar or it feels like my teeth will vibrate out of my head.

When no one's around, I hold Myla's hand. Kiss her eyes. Whisper to her, saying how she'll wake up soon. All the while, she stays in a cold sweat. I'm starting to worry when, at last, a pulse of warmth moves across her skin. Myla whispers my name.

"Lincoln."

Then, she smiles.

One thing I'll give to Camilla. That woman may be in another room, but she still has the same gifts for extreme maternal hearing as Octavia. A moment after Myla speaks, the bedroom door whips open. Camilla stands there in sweatpants and a long T-shirt. Her eyes widen with excitement.

"What was that?" she asks.

"Good news," I reply. "She's past the worst of it."

Camilla steps to the bedside and touches Myla's hand. "Oh, she's warming up." Camilla leans in to examine Myla's skin. "Her coloring is coming back as well. I'll fetch the doctors to confirm." With that, Camilla leaves the room. Another parade of doctors come through, but since no one knows anything about the Great Scala, they can say little except agree with us.

Myla seems better.

Hours pass. Perhaps days go by as well. It's hard to know. At some point, Camilla stands in the doorway again.

"When was the last time you slept?" she asks me.

I scrub my hands over my face. "A while."

"You should get some rest."

"After you," I say. "I've only had one patient to deal with."

Camilla yawns. "Xavier is better as well." She tilts her head, eyeing me carefully. The question is there, *is he really fine without sleep?*

"Get some rest, Camilla," I say gently.

And so Myla's mother goes off for a well-needed nap. I stay by my girl's beside, holding her hand and cherishing the warmth that courses through her once more.

~

When I do rest, I decide to crash on Walker's floor. No need to get too far from my girl. When I awaken, it's to Walker's colorless face looming over mine. "What happened to your baculum?" he asks.

It's the classic way for Walker to start a conversation. No *hello* or *why are you asleep on my floor?*

I roll over and stretch. "I left it with Myla. She needs to practice her battle moves."

Walker steps back. "You left a weapon with Camilla? She can be a little uptight, you know. The woman may call in a bomb squad."

"I explained it all to her. She understands." I sit upright and check my watch. While I've been taking care of Myla, I've been in human clothes. Modern conveniences like watches are a perk. The downside is when *said watch* confirms I need to be on demon patrol in an hour. "I must get to Antrum."

"Really?" asks Walker.

"I've already asked for three extensions to stay by Myla's side. The royal physicians just confirmed she's recovering, and so I'm out of excuses. Aldred is also being a pain in the ass, so I need to focus again on my anti-Acca treaty."

Walks nods. "You want a portal?"

"Funny you should ask that. If my guess is right, Nightshade is outside. I can ride back to the old camp and use our temporary transfer station there. That said, I would like some portal help later when I'm on demon patrol."

"Who's on point?" asks Walker.

"Gurith." That's Mother's house.

"Let me guess. You want me to sneak you away so you can see Myla."

I wink. "It's like you're my best friend or something, the way you read my mind."

Walker grins. "Sure thing. I'll take you."

"Many thanks." I rise, feeling the creaks in my joints from sleeping on the floor.

Walker folds his hands into the loopy sleeves of his ghoul robes. "Are you going back to your cabin?"

"I am."

Walker smacks his lips. "I thought you'd gone back to Antrum."

"Everyone else has. I've been at Myla's place all this time." I give Walker the side eye. "What's up?"

"If you notice anyone has gone through your personal things, that would be me. I've been camping out at your place and working on your puzzle."

"So you're hiding from the ghouls, too."

"They know all my other addresses and want constant updates. My people aren't thrilled to be out of power. They're very needy."

"You can stay there anytime. Knock yourself out."

"Much appreciated."

The puzzle brings back a memory. "The Tithe."

"What about him?" asks Walker.

"I've forgotten all about the guy, what with all the drama from Armageddon. He sent minister Jali after me. I'm concerned he's still interested in Myla for some reason." I rub my neck, thinking. Nope, no new revelations come to mind. "You haven't gotten any new ideas on the subject, have you?"

"I'm afraid not. Although the puzzle is most distracting."

"Glad I can help entertain you."

And with thoughts of the Tithe still in my head, I leave Walker's place. As expected, Nightshade awaits me outside. She really is the best.

*A*n hour later, I stand outside the Eko supermarket in Helsingborg, Sweden. Light snow falls around. Humans stream in and out of a one-story structure.

Welcome to demon patrol.

Today, our fighting group consists of myself and three other lady warriors. The House of Gurith is one of the few that encourages women fighters. We're all in body armor, although we've activated charms so the humans don't see us.

Helga, the troop leader, is first to speak. "There's something in the herring section of the supermarket." She speaks Latin, the universal language of thrax. "We've never seen a demon like it before." Helga's a short powerhouse of a woman with heavy limbs, a square face, and a no-nonsense attitude. Her long blonde hair is braided down the back.

"Is it contained?" I ask.

"For now," replies Helga. "We placed charms around the creature. Humans who approach the area get confused and walk away. But you know how it is with charms. They only last so long. At some point, it will be suspicious that no one's buying fish."

"All right, plan Rho Sigma." That plan calls for reconnaissance before any attack.

Helga nods and turns to her squad. "Fall out."

Together, we all march into the grocery store. It looks like human markets everywhere. The big difference here is that the aisles are very slim, heavily packed, and all the writing is in Swedish. And, of course, there's an extended section here for all kinds of fish. Pickled. Salted. Imported. Roasted. You get the idea.

It's always strange to walk around while under an avoidance charm. Invisibility is one thing. You have to be careful not to push someone over or cause a disturbance. Avoidance is far easier. The humans don't even look you in the eye, they just … get out of your way. Within minutes, we reach the herring area.

There's no visible sign of a demon.

"What's the damage?" I ask.

"Two heart attacks in this aisle in the last week. Humans think it's a coincidence, but there's a demon around here somewhere."

I scan the aisle. "I can tell your problem right now."

Helga raises her brows. "Really?"

"Lobster tank. It's imported from the Northern Americas. That isn't water in the tank. You've got a full grown dissolus in there."

"Dissolus?"

"Sure. There's an infestation in North America. Make sure they don't start one here."

Dissolus turn acidic when attacked, but they don't use acid on their prey. Nope. An active dissolus can suck out a human's soul in three seconds. The mortals don't even know it happened. Heart attack is a common post mortem diagnosis.

Helga steps closer to the tank. "Well, I'll be. No bubbles in the water. That's a dissolus, all right."

"You know how to kill them?"

"Certainly," says Helga.

If another house said that, I'd worry. But Gurith are top notch. "In that case, do you mind if I leave early?"

"Officially?"

"Decidedly not."

"May I guess the reasons?" she asks. There's a knowing gleam in her eyes which makes me curious.

"Go on."

"You've a new girl you're watching over."

"True." I smile. "You said reasons, as in plural."

"Aldred is also threatening war."

I nod. "That as well. Would you be interested in joining an alliance against him?"

"Come find me after you see your woman. We'll discuss it. My people are well trained, but we don't have enough equipment."

I've seen the prep reports. Gurith is low on armor and swords. That's easy enough to fix. "May I ask why you're so open to the idea?"

"Aldred gives Octavia no end of trouble. She's one of our own. We've wanted the Earl of Acca dead or neutralized for ages. Patrol ends in four hours. Come back and talk before then?"

"I will."

"Good." Helga turns to her troop and starts planning their dissolus attack.

A low hum sounds behind me. *Ghoul portal.* A moment later, Walker steps into my line of vision. He seems positively comical here: a seven foot tall ghoul in long robes, standing the imported fish area of a Swedish grocery store. And he's invisible to the humans, thankfully.

"Your portal awaits," says Walker.

"I'd ask you how you knew when to arrive, but you always say—"

"A good ghoul never shares his secrets," finishes Walker.

"Yes, that."

Walker and I step into the ghoul portal. When we march out once more, I'm back in Myla's room. It's the middle of the night here in Purgatory. Myla shivers under her blankets.

That's simply not acceptable.

Once Walker leaves, I slip under the covers, pressing Myla's back to my chest. My girl stops shivering. A few blissful hours pass before Myla stirs. I can feel the moment she knows I'm here. Her entire body goes rigid. I whisper in her ear. "Hello, Myla."

She twists to face me. "Hi, Lincoln." She gives me a sleepy grin. "How did this awesomeness happen?"

"Walker brought me here from earth. I'm playing hooky from demon patrol."

"Mmm." She gets back into position, back to my chest, resting her head against my arm. "Walker brought you all the way here to cuddle?"

"No, this is my idea." I kiss the tip of her ear. "I decided it has therapeutic value."

"It does. Thanks for sneaking away."

"I can't stay long. The Earl of Acca's threatening war."

"That family is hell on toast." She turns back to face me once more. "Is he still pushing for you and Adair to get married?"

I nod. "But I'm recruiting more of the lesser Houses to the Alliance. I'll stop him, Myla." I exhale. "Actually, I'm supposed to be with the House of Gurith right now, convincing them to join up. I'm afraid I must leave in a few minutes."

A heavy pause hangs in the air. "I'll miss you, friend."

"This doesn't have to be goodbye. Walker told me your summit begins in a few weeks." This is the event where the new government of Purgatory will form. "If you're feeling up to it, perhaps you can visit Antrum before everything starts." I stroke her upper arm. "Maybe we visit the House of Striga, find a way to remove the igni." It's something Myla talked about back in the bunker.

Myla nibbles her lower lip. "Do you ever think about leaving Antrum?"

"Sure. I have my days." I give her a shy grin. "I have a fantasy that you and I go to Earth and find a tropical island."

Her eyes widen. "What do we do there?"

A blush colors my cheeks. "Fool around, fight demons." I run two fingers up her arm like they're a pair of legs. "Have little thrax."

Once the words leave my mouth, I wish I could take them back. I didn't mean to mention children. Myla may need time to adjust to the whole idea of a family.

Myla giggles, her eyes alight with joy. If the concept of a family worries her, she doesn't show it. I smile so hard, my face hurts.

"And how do we do stuff like make money or find food?" she asks.

"It's not that kind of thing. I put a lot more thought into what you're wearing and the demons we kill together." *Many hours, actually.*

"So, you *have* thought about leaving." Myla's smile fades. "Why don't you?"

"The same reason you're not interested getting rid of the igni anymore." I kiss the tip of her nose. "You aren't interested now, are you?"

Now, it's Myla's turn to blush. "No. Definitely not."

I lift my brows. The words are there yet unspoken. *Go on.*

"I've complained about life in Purgatory for ages. But the problem's bigger than being told how to dress or serve. The way the ghouls ran things, a lot of good souls were destroyed. Now that I'm the Scala, I think I can change things. I need to stay here and prepare for the summit."

My beautiful girl, lovely inside and out. "I understand. You can make a difference, so you have to try. Not everyone gets that chance." A weight of sorrow settles into my bones. "I know the feeling well." I press the sadness aside. There may be a time that we have to spend apart, but it won't last forever. I refocus on my girl. "As Scala, you'll have diplomatic duties to attend to, eventually."

She mock-frowns. "None that I know of."

"Perhaps you'll be surprised by an invitation to Arx Hall."

"I don't know, unexpected invitations haven't worked out for me."

Myla trembles. This is overwhelming for her. Going from normal-ish quasi girl to demigoddess. I set my knuckle beneath her chin, gently guiding her mouth toward mine. Our lips brush. With this kiss, I want to show her the truth of her life going forward.

It may be strange, but she'll never be alone.

Myla breaks the kiss. "But if the thrax High Prince asks me, I suppose I can't say no."

That's the spirit. "Come to me at Arx Hall."

"I really don't know when I'll–"

"Whenever you can. I'll be waiting." I lower my voice. "Say yes."

She sighs. "Yes."

"Good." Myla yawns. I forget how she's still recovering. I slide out of bed. "I'd better get going." I pause, waiting for Walker to open a ghoul portal. I don't know how Walker knows when to show up. He just always does.

Nothing happens.

Huh. Maybe Walker got caught up.

I step back to Myla's bedside. She's already fallen back asleep, so I kiss her forehead and then slip out of her room. Since everyone's asleep, I can steal out the front door.

Outside ,Nightshade is waiting for me. I step up and pat her neck. "For being Myla's horse, you're spending an awful lot of time with me."

She scrapes at the ground with her hoof, giving me a look that says. *Yeah, right.* I know what she means. Helping me now helps Myla. My horse is nothing if not loyal.

I hoist myself onto her back. "Let's return to camp, girl."

We take off at a gallop.

4 4

*a*s Night and I close in on camp, I slow my horse to a walk. At this point, there shouldn't be anyone running around the compound, but you never know. My horse's hooves make sloshing sounds in the mud as I navigate through the labyrinth of cabins. Some places are neatly closed up. Others have doors open, the cabin's interior showing as a mess of quickly piled belongings. Once Armageddon invaded, everyone had to evacuate through the temporary Pulpitum station. Clearly, some people handled the rush better than others.

I make a mental note to send servants back here to go through the cabins, inventory leftover items, and ensure they get to their rightful owners. My court wasn't pleased to be stuck in Purgatory. Leaving in a rush for Armageddon would only make things worse. The least we can do is ensure they get their things.

I turn down the so-called street which holds my old cabin.

Beyond the spindly trees, the horizon line starts to lighten. Between nightfall and morning, there's a certain kind of magic in the air. That power attracts some demon breeds to cause trouble. Shape shifters, mostly. And although there haven't been many demons by our compound, that was mostly because the place was overrun with thrax. Now that my people have left, I'd expect more demons to poke about.

All of which is why I'm not surprised when I see a wispy shape before my cabin. Could be a shape shifter. Muto demon. False vision from a hedge witch. As Night walks me closer, my blood freezes. The shape is none of those things.

It's Myla.

And she's a ghost.

Terror rattles through my nervous system. I slide off Night and race over to the spectral version of Myla. My girl hunches over in pain.

"Lincoln," she moans.

I kneel before her, tilting my head to catch her line of vision. "I'm here."

"Some thrax asshole in a toga showed up. He wants me to serve him for eternity." She hisses in a breath. "I told him to fuck off."

I recall what happened with Devak, Silvinio and Jali. "This happened to some of my ministers. They were approached by the Tithe, too."

She hisses in a pained breath. "What does he want with me?"

"You have angelic blood; he's obsessed with angels. Beyond that, I don't know."

She hunches over into a crouch. "It hurts."

"That happened to Jali. It's because you're not accepting the change. Keep fighting. If you stop and give in, he'll turn you into an effigy."

She looks up at me through her mass of hair. "A what?"

"A stone solider that will serve him forever. That won't happen, though. I'm coming for you."

"Then we'll kill that dickhead."

"Yes, we will. I promise."

"Good." Myla falls over and moans. A moment later, her ghostly self vanishes. I race over to Night, ready to hoist myself back on her saddle and return to Myla's house. Her body is still alive, even if her ghost has been separated. At least, that's what happened with Jali, Devak and Silvinio. I must get her physical self to safety. I set my foot in the stirrup, ready to mount Night and take off. That's when I hear it.

A low moan.

And it's coming from my cabin.

All the hair on my neck stands on end. I'd know that particular voice anywhere.

It can't be.

Once again, I set both feet on solid ground. My hurt thuds against my rib cage. I rush over to my cabin and throw open the door.

Walker lies on the floor. The back of his head is a mass of blood.

I race inside. "Walker!"

He opens his eyes a slit. "Working on map … statues attacked from behind … thought I was you."

I help my friend onto the bed. The blood has already dried up and his wound have started healing. Still, there could be internal damage. "Can you recover alone? They got Myla."

Walker gives me the barest of nods. "If it doesn't get better … Group Think."

No question what Walker means here. If he doesn't self-heal fast enough, Walker can contact other ghouls through his Group Think and get help. But what can Myla do? She has only me to fight for her.

"I hate to leave you," I whisper.

"No, I loathe to see you go alone. I'll find you when I can. Trust me."

A chill of realization prickles over my skin. *The Map. Heaven.* "Walker, did you figure out where the Tower of Wonders is in relation to Heaven?"

Walker tries to speak but hisses in a pained breath instead. At last, he nods.

The time has come to multitask. While I chat with Walker, I change into fresh body armor and pack in every charm I have laying around. The ones I have are the equivalent of strange thing you find under a couch cushion.

Extra speed. That one's not too bad.

Minor glamour. It's pretty weak, but

Weather. Powerful, but I have no idea how to use it. Which is why it's sat in my drawer for months.

Oh, well. No time to go back to Antrum for supplies. While I set the charms into my pockets, I address Walker once more. "Don't speak if you don't need to. Just tell me one thing. Is the Tower of Wonders directly *under* Heaven's Citadel?"

Walker fixes me with his all-black gaze. "How did you guess?"

"The Tithe said something about revenge, hates the Citadel, and is obsessed with warriors. Xavier and Aquila founded the Citadel. Revenge must mean going after Myla."

Walker thunks his head against his pillow. "Oh, no. I'll come as soon as I can."

"Just be safe."

After racing out the door, I mount Nightshade and take off for Myla's house at a gallop. All this time, I thought the Tithe was somehow focused on Aquila. It's Xavier he wants. Something happened between Myla's father and the Tithe. I simply must understand what that is.

It's time for a serious talk with Xavier.

*T*he thrax camp fades into the distance as Nightshade gallops away at a supernatural pace. Even so, it feels as if we inch along the path to Myla's house. At last, we arrive. I slip off Night's barrel and race to the front door.

Camilla opens it before I have a chance to knock. "What's wrong?"

"How is she?" *No question who I'm referring to here. Myla.*

"Asleep. She's fine." Camilla scrunches up her nose. "Are you all right?"

"May I see her?"

"Sure." Camilla steps back, allowing me room to enter. I speed into the house and tear open Myla's door. My girl lays motionless on the bed, her chest rising and falling in a steady rhythm. Camilla steps up behind me.

"See? She's perfectly well." A moan sounds from the master bedroom. "Oh, that's Xavier. I'll be right back." Camilla steps away. My head turns foggy with worry. Moving forward, I take Myla's hand. It's chilly to the touch once more. *So cold.* I kneel beside her.

"Myla," I whisper. "Wake up."

Please, let her be all right. People under stress get visions all the time. Perhaps that's what happened to me.

Myla doesn't flinch. I lean in and kiss her eyelids. "My love. Wake up."

Nothing.

My skin prickles. Every hunter's instinct in my body tells me that someone's in the room, watching. I remember what happened with the Minister of Horus. When I grasped Jali's hand in my cabin, I could see the Tithe. Will the same thing happen now? I keep my hold on Myla's hand.

Little by little, I turn my head.

He's there.

The Tithe.

He appears as he did before. A grizzled old man in a threadbare toga. Dust covers him from head to toe. The loose leather satchel hangs over his left shoulder. His right arm is now made of stone. Which makes sense. He lost his left in our battle at the Pulpitum. Little by little, the Tithe's wide mouth cinches into a frown. "How are you still alive? My effigies killed you."

Keeping Myla's cold palm gripped in my own, I rise to face him. "I'm not easy to destroy."

"Doubtful." The Tithe sniffs. "I know your kind. Study at the Citadel but know nothing of power."

"Listen to me carefully." My voice deepens with rage. "Release Myla from your spell or it won't be your arm you lose this time. It will be your life."

"You? A little thrax princeling?" asks the Tithe. "That was luck, when you took off my arm."

"It wasn't a matter of chance. I've skills you can't imagine. Myla does as well. You've no idea what we're capable of. Set her free this moment or we will hunt you down."

"You two can try." The Tithe reaches into his satchel and pulls out a mallet. With the chisel still set in the satchel, the Tithe lifts the mallet. With a slight motions, the Tithe then taps the chisel's blunt end with his enchanted mallet. A swirl of white dust erupts from the spot. He's casting a spell. A vortex of white powder and brightness whips across the bedroom, enveloping Myla.

"No!" I cry. Somewhere in the back of my mind, I'm aware that Camilla has rushed into the chamber. She now stands beside me.

"What in the after-realms is happening?" she cries.

The swirl of magical dust glows more brightly, then it vanishes, taking the Tithe along with it.

I exhale. *Good riddance.*

All of a sudden, another burst of magic and power surrounds Myla. Then her body vanishes as well. I want to howl with pain, but I'm well aware that Myla's mother is still here. Now is not the time to mourn. I must fight.

I round on Camilla. "Remember our conversation the morning before Armageddon's invasion?"

Camilla sets her fingertips against her lips. "The Tithe."

"That's the one. He's taken Myla."

"Can you save my baby?" Camilla's voice cracks with worry.

"I can, but I must speak with Xavier first."

"Don't tell him Myla is gone. That will kill him."

I nod. "I can get the information I need without worrying him."

"Thank you." Camilla speeds from Myla's room to pause outside Xavier's door. She knocks gently. "Xav? Someone here to see you." Low mumbles sound from within. Camilla looks to me. "He doesn't say much yet."

"I understand."

Camilla pushes open the door. I step inside. Myla's father lays on the bed. He's a skeletal figure under the thin coverlet. His cocoa-colored skin hangs loose from his bones. Bruises cover his face and neck. Camilla rushes to his side. "Xav, this is Prince Lincoln. He has some questions for you."

Xavier opens his eyes a slit. "Linc …. Lincoln." His voice sounds rusty, as if he hasn't used it in many years. I think back to what I discovered the day Myla fought Armageddon. Xavier has spent decades being tortured. The poor man probably only spoke to scream.

Pulling up a chair, I sit beside him. "Do you remember the Tithe?"

Xavier closes his eyes and for a moment, I think he may be falling back asleep. Eventually, he opens them again. "Yes."

"This is very important," I say. "Does the Tithe have a reason to hate you?"

Xavier laughs, but the sound comes out as more of a cough than anything else. Camilla rushes him a sip of water and settles him back onto his pillow.

"The Tithe … yes, he loathes me," answers Xavier at last.

I lean forward, gripping the wooden arms of my chair. "Why?"

"Aquila gave him power." Xavier's voice is a low croak. "Started off fine. Made effigies of dancers, law makers, that kind of thing." Xavier smacks his thin lips. His eyes flutter shut.

Camilla squeezes his hand. "Then what happened, Xav?" I must admit, she does a good job of hiding her fear. You wouldn't know the woman saw her own daughter just get abducted.

"The Tithe wanted to create an army," continues Xavier. "Warrior effigies. No more angel fighters. He sought to replace the Citadel. So I limited his powers. Only five effigies each year." Xavier chuckles, but the sound comes out as another cough. "That slowed him down."

"Effigies don't die," I state. "What happens to them, do you know?"

"As long as the Tithe's alive, then they live as well." Xavier yawns. "But if the Tithe dies, they can move on. Souls … Purgatory …" He looks to Camilla and grins. "The Great Scala."

Xavier and Camilla share a sweet smile. I know they're thinking about how their daughter is now the Great Scala and can send the effigy souls to their after-life. Still, I need more information in order to keep said daughter alive.

"Word is," I continue. "The Tithe can't be killed by anyone living. Is that true?"

Xavier nods. "Another gift from Aquila," he says in a low rumble. "She gets carried away. But now the Tithe helps thrax, isn't that right?"

"Yes," I reply. Somehow, I'm able to answer without screaming. "He chooses thrax and makes their dreams come true."

"That's good." Xavier leans back into his pillow. "One day … must make a list of all my haters." His voice fades to a whisper. "When you're alive from the dawn of time…" His words trail off. Even so, I know what he means. I've only been a leader for less than two decades, and I already have a long list of people who want revenge. I can't imagine being alive since the dawn of time.

Camilla lifts her voice. "Xav?" The archangel's chest rises and falls in a slow rhythm. Camilla turns to me. "He's out." She releases his hand and sets it on his chest. After that, she steps out the bedroom door. I follow, my mind whirring through everything I just learned.

Once the door is closed behind us, Camilla focuses on me. "This Tithe," she begins. "Did he make Myla into an effigy?"

"He's trying. She's not an effigy yet."

Camilla clasps her hands by her throat. "So my baby's still alive."

"Yes, but I need to get to her before the Tithe finishes his work."

Camilla's mouth quivers. "How long?"

I look around the room, my mind making calculations. "The Tithe took one of my ministers, Jali. That thrax fought the process for a few hours. Myla is tough. She can last at least that long."

Camilla inhales a shaky breath. "But Myla's not at her strongest right now. I wouldn't count on her having much time at all. You must hurry." Reaching forward, she grips my shoulders. "Bring my baby home to me."

When I speak, I force all my will into the words. "You can count on it." Stepping backward, I bow to Camilla. "I'll be off."

"Where are you going?"

"To visit the mermaids."

Camilla slowly nods. I take that as the most approval I'll get for this plan. Turning, I head out the front door. Nightshade awaits; I hoist myself onto her saddle. As Night and I gallop of to the temporary transfer Pulpitum, I think through everything that's happened since I met Myla.

At first, I felt it was my duty to leave Myla alone. Then I gave in and trusted my love for her. Now I simply can't lose her. Even when she fought Armageddon, I never lost faith in Myla's abilities. But now, an enemy is targeting her when she's already ill.

I have fought my emotions.

Feared them.

Embraced them.

Now I'll burn down the after-realms before I'll allow someone to hurt my queen.

46

*N*ightshade's hooves pound across the marshy hills and through the sickly forest. Within minutes, I stand outside the round tent that marks the temporary Pulpitum station. We'd planned to keep it open for a few weeks after evacuation, just in case.

I never thought I'd need it for a rescue mission.

Sliding off Nightshade, I call around. "Walker? Convincing Transfer Central to hide my platform journey won't be easy. If you're going to show up, now would be a great time."

Nothing.

Ah, well. Worth a try. I rush inside the tent.

"Activating temporary station. Lincoln Vidar Osric Aquilus." From the top center of the tent, a grid of white laser beams crisscross the space, scanning me.

Once again, Cassandra's voice echoes through the space. "Identity confirmed. You aren't scheduled for transfer today, my prince." Beyond Cassandra, there's the sound of other operators in Transfer Central.

"Can we switch to private comm?" I ask.

"Yes." Clicking sounds echo through the chamber. When Cassandra speaks again, I hear her voice alone. No background noise. Whatever we say now, it will be private. "What do you require?" she asks.

"I need transfer to Earth, New York Harbor Station."

"That's not on the schedule. I'll need to do an emergency alert."

I pinch the bridge of my nose. "And those alerts go to my parents and Aldred, correct?"

"I'm afraid so."

I shake my head. We thrax are diligent about security. Any passage in or out of Antrum must be scheduled. All emergency transfers get an instant alert. It's the equivalent of a big red siren going off in the palace. If my parents discover I'm making a rush transfer, they'll panic. In seconds, I'll have half the Rixa army and all the nobility racing to New York Harbor. Even worse, Aldred will insist on joining them as well. I can't rescue Myla if I'm dealing with that amount of nonsense.

"Can you transfer me now and wait two hours to send the alert?" I ask. "This between Purgatory and Earth. Antrum isn't involved. It's not a security risk."

There's a long pause while Cassandra thinks things over. "But you're our prince. Your safety is paramount."

"All I'm asking for is two hours. System glitches stall out alerts all the time." I shift my weight from foot to foot. All this waiting is making me nuts. "This is important."

Moments pass. My fingers curls into fists. First Walker can't help by creating portals. Now Cassandra's getting cold feet about a simple two-hour alert delay. Meanwhile, Myla's very soul is at risk. I travel the after-realms constantly. There's never this level of hassle. Why today of all days?

Finally, Cassandra speaks. "Two hours." Another click sounds; the background noise returns. "Confirmed and ready at your signal."

I exhale. "Launch transfer on my mark. 3, 2, 1."

Beneath my feet, the transfer platform hurtles into the ground. I stream past magma and stone. At some point, we also pass the magical barrier between realms, but my platform moves too quickly for it to register to the naked eye. Soon the metal disc slams to a halt inside a metal shipping container. A lone light bulb hangs from a single cord above me. I push open the rusty door and step out onto a misty New York night. Haze obscures the city. Odd lights blink in the mist.

It's a welcome sight.

I race to the end of the Pier 34 and cast the required charms to hide all trace of myself and the mermaids. Then I step down the side ladder to the harbor, swish my hand in the chilly water, and wait.

Thankfully, the pause isn't a long one.

Soon Cordelia and Dwyn surface nearby. "Are you here about the dissolus?" asks Cordelia.

I blink hard, remembering. That's right. There's an infestation here. "Not tonight."

Cordelia tosses her seaweed hair. "The thrax warriors said it would be fixed and soon," she complains. "The dissolus are frightening our flocks."

"This is Acca patrol territory. They'll return within twenty four hours and fight the dissolus. I swear it." In my mind's eye, I picture punching Aldred in the face. The earl promised he'd fix this. Many times. And yet it's still an issue. "Right now, I need you to take me to the Tower of Wonders."

"To kill the Tithe?" ask Dwyn and Cordelia together. The hopeful look on their scaled faces makes one thing clear. When it comes to this pair, killing the Tithe might be rather motivating.

"Absolutely," I state.

"We're in," says Cordelia. "And you don't even have to kiss us."

"No kisses," confirms Dwyn. "I'll get a boat."

"Please hurry," I entreat.

There's barely a sound as Dwyn disappears under the water. Nervous energy rattles through me. I need to do something and focus. I turn to Cordelia.

"Why so much hatred for the Tithe?" I ask.

Cordelia bares her pointed teeth. "When it comes to scaring our flocks, he's worse than the dissolus. Effigy warriors tramping around all day and night. Most of the Tower of Wonders is underwater, you know. That's a lot of noise for fishy ears."

"I can imagine."

A small rowboat streams across the harbor, stopping beside the pier. Dwyn surfaces beside it. "Your ride."

There's no mistaking the boat's name. Municipal Dinghy #716 is written in faded paint on the bow. Oh, well. At this point, there's no time to procure a boat that isn't stolen. I climb into the small vessel.

The moment I'm seated, the hull shimmies as thousands of fish swim beneath it, pressing the boat forward. I release more charms to hide our supernatural progress through the harbor. Within minutes, we're speeding out to sea. Most of the ocean is choppy, with whitecaps and mounting waves. However, the area around my little boat always stays calm as glass. That's Cordelia's doing.

Wind howls in my ears as we rush toward the spot that will resemble an oil rig, but will really be the Tower of Wonders. I've stared at maps of this spot for so long, I can easily calculate how much time it will take to reach the tower. Ten minutes.

Five minutes.

One.

Suddenly, the mist parts. An oil platform looms above us. It's a mountain of a structure, with four hefty pillars, a wide base platform, and rusted machinery climbing into the night sky. The glamour on it is old, though, and it doesn't take much concentration to see beyond the magical illusion.

I focus and it soon appears.

There's a white tower, round and multi-leveled, with tiny slotted windows. When Cordelia first showed me the Tower of Wonders, it was a model made from dark harbor water. Now, seeing it in real life, it's obviously made from white stone and built to copy Heaven's Citadel. But while the heavenly school is all arched windows and twirling spires, this structure is squat and dull. Xavier's words come back to me.

The Tithe sought to replace the Citadel.

Well, the Tithe didn't do the best job, at least from the design side. Another revelation appears. *The countdown.* If the Tithe wanted to replace the Citadel, then the countdown is part of that. He needs a certain number of souls to accomplish his goals. But what for what purpose? Does he want enough warriors to fight off the angelic force protecting the Citadel? Or is there another plan in place? There are still too many puzzle pieces that don't fit. The Tower of Wonders ... the Echo Vortex ... the Citadel ... and Myla.

I stiffen my spine. At one time, I wanted to wait until I understood the Tithe's plans. I wouldn't march into an enemy stronghold solo.

Then the Tithe took Myla.

Now, it doesn't really matter what the Tithe's full scheme may be. I'm getting my girl.

I turn to Cordelia. "Where's the main entrance?"

"On the sea floor," she replies.

I rub my chin, thinking through my remaining charms and the best ways to take down stone warriors. Another idea appears. I refocus on Cordelia. "Can you clear out some of the floor for me? I can take down the Tithe's warriors, but I need to approach on foot."

Cordelia flares her nose holes. "That won't be easy."

I tilt my head and give her a winning grin. "But you want the Tithe dead."

"Dead, dead," echoes Dwyn.

The mermaids share a long look, then raise their arms high. All around the Tower of Wonders, water begins to swirl. A great vortex forms, pulling the ocean down lower and lower. Cordelia and Dwyn both grit their teeth. Their gills flex with heavy breathing. The water continues to drop until the ocean floor is exposed, revealing a swath of seaweed and rock. It's a four story fall to the bottom.

"You better hurry," says Cordelia. "I don't know how long we can hold back the ocean."

"Focus, focus," echoes Dwyn. Keeping a spell going is never her strong suit.

Nodding, I dive off the boat's side and swim toward the sea floor. To my right, there's the magical mermaid barrier; it's like a sheet of undulating glass that keeps the ocean in place. Once I'm closer to the bottom, I swim through that barrier, tumble through the air, and fall toward the soggy ground.

Looking down, I realize that this move could kill me.

A major dissolus nest sits directly on my landing spot. To human eyes, it would appear to be nothing more than a large boulder. But my angelic vision can see through the disguise. It's actually thousands of dissolus eggs piled high, each one the size of a sesame seed. That's a ton of demons hiding, right there. If I disturb them, they'll expand to full size. I'll be encased in acid.

Turning, I jam my left arm into the clear wall of water beside me. The motion pulls my fall to one side. It's barely enough to land me just outside the dissolus nest. Soggy ground sloshes as I hit the ocean floor. High above, a light mist pours over the edge of the water and into the pit below.

Now, there's nothing left to do but wait. Tough though it may be, it's the only way for my plan to work. So I stand by the water wall. To pass the time, I flip charms through my fingers. The ones I grabbed are made to look like quarters. Yet as with all things Striga, if you look closely enough there are runes and writing. Magic.

About twenty yards away, there sits the base of the Tower of Wonders. A large and open archway marks the entrance. The white stone exterior is pockmarked with barnacles. Bits of seaweed cling to its surface.

Come on, Tithe. Take the bait.

Sure enough, white stone bodies march out under the archway and cross the exposed ocean floor. The Tithe leads at the head of his army. I count at least five thousand warriors. I scan the faces, looking for Jali, Devak or Silvinio. None of the effigies look familiar. The stone warriors settle into neat rows that fan out from the tower's base. The Tithe walks out before them all, pausing right before me. He's changed into white Roman armor of the occasion. He's even replaced his missing arm with a stone one.

"Greetings, my little princeling," says the Tithe. "I've good news for you. I've added new spells onto my effigies. You can't strike them with metal or weaken them with fire. All my careful scouting of your skills has paid off. This is now an unbeatable army. With these soldiers, I shall invade Heaven itself and replace the Citadel with my own greatness."

"Listen to me carefully," I announce. "Bring me Myla, whole and alive, or you will die. Painfully."

The Tithe grins, showing off a mouth of blackened teeth. "Attack him, everyone!"

I match his smile with one of my own. Tossing my Striga coins onto the sea floor, I call out three words. "Consume the effigies."

And so it begins.

*a*s a rule, I've a mind for details. Names. Faces. Statistics. All are accessible to me. Then come moments like this one, where my mind records even more information. Every last scintilla of this time becomes seared into my memory: The rows of white stone soldiers fanning out from the tower like petals on a daisy ... The overcast night sky ... Thin tendrils of mist curling down the edges of the water wall ... And the Tithe, a dusty figure with a scraggy face and mismatched eyes, who leers at me triumphantly, all while a handful of purple coins tumble to the muddy ground.

The charms hit the ocean floor and everything changes.

Long arms of ice spread out from the impact point. Lines of prickly icicles jut up from the trails they make, reminding me of so many silver blades slicing up from the earth. The spell expands, encasing every effigy in a sheath of ice. They're all captured in some state of attack as they race toward one spot.

Me.

Even the Tithe is trapped inside a shell of frozen water. Up close, I can see the smattering of salt atop of the slick surface. Nothing stops ice.

Across the ocean floor, one figure moves. A spirit. My blood thumps harder in my veins.

"Myla!"

I race through the forest of icy figures, closing in on my girl. She's hunched over in pain. Still a ghost, alive and fighting. My Myla.

"I'm here," I say. "Where are you?"

"I see you," says Myla. "You're in my cell. But you keep walking away." Tears stream down her face. "Why would you do that?"

"It's an illusion. Describe where you are."

"Dark room. Walls with writing. Coned roof. Small barred windows."

I scan the Tower of Wonders. There's one spot that meets that description perfectly. "He's got you in the peak of the tower. I'm coming. Do you hear me? What you saw; that's not me. I'm on my way."

Myla's teeth chatter as she curls forward. "Lincoln!"

My girl disappears.

Behind me, the statues start moving. I'd warn them to stop. As it is, they'll only kill themselves faster if they try to race after me. But they won't listen. And at this point? I'd like to see them all destroyed. It buys me time to get Myla.

I rush into the tower. Inside, it's a wide open interior, like a tall empty column reaching up to the sky above me. A corkscrew walkway lines the entire space. Basically, it's long curling ramp with no railing which encircles the interior like a ribbon. Everywhere I look, the stone walls hold murals of more warriors. Their all-white eyes seem to peer out at me.

Assessing.

Scheming.

Hungry.

I pull another charm from my pocket. My last one. It's a candy heart for speed. I bite down on the treat. Power pulses through my limbs. Fresh energy charges through every muscle in my body. I race up the winding walkway with one thought in mind.

Myla's at the stop of this place.

Below me, the frozen effigies lurch into the tower. The coin charm will keep them in solid ice. But the more they move, the more the water surrounding them fights back. And living in a stone world, I've learned a few things over the years.

Every stone has its imperfections.

Water finds each crevice.

And frozen water? It expands over time.

With every move the effigies make, the deeper the water goes, and the more ice spreads throughout their stone bodies. Soon it will happen.

Cold.

Expansion.

Explosion.

It's only a matter of time.

As I race upwards, the effigies follow along. Even with my speed spell and their icy casings, they quickly close in on me. Glancing over my shoulder, I see them. Tall all-white figures dripping with frost and icicles, racing for me. Nearer.

I must reach the top.

The door to Myla's cell is only yards away when a chilly hand grips my shoulder. More latch onto my ankles, pulling me down. I land on my back with a thud. A massive effigy looms above me. In life, this thrax stood seven feet tall and seems almost as wide, what with his heavy armor and wide shoulders. Icicles stick out of him from at every angle, the ends glinting and sharp.

I writhe under the grip of my attackers. At least five effigies hold me down while a sixth gets ready to slice me in two. Just as the Tithe said, their faces are now carved with spells to protect them from fire and metal. I can't use my old schemes against them any more.

This can't be how I end. So close to Myla and unable to save her. *No, no, no.*

The mountainous effigy raises his sword high, ready to attack. I glare at him straight on.

If this is how I die, I'll do so with my eyes open.

Then I hear it.

The telltale pops of stone cracking. The man-mountain effigy above me pauses, then brings his sword down toward my neck. The blow never connects. Instead, the effigy's body shatters into countless pieces. The other warriors who held me down all suffer the same fate. Their bodies burst apart. Below me, thousands of warriors crumble and are no more. The chips of their stone forms cascade from the spiral walkway, tumbling into the center of the tower's floor. I exhale.

That was close.

I hop to stand, kicking the extra stone bits from my path. The thought hits me that, although I almost lost my life, it's still been rather easy to reach Myla. After all, the warlock wields considerable magic. Is this all he can throw at me?

Shaking my head, I set such thoughts aside and focus on the heavy wooden door at the top of the winding walkway. A thick metal slider locks everything in place. Pulling out my baculum, I ignite them into a long sword and slice through the steel bar like paper. Leaning on my back foot, I kick the wooden slats into fragments.

The door is open.

It's time to get my girl.

I rush into the chamber. It's a small stone room with a conical roof, just as the ghostly version of Myla described. Tiny barred windows cast thin beams on moonlight across the scene. The walls are lined with scribblings in chalk. Myla lays huddled on the floor, shivering. I scoop her body into my arms. Every inch of her feels chilled through. Pressing her against my chest, I turn for the door.

The spirit version of Myla blocks my exit. Like the physical Myla, the ghostly version is barefoot and in sweats. "If you take us from this room," she says. "We'll die. Which for the record, I'd rather have happen than turn into an immortal Barbie doll made of rock."

"How? Why?" Then I see it. The writing is literally on the wall. I've seen those kind of markings before. They're on every charm that Striga creates. The patterns are meant to look random, but if you know what to search for, the meaning of the spell is clear.

Still holding Myla in my arms, I step around the room, scanning the marks on the walls. While at first glance, they seemed to be made from chalk, the writing is actually carved into the rock itself. Most likely, the Tithe used his enchanted mallet and chisel.

"The spell says you can't leave," I read. "Unless you're one."

"One what?" asks Ghost-Myla.

"You must become one person again, both spirit and body."

"Let me guess." Ghost-Myla points to a specific spot on the wall. "Those numbers? They're a clock that says we've got four minutes left to bring me back together, or I become an effigy forever. "

I scan the runes. Sure enough, there's a bit written in Latin. And it's changing. Counting down. "How did you know?"

"Lucky guess," says Ghost-Myla. "I could read the countdown part because it's in Latin numerals, but the rest? That's just how my life sucks. If nothing else, my existence is consistent." She's smiling, my there's no missing the pain in her eyes. My girl is hurting.

"No," I lean over, pressing my cheek against physical-Myla's forehead. "There must be something." My eyes widen. "What about your powers? Can you summon igni?"

"Sha. I've been sitting here alone for-fucking-ever. Summoning my igni was the first thing I did. No go. Turns out, they're unreliable little lightning bolt shaped bastards."

"Did you try summoning them from other places?"

"Sure, ghost-me can move around. I float-walked to a ton of different places. Still didn't work." She hisses as she leans over. "That's an owie. Damn."

Still holding the physical Myla, I scan the walls again. *There must be something I'm missing.* My muscles tighten with nervous energy. I scan the numeral-clock on the wall.

Three minutes.

"Let me try my igni again." The ghostly Myla closes her eyes and raises her hand. It's a movement I've seen a number of times. I press the physical Myla more closely against me. Her slow heartbeat thumps against my chest.

Please, let this work.

No igni appear.

"Ugh," groans Ghost-Myla. "They really are supernatural prima donnas."

A rhythmic sound fills the air. Clapping. It's the Tithe. He steps into the room, passing directly through the ghostly Myla in the process. She shivers.

"Eew, eew, eew," sneers Ghost-Myla. "There's a thing called deodorant, buddy."

Even though we're trapped in a cell with an arguably evil thrax … and possibly about to die … and *definitely* about to get into trouble … I can't stop my smile.

Everything is better with Myla nearby. Even this.

The Tithe limps toward me. His right leg is a solid log of ice. His false arm popped off thanks to the ice spell, so there's that. Light patches of frost cover his skin. I make a mental note to thank Lucas for his excellent freezing charms. That is, if we survive this encounter.

"How lovely to have lured you both here," says the Tithe. "You did notice that was my plan, I hope?"

"I noticed you're a dick," says Ghost-Myla.

I nod. "What she said."

The Tithe focuses on me. "All the effigies I sent after the you, my little princeling. Yes, I wanted to see if you'd disavow the demon girl."

"I have a name," snaps Ghost-Myla.

The Tithe glares at her. "We'll get to that in a moment." He returns his focus on me. "But what I really wanted to see was how a Citadel-trained warrior stood up against my effigies. And I'm happy to report that—despite a few stone-related specialty attacks that you came up with—my warriors are invincible."

Myla raises her hand. "Not sure if you saw, but my man popped all your warriors with ice. And your arm is gone, too. So not sure where you're getting the invincible stuff from."

The Tithe rounds on her. "Because when I reform my army again, they'll have new runes that protect from ice. You two ..." The Tithe gestures to me and Myla with his remaining arm. "You're creating my perfect army."

Myla bites back a pained moan. "I hate this. And you." She glances at the wall clock. So do I.

Two minutes.

"This is all your father's fault," snarls the Tithe. "Xavier should have seen my greatness. He should have allowed me to run the Citadel!"

"*That's* what this is about?" asks Ghost-Myla. "The Citadel? And you have some thousand-year-old grudge against my dad?" She looks to me. "Really?"

I shrug. "Afraid so. I'm pretty sure he wants to break into Heaven, empty out the Citadel, and replace it with his creations."

The Tithe points at me with his good hand. "You said it perfectly. You see, the archangel Aquila gave me the power to create effigies. My magic forms unstoppable warriors. Xavier had no business limiting my greatness. Only five effigies a year? Bah! It slowed my plans to a crawl, and yet I persevered. With you, Myla, I will have enough souls to power my plan." The Tithe steps closer to Ghost-Myla. "Which means you're going to suffer as my slave."

"Fuuuuuuuuck." Ghost-Myla grits her teeth. "I just got done being slave to the ghouls. Not doing it again. Especially not for some thrax hobo who hasn't washed in a generation."

The Tithe gasps. "How dare you speak in such a way to me?"

Ghost-Myla shrugs. "It's what I do. The fact that it bothers you? Well, that just makes life worthwhile." She blinks her eyes in pretend fascination. "Tell me again how awesome you are, despite the fact that all your effigies are now a pile of rock chips."

"Impertinence!" cries the Tithe. "My effigies may be down, but that is nothing to me. I can merely reform them all again. And when I reshape them next time, I will create into the perfect beings to ruin the Citadel." The Tithe pats his leather satchel for emphasis. "I am the only one with the power to do so."

"How fascinating." Myla winces in pain. "You suck."

My gaze locks on the numeral clock.

One minute remains.

While Ghost-Myla keeps the Tithe distracted, I keep scanning the walls, looking for any hint of how to get Myla's body and soul back together. The symbols for *magic* and *tools* keep appearing. I glance at the leather satchel the Tithe carries on his shoulder.

The enchanted mallet and chisel. Perfect.

Kneeling down, I rest the physical Myla against the floor. It hurts my heart to set her down, but I must get my hands on that mallet and chisel. Ghost-Myla gives me a sideways glance. The question is there if unasked, *what are you doing?*

I fix Ghost-Myla with a steady gaze while I speak to the Tithe. "I can read these runes, you know. They tell me exactly how to destroy your effigy army."

"They do not." Yet the way the Tithe says these three words, it's more of a question than a statement.

"Look for yourself if you don't believe me." I gesture to a far wall.

The Tithe takes the bait. Turning his back to me and the Mylas, the Tithe strides over for a closer look. With Myla's physical body on the ground, I make eye contact with the ghostly version. My pulse pounds so hard, I feel the whoosh of blood in my ears.

This simply must work. Only seconds remain.

Once I have Ghost-Myla's attention, I set my hands above the Myla's physical body. I mime holding a chisel in one hand, and a mallet in the other, the way I've seen the Tithe do before. With a swoop of my arm, I pretend to strike the mallet and chisel into Myla's physical shoulder.

Ghost-Myla nods. She points to the Tithe while mouthing the word, *distract?*

I nod. *Yes.*

Ghost-Myla hisses in a pained breath and saunters over to the Tithe. "Hey, douchebag."

I pat my pockets. There are no charms left. I must rely on my hunter's skills. With silent steps, I steal up behind the Tithe, who's still staring at the rune-covered walls. Once I'm directly behind him, I reach into his satchel. The Tithe pauses.

Does he sense I'm behind him?

Ghost-Myla pops up in front of the Tithe. "I can read these, too." She points to a section of wall. "This part here says you have a totally limp dick."

That's an attention grabber. "What?" howls the Tithe.

The warlock is so enraged, he doesn't feel me pull the mallet and chisel from his satchel. Ghost-Myla goes on to list the ways his manhood is probably diseased, and I use the opportunity to race over to the physical version of Myla on the floor. Leaning over her body, I set the chisel against her shoulder and pound it with the mallet, just as I'd seen the Tithe do before.

Nothing happens.

Is it too late?

A chill of despair settles into my heart. I fought her, found her, loved her. And now, I really will lose her. I look over to ghost-Myla. She stops speaking.

This is it. The moment she becomes an immortal slave to the Tithe.

All of a sudden, a burst of light flares out from Myla's physical body. Tiny particles swirl through the air. Ghost-Myla's form exudes white brightness as well.

"Hells, yeah!" cries Ghost-Myla.

Bands of white light whip across the room, creating cords between the spirit and physical Mylas. A deep roll of thunder sounds as the two halves of my woman get drawn back together again. Another burst of light and energy erupts. Then all is silent. After so much light, the shadows feel like utter darkness.

I blink hard, forcing my eyes to adjust to the light.

There she is, standing before me. My Myla, body and soul together once more.

She grins. "Hey."

"Hey," I reply.

Myla turns to the Tithe. "Guess what? Buh-bye, revenge."

"This ends nothing!" yells the Tithe. "You think you've seen the full scope of my power? The Tower of Wonders isn't just home to effigies. It *is* effigies."

Around us, the walls transform. The etchings and runes disappear. Murals of more warriors appear in their place.

After that, the fighters in the walls step out. No longer are they raised images on stone panels. Now, thirty stone warriors surround me and Myla. Plus, new runes and markings have been craved into their faces. This time, the spells include protection from ice. I have to hand it to the Tithe. He works quickly. I grip the mallet and chisel more tightly. These are our best and last weapons.

The Tithe rounds on Myla. "My plan was for you to be the last effigy. But now? It seems that joy will fall to me."

A chill crawls up my limbs. All along, I've had a sneaking suspicion that the Tithe has far more to his master plan than I could ever guess.

And now? That same suspicion tells me that his full scheme is about to be revealed.

49

*T*he Tithe snaps his fingers. The enchanted mallet and chisel fly out of my palms and return to the Tithe's satchel. With a howl of pain, the Tithe then jams the sharp end of the chisel into his chest, right at his own heat. Not what I expected, that. He grasps the mallet next, and drives the chisel deeper into his flesh. A burst of magical light erupts from his body. The Tithe transforms into an effigy, but not like any I'd ever seen before. He's a mixture of flesh and stone, a mottled being covered in a patchwork of runes.

"And now, my friends?" asks the Tithe. "You shall witness my revenge."

My thoughts race. I'm out of charms. I'm surrounded my effigies. My weapons and attacks—cracking, burning, freezing—they've all been discovered and counteracted. I set my hand by my mouth. "Walker, if you're going to show up, now would be another great time."

"What he said," adds Myla.

Moments pass.

No Walker.

At least, Myla and I are together. That simply has to be enough.

The Tower of Wonders rumbles beneath our feet. Long cracks form along the walls. Ear-splitting booms echo through the air. Myla's eyes widen. "What's happening right now?"

"The whole place is collapsing," I explain.

"Oh, okay. Because I thought we were about to be really fucked over again. Guess I'm right. Gah!"

The Tithe watches us and grins. "Soon you'll be crushed to death. I've heard it's an awful way to die." He mock-pants. "Ugh, ugh. I can't breathe."

Myla points at his nose. "You can just shut the Hell up."

A large chunk of wall tumbles out of place, leaving a gaping hole in the chamber. Myla and I share a long and questioning look that says, *how do we get out of this?*

I've got nothing.

Myla's eyes widen. My girl has a plan. "What about the Tumtum tree?" Myla asks. "Only, you know, we slice our way down the trunk."

"I love this idea," I reply.

And I'm not kidding. Not only do I absolutely understand what Myla is going for here, but I also think it's brilliant. My girl can think on her feet like nobody's business.

Hand in hand, Myla and I then race toward the new gap in the wall. Behind us, I hear the Tithe's laugher.

"Death by falling," he chuckles. "It's not much better."

It's on the tip of my tongue to correct him. Myla and I aren't killing ourselves, we're escaping. But the Tithe is keeping his soldiers back, so there's no point in contradicting him.

Plus, there's a very large hole in the wall and I'm about to jump through it. That's rather distracting.

As we close in on the opening, I pull out my baculum, igniting them as a long sword. Myla arcs her tail over her shoulder. Once we step out into the air, Myla jams her tail into the tower's exterior. Flipping about, I thrust my baculum into the stone as well. The friction from my blade slows my fall. The same happens with Myla's tail. Nothing stops dragonscales.

My muscles strain to keep a firm grip on my baculum. Trouble is, huge chunks of the tower break away as we descend. The trick is to dodge falling debris while keeping your blade—or in Myla's case, her tail—firmly lodged to slow us down. We call out directives to each other. This is a team sport.

A massive chunk of tumbles toward me.

"Veer left!" Myla cries.

I shift my grip and avoid getting squashed.

An entire floor implodes. "Go right," I call to Myla.

Myla leaps in a new direction, her tail catching a fresh section of solid wall.

At last, we reach the ocean floor again. There's no time to celebrate, though. A series of ear-splitting blasts sound as the tower fully collapses on itself. Rubble lies in a messy pile on the center of the cleared ocean floor. It reminds me of what happened when I first defeated Devak. Only now the pile of chipped stone is far higher. And atop that small hill, there stands the Tithe. Moonlight reflects off the stone parts of his body, making him seem luminescent.

"What do you think he's up to now?" asks Myla.

"Nothing good," I reply. Turning, I look her over carefully. My girl's been through a lot. "Do you want to leave now? I wouldn't blame you. There are some mermaids nearby. We can make a run for it."

Myla scrunches up her face into a look that says, *are you crazy?* "I'm not going anywhere. The Tithe wants to invade Heaven. I think we should stick around. Plus, you totally vowed to kill him if he wasn't nice to me."

I shake my head and smile. *My Myla.* "Yes, that's true. We should hang out and see what happens."

"Oh." Myla points. "He's on the move."

Atop the rubble pile, the Tithe raises his arms. Beneath him, the chips of effigies shimmy and twist. Then they take form. A whirlwind of rubble swirls around the Tithe, stretching far above the ocean floor.

It takes a new form.

Myla tilts her head. "Is that looking, you know…"

"Humanoid?" I ask.

She snaps her fingers. "That's the word."

"He said something about it taking a specific shape to attack heaven."

"I can't wait to see what he comes up with."

The bits of rubble solidify into a massive stone figure. Somewhere in the center of that huge avatar, there's the Tithe, controlling the new and massive puppet with his magic.

The last pieces of the giant creation fall into place.

Myla gasps. "I can't believe it."

I wince. "Well, he said he wanted revenge on your father so …" I bob my head, searching for the right name for what looms ten stories above us. "He created Myla-zilla."

Sure enough, the Tithe has merged all his effigies into one giant stone version of Myla, complete with tail. Myla's real tail bounces over her shoulder. She pats the arrowhead end. "I know, boy. It's like we're famous now or something."

Myla-Zilla raises her arms. Light flashes in her palms as a supersized mallet and chisel appear in her hands. She kneels down. It's a slow-moving business considering all her bulk. I extinguish my baculum and watch the show.

"What do you think *I'm* up to?" asks Myla.

"No idea."

Myla-Zilla sets the chisel against the ground, raises her mallet high, and slams down on the knife-like instrument with all her strength. A massive pit opens in the ground below.

"How am I doing that, do you think?"

"My guess?" I rub my chin. "All the angelic soul power from so many effigies is combining to super-charge his gift from Aquila. The Tithe used that energy to create that Myla super-suit around him. Now he's casting more spells with his extra power."

"Clever. We'll need to stop him soon, you know."

"Yeah, I'm working on it." *Nothing's come to mind yet, however.*

Myla-Zilla then aims the chisel toward the empty hole, and strikes the back of the tool with the mallet once more. A bolt of white fire spews out from the chisel's end, flaring right into the pit.

My stomach sinks. "I know what he's doing."

Myla lifts her brows. "Starting a barbeque?"

"No, he's igniting the Echo Vortex. It's in Antrum, right below our feet. And it's what keeps all my people alive. He'll use that power to break into Heaven."

Myla nods. "Then he'll take down the Citadel with his little Happy Carpenter toolset."

"Sadly, I think you're right." I press my palms against my forehead. "Trouble is, if he ignites that vortex, everyone in Antrum will die."

"That wouldn't be good, especially how I was pulling to be their queen one day."

I love the queen comment, by the way. Something to contemplate later.

"We better save them." My thoughts race. I'm a planner. Someone who memorizes names, lays out schedules, and follows procedures. There's no training manual for what to do when a maniac warlock creates an oversized version of your girlfriend in order to kill your underground realm. I look to Myla. "Any ideas?"

She tilts her head. "When I was floating around before, I saw this dissolus nest nearby. Could be handy." A slow smile curves across her lips. "What do you think?"

I share her slow smile. Fire, ice, and metal all destroy rock. So does acid, especially the magically enhanced kind that fills up a dissolus.

"I think you're brilliant." *And I mean it.*

"Sha. Now let's go kill that Mega Myla."

"I thought we decided on Myla-zilla."

She winks. "We can discuss along the way."

And with that, we take off for the dissolus nest at a run.

50

*M*yla and I race across the ocean floor. Between the rocky ground, piles of seaweed, and massive Myla-zilla stomping around, the path is a bit of an obstacle course. The one good thing is that the Tithe sucked up all his other effigies in order to create his oversized Myla. There are no sentries left around to alert him that we aren't dead.

Again, if the warlock had taken the time to get an actual education at the Citadel instead of deciding he knew everything and could just destroy it, then he'd know all about sentries. And there would certainly be some effigy guards running around.

But I digress.

Soon Myla and I run across the oversized boulder that's actually a dissolus nest in disguise. At first glance, it looks like a massive brown lump of rock. But when I focus, I can again see that it's actually hundreds of thousands of tiny white eggs, each one about the size of a sesame seed. And every one of those eggs can balloon into a full-sized dissolus, just like the one I fought in the royal stables.

Waist-high.

Slimy.

Murderous.

I turn my baculum over in my hands. "I could create a spear made from angel fire and stab at the nest's center."

Myla sighs. "No."

"Ignite a fiery bow and arrow?"

"Nope."

"Kick it and run?"

"You'd lose your leg, and that's if you're lucky."

"I've said the same thing." I groan. "There's only one way to disrupt this nest. For the record, I hate this part of the plan."

"It's not my favorite, either. But you know how dissolus are."

I nod. "They'll hunt whoever disturbs their nest."

"And no offense, but it's not like the Tithe decided to take the form of Mega Lincoln."

"Myla-zilla."

We both turn to look at the monster in question. The stone Myla-zilla stand over the newly created pit to the Echo Vortex, slamming the hammer against the chisel, over and over. Each time, another blast of angel fire pours out from the chisel's sharp end and flows into the vortex itself. At some point, there will be enough of a charge to light the vortex and destroy my homeland.

We must stop the Tithe. It's just ... I really hate the idea of a hundred thousand dissolus chasing after Myla, trying to melt her with acid. I'm a protective boyfriend that way.

And don't think I missed Myla's comment about how she wants to be my queen. That's a major relationship milestone. You don't let your prospective wife say something like that and then let her poke a nest of dissolus.

Myla sets her hand on my shoulder. "Lincoln, this is my choice." Stepping over to the nest, she arcs her tail over its peak. She lifts her chin. "Five ... four ... three ... fuck it." The arrowhead end of her tail punctures the nest. "RUN!"

We race toward Myla-zilla. Well, Myla races forward. A hand holds me back. It's Cordelia. She's left the water wall and is walking around on her nest of wiry legs. Think about a jellyfish's bottom, only with scales, and that's the general idea. Not sure where humans got the fish tail concept.

"Will you need much longer?" pleads Cordelia. "This requires way too much focusing for Dwyn."

"Me, me," exclaims Dwyn. In fact, her overlarge eyes do look rather bloodshot. This is really taking a toll.

"Any second now," I tear my arm from Cordelia's grip. It isn't easy. Mermaids are strong.

Turning away from the mermaids, I watch the scene before me. My girl has climbed waist-high up her Myla-zilla counterpart. A long line of white blobs roll along behind my girl, creating streams of slime that stripe Myla-zilla's lower body. There are thousands of dissolus. Beside me, the nest spews out a steady geyser of what look like white sesame seeds. Only when these tiny orbs hit the ground, they expand into waist high mayo monsters that take off for Myla. Or Myla-zilla.

For her part, Myla scales around the back of her massive counterpart. The process involves a lot of cutting hand and foot holds with her tail. Fortunately, Myla-zilla is all stone, so my Myla can hack away and it doesn't cause any pain. And damn, but my girl is a sight. She shimmies, catapults, and somersaults her way around a giant version of herself like she'd been doing it her entire life.

At the same time, Myla-zilla is still hard at work, slamming the massive mallet against an oversized chisel. With each blow, fresh bursts of angel fire ricochet into the vortex. During the last few strikes, a few sparks erupt from the vortex below.

The Tithe may be a dip, but he has a solid plan.

He'll destroy Antrum if we don't stop him first.

Rushing away from the mermaids, I halt at the base of Myla-zilla and freeze. There's no way I can climb after my girl. The entire lower surface of Myla-zilla is now covered in dissolus. The slime balls pulse and shimmy as they ooze their way towards my girl. If I climb now, I'll activate their acidic defense for certain.

I step backward, hoping to get a better view of Myla. She's now taken to scaling the Myla-zilla's tail. The stone appendage moves with whip-like speed. Shock freezes me in place. I can only watch as Myla rides the tail in every direction. At last, she somersaults off and lands beside me on her feet because, after all, this is Myla.

She crosses her arms over her chest and grins. "That was awesome."

"It was and you are." I kiss her cheek. "Now never do anything like that again."

Myla chuckles. "How long before we know if the acid works?"

I scan the dissolus. Some of the bulbous shapes are already flattening out and releasing their acid. Fortunately, Myla-zilla is still moving wildly about as she tries to ignite the Echo Vortex. Nothing pisses off a dissolus more than jerky movements. "The dissolus are starting to attack. Let's hope they dissolve Myla-zilla."

A long pause follows. "Mega Myla."

This may be a near-disaster, but I can't let that go. "It's a massive you-shaped monster that's tearing up the ocean outside New York. I think that's Myla-zilla."

"Two words: Mega Myla. And we need to stop flirting and pay attention."

"Why? I like flirting."

"Because." Myla rubs her palms together. "The dissolus demons are finally spewing their acid. Even I can see that. The surface of Mega Myla looks all gooey. This is really something."

Indeed, my girl has a point. Sentences like, *the dissolus demons are finally spewing their acid* don't come along every day, even in my rather strange world.

Sure enough, huge chunks of Myla-zilla start to vanish. An elbow. Some hip. And each time something disappears, what looks like a white cloud rises up to the sky. I squint.

"Those aren't clouds, are they?" I ask.

"Nope, they're ghosts."

As parts of Myla-zilla vanish, the entire body begins to shrink. Within seconds, the massive figure is down to five stories high.

Four.

Three.

It's definitely working. And more ghosts are being released as well. I glance to Myla. "This is the most fun I've had …" I shrug. "Well, since you released those reperio demons at dinner."

"I know, right? Your life pretty much sucked before I came along."

There's only one thing to do when your girl says something like that.

Lean in and kiss her.

Hard.

So that's what I do.

Wrapping my hand around her neck, I pull Myla to me and press our mouths together. For a long moment, I do nothing but taste her. *Cinnamon and sunshine.* I break the kiss. My girl is breathless.

"I love you, Myla Lewis."

"And you're telling me this again in the middle of a huge battle against Mega Myla?"

"Myla-zilla. And that's right."

Her big blue eyes turn watery. "That's the best." She clears her throat. "I love you too, Lincoln *with the long name I can't totally remember.* There was an Osric in there, right?"

"Yes."

"Excuse me," comes a low and snarling voice.

Myla and I look over. And it's the Tithe, back to his regular size and absolutely mortal again. Which means he's back to one arm as well. It helps to keep track of these things.

"Damn," says Myla. "We missed the part where mega-you got eaten down by acid until you were regular size again. Although …" she looks at me and winks. It really was a good kiss.

The Tithe holds up his chisel. "I've ordered others kill you. All have failed. Now, I shall do it myself."

Myla holds up her pointer finger. "One question first. Why aren't you dead? I was really looking forward to seeing you get eaten by acid."

"Fool!" cries the Tithe. "Nothing that lives may kill me. Which is why you shall now die at my hands."

"Hand," corrects Myla. "You've only got one now."

The Tithe holds up the chisel and points it at Myla's face. "You'll die first, demon wench."

Myla curls her fingers at him. "Bring it on."

Now, normally I'd ignite my baculum at this point. However, while Myla and the Tithe were talking, I happened to notice a large black rectangle opening up nearby. A ghoul portal.

Walker now marches over in our direction. He does not look happy.

The Tithe lunges for Myla. At the last second, Walker steps between them. Instead of striking Myla, the Tithe embeds the chisel in Walker's shoulder.

Walker glowers. "Ow."

The Tithe stumbles backward. "How are you not killed?"

"Because I'm already dead." Walker pulls the chisel from his shoulder and rams it into the Tithe's chest. "And *that's* what happens when you attack Myla-la."

A flash of white light erupts from the spot where the chisel meets the Tithe's chest. The brightness grows until it surrounds the Tithe's entire body. His skin turns grey and withered. The chisel blackens. Strips of flesh fly away from the Tithe's bones. Then the bones themselves crumple into ash.

Myla steps forward and toes the ashes with her boot. "Now that's what I call dead. Thanks, Walker."

"You're most welcome." Walker grins. "Looks like you cleaned out that dissolus infestation, too."

"We're multi-taskers," says Myla.

"Yoo hoo!" calls Dwyn. "Mister ghoul guy!"

"Oh, no." Walker winces. "How did she end up here?"

"Dwyn," snaps Cordelia. "Stay focused."

A great rumble fills the air. Wind rushes around the clearing. Alarm rattles down my spine. The water wall. Cordelia can't hold it on her own. It's going to collapse. We'll be drowned.

I grasp Myla and Walker's hands, then turn to my friend. "Walker, open a portal now."

"Why? I don't think she's that beautiful." Walker sighs. "Or maybe she is."

"Walker!" I cry. "Portal!"

"All right, fine." Walker opens a ghoul portal behind us. Up ahead, a great water wall comes rolling over the ocean floor. However, Walker doesn't take a single step toward exiting the area.

"Lincoln." Myla gestures to the oncoming tsunami. "Do you see that?"

"I do."

"Why isn't Walker moving?"

"He's under an enchantment from the mermaids."

"Oh." Myla turns around and sets her shoulder against Walker's stomach. I see where she's going with this. It's a short shove to get into the portal. "On my mark. Go!"

With all our strength, Myla and I press against Walker. It isn't easy, but with both of us shoving along, we're able to get him into the portal just as the first water hits. A moment later, we tumble out onto Myla's living room floor.

Camilla stands above us. "What is this?"

Myla blinks. "What do you mean?"

"Water." Camilla gestures to the floor. "All over my rug. And you." She points to Myla. "Should be in bed. And you." She turns to me. "Are the single greatest man ever."

Walker clears his throat. "Next to Walker," adds Camilla.

"Hey," comes a voice from the other room.

"And my husband," adds Camilla once more.

"I'm honored." And I mean it with all my heart.

After hours filled with dissolus demons, Myla-zilla, and the Tithe, I can think of no better greater honor than being grouped with Walker and the archangel Xavier. And let's not forget my kiss with Myla, or the fact she wants to be my queen.

All in all, this is what I call a great day.

TWO WEEKS LATER

J step into the back of the kindergarten at Purgatory Children's School. Actually, the sign outside reads Ghoul Kids Education Camp GP-9170, but they haven't had time to get a new sign made yet. Best to respect the reformed government. Today I'm in human clothes and wearing sunglasses. With any luck, I won't be recognized.

Surprisingly enough, even though the country is still recovering from war, the tabloids are functioning perfectly. They've quickly figured out that they have a new local girl turned demigoddess. They've also discovered that Myla and I are dating. The theory is that I'm a spiritual gold-digger who wants some of Myla's limelight. My servants get me copies of all the magazines. I keep copies of them in the royal archives. Cracks me up.

The classroom is a long space with a small *circle time* area up front. Myla sits on a chair surrounded by tons of adorable children, all with different kids of tails. Puppy. Kitten. Lizard. Every young face is locked on the Great Scala as she tells the story of her fight against Armageddon. Myla even wore her white Scala robes of the occasion. She looks especially lovely.

"So then I sent all the demons back to Hell," says Myla. "And I did it all from inside my soul column. But do you know who got in there, too? Armageddon. And he fought me hard, only he used his mind. In fact, he made me wonder what I could really do. I felt so sad and empty. Do any of you ever feel that way?"

All the kiddo's tails wag. Some raise their hands. Others nod. *So sweet.*

"Well, feeling like that isn't fun. In fact, I was about to give up. And then, I thought: I am this fight. I can do this. I opened up a great pit to hell and —*whoosh*—Armageddon fell into it. And he's staying there forever now."

The kids cheer. So do the adults. I should know, considering how I stand with all the grown-ups in the back of the space. This part of the classroom is packed with parents taking snapshots of their children and the Great Scala. It's fun to be near their energy. They're so thrilled to see my girl.

"Now," says Myla. "Do you have any questions?"

The girl with a kitty tail raises her hand. Myla points to her. "What's your name?"

"Donna."

"Well, Donna. What's your question?"

"Are the new-old ghosts here?" asks little Donna.

"Always," replies Myla. "Millions of ghosts come to Purgatory each month. It's our job to sort them into their best afterlife. Then I move them to Heaven or Hell, assuming I agree with the choice."

"No, I mean the new-old ghosts. My dad says these ones are really, really, really, really old."

"I think your father means the ones from the Tithe?" asks Myla. Donna nods. "Yes, they're all here and safe. I'll move them very soon."

"Why not now?" asks Donna.

Myla worries her lower lip with her teeth. She's had trouble with her powers lately. Turns out, the ghouls have hidden a magical item in Purgatory called Lucifer's Orb and it can block Myla's abilities. The ghouls hope that if everything goes haywire, the quasis will invite them back to rule. Not going to happen. That said, I don't think it's time to worry about the orb just yet. The backlog of souls isn't too dangerous.

"Lady Adair came to our school last week," adds Donna. "She said the soul towers will burst and kill everyone, since you don't know what you're doing."

Myla smacks her lips. "Lady Adair is a very sad person, even if she now serves as the official thrax diplomat to Purgatory."

I shake my head. Unfortunately, Adair really is a diplomat now, and she's used her position to do annoying things like trail Myla around and scare school children. Thank Heaven I never signed that betrothal contract. Speaking of which, Aldred has officially dropped all talk of marriage or war. Instead, he's vigorously promoting his daughter's diplomatic career. Clearly, he's scheming something new. We'll find out what he's up to eventually. If nothing else, it's taken the pressure off Lucas. Aldred's dropped whatever he was holding over Gianna. The girl is safe once more.

"Does anyone else have questions?" asks Myla. "Perhaps someone in back?" Her tail arches over her shoulder and points directly at me. Myla hasn't noticed me yet, so I take the hint and raise my hand. My girl catches the movement, spies me, and pales. "Is that … you?" she asks.

"Yes," I reply. "And I was wondering. How much longer are you supposed to be here?"

"Oh." Myla beams. "I was just finishing up."

"In that case, do you want to leave here and get into trouble with me?"

Half the room gasps. Almost everyone turns to stare in my direction. Whispers echo nearby.

"That's the thrax prince."

"He's Myla's boyfriend."

"Snack time!" That's the teacher. All the kids rise up and rush toward the lunch room. I make a note of the instructor's name. I'll be sure to send him a thank you gift later. Quasis seem to enjoy mix tapes from the 1980's earth era. Ghoul technology has them stuck in that time period and everyone loves a good mix tape.

As the kids and parents retreat, I step closer, my gaze locked on Myla. "Well? What do you think?"

Myla stands. "I'd love to."

We share a smile, and that's everything I need in this world.

Stepping forward, I link my hand with Myla's and we walk off into a rainy Purgatory afternoon. Because if there's one thing I've learned since I first met Myla, it's that even the Heavens can fall when you least expect it.

Yet as long as Myla and I have each other, we'll still be happy.

Perhaps definitions of duty can change, after all.

The End

Lincoln's story continues with TRICKSTER, Book 3 in the Angelbound Lincoln Series.

ALSO BY CHRISTINA BAUER

TRICKSTER

ANGELBOUND LINCOLN BOOK 3

The adventure continues with TRICKSTER, Book 3 in the Angelbound Lincoln Series.

ANGELBOUND

Revisit ANGELBOUND, the kick-ass paranormal romance with more than 1 million copies sold!

OFFSPRING

The next generation takes on Heaven, Hell, and everything in MAXON, Book 1 of Angelbound Offspring!

FAIRY TALES OF THE MAGICORUM

A modern fairy tale that *USA Today* calls a 'must-read!' Check out WOLVES AND ROSES!

DIMENSION DRIFT

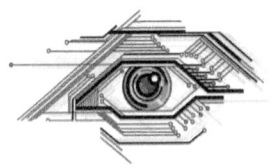

A kick-ass heroine + a swoon-worthy prince + an all-girl heist = the DIMEN-SION DRIFT series!

BEHOLDER

Medieval mages … Slow-burn love … And heart-pounding action! Check out the BEHOLDER series!

PIXIELAND DIARIES

PIXIELAND DIARIES tells the story of sassy pixie Calla and 'her' elf prince, Dare.

APPENDIX

IF YOU ENJOYED THIS BOOK...

...Please consider leaving a review, even if it's just a line or two. Every bit truly helps, especially for those of us who don't *write by the numbers*, if you know what I mean.

Plus I have it on good authority that every time you review an indie author, somewhere an angel gets a mocha latte. For reals.

And angels need their caffeine, too.

ACKNOWLEDGMENTS

If you're reading my freaking acknowledgements, chances are, I should thank you for something. So, for the record: you are awesome, dear reader.

That said, huge and heartfelt thanks must go out to my husband and son for their rock-solid support. Writing means a lot of early mornings, late nights, long weekends, and never-ending patience. You two are the best guys in the universe, period.

After that, I must thank the extensive network of reviewers, friends and colleagues who helped me build my writing chops in general. Gracias.

Finally, deep affection goes out to my late, much loved, and dearly missed Aunt Sandy and Uncle Henry. You saw the writer in me, always. Thank you, first and last.

COLLECTED WORKS

Angelbound Lincoln
The Angelbound experience as told by Prince Lincoln
1. Duty Bound
2. Lincoln
3. Trickster *(coming 2020)*
ALSO: Lincoln Box Set *(Books 1-2)*

Angelbound Origins
About a quasi (part demon and part human) girl who loves kicking butt in Purgatory's Arena
1. Angelbound
2. Scala
3. Acca
4. Thrax
5. The Dark Lands
6. The Brutal Time
7. Armageddon
8. Quasi Redux *(coming 2020)*
ALSO: Origins Box Set *(Books 1-5)*

Angelbound Offspring
The next generation takes on Heaven, Hell, and everything in between
1. Maxon
2. Portia
3. Zinnia
4. Rhodes
5. Kaps *(future)*
6. Huntress *(future)*

ALSO: Offspring Box Set *(Books 1-3)*

Fairy Tales of the Magicorum
Modern fairy tales with sass, action, and romance
1. Wolves and Roses
2. Moonlight and Midtown
3. Shifters and Glyphs
4. Slippers and Thieves
5. Bandits and Ball Gowns *(coming 2020)*
6. Evil Queens and Goblin Kings *(future)*
ALSO: Magicorum Box Set *(Books 1-3)*

Dimension Drift
Dystopian adventures with science, snark, and hot aliens
1. Scythe
2. Umbra
3. Alien Minds
4. ECHO Academy *(coming 2020)*
5. Drift Warrior *(future)*
ALSO: Dimension Drift Box Set (Books 1-3)

Pixieland Diaries
Sassy pixie Calla loves elf prince Dare. Too bad he hasn't noticed her. Yet.
1. Pixieland Diaries *(coming 2020)*
2. Calla *(future)*
3. Dare *(future)*

Beholder
Where a medieval farm girl discovers necromancy and true love
1. Cursed
2. Concealed
3. Cherished
4. Crowned
5. Cradled
ALSO: Beholder Box Set *(Books 1-5)*

ABOUT CHRISTINA BAUER

Christina Bauer thinks that fantasy books are like bacon: they just make life better. All of which is why she writes romance novels that feature demons, dragons, wizards, witches, elves, elementals, and a bunch of random stuff that she brainstorms while riding the Boston T. Oh, and she includes lots of humor and kick-ass chicks, too. Christina lives in Newton, MA with her husband, son, and semi-insane golden retriever, Ruby.

Stalk Christina on Social Media

Blog:
http://monsterhousebooks.com/blog/category/christina

Facebook:

https://www.facebook.com/authorBauer/

Instagram:
https://www.instagram.com/christina_cb_bauer/

Twitter:
@CB_Bauer

VLOG:
https://tinyurl.com/Vlogbauer

Web site:
www.bauersbooks.com

COMPLIMENTARY BOOK

Get a FREE book when you sign up for Christina's newsletter:
https://tinyurl.com/bauersbooks

BEVERLY
HILLS
VAMPIRE

A NOVELLA BY
CHRISTINA BAUER

ONE LAST AUTHOR NOTE

Dear Reader,

If you've gotten this far and are still with me, I thought you might want some additional background on LINCOLN. While writing ANGELBOUND, I penned a few future chapters so I'd know where the overall story arc was going. Originally, I wanted Lincoln to marry Adair. *I know, eew.* Even worse, Lincoln would only do so after he and Myla shared one night of passion. Maxon would be the result.

Sometimes my characters talk to me.

In this case, Lincoln said: Absolutely not—I shall always watch over Myla! In what universe would I *not* know of her pregnancy? Or avoid caring for my own son? Are you insane, woman?

And he was right. At the core of Lincoln, there's only duty and honor. He may act like an anti-demonic douchebag, but it's only because he thinks it's the right thing to do. So, even as I finished ANGELBOUND, I knew there would be a whole side to the story that explained Lincoln's actions. The specifics about the Tithe and mega Myla came later, but when they appeared, I knew this had to be a full novel.

So, if you were hoping to hear Lincoln wax poetic about how demons suck, apologies! That's not our Lincoln.

So you know, I had a lot of fun (and also self-torture) going through events in ANGELBOUND and re-examining from Lincoln's point of view. Turns out, in some ways Myla and Lincoln are similar. Both are happily surprised to find that there is someone else in the world like them. They share the same values when it comes to battle. Sometimes they describe things in a similar way. Both count down the time to cherished activities.

When they meet, both instantly become obsessed with the other. It's an expression of how similar the two of them really are. Myla expresses an overt passion for life; Lincoln holds the same intensity, only his is hidden. In my opinion, this is what 'love at first sight' is all about. I do think it happens, but it's when two unique people recognize their other puzzle piece. That's what happened with Lincoln and Myla. Where that gets tricky is if you have one person equation who is acting controlling or faking it. Lincoln isn't giving Myla expensive gifts and solely fawning all aspects of his girl that she has no control over, like her physical appearance. The big thing that grabs Lincoln is Myla's passion for life, which he sees from the moment she appears from the lake.

In other ways, the pair are radically different. Stuff that impresses Myla—such as the thrax way of life—are things Lincoln sees as ho-hum. This is his world, after all. There's no way he'll spend three pages describing how the House of Horus rides chariots. Plus, if he's experiencing anything Adair-related, like her awakening ceremony, the details just don't grab his interest. For example, Lincoln spends much of Adair's awakening ceremony doing the equivalent of planning his grocery shopping list.

Easter Eggs

Okay, so I built in a ton of stuff that you may or may not have caught. In case you're interested, here's what I hid. ***Warning: spoilers ahead***

- The Arbiter (a character from ACCA) is actually an effigy that survives the Tithe dying. She's one of the early ones that the Tithe created, before he decided to only create soldiers.

- The Furor dragon, Epsilon, shows up again in PORTIA, Angelbound Offspring Book 2. I built out a whole storyline for him where he falls in love and adopts a child. It's out there; I'll get to it one day!

- Myla's tail and Lincoln have always had a special relationship. In this book, we find out why.

- Ethan is mentioned as the person who will take in Acca when they leave Antrum. His character returns in THRAX and yes, the guy is a dick.

- Walker's mission for a water elemental is actually for Lianna from the book MAXON.

- Lincoln mentions a change in Adair's scent. That's a teaser to some changes in Adair which we discover in SCALA.

- In ACCA, Octavia mentions how a young Lincoln used to chase his cat with a sword. In this book, that feline is given some more personality as well as a name. Perkins.

- This next thing is just a general note since I couldn't fit it into the book in an organic way. Lincoln is named Lincoln because his parents (okay, mostly his father) wanted him to unite the houses of Rixa and Acca. Connor knew the American President Lincoln kept the United States together, and hoped the Thrax Prince would do the same for the two houses one day. The bloody civil war part was somewhat ignored.

So that's it! I hope you enjoyed LINCOLN. It was fun getting to know the prince in a new way. The story continues in SCALA!

www.ingramcontent.com/pod-product-compliance
Lightning Source LLC
Chambersburg PA
CBHW022023240626
47154CB00007B/2239